Iguana
Dreams

Iguana Dreams

NEW LATINO FICTION

Edited by Delia Poey
and Virgil Suarez

WITH A PREFACE BY OSCAR HIJUELOS

HarperPerennial

A Division of HarperCollins*Publishers*

For Alexandria

A Background Note for the Popular Muse Belongs to Everybody

The muse has been turned into powder
Sprinkled into the ocean
It has ventured back out upon the
Tongue of a lizard
To make trees and plazas
And the edge which is where
I fall between the balconies
Yellow dresses adjacent
To lush encounters
Between a thought and hanging
Sweetness

At any moment it has no place
Who would own it tries
To imprison the wind
It makes desires that take
Shape
Worth more than Catholic
Churches made of gold

It could be a frog
Or a song
The seams of dresses
The drop of tropical
Land in azul *water*
The height
The low

It paid rent at the formation
And talks with feet eyes and
Rocks
It could be standing next to you
and no where to be seen
I wait with a gourd full
of gasoline
For a chip to fall from
The festival fireworks
To favor me
And set me on fire.

—Victor Hernández Crúz

Contents

Preface

The enchanting title—and contents—of this anthology, *Iguana Dreams*, puts me into a mischievous frame of mind, dense with thoughts about the "good old days" in literature when people were really letting go. George Orwell's *Animal Farm* comes up when I ask myself, Just whom or what does the "Iguana" of the title represent? True iguanas crawl along through jade plants and blossom-thick yards; they sometimes sit, unnoticed, among a piling of stones, or scamper about on a house coping in the dead white heat of a tropic day. But this Iguana, this literary entity, this being, must carry the burden of enticing the citizenry of the world into its lair of dreams and stories and is not, I swear, a beast of fiber and scale and claw. This Iguana, slinking along, embodies the spirit and imagination of this book, a little startled because while slinking along it has found itself—to stay with this allegorical and nature-oriented metaphor—in the garden of mainstream American literature where its proper job is to lick, bite, alert, and, yes, charm the inhabitants of the garden (beasts and human alike).

To that end, this anthology (or "garland of flowers" as folks used to say, and quite appropriate to the garden when the Iguana crawls) does its work well. The writers represented here are not only feisty and lyrical and brilliantly entertaining, but they also do the work of literature, which is to bring into the world the life, heart, mind and imagination of writers. In this instance, they are writers of diverse Latino background with much to say and give.

—OSCAR HIJUELOS

Acknowledgments

This anthology would not exist today without the help and encouragement of many individuals. It is to them we are forever indebted.

When the idea for this book surfaced, Rudolfo Anaya and Carolina Hospital got us in touch with many of these writers. Having edited anthologies before, they provided us with a lot of valuable information.

Also, we are grateful to all those writers with whom we made contact in the early stages to ask them to rush us their stories so we could prepare a small sample of what was yet to come and present that to our agent. Among them were Roberto G. Fernandez, Pablo Medina, Cecilia Rodríguez-Milanés, Marisella Veiga, Guy Garcia, Wasabi Kanastoga, and Elías Miguel Muñoz.

Our agents, Elaine Markson and Karin Beisch, came through for us with energy and enthusiasm for this project. They placed it quickly in the hands of Terry Karten, our editor at HarperCollins, who kept us going during some very crucial and tough moments. And special thanks to Charlotte Abbott whose assistance became our safety net.

We would also like to thank Federico Poey Sr., and Jr., and Bernardo Pestano at AGRIDEC where we ran up their utility bill using their computers, manpower, and facilities.

Special thanks go to Susan Bergholz and her agency for working with us, helping us, and selling to us the incredible Latino talent she represents: Ed Vega, in particular, who got us in touch with new and emerging Puerto Rican writers.

Our parents offered us love, baby care and, as always, fattening delicious food which nourished us.

Erica Babin at Louisiana State University and Virginia Trujillo in Miami helped us with the typing and proofreading of the manuscript.

And finally to all the writers in this anthology (and also to all those who for technical reasons were not included) who have struggled against the odds to keep writing and producing so many fine, unique, and memorable voices—this is their book.

D. P. & V. S.

Introduction

The idea for this anthology developed slowly as a result of discussions over the years with family, friends and acquaintances regarding the Latino experience in the United States. These discussions, some casual, some passionate, dealt mainly with the issues of identity, assimilation, cultural heritage and artistic expression. We sought out works by Latino writers, curious as to what they had to say and how they said it. We celebrated the recent attention paid to these writers by New York publishing houses and the recognition some received through prizes like the Pulitzer, National, and American Book Awards, as well as many other important literary awards received throughout this country.

Over time we discovered that while there are many excellent anthologies representing individual groups, so far there had been no one volume attempting to showcase writers from all Latino cultures and offering their lively literature in the United States. This seemed surprising. Upon reflection we understood that factionalism along national lines is only natural, for our own discussions had sometimes dealt with the forced nature of grouping so many distinct and separate cultures under the term *Latino*.

A negative consequence of this grouping is that, in the eyes of many Anglos, the diverse Latino cultures are interchangeable. Thus, Hollywood will create absurdities such as Cubans eating tacos, or Anglo actors cast in Latino roles only because they have dark hair and a tan. In gathering together Mexican- , Puerto Rican- , Cuban- , Chilean- , and Dominican-American writers we are in no way repeating this all too common error. Our intent is rather to unite, and in so doing allow the reader to determine for him/herself what we share and what sets us apart from one another. Bringing all these cultures together in one volume may be comparable to the tension of sharing a meal with distant relatives—there is a separate history and experience, yet there exists a bond of recognition, a family camaraderie.

The central point of our unity is language. While we may speak with different accents and use different expressions, we all share the experience of bilingualism. The ability to communicate in two languages, and more importantly to think and feel in two languages, brings with it the phenomenon of at times being unable to express oneself fully in only one. Linguists term this "interference," and generally view it as a negative trait, or shortcoming. We, as Latino writers and readers of Latino fiction, however, assert that the intermingling of the two languages is an effective means of communicating what otherwise could not be expressed. Thus many Latino writers use Spanish in their work because it is an integral part of their experience.

In putting this manuscript together, we made the decision to italicize all Spanish words for the sake of uniformity. Several writers questioned this, explaining that in the lives of their characters Spanish is not a "foreign" language, but rather a vital part of everyday speech and as such should not appear in italics. We respected this line of reasoning and prepared the final draft accordingly. We mention this in order to emphasize the importance of Spanish and its role in Latino literature. The writers in this anthology express themselves in English—the language of the mainstream (whatever that may mean)—but are resisting the destruction of their culture and thus preserving their identity by using Latino expressions, points of reference and experiences. Hopefully this will become accepted not as "exotic" (read foreign), but rather part of a redefined mainstream in the arts.

A second facet which all Latino cultures share is the need for cultural survival. This is a controversial issue among Latinos, since it deals with the question of assimilation. How much of our culture should we be willing to lose or suppress in order to participate in mainstream society? The answers to this important question vary, yet it is an issue that all Latino writers must tackle either directly or in more subtle ways. For example, Guy Garcia's story "Frazer Avenue," Judith Ortiz-Cofer's "American History," and Julio Marzan's "The Ingredient" all touch on it in radically different ways.

Cultural survival is nothing new in Latino culture. It has strong roots even outside the United States, and must be placed in a historical context. Octavio Paz in his book *The Labyrinth of Solitude* places it as a central factor influencing the Mexican psyche. When the Spanish conquest defeated and literally toppled the Aztec gods of Tenochtitlán, the Aztec name for today's Mexico City, the indigenous people were forced to adopt aspects of Spanish culture and religion in order to survive. Even today, Paz points out, Mexicans use *el disimulo* or "the process of concealment" in everyday life. Testimony to the strength of the indigenous culture is the fact that a merciless Spanish rule and five hundred years of history have not been able to eradicate indigenous myths, culture, values and languages. The Mexican Department of Education recently issued a report which revealed that there are to this day fifty-two indigenous languages in use in the country. Thus Mexican-Americans carry a legacy as cultural survivors with strong ties to their ancestral roots.

Paz's term of *el disimulo* can also be applied to other Latino cultures in the United States. Like chameleons, Latinos camouflage and adapt to new environments without losing their identity. *El disimulo* entails adopting characteristics of the mainstream; this is an effort to disguise the true self, which might be deemed unacceptable. Virgil Suarez's "Settlements" and Ed Vega's "The Clocks, Ribbons, Mountain Lakes, and Clouds of Jennifer Marginat Feliciano" serve as examples of this.

Although the ties that bind all Latino cultures are strong, there are many significant differences that are at times not obvious to a mainstream American public. For instance, Mexican-Americans have a peasant or *campesino* tradition which is rural and carries with it strong ties to the land. José Antonio Villarreal's sketches "The Last Minstrel in California" and "The Laughter of My Father" as well as

Leroy V. Quintana's story "La Yerba Sin Raiz (The Weed Without a Root)" spring from this tradition. Puerto Rican- and Cuban-Americans on the other hand, being islanders, have strong ties to water as illustrated in Gustavo Pérez-Firmat's piece "My Life as a Redneck."

Urban life in the United States has given rise to a new tradition in Latino fiction, that of the *barrio*. While for Mexican-Americans the barrio is likely to be in California, the Southwest, or Chicago (as in Sandra Cisneros's "Salvador Late or Early," and Wasabi Kanastoga's "City for Sale"), for the Puerto Rican-American the barrio is in New York as is the case in Ed Morales's story "The Coast Is Clear" and Abraham Rodriguez, Jr.'s "Roaches."

For Cuban-Americans, being Latino in the United States means also dealing with the dilemmas and frustrations of political exile. Their characters often feel a yearning and sense of loss for a homeland to which they cannot return. This is most obvious in nostalgic stories set in the idyllic Cuba of the past, as well as those speculating on the Cuba of the future as in Ricardo Pau-Llosa's "Martes."

There are also differences in religion. Although due to the Spanish conquest and colonization, Latin America is predominantly Catholic, each region has its own brand of Catholicism. In Cuba and Puerto Rico the influence is African, because the natives were subjected to genocide roughly eight years after the discovery of the new world by Christopher Columbus. Elías Miguel Muñoz's story "The Movie Maker" has elements of Santería, a religion that blends Catholicism and African religions. For Mexicans, the influence is indigenous, as in Ana Castillo's "On Francisco el Penitente's First Becoming a Santero and Thereby Sealing His Fate." Lionel Garcia's "Confession" also shows a child's perspective on the strict Catholicism brought by the Spanish.

The Latino experience has many points of divergence from that of the mainstream, so it follows that our literature does too. However, there are common experiences that we all share as human beings, experiences that transcend cultures and find expression in Art, making it universal and timeless. Coming of age, for instance, is a theme commonly explored in literature, as it is in stories like Alberto Alvaro Ríos's "Saturnino El Magnífico," and Wasabi Kanastoga's "City for Sale." War, unfortunately, is another common human experience, and Rolando Hinojosa-Smith's "The Useless Servants" reminds us of Latinos' role in the United States' armed forces. "Tito's

Good-bye" by Cristina Garcia, "Spider's Bite" by Pablo Medina, and "In Search of Epifano" by Rudolfo Anaya all deal with a third universal truth, death. It is important to note that, even when dealing with universal themes, Latino writers are still drawing from a specifically ethnic experience, giving their work a unique point of view that has been overlooked or ignored in mainstream American literature.

Each of the stories in this collection gives an individual perspective on the Latino experience, a testimony that you can't go home again, but you can come close by tapping into the collective subconscious fed by recollections, tradition and history. Each is a world apart from the others in matters of voice, style, experience, and a different definition of what being Latino means. This anthology is in no way intended as a canon of Latino fiction, but rather a resource for discussion, interpretation, and future inspiration in creating and defining this genre. In an effort to allow each story to stand on its own, we thought it best to arrange them in alphabetical order by author rather than grouping them by nationality.

We hope this collection will whet readers' appetites for Latino fiction and enrich their imagination, as well as provide the same profound enjoyment we had in putting it together.

Gracias y saludos,
The Editors,
DELIA POEY & VIRGIL SUAREZ
Baton Rouge, Louisiana, 1992

Iguana
Dreams

Customs

Julia Alvarez

JULIA ALVAREZ was born in the Dominican Republic and came to the United States when she was ten years old. After receiving her undergraduate and graduate degrees in literature and creative writing, she spent twelve years teaching poetry in schools in Kentucky, California, Vermont, Washington, D.C., and Illinois. *Homecoming*, her first book of poetry, was published in 1986. Her novel-in-stories, *How the Garcia Girls Lost Their Accents*, was published in 1991 by Algonquin Books of Chapel Hill and was named a NYTBR and ALA Notable Book of the Year. She lives with her husband in Middlebury, Vermont, where she teaches at Middlebury College and is at work on a new novel.

At Customs they had her unpack the tent even though she warned them it was going to be more trouble than it was worth to fold it back into its cloth sack. But they insisted, four minor officials, three more than were needed, unfolded the flaps, checked the case, found the instructions Steven had written out for her tucked inside. By the time Tío Mundo came through the guarded doors with the man in charge, the officials had draped the canvas over the conveyor belt and were prepared to unfold it further, blocking the passageway.

"They didn't believe me," she said to her uncle about the four men still fumbling with the tent. "I told them it was just a tent."

"A tent!" Tío Mundo pulled a long face. "What on earth does my pretty niece want with a tent?" He turned to his buddy in Customs, who was ordering the officials to put stickers on Yolanda's things and detain her no longer. "These girls of Carlos come down and each time it's something new!" The head official wiped his mouth with the back of his hand and smiled vaguely. His lips still looked greasy, as if he'd been eating a fried snack in his office when Don Mundo had dropped in to ask if they couldn't do him a little favor and speed his niece through the line.

In no time the inspectors had zippered shut Yolanda's bags, but as she had predicted, they were unable to fold the cumbersome tent back snugly into its case. Two porters carried it between them, hammock style. There could have been a body hidden inside it.

Outside, the limousine had pulled up to the entrance. Through the tinted green glass, Yolanda could make out Lucinda and Carmencita and Tía Carmen. She rushed forward to say hello to her favorite cousins and aunt, but before she had reached the car, a young man shot out from behind the lifted trunk and hurried to open the door. He had such an eager look in his eye that Yolanda felt he must have met her before. He was a slim young man, no taller than she, though he looked to be a few years older, in his early twenties possibly. Her uncle came up between them and patted the young man on the back. "This is Francisco," he introduced the new chauffeur, so there would be no mistaking him for one of the darker-skinned cousins. Francisco touched his forehead. "At your orders, señorita."

The ride to the compound was catch-up. Who had married whom and what the forecast was on their happiness. New babies and whom they looked like, who had died and who was ill. Tía Carmen stopped in the middle of the news. "You seem—" she cupped her niece's cheek in her hand, "happier this year."

Her aunt was right. There was a man in Yolanda's heart, but she was not about to confess and go through grueling interrogations. Besides, her Dominican aunt seemed to have psychic powers. Those dark, soulful, loving eyes could see through to their niece's heart. They could see at the bottom of her overnight case the birth control packet Yolanda was finishing off.

"Maybe it's just I'm a little heavier this year," Yolanda said. Her aunt always equated weight with well-being. Quickly, she changed the subject to politics. "How are things?" A new president had been elected after years of unrest.

Her uncle had turned around in the front seat where he'd sat because the car was too crowded. He flipped his hand front and back. "Things are así, así," he said, shrugging.

"To tell the truth, no one's thinking much about politics these days." Tía Carmen shook her head tragically. In her elegant, dark mourning dresses—there was always a fresh death to mourn in such a large family—her words had the ring of pronouncements. "Betsy hit us so hard, we're still catching our breath."

"Just like a woman!" Tío Mundo winked at Francisco, and the two men shared a manly chuckle.

"Ay, Papi," Lucinda groaned. But there was no affection in her voice.

Her uncle continued. "The new president, I'll say this for him, he's on the ball. The new highway will be ready next month. There's construction now up in Bonao—"

"With your permission, señor," Francisco interrupted. "A highway is not a house. Many are without a roof over their heads." He pointed past Uncle's face. Yolanda looked and saw empty fields on both sides of the road, bare of the usually feverishly lush vegetation. Here and there, four wobbly poles held up a thatched roof of palm branches. "The hurricane took the trees so there's no palm wood to finish the walls of those huts."

"People live there?" Yolanda shook her head. She had thought they were shade stands for the merchants on the side of the road. But even as she acknowledged Francisco, she was aware of the uncomfortable silence that had fallen inside the car. The chauffeur had spoken out of place. Someone was going to have to take the new man aside and instruct him on the do's and don'ts of working for the clan.

"What about you, young lady?" Tío Mundo covered the hand she had put on the front seat to pull herself forward when Francisco had spoken. "The boys up there must be lining up! Let them look all they want. You come back and marry one of your own!" Tío nodded at his daughters. "What's that saying of the Americans? No charge for looking at the merchandise?"

This was the kind of moment Yolanda would later recount to Steven, and he would shake his head. "It's like going back to the nineteenth century," she would roll her eyes to the ceiling. "Chaperones, virginity, girls can't do this, girls can't do that." Sometimes, Yolanda had to admit to herself, she enjoyed the fuss. It made her feel like a romantic heroine, valued and important, instead of anonymous, one of several hundred co-eds crowded into a lecture hall, her foreign name mispronounced. Except for Steven—he made her feel plenty important. She had not told her parents about her long-haired, bearded young lover who had applied for c.o. status and was one of the campus agitators against the war. Her parents would have forbidden her to see him, no less camp out with him in the very tent she had brought down. In a way, she was getting back at them by bringing the contraband tent into the country!

Yolanda had tried talking her parents into letting her stay in her college town that summer working and sharing an apartment with "friends." But the answer was no, *n.o.*, spelled the same way, Spanish or English. Until she graduated from college and was on her own, she was to spend her summer with her Island family. She knew the ground plan—what her uncle had nodded about to her aunt—that she should meet and marry a young man from a prominent family, maybe one who had also been to school in the States. That way her education would be an asset, not a liability.

Having been forced to come against her will, Yolanda was determined to be here on her own terms. But this was nothing new. She always brought new ideas. Hippie ideas; one of the aunts had read about the phenomenon in a magazine her husband had brought her from the States. A few summers back it was vegetarianism. Everything in life, Yolanda explained, had a soul, and you built up karma like cholesterol you had to work off. Last summer, Yolanda wasn't eating at all, fasting, she called it, to cleanse and stroke the organs. But she looked as skinny and pitiful as the country poor in a drought year. She read Zen poetry in translation to Yuri, the gardener, who said that if the señorita said so, the sound of one hand clapping made sense to him. It was no more riddling than the Virgin Mary giving birth to a human god baby. This summer, she was reading Steven's trouble-making books. The class system was wrong. All the people should own the means of production. Her aunts and uncles were up in arms defending themselves.

Several times she went out back of the kitchen to a small courtyard enclosed by concrete blocks with a filigree design, where the servants gathered to relax during lulls in their work day, after meals or late at night. They welcomed her warmly, but always with so much protocol that she felt she was intruding. "Please señorita." They all stood and offered her their chairs. "I can stand too," she reminded them.

Her parents had emigrated when she was still so young that, unlike her cousins, Yolanda had never gotten used to the idea of servants. What were their work conditions like? How could they be improved? The servants spoke openly to her. Yuri didn't earn enough to buy himself cigarettes. Iluminada, the cleaning maid, had a rotten tooth, but she couldn't afford to have the dentist pull it. The cook, Zoraida, wanted to get her hair straightened but she didn't have an extra cent to her name. Always, the complaint was followed by a request for a handout. Yolanda felt as if all they really wanted from her was money, not a true exchange of ideas. After a few times, she stopped dropping in for her visits. Her aunt, she could tell, was relieved.

Francisco, the chauffeur, was different from the others. He listened attentively when Yolanda talked about the States, about how students went on strike to protest a war that was going on in a little country not unlike this one, about how workers could do the same thing against bad working conditions. "But señorita, begging your pardon," Francisco explained, "don't you see, if we workers strike, we'll just all be fired, and a whole new crew hired, willing to work for half what we earn?" Yolanda didn't know what to propose. She wished Steven or one of his radical, well-informed friends were here to be specific.

One specific thing she did want to put a stop to. "Please don't call me señorita, Francisco." He had come to pick her up after one of her obligatory visits to a great-aunt, and she had wanted to take the front seat next to him. But he had insisted: "Unless the car is filled up, if you're seen in front, I could lose my job." Obviously, somebody, probably the head chauffeur, had been taking the young man in hand and training him in the fine ways of being a chauffeur. He had lost his novice eagerness and was learning to deliver expert, silent service. "Okay, I'll ride in back," she had agreed, but she drew the line at señorita.

"But it's no offense, señorita. It's the custom here, a title of respect—"

"I don't need a title, Francisco. I've got a name." She had come forward, folding her arms on top of the front seat, propping her chin upon them. "Yolanda," Yolanda said, coaxing him. "Say it, go on, Francisco. Yo-lan-da."

He looked at her in the rear view mirror, his gaze lingering a second too long. "You are very pretty, Yolanda," he said. His voice had changed, become intimate and husky. Yolanda sat back in her seat. Her aunt had warned her that by befriending the servants, she confused them. They took advantage of her or misunderstood her friendliness as flirtation. But, unless someone took new steps, things were never going to change. If Francisco had gotten the wrong idea, the thing was, not to abandon the friendship, but to let him know delicately, so as not to hurt him, that she was not interested. She already had a boyfriend in the States.

The occasion came as a result of another of Yolanda's schemes: six weeks had gone by, and she had yet to use the tent Steven had loaned her. She had been with him when he had bought the tent at the army surplus store in her college town. "A good recycling of military industrial crap," he had said. But politics had not been the issue. They had used the tent that spring in order to sleep together and not put out one or another of their roommates in the dorms. They set up the tent out on the soccer field during the school week. Weekends, they headed for the Green Mountains. When their plans for the summer had fallen through, the tent had been a kind of consolation prize to her. Yolanda should scout out good campsites in her native land, Steven comforted her. Someday soon, they would go down together, and she'd know the best places to take him. Although Yolanda had never liked camping in and of itself, using the tent now would be a way of feeling close to Steven.

After the fiasco at Customs, the tent had been aired out on the wash line in the laundry yard, then folded neatly into its case by Francisco and Yuri and handed over to her uncle. Yolanda began talking up a camping trip among her cousins. Every meal the young people lobbied the old guard for permission. Negotiations whittled them down. The boy cousins lost interest when they realized they would basically be chaperoning a bunch of younger girl cousins. The girl cousins lost their nerve after their mothers took them aside and warned about tarantulas, mosquitoes, guerrillas, which they mispronounced *gorillas*, purposely, Yolanda believed, in order to get double the fear quotient out of the word. "Remember the countryside is still a mess after Betsy. People are desperate. Anything can happen," her uncle warned ominously.

Finally, only Yolanda and Lucinda and Carmencita, and two little cousins who were eager to come along on an adventure with older girls were left lobbying to go. At last, Tío Mundo consented. He couldn't stand to disappoint his girls, he said. They could go for an overnight to the family rancho just outside the capital.

"Ay, come on, Tío," Yolanda pleaded with her uncle. "The rancho'd be like camping in the backyard."

"*Ya, ya,* girls." Uncle threw up his arms, and then like Pilate, he wrung his hands, washing them clean of the matter. "You're on your own." He spoke to the chauffeur in front of the young women, narrowing his eyes to make his point. "Francisco, take them wherever they want to go! They want to be *conquistadores*, let them go explore." The tone in his voice was that of the villain in a fairy tale: they-will-be-sorry-they-asked!

Off they went, five girls in a merry mood from at last flying the coop. The older cousins lit up cigarettes the minute they were off compound limits, and the young girls worked the automatic windows up and down until Francisco put a stop to them. "You'll break them, señoritas." Yolanda sat in front, her back against the door, so she was half turned to face Francisco and her cousins in the rear of the car. She told them all to be on the lookout, enumerating the qualities of a good camping site. Pointedly, she added, "*Mi novio* taught me how to scout for one."

"Among other things!" Lucinda bit the fleshy part of her lower lip. Yolanda gave her the eye, but she was glad to see that although the younger cousins had begun looking eagerly out the windows for a level spot with shade trees and running water, Francisco had caught her older cousin's hidden intent. Now he understood—if he had had any doubts before—that Yolanda had not been flirting with him. And since *novio* could mean either a boyfriend or a fiancé, for all Francisco knew, Yolanda was on the brink of marriage.

Once out of the city limits, the countryside began to change. Unlike the cleaned-up strip along the airport highway, the landscape here seemed mined: acres and acres of burnt fields. The cousins did not know what had happened. Francisco had grown quieter and did not volunteer an explanation until asked. This had once been a beautiful forest until the gringos had burned it down.

"Why on earth?" Yolanda asked. But the explanation had already been spotted.

"Look," one of the little cousins called out. Up ahead, a sign on a tipped-over pole had been defaced with a black cross. "United States Marine Camp." Yolanda's little cousin stumbled over the English words. The marines had spent a good part of last year here in this occupation camp while civil war raged in the capital. Francisco spoke up: "We've had two bad hurricanes, Betsy, and the Yanquis."

"Let's go see it, Francisco." Yolanda sat up and looked eagerly out her window, half-expecting to see a troop of blonde G.I.'s like the R.O.T.C. guys on campus Steven and his friends were always demonstrating against. The camp had been deserted for the good part of a year, Francisco explained. But he was at her service.

Off he swerved, down a bumpy road that came to a dead end at a cleared field. The girls climbed out of the car and looked around. Up and down the length of the field were poured cement floors, embedded with iron rings. Patches and tufts of grass were breaking through the cracks in the cement: the land was taking back its own. Rainy season was working its magic. At the bottom of the hilly plain, the flooded river was spanned by a chain link bridge that swayed and jingled in the breeze. Beyond were blessedly green rolling hills. Yolanda began crossing over and waved to her cousins to follow her.

"That thing looks dangerous," Lucinda called through the megaphone she had made with her hands. "Come back here!"

But Yolanda kept going, stopping midway to contemplate the rolling, rushing water through the links below her feet. Dark green seagrasses tossed wildly in the current. They reminded Yolanda of helicopters landing in the Vietnam jungles on the news every night in the States, tossing the nearby trees and grasses with the wind of their descent.

Francisco joined her on the bridge. He looked at her a moment before he spoke. "I did not know you had a *novio*."

"I don't let it be known, Francisco, or my family—you know how they are."

"So your *novio*, he is a—" Francisco hesitated, searching for the polite term, Yolanda was sure. "He is an American man?"

Yolanda looked down and saw her hands were gripping the chain link fence, so her knuckles shone white. "You do not like the Americans?"

Francisco shook his head. The bridge beneath their feet swayed. Yolanda held on tighter to the guard rail to keep her balance.

"You know, Francisco," Yolanda offered, "not all Americans are alike. Steven, *mi novio*, for example, doesn't agree with the American policies here or in Vietnam."

But Francisco did not want to talk politics. "This *novio*, if he is serious, why doesn't he declare himself to your family?"

"Things are different in the States."

"And you go along with their custom?"

"Yes, I guess when it comes to this, yes."

He turned to face her, and she felt that now he had something more personal he wanted to say. Afraid, she turned away. On the surface of the water, little rings began to form, linking with each other like a chain, then widening and disappearing. New links formed as more drops fell.

"It's raining!" Wild shouts came from the shore. There was a stampede of cousins toward the car. Yolanda and Francisco hurried after them. Once inside the car, they dried themselves off with towels from their knapsacks; the cousins debated whether to turn back.

"No way I'm going back now," Yolanda announced. "It's nothing but a little shower." Big drops fell on the car top, with the sound of insects smashing on the windshield as the car sped down the pebbly road.

They turned into the main highway, then veered off again over rough terrain. Francisco wound around and around hillsides until Yolanda felt they were traveling deeper into the heart of the country than the agreement with her uncle had allowed. Soon they were thrashing through a dark, dense jungle of vegetation. Beyond the tinted windshield, vines fell in thick coils from the branches of arching trees. Yolanda gaped at the sheer drop of a ravine to the river below: the land looked as if someone had hacked it open and exposed its dark, wet, beating life.

By the time they came through the tunnel, the sun was shining brightly. The sky glowed a picture-postcard turquoise. Ahead was a grassy, gently rolling plain, watered by a small brook and shaded by a grove of thriving mimosa trees. It was a little garden spot the hurricane had bypassed, cradled between the hills, a place Steven would have chosen to camp! "This is perfect, Francisco," Yolanda congratulated him.

The girls climbed out of the car and raced eagerly up a small hill. To the south was the deep blue ocean—or sky? Only when a carrier or cargo ship or tourist boat appeared on the horizon was there a reminder of a seam between heaven and earth. To the east was the capital. Modern office buildings were going up, and in the more exclusive residential neighborhoods, old world stucco and salmon-colored houses sprawled over kempt green lawns. Then, to the northwest, lay the disgrace of the shanty village where most of the damage from the hurricane had been concentrated. Finally, the barracks that strategically surrounded the wedding cake of a presidential palace where most coups and revolutions got started.

Carmencita pointed to a complex of houses surrounded by lawns. "Look! Our house! We sure seem close."

Francisco did not respond. He turned back down toward the car, his hands jingling the loose change in his pockets, a sound that reminded Yolanda of the jingling of the chain link bridge in the breeze. The girls followed him, trying to break their hillside run. They hoisted their gear out of the trunk, Francisco lifting the tent to his chest as if he were carrying a small child. "Shall I set it up for you, señoritas?"

Yolanda reached for the tent very much as if it were her child. "I've been setting it up all spring," she lied. In fact, she had mostly helped Steven by handing him stakes or holding one of the complication of flaps as he sorted them out. "No problem, Francisco."

She turned away and began taking the tent out of its case, not daring to look over her shoulder, so the young man would not be encouraged to stand by. The car engine started, and the black limousine moved slowly down the narrow dirt road, disappearing into the green tunnel.

Yolanda and her cousins set to work on the tent. As she unpacked it, Yolanda looked for Steven's instructions, handwritten on yellow, legal-sized paper, the letters tilting in the wrong direction as if some wind of passion were blowing through what he had to say. The instructions were supposed to be in the center of the coiled tent. Vaguely, she recalled the officials at Customs finding them, handing them to her. What had she done with them? She patted the pockets of her jeans as if just now the transaction had occurred. She remembered specifically slipping them back in between the canvas flaps. Again, the cousins spread the canvas out, rummaging in its folds, until it lay, a confused heap at their feet. But there was no sign of the yellow sheet of paper.

"I thought you said you knew how to set this thing up?" Lucinda's hand was on her hip.

"Not without the instructions," Yolanda said. This was not one of the newer, spiffy sporting goods tents, but an old, complicated contraption already outdated even in the army. Yolanda was disappointed, of course, since the whole point of the camping trip had been to use the tent. But something had been gained: for the first time the girl cousins had been allowed out for an overnight on their own. They must make this first freedom into a great success. "Look, you guys. It's no big deal. Most people wouldn't even be using a tent in this weather." The group looked up worriedly at the sky.

They spent most of the afternoon arguing with each other. The mosquitoes or horse flies, or whatever they were, came up from the brook. Whoever said she was going to bring it had forgotten the bug spray. Carmencita would die if the insect she was allergic to bit her. Lucinda had cut her finger on the tin of sardines. She would have lockjaw by morning. The cousins were in foul moods and blamed their imminent deaths on each other. They turned in early to avoid the bugs, bypassing dinner, after snacking all afternoon on the dainty party sandwiches Zoraida had packed in the cooler.

Late that night, Yolanda stirred in the darkness. She listened to the breathing of her sleeping companions. A distant cock crowed. Then the sound of thunder, faint rumbles, getting closer and closer. But the sound which made her body jolt, fully awake, was that of a man's cough. She was sure of it. A gruff voice amplified by a failed attempt to muffle the sound in the fist. Ever so slowly, Yolanda rolled over toward the others, hoping to nudge them awake.

Suddenly, the sky lit up. There was a thunderous explosion. The cousins woke with a start; they had been through so many in the last seven years, they were sure this was yet another revolution. But a second flash of lightning revealed the rolling hills, the palm trees doubling over in the high winds. A heavy curtain of rain began to fall. The girls lifted the tent they had placed as a dry pallet on the ground over their heads and huddled close to the trunk of the largest of the mimosas. It was good to have been spared a revolution, but once soaked, a rainstorm was bad enough. The youngest of the cousins began to cry, "I'm going to get pneumonia."

In the next flash of lightning, they saw a dark shape hurrying uphill towards them in the driving rain. One of the little cousins screamed, and the others followed. Yolanda was sure the band of desperate *campesinos* had come for them. They could hold the girls hostage. Her cousins, at any rate, would bring in a handsome ransom. Their father was a big industrialist, who had been part of the junta the Americans had put in place to conduct the country's business before the elections could be held.

"It's just me, señoritas." The familiar voice was muffled by the splattering of rain and rumbling of thunder.

"Oh Francisco, Francisco!" The young women reached out their arms, urging him to come quickly under the cover of the tree. They lifted the canvas over his head and waited for the rainstorm to end. One of the cousins told the story of the lost instructions. "I think they must have dropped out in Customs," Yolanda explained. "They were on a yellow piece of paper."

"Oh . . . that paper," Francisco remembered it well. "Yuri and I found it when we were packing up the tent; we gave it to your uncle so it wouldn't get lost."

So that's where the instructions had gone! Briefly it crossed Yolanda's mind that her uncle had kept the paper in order to sabotage their outing, and teach the girls a lesson. Now, more than ever, she was determined to prove him wrong. There was no way, even if a hurricane was on its way that she'd head back home this very night.

A plot began to hatch: as soon as the rain eased, they would make a dash for the car. It was parked not too far from this very spot, Francisco explained. "All we have to do is hike down the back of this hill, and we'll be at the little bridge. Remember?" He lowered his voice as if he were referring to a private rendezvous Yolanda and he had enjoyed there.

"We must be farther than that, Francisco?" Yolanda had grown suspicious. "Why, we drove away from there for over an hour." And then, just as the lightning shone for a moment on the outline of the landscape around her, Yolanda saw the bits of evidence coalescing: her uncle's look, the stolen instructions, the compound so close by when they looked towards the capital at the summit of the hill. They had been tricked! They had been led to believe that they were truly in the interior, winding around and around over rough road, and here they were just a hop, skip, and a jump from the new highway! She was surprised, not at her uncle, but at Francisco. Despite his progressive ideas about politics, the old customs about women still held. He had fallen in with her uncle.

As soon as the rain let up, the group gathered up their gear. Francisco led them, down the hill, through a thin grove of trees, and there they were at the river bank. The sky had begun to clear; here and there a star sifted through; the moon, almost full, radiated through the thinner and thinner layers of cloud so that the sky shone with a strange iridescence. At the bridge, the cousins hesitated, but Francisco urged them across. They held the tent and sleeping gear in a single file flank to their left while with their free hands, they grasped the guard rail nervously.

Parked on a cement slab was the car. The girls argued about whether or not they should return to the compound this very night. "Look, I get to leave at the end of the summer," Yolanda persuaded, "but you guys will never hear the end of it. Besides, if we try setting out tonight on these back roads, we'll probably get stuck in the mud. Right, Francisco?"

"At your orders, señorita."

They draped the damp bedding over the top of the car to drain, so that the sheets and light flannels fell over the windshield and windows. Inadvertently, the girls had found a way to curtain off the early and bright tropical dawn. They would get some sleep this awful night. But what about Francisco? He would not come into the car with them. "He won't sleep with us," Lucinda explained. "It just wouldn't look right."

"Look right to whom?" Yolanda snapped. She was fed up with all of them. In spite of her resolve never ever to order the servants around, she commanded the chauffeur from her front seat, "Francisco, you come in here right now!" But the chauffeur merely chuckled and begged off. "Should you need me, señorita, I'll be right outside. At your service."

For a while, between sleep and waking, Yolanda heard the humming of the air conditioning and the breathing of the others in the sealed interior of the car. Later, she heard the door click open, the windows whirled down a crack from the control panel on the driver's armrest. The engine was turned off. Through her opened window, she would hear the chiming of the chain links on the bridge. Several times that night, Yolanda woke up, disoriented, but the sound of the chains would recall her to where she was.

In the morning, she woke to cock crow, and it was as if they were in the tent, all the windows covered up by their sleeping gear. Quietly, so as not to wake the others, Yolanda opened her door and let herself out. Just ahead sat Francisco, fast asleep, his back against the trunk of a palm tree, the green canvas of Steven's tent draped over his shoulders like a poncho.

Yolanda stood so close that she noticed the way his hair waved back from his forehead in tight curls, his shoulders rose and fell. Just so Steven slept, his mouth slightly open, his body limp and sweet beside her. She felt a surprising tenderness. Why hadn't it struck her before, so viscerally? Because he was the chauffeur? Because her family would consider such attraction taboo? Some things did come of being part gringa, she thought. She had sprung free of the old customs. Well, almost.

Francisco stirred awake, sensing a presence. Slowly, he rose to his feet.

"So, you took us to the interior, eh, Francisco?" There was irony in her voice he might have mistaken for play had she not looked directly into his eyes. This time, his were the first to look away.

"Your uncle's orders," the young man admitted, as if she should take it up with her own family. "I wasn't to lose sight of the señoritas for a moment. And it's a good thing too, or you would have gotten drenched." He indicated the tent draped in folds at his feet. There was still water caught in those folds.

"But we wouldn't have gotten drenched if we'd been able to set it up," Yolanda reminded Francisco. "You said that my uncle kept the yellow sheet of paper with the instructions?"

The young man nodded slowly as if for the first time he too comprehended, link by link, the whole chain of events that led to their shared helplessness this moment.

Both gazed a moment at the dark green canvas as if neither knew quite what to do with it. Then, bending, Yolanda took up one of the flaps. Francisco bent to help her, picking up two and handing her another of the flaps. They backed off from each other until there was a large, taut canvas plane between them. They tilted it to make the water run off, and then, as if it were a dance whose steps they knew by heart, she stepped toward him, he stepped toward her, corner to corner, they doubled forward and back until the tent was folded up so snugly it slid easily back into its cloth sack.

In Search of Epifano

Rudolfo Anaya

(Photograph © 1992 by UNM Photo)

RUDOLFO ANAYA is the author of *Bless Me Ultima*, an award winning novel and an essential work in the canon of Latino-American fiction, as well as *Heart Of Aztlan, Tortuga, A Chicano In China, Lord of Dawn*, and several other important works. He is a full professor and teaches creative writing at the University of New Mexico, where he also edits *Blue Mesa Review*. Being an important figure among Latino writers, Mr. Anaya's work has received high international as well as national critical praise and attention. He lives and writes in New Mexico.

She drove into the desert of Sonora in search of Epifano. For years, when summer came and she finished her classes, she had loaded her old Jeep with supplies and gone south into Mexico.

Now she was almost eighty, and she thought, ready for death, but not afraid of death. It was the pain of the bone-jarring journey which was her reality, not thoughts of death. But that did not diminish the urgency she felt as she drove south, across the desert. She was following the north rim of El Cañon de Cobre towards the land of the Tarahumaras. In the Indian villages there was always a welcome and fresh water.

The battered Jeep kicked up a cloud of chalky dust which rose into the empty and searing sky of summer. Around her, nothing moved in the heat. Dry mirages rose and shimmered, without content, without form. Her bright, clear eyes remained fixed on the rocky, rutted road in front. Around her there was only the vast and empty space of the desert. The dry heat.

The Jeep wrenched sideways, the low gear groaning and complaining. It had broken down once, and had cost her many days' delay in Mexicali. The mechanic at the garage told her not to worry. In one day the parts would be in from Calexico and she would be on her way.

But she knew the way of the Mexican, so she rented a room in a hotel nearby. Yes, she knew the Mexican. Part of her blood was Mexican, wasn't it? Her great-grandfather, Epifano, had come north to Chihuahua to ranch and mine. She knew the stories whispered about the man, how he had built the great ranch in the desert. His picture was preserved in the family album, at his side, his wife, a dark-haired woman. Around them, their sons.

The dry desert air burned her nostrils. A scent of the green ocotillo reached her, reminded her of other times, other years. She knew how to live in the sun, how to travel and how to survive, and she knew how to be alone under the stars. Night was her time in the desert. She liked to lie in her bedroll and look up at the swirling dance of the stars. In the cool of evening her pulse would quicken. The sure path of the stars was her map, drawing her south.

Sweat streaked her wrinkled skin. Sweat and dust, the scent commingling. She felt alive. "At least I'm not dry and dead," she said aloud. Sweat and pleasure, it came together.

The Jeep worried her now. A sound somewhere in the gear box was not right. "It has trouble," the mechanic had said, wiping his oily hands on a dirty rag. What he meant was that he did not trust his work. It was best to return home, he suggested with a shrug. He had seen her musing over the old and tattered map, and he was concerned about the old woman going south. Alone. It was no good.

"We all have trouble," she mumbled. We live too long and the bones get brittle and the blood dries up. Why can't I taste the desert in my mouth? Have I grown so old? Epifano? How does it feel to become a spirit of the desert?

Her back and arms ached from driving; she was covered with the dust of the desert. Deep inside, in her liver or in her spleen, in one of those organs which the ancients called the seat of life, there was an ache, a dull, persistent pain. In her heart there was a tightness. Would she die and never reach the land of Epifano?

She slept while she waited for the Jeep to be repaired. Slept and dreamed under the shade of the laurel in the patio of the small hotel. Around her Mexican sounds and colors permeated her dream. What did she dream? That it was too late in her life to go once again into the desert? That she was an old woman and her life was lived, and the only evidence she would leave of her existence would be her sketches and paintings? Even now, as weariness filled her, the dreams came, and she slipped in and out of past and present. In her dreams she heard the voice of the old man, Epifano.

She saw his eyes, blue and bright like hers, piercing, but soft. The eyes of a kind man. He had died. Of course, he had died. He belonged to the past. But she had not forgotten him. In the family album, which she carried with her, his gaze was the one that looked out at her and drew her into the desert. She was the artist of the family. She had taken up painting. She heard voices. The voice of her great-grandfather. The rest of her family had forgotten the past, forgotten Mexico and the old man Epifano.

The groaning of the Jeep shattered the silence of the desert. She tasted dust in her mouth, she yearned for a drink of water. She smiled. A thirst to be satisfied. Always there was one more desire to be satisfied. Her paintings were like that, a desire from within to be satisfied, a call to do one more sketch of the desert in the molten light before night came. And always the voice of Epifano drawing her to the trek into the past.

The immense solitude of the desert swallowed her. She was only a moving shadow in the burning day. Overhead, vultures circled in the sky, the heat grew intense. She was alone on a dirt road she barely remembered, taking her bearings only by instinct, roughly following the north rim of the Cañon de Cobre, drawn by the thin line of the horizon, where the dull peaks of las montañas met the dull blue of the sky. Whirlwinds danced in her eyes, memories flooded at her soul.

She had married young. She thought she was in love; he was a man of ambition. It took her years to learn that he had little desire or passion. He could not, or would not, fulfill her. What was the fulfillment she sought? It had to do with something that lay even beneath the moments of love or children carried in the womb. Of that she was sure.

She turned to painting, she took classes, she traveled alone. She came to understand that she and the man were not meant for each other.

She remembered a strange thing had happened in the chapel where the family gathered to attend her marriage. An Indian had entered and stood at the back of the room. She had turned and looked at him. Then he was gone, and later she was not sure if the appearance was real or imagined.

But she did not forget. She had looked into his eyes. He had the features of a Tarahumara. Was he Epifano's messenger? Had he brought a warning? For a moment she hesitated, then she had turned and said yes to the preacher's question. Yes to the man who could never understand the depth of her passion. She did what was expected of her there in the land of ocean and sun. She bore him a daughter and a son. But in all those years, the man never understood the desire in her, he never explored her depth of passion. She turned to her dreams, and there she heard the voice of Epifano, a resonant voice imparting seductive images of the past.

Years later she left her husband, left everything, left the dream of southern California where there was no love in the arms of the man, no sweet juices in the nights of love pretended. She left the circle of pretend. She needed a meaning, she needed desperately to understand the voices which spoke in her soul. She drove south, alone, in search of Epifano. The desert dried her by day, but replenished her at night. She learned that the mystery of the stars, at night, was like the mystery in her soul.

She sketched, she painted, and each year in spring time she drove farther south. On her map she marked her goal, the place where once stood Epifano's hacienda.

In the desert the voices were clear. She followed the road into Tarahumara country, she dreamed of the old man, Epifano. She was his blood, the only one who remembered him.

At the end of day she stood at the side of a pool of water, a small, desert spring surrounded by desert trees. The smell in the air was cool, wet. At her feet, tracks of deer, a desert cat. Ocelot. She stooped to drink, like a cautious animal.

"Thank the gods for this water which quenches our thirst," she said, splashing the precious water on her face, knowing there is no life in the desert without the water which flows from deep within the earth. Around her, the first stars of dusk begin to appear.

She had come at last to the ranch of Epifano. There, below the spring where she stood, on the flat ground, was the hacienda. Now could be seen only the outlines of the foundation and the shape of the old corrals. From here his family had spread, northwest, up into Mexicali and finally into southern California. Seeds. Desert seeds seeking precious water. The water of desire. And only she had returned.

She sat and gazed at the desert, the peaceful quiet mauve of the setting sun. She felt a deep sadness within. An old woman, sitting alone in the wide desert, her dream done.

A noise causes her to turn. Perhaps an animal come to drink at the spring, the same spring where Epifano had once wet his lips. She waited, and in the shadows of the palo verde and the desert willows she saw the Indian appear. She smiled.

She was dressed in white, the color of desire not consummated. Shadows moved around her. She had come home, home to the arms of Epifano. The Indian was a tall, splendid man. Silent. He wore paint, as they did in the old days when they ran the game of the pelota up and down las montañas of the Cañon de Cobre.

"Epifano," she said, "I came in search of Epifano." He understood the name. Epifano. He held his hand to his chest. His eyes were bright and blue, not Tarahumara eyes, but the eyes of Epifano. He had known she would come. Around her other shadows moved, the women. Indian women of the desert. They moved silently around her, a circle of women, an old ceremony about to begin.

The sadness left her. She struggled to rise, and in the dying light of the sun a blinding flash filled her being. Like desire, or like an arrow from the bow of the Indian, the light filled her and she quivered.

The moan of love is like the moan of life. She was dressed in white.

The White Bedspread

Elena Castedo

ELENA CASTEDO was born in Spain and grew up in Chile. She has held dozens of jobs, among them as teacher, translator, demonstrator of electrical appliances at shopping malls, model, and editor of a trilingual scholarly magazine. She holds an MA degree from UCLA, where she received the 1968 UCLA Master's Award as the best student in all humanistic fields, and a Ph.D. from Harvard University. She has received a Woodrow Wilson as well as fellowships from Harvard University and the American Association of University Women. Her first novel, *Paradise*, was nominated for the 1990 National Book Award. Mrs. Castedo is married and lives in Virginia near her three children and five grandchildren.

Approaching the closet, Audolina meets Maria in the mirror. Maria is her name in the Anglo houses. They are all Marias here, nobody can remember "Audolina," "Filomena," "Mirella," such simple names. Audolina places her ear against the door one more time, then takes the carefully folded Garfinkel's bag la Señora gave her from the closet. This is the most delicate operation of the whole week, the most dangerous and eventually the most satisfying. It requires speed and precision.

Someone's coming up the stairs! Maria drops the bag and looks in the mirror to take a hairpin from her chignon, then puts the pin back. Even with her face all flushed from the scare, her image looks so dignified in front of the attic room, like the pictures of saints with landscapes behind them. *La Virgen Dolorosa* be praised; a bed white as a dove, with her own bedspread, in a room with a door that stays closed all night long.

The sound of steps is interrupted. Then they go down. Audolina takes a deep breath, opens the Garfinkel's bag and carefully places a pork chop, wrapped in double tinfoil, to keep the cursed dog's nose out of it.

Steps come up the stairs again. Audolina drops the bag nervously. She observes Maria in the mirror remove her apron. When the lines of the chest and the rump go flat, and hair shows gray, and the months are put to rest, it's the way the body shows what goes on in the soul. Then a woman can become pure again.

The steps are almost at her door. She walks around the bed, caressing out every nonexistent wrinkle. How beautiful. How lovely. Finally, her own bedspread, a dream for more than four times as many years as she has fingers.

The girl opens the door without knocking and walks in, wearing a slip and teen bra.

For the Sacred Virgin, still flat as a tortilla, wearing a bra . . .

"Maria, hook this bra tighter for me, will you?"

Audolina joins the two ends of the satin cloth; it feels dry compared to the live satin of the girl's back. Rougher patches announce her skin's imminent changes.

"Maria, if you stay this Sunday, you could tell me stories. Like the one about the delivery man. Did he really leave you a red rose? Are you sure you didn't make it all up? You can tell it to me again." The girl's lips stretch an unsteady smile over braces.

"Why you ask me to stay, Missy Jenny? You know I got and see the friends in la Mamplesa."

"Give me a break, Maria! It's not Mamplesa, how can you be so ignorant! It's Mount Pleasant."

"Is what I say, Missy Jenny, Mamplesa. I get ready now; in a minute la Señora, your mama, she take me to the bus stop. I got to fix my hair now, I got to change now." She lifts her arms to take out the same hairpin and puts it back.

"You're so vain, Maria, always smoothing your hair to the back of your neck, and always putting cream on your hands. Don't tell me old women have boyfriends in Mount Pleasant! Wouldn't that be a riot!"

"Vain no, Missy Jenny. A woman have to be neat and clean, and, when the woman is young, she . . . well, she got to have no choice, but all the bad times have the end, then a woman is not so young, then a woman can be neat, a woman can be . . . clean again. Miss Jenny, you eat more, you put some meat up front, not a good for nothing bra you have. Next week we are together, and I fix you the most best *sopapillas*. Delicious, O.K., child?"

"Child? Have you gone nuts? I'm not a child! You know very well I'm not! It's been five months now; I'm a woman! And I'm almost taller than you. Look, see? And what makes you think I need you around all the time? I have friends. I have a friend called Megan. If her parents hadn't forced her to go to the Greenbriar with them, she'd be right here with me, right here. And other friends too. And I'd rather not have you around at all. You can leave, just leave!" The girl slams the door as she walks out.

Audolina listens to the door. She must work fast. From the wastepaper basket she retrieves the small packages and tiny jars. Who'd look there, even if they should get suspicious? The rich have a fear of trash. She's so clever it makes her smile. She places the banana—also wrapped in tinfoil, so the child won't pick the aroma. Then the scissors that appeared—a joyous miracle—inside the family room's old couch while she was vacuuming it. She'll admire them later. Maybe she'll trade them for Corina's canned artichokes, or a scarf, or a belt; Corina's very bold; she'll take anything from her Señora. Now some of the little jars; Audolina's very conscientious about collecting small containers ahead of time; never leave things for the last minute, her grandfather used to tell them. Actually, nowadays she could buy some of these things if she wanted to, but it's for prevention and, why not; she's very good at it. Empty prescription jars are the best; light, small, easy to pack and ideal for a Sunday's supply. Plus some left over, to go on filling the larger containers in the room she rents from her countrywoman, Doña Rosa.

Ave Maria! Steps up the stairs again! Audolina dumps all the small jars with the lilac bath salts, dish soap, cooking oil, vinegar, laundry soap, bicarbonate of soda and butter into the bag and drops it in the closet. There's no peace to be had. The steps go down the stairs. *Virgen Santa*, out with the bag again. The little jar with face cream fits snugly. Yes, she's still vain in some ways, Up Above forgive her. Last is the whiskey. She'll invite Doña Rosa and Corina, and they'll go to La Latina to buy the best *empanaditas* and *croquetas* and olives in all of la Mamplesa, and come back to listen to Celia Cruz sing those Ayayay! merengues on Radio Borinquen, and drink on the rocks, and laugh until their cheeks hurt. She brings no perfume; none of that rich woman's perfume; the smell still tugs at her stomach. In the houses of diplomats from her own country, every time she heard those faint male steps come into her room at night, instead of asking aloud "Who is it?" or turning on the light, she would dab la Señora's perfume—kept in a Kaopectate bottle—in the dark . . .

Steps run up the stairs and the girl bursts in with shiny eyes. "Look what I brought you, Maria! The jewel box my father gave me; it's for you." The girl puts the box on the night table and opens it. "Isn't it beautiful music? It says here it's Rachmaninoff's Prelude in C. You're going to stay, aren't you, Maria. We can do fun things. If you want to, we can watch *telenovelas* on the Spanish channel; nobody'll be home but us."

"Gracias, gracias, Missy Jenny, but this is not for me, but it is for you. I come back Monday and now I get ready."

"Well, I don't care if you go away for all of Sunday, or the whole weekend for all I care! You think I'm going to be begging you to stay? No way! You really think you're the cat's miaow, don't you. Well, there're lots of things you don't know. I bet you don't know I don't have a thing under my slip; no panties. Sexy, huh?" The girl lifts her slip playfully above her bony knees. "Ayyy! Shame, shame!"

"Missy Jenny, you go, pleese; and take the pretty box; your mama, la Señora, she very busy and she go to her office, and she call me in a minute . . ."

"C'mon Maria. Pretty soon you'll be telling me your sob stories about no father, and 'thees vallee of teers' and working in houses where your soul split and all that crap. I know it's nothing but lies, because you won't tell me why your soul 'split.' What nonsense. And you won't stay and tell me. And your stupid stories; a red rose, give me a break! . . . Maria, Maria . . . I, didn't mean it, I like your stories; I want you to stay, and you can tell me whatever you want. O.K.?"

"Pleese, Missy, you go now, pleese, I get ready now . . ."

"Listen, why don't we pretend that my mom and step-dad are going on a trip today, instead of just going to their offices to work all weekend, that way we can walk to the bus, and we can go to the space museum and get ice cream, like we did when they went on trips. Hey! We can go to the river again, and walk there, and sit on the rocks under the bridge, and watch the water, and you can tell me things, all right?"

"Missy Jenny, now I pack to go; things I need for the Sunday. Your mama; ask la Señora . . . ask el Señor to take you . . ."

"C'mon, Maria, you know perfectly well that my mother can't; she has all that law work to do. And my father lives in Chicago, of course, he can't. And my step-dad; he always has work to do; always, always."

"Well, your Señora mama she is a lawyer very important. You call some friend from school, Missy, you play."

"Play! Listen, Maria, why don't you get it through your thick head; I'm not a little kid! I'm a woman. And kids from school, they are busy; they have to go shopping with their parents, and they have to go eat out, and all that. And . . . they'd come but they can't . . ."

The girl observes Maria. Maria's standing firm. The girl goes to the bed; with a gesture that follows the music, she picks at the bedspread, leaving a big wrinkle.

"Missy Jenny, pleese, the bedspread is very good, very good bedspread, you know I paid the money for a new, white bedspread, is not for play."

Another big gesture, another tug, another big wrinkle on the bedspread.

Audolina freezes.

"Do you want me to leave you a red rose on your bedspread, Maria?"

"Missy Jenny, the bedspread is very important . . . like the bra for you. Pleese, for Santa Catalina, *protectora* of young girls . . . "

"Mariaaaaa! Why aren't you downstairs! I'm in a big rush!"

"*Ay! Virgen Santisima!* La Señora, see? I said to you . . . now you make me very mad." Audolina attempts to bring the girl to the door. They push and pull.

"Let me go! Let me go! You're scratching my arms! You horrible old woman! You're the worst maid I ever had!" The girl wiggles free and runs to the bed. She lifts her slip and sits in the middle of the bedspread. "Guess what, Maria, guess what time of the month it is for me-e." The braces shine as she forces a smile.

"Missy, pleese, Missy, I not can buy another bedspread, pleese . . . go, go now . . . "

"Mariaaa! Are you coming or not! Jenny! Where's everybody!"

The girl gets up and leaves the room with dignity.

In the middle of the white bedspread there is a red spot. Audolina forcefully pushes back a savage assault of unending trampled territories. Where, where is that territory that can't be trampled on. With a flushed face, she quickly rearranges the ham piece and the sandwich baggy with oatmeal. She drops a sweater on top of the bag. This sloppy work is against her principles, but she has no choice. The music stops. Maria closes the door and rushes downstairs, taking care not to jiggle the bag, holding it so it appears very light, saying loudly, "Si, Señora! Si, Señora!"

On Francisco el Penitente's First Becoming a Santero and Thereby Sealing His Fate

~~~~~~~~~~

Ana Castillo

ANA CASTILLO, in addition to being a widely published poet, is a novelist, essayist, translator, editor, and teacher. She is the author of several books, *Women Are Not Roses*, *My Father Was a Toltec*, *The Mixquiahuala Letters*, and *Sapogonia* among them. A nonfiction work, *Massacre of the Dreamers: Reflections on Mexican-Indian Women in the U.S.*, will be published by the University of New Mexico in 1994; her novel, *So Far From God*, is forthcoming in 1993 from W.W. Norton.

Francisco el Penitente was not always Francisco el Penitente. As a boy at Our Lady of Sorrows School and to his pals in the playground he was Frank. To his six other brothers and his father he was el Franky. To his Mexican Godmother, la Doña Felicia, however, he was Panchito and sometimes Paquito, and as he grew up, her *Paco*. But to his buddies in Nam he was Chico.

He didn't like Chico—which back home meant a roasted corn.

Or just a hard kernel.

He didn't like Chico no more than the Navajo that was also in his platoon went for the nickname "Chief," nor did the Puerto Rican from Rio Piedras, just shy of finishing his Ph.D. when he was drafted, like to be called Little Chico. Francisco el Penitente (who was not a Penitente then) was a lanky six feet in height compared to Little Chico's five feet eight inches, and to the white and black soldier majority, all "Spanish boys" were "Chico."

It was much later, at the age of thirty-three when Franky joined his uncle's *morada* up north, over ten years after he undertook his uncle's vocation of *santero* for himself, that he sealed his fate as part of the intrinsic religious belief system of his people and his land as both *santero* and *penitente* and from then on became Francisco el Penitente.

There were many signs throughout Francisco el Penitente's life that indicated such a destiny for him, but they were never so blatant that anyone like Doña Felicia, his father, or his tío Pedro would have readily detected, never nowhere near the "miracle-strain" inherent in some others' lives, like that of the famous family of women from Tomé.

Signs that pointed to a special fate came to him rather like his third grade teacher Sister Prudence used to say, "Remember, children, God writes straight with crooked lines!" For example, Francisco was the seventh son, but not of a man who was the seventh son. Francisco's own father, in fact, had been the first son, and as such, had only known a life of family obligation rather than spiritual aspiration.

His *tío* Pedro, the seventh son, inherited his father's gift for making *santos* at a very early age. Francisco was not sure if his grandfather had also been a seventh son because his grandfather did not live to see his youngest grandchildren, and his own children were not as interested in knowing such ancestral details that were so important to Francisco who was intent on a divine sign to reveal to him his role on earth. Thus, the crooked line of God passed the seventh son's gift to a seventh son although not in direct lineage, and for the time being Francisco had to settle for that much.

Being a *santero* means many things in many places, which Francisco discovered when having a conversation with Little Chico about his *tío* Pedro one night while they shared a joint and waited to be killed if they didn't kill first. "Hey, no kidding?" Little Chico laughed. "My uncle in Carolina, Puerto Rico, is a *santero*, too!" But no, as Francisco discovered when they got into it more, that Little Chico's *santero tío* practiced a very distinct variation of the Catholic influence on the New World—a Yorubic blend of adapting the names of European and Hebrew saints to African gods.

The Caribbean *santero* maintained a kind of secret membership as the Penitente Brothers of Francisco's *tierra* did; however, theirs included women as much as men and were not based on medieval Catholic rituals seeking absolution through penance and mortification, but on ancient African rites, with drums and frenzied dance and much more, when the *santero* himself contained the power to answer prayers, perform miracles, and cast out demons from the possessed.

No, Francisco explained, a *santero* in *Nuevo Méjico* was a simple man, often given to solitude, who worked alone. Sometimes a woman succumbed to the vocation, but this was rare. The *santero*, in and of himself, had no divine powers except during the time he was preparing a *bulto*, a wooden sculpture of a saint. His expert hand was not guided by the aesthetic objectives of artists, but by the saint himself in heaven, as permitted by God, because that wood turned *bulto* would become the saint's own representation on earth to aid those who were devoted to him.

The *santero* used but humbly ignored the artistic talent granted to him as a creative individual and with the same deftness which he applied to his fields, to the care of his animals, and perhaps even the love he had for his woman, he prepared his materials for his *bulto* or *retablo*. Not every man or just any man who decided to produce such holy icons for his church and community had the stamina to make it his life's vocation. And while a *santero* received a certain amount of respect for his work, it was nothing in comparison to that recognition that artists have aspired since the Renaissance when all work—secular and sacred—began to be signed with the illustrious name of the individual who designed it.

El tío Pedro never expected anyone in his own family to follow his path, because although times changed slowly for him, around him he knew the world was transforming beyond comprehension. But when his nephew came back from the war in Vietnam and visited him so many times and finally asked to try his hand at a *bulto*, he considered that perhaps it was possible, after all, that the family tradition of over two centuries was not ready to die out yet.

Francisco, or el Franky as his *tío* Pedro still liked to call him, was the youngest born to his sister-in-law, and while an unquestionably sensitive child—something which Don Pedro tended to attribute more to being "spoiled" by his mother as the youngest boy and later by his godmother—he showed no indications of being special in any way.

Pedro's eldest brother insisted on yet another child after the birth of his seventh son because although it had been a good thing as a rancher to have so many boys, his heart yearned for a daughter. And so it was that the eighth and the last of his brother's children was a beautiful little girl, Reinita, after her mother, Reyna.

When Franky started school at the age of six, both his mother and baby sister, who were not vaccinated as had been all the boys in school, became very ill and died of smallpox, leaving Franky's father alone with the seven boys.

The youngest boys were sent to their respective *padrinos* and the oldest ones stayed to help their father with the ranch. When Pancho was ready for high school he left his godmother Felicia's home, where he had been treated like a little prince without so much as ever being expected to fix his bed in the mornings, and went back home to help his father with the laborious tasks of farming.

Doña Felicia, because of her advanced age, was more of a grandmother to Francisco than a substitute mother and as the years went on his mother, ever ascending toward heaven, became more remote as a former human being and more akin to a celestial entity. To Francisco, yes, his mother was no less than a saint. Many men say this of their mothers, of course, who sacrifice themselves to their children and husbands, but for Francisco, what else could his mother be at that moment when he found himself a small child with his large family gone from him, if not *una santita en el cielo* watching over all of them to make sure that they completed the tasks she had labored so hard to bring each into the world to do?

In Doña Felicia's home, at that time she lived in Tomé near the church and was, in fact, the keeper of the keys and the caretaker of the *santos* there, there was always something good and satisfying on the stove when he got home from softball practice, his denims were patched but clean, his shirts ironed; in short, he was well cared for by the old woman. And the little house was anything but gloomy, since it was always bustling with all kinds of *gente* from the community who came to get massaged, receive consultation for family dilemmas, be "cleansed," or to get herbal remedies from the old healer woman.

Many times Francisco assisted, glad to help his *nina* but not completely aware of what all the details of the *remedios* meant or whether they in fact helped, although of course they had to help, since people held her in the highest regard and they always came back, moreover recommended others to her as well.

So Francisco learned a little about being a diagnostician of physical and spiritual ailments, and which symptoms were caused by something physical and which were caused by the bad intentions of mal-wishers. But Francisco did not like to talk about these things too much with people, not even with his brothers once he went back home, who being practical men tended to find his godmother more of an eccentric than someone to turn to for medical attention.

His father, however, did often go to Doña Felicia for massages although he never followed the tea prescriptions she advised, and he also managed to get Francisco to give him a massage at the end of a day in the field on occasion or a *ventosa* treatment when his rheumatism acted up.

Francisco watched his *tío* Pedro prepare to make a *bulto* many many times before he went to him one day after a philosophy class at the university to ask him to teach him the work of the *santero*. Francisco was attending college but was not pursuing anything in particular. He had learned to be a mechanic in the army and he could always work at that to earn a living, and in fact as it turned out, ended up doing that to get by most of the time. But when he came back from Vietnam it was hard for him to concentrate on things, to take a steady job and spent nearly a year doing little more than wandering around the streets of Albuquerque, usually stoned on pot.

As it turned out, as it usually is with young romantic men, it was for the love of a "pretty girl" who persuaded him to enroll at the university. She was to Francisco the epitome of loveliness, with sky-blue eyes and long blond hair, her loveliness was that much more enhanced by her lack of encumberment by material things like money, that "just didn't matter" as so many youth felt in 1969—at least those who did not go to Vietnam, or who did not live in *barrios* or housing projects.

She took Francisco home to her parents' house and fed him *gringo* food—nothing like the blue corn tamales, posole and green chili he was raised with—but a little closer to the army food he was fed for two years, only tasting better, things like mashed potatoes, string beans, and steak. She made love to him under the stars (we may not say in this case "with" him because Francisco was in a kind of mummified state when he came back from the war, in addition to the fact that he thought this young woman was less real than a flashback from the LSD he took in the army—so free was she from worldly preoccupations, it seemed her barefeet hardly touched the ground—so he hardly did more than respond during their sexual encounters).

So it was because of this young woman, whom he was as close to being in love with as he had ever been (the glossy pin-ups in the army barracks could not be counted as having been in love, he decided once he had a taste of the "real thing"), that he acquiesced to the idea of enrolling in college, but no sooner was his angel on to other men as earth-bound as himself, than Francisco lost all interest in being a student.

He also lost interest in being a lover, not just a lover of privileged white college girls, but all women. It was not within Francisco's scope of imagination to be a lover of men, neither, by the way. Although it may be said that until he came across la sublime *Armitana*, and with the exception of his godmother, he only loved men, even if only in *el platonic* sense.

He loved the strength and tenacity of his father and each of his brothers who—except for his brother James who seemed to find it easier staying in jail than out—were all family men devoted to their homes and land. He loved his *tío* Pedro above all his *tíos* for maintaining the religious tradition of their ancestors. Above all, he loved Christ, his heavenly Lord. He loved God, too, of course, but God was too great and too remote to have a fixed picture in his head of that entity or presume any direct contact with Him—at least that is what he felt for a long time until the day he took his knife to a piece of wood and began to carve out his first *santo*.

He and his *tío* Pedro went out on his uncle's land one morning and felled a pine; one that was a straight and healthy and as perfect as their eyes and hearts could tell. They each cut a log for themselves approximately two feet in length. Next, they trimmed the front and back with a hand axe and knife, then smoothed it with a stone just as one would use sandpaper for refining a surface.

Without too much pondering over his first subject, Francisco began to carve the image of the pious Saint Francis of Assisi, for whom, of course, he was named. His *tío* Pedro approved but sparingly offered guidance, knowing that at best all he could do was educate his nephew on how to handle his tools and the wood, but not on what his *bulto* should look like, that is, what would be correct or incorrect about the representation of his image. For that, Saint Francis himself could only guide Francisco's hand since it wasn't Saint Francis the holy man whom Francisco was imaging, the one who had cared for the poor, the infirmed and the hungry, the orphaned children and all the innocent creatures on earth, but Saint Francis in his rightful eternal place in heaven, from which privileged place he was able to work miracles for the all too human left on earth.

Francisco's first *bulto* was no more than three feet high, angular, much like himself, a thin, undernourished monk with hands stretched out before him. He was barefoot and although Francisco did not have the patience to carve out little things like individual toes or face details like nostrils or pupils, he did take the time to shape each small round bead of the rosary hanging around the saint's neck, repeating all the while the Our Father or the Hail Mary, depending on which prayer pertained to the bead he was carving.

When the figure was done (although one leg ended up uneven with the other and *tío* Pedro advised against Francisco trying to do anything about it, lest he end up with a truly *cojo bulto*), *jaspe* or gesso was manufactured out of gypsum to prepare the wood for painting.

Their paints, too, were manufactured by their own hands—gathered from earths and plants and carbons from charcoal or soot; their brushes were made from yucca fronds and chicken feathers tied together and from horse hair. In other words, nothing was store-bought because everything that went into making a *bulto* must be prepared with the utmost reverence; and although they did not have the actual relics of the saints to mix with their paints like the Russian monks who produced Byzantine icons, they labored with the natural elements, sun, air, and earth and prayed all the while as they worked together in silence—like their Spanish ancestors had done for nearly three hundred years on that strange land they felt was so far from God.

Chata

Denise Chávez

DENISE CHÁVEZ is a native of New Mexico. She is the author of numerous plays, works for children, and stories that have won several important literary awards. Her collection, *The Last of the Menu Girls*, won the Puerto del Sol fiction award for 1985. She holds a Masters' degree in Creative Writing from the University of New Mexico. She tours the United States with her one-woman performance piece, "Women in the State of Grace," from her home base in Las Cruces, New Mexico, where she is working on her new novel, *Face of an Angel*.

Chata was coming to clean Soveida's house on Fir Street. It was the third Monday of the month, an occasion Soveida was always grateful for and yet dreaded.

Since Soveida had known Esperanza "Chata" Vialpando her fees had slowly climbed. In the mid-seventies she had charged $15 a day, raising that to $20 in the late seventies and $25 in 1980. In 1985 she went to $30 and had remained constant there. Soveida never hesitated to always give her extra money as well as all the rummage she could find and whatever canned goods and food she didn't want or couldn't use. In addition to all these things, Soveida made sure Chata always had a good lunch, usually hot and store-bought. Every three weeks they would decide what they felt like eating on Cleaning Day.

Monday was Soveida's day off, and yet on those days Chata came to clean she was sure to be found at home. It never entered her mind to leave Chata alone to clean house, and so every third Monday the two women scraped, scoured, washed, rinsed, polished and then dried everything as best they could. Soveida would be dressed in her usual cleaning outfit: an old pair of black running shorts and a very

large white paint-flecked T-shirt she'd worn to paint every house
she'd lived in in the past ten years. On her head was a tattered red
bandanna that had also seen better days. A pair of gouged rubber
thongs completed her outfit.

Chata, on the other hand, was meticulously dressed in a pleasant
nylon shirtdress, sturdy brown walking shoes that laced up, and dark
pantyhose. Chata carried a special apron with her to all her jobs, and
each third Monday morning at nine a.m. she would ceremoniously
remove it from a webbed blue and white plastic satchel made in
Hong Kong. Unfolding it tenderly, she would unfurl it as Soveida ran
around the house organizing the cleaning supplies, noting that once
again she was low on soap pads and that she needed to go to the grocery store to get her 409 multi-purpose cleanser as well as a new pair
of rubber gloves. It never failed that she was low on some supplies,
but Chata took this all in stride, and did miracles with a little ammo-
nia and some rags from a plastic bag Dolores, Soveida's mother, had
given Soveida that week containing her father Luardo's softened T-
shirts and torn cotton boxer shorts.

Working with seemingly tireless concentration, efficiency and
speed, Chata worked hard all morning, only stopping briefly for
lunch with Soveida around noon. That day the two women had
decided on fried chicken. Soveida left the house secure and happy in
the knowledge that Chata was "at home" in her house cleaning.
There was no question of trust. None whatsoever. That in itself was
very wonderful. Soveida knew she could leave Chata all day if she
ever had to, even all night, and that nothing irregular would happen.
Everything would be in its place, or the place Chata felt it belonged,
because it was Chata who ordered where the knifes would be better
placed and what system would work best in each cabinet, the glasses
on the left with the plates and the cans of food on the right with all
the spices. Oh no, nothing would be broken or hidden or stolen as
long as Chata was there.

Soveida had known Chata since she was in high school, and that
was a long time ago. Chata was a young woman then, and "in her
flesh" as she liked to say about herself, with everything to look forward to, including laying down next to a man for the very first time.
Now they were older women together, both of them dear friends,
years apart, but very close.

Who was this woman called Chata? She was a short, compact,

flat-nosed little woman with the most incredible hands. They were unlike any others Soveida had ever seen on a woman. Once Soveida had seen a photograph of Pablo Picasso's hands in a book. His short squat fingers seemed highly unartistic. They were the hands of a laborer, not the hands of a great artist. Chata's hands were like Picasso's. They were thick, no-nonsense hands absolutely adept at any task. They were hands unafraid and willing to reach out. They were hands that could just as easily comfort a child and pull long, tangled clumps of dark hair out of a clogged bathroom drain. Chata's hands were not repelled by moldy food or liquid slosh of any kind. They never balked at objects sharp or rough, warm or cold. They were hands that never recoiled at soft, sick flesh, or untidy corners full of dark brown roach droppings. They were never repulsed by stoves crowded with the usual dried macaroni, the burners sticky with rivulets of gummy brown grease. They were hands that never used plastic gloves. "Pa'qué? What for? If I use them, I can't feel anything!"

Chata's hands were no strangers to toxic matter, and continued to dare plunge into burning water to get the job done. No poison was unfamiliar to these hands, no Drain-O, no Oven-Off, no lyes, or dyes, or scalding water or full strength bleach, because to Chata, to feel was everything. "And because, Soveida, one of the best of God's inventions has to be the fingernail. You can keep the earlobes, they're useless unless you wear earrings, and the breast, well, it has its use with babies, but for an old woman like me, breasts serve no purpose that I can see. They just get in the way. The same goes for an old man's penis. It's even more useless than a breast, or worse yet, two breasts. For all the trouble they give men and you hear of prostate problems in old men like you hear about the weather, well, they're just in the way, you might as well just fold them up and forget about them. There are other useless body parts, I don't know what God was thinking about. I've just covered a few of the most important. But a fingernail. A fingernail! God knew what he was doing when he invented the fingernail. And when you think about it, God had to be a woman to invent the fingernail. That's what I say. Only a female God would invent the fingernail. Think about it for a moment and you'll see what I mean. What would we do without fingernails? If I had money I'd invent a cleaning tool, like a scrapey-scrapey thing made out of fingernails. Nothing tougher. If you give me those gloves, muchacha, I can't feel my way in the dark and pick my way into the light. You know how in Mexico they make those things out of bone, like Don Quixote figures and all kinds of stupid things to collect dust? Well, maybe I could invent something with fingernails. If I had money, I would look into it. Just think about all those fingernail clippings that go to waste! We could start collecting them. And who knows? Someday you'd see a thing called "Chata's Scrapey-Scrapey" for a dollar sixty nine in aisle five at the Piggly Wiggly or the Jewel. That's if I had the money. Now hand me the paper towels on that shelf."

Chata was fond of cleaning metaphors. A house was as clean as an old man's ears. As clean as a widow's windows. As clean as a baby's chin folds. As clean as a virgin's ombligo. As clean as the corner of an old dog's eyes. Here is a woman, Soveida often thought, to whom cleanliness is a state of grace, the highest virtue known to any living soul. Chata was good at cleaning, and fast, faster than anyone Soveida had ever known. Chata was faster than any of Mamá Lupita's girls or her mother Dolores' helpers. Chata was even faster than Soveida, and that was something.

Chata had briefly worked for Dolores' mother, Doña Trancha, but that experiment was short-lived, as the old woman was quite blind by then and in ill health. "Oh, I could have taken her dishes all stained with egg and her foul bathroom like an open sewer pit, but what I couldn't take, and I'll tell you this, girl, now don't be telling your mother, I couldn't take that old woman's infernal stinginess. Not once, during that four months that I was with her, did she once offer me lunch. I'd start at six in the morning when it was still dark and I'd finish after the sun set, this was still when I was 'in my flesh' and there was no food in between, or time to eat anything if I'd have brought it. That old woman, Doña Trancha Loera, the devil's own mother, may she rest in peace, had me working like a prostitute in hell, and I could have taken it, I was younger and stronger then, and 'in my flesh,' but what I couldn't take was her not offering me lunch, not to mention any other small kindness. One day I just looked her in that eye of hers, the other one was white, like a dead fisheye, and I said, I'm sorry, Señora Trancha, but I'll be leaving next week, I have another job. Now I didn't have any sort of job, but I had to say something, who wants to live like a whore in hell? Oh, the old woman carried on and then I walked her into her bedroom with that walker of

hers and she lay down, still angry. And she asked me why I was leaving and I didn't bother telling her Pa'qué? Why? She was too mean to
change and I just knew something else was waiting for me. I was 'in
my flesh' then. Shortly after that your mother, Dolores, put your
grandma Doña Trancha, kicking and screaming, into the Del Valle
old folks home where she later died. I never felt guilty. Why should I?
Let her yell at those people up there at the Del Valle Nursing Home
and see if they forget her lunch! Pobrecita, but she was a mean old
woman. Cold. Like the inside of this freezer, Soveida. You broke
another bottle of that carbonated water in here again. Why don't you
let it cool in the icebox naturally. You're always in a hurry, girl! Well,
your grandma was cold, and I'm not saying she didn't have her reasons. She was cold and jagged like this ice, may she rest in peace. If
hell is hot, she'd sure be there for the warmth. From there I worked
with your other grandma, Mamá Lupita, but she didn't want to pay
me my full due and tried to bargain me out of my time and wanted to
subtract for my lunch and so I decided to move on to the Americanas.
They pay me what I'm worth. And they give me their old furniture
they don't use anymore and their old clothes which are very nice, not
the rags your grandma, Mamá Lupita, tried to give me, and they give
bonuses for Christmas. Las Americanas, Soveida, they're good to me.
And I love my little ladies, La Señora Bixler, La Señora Williams, La
Señora Pringler and especially La Señora King-Kelley. I don't have
anything against my own people, except they don't feed you or pay
you what you're worth. The men run after you when their wives are
gone and try to lift up your skirts when you're hunched over cleaning
out their toilet bowls, and the women, I speak from experience, don't
have no pity for you if anything goes wrong. They start on how
you're a Mexican and nobody from Mexico can do anything right
and how Mexicans can't be trusted and so on. And they forget they're
Mexicanas too. Maybe they should look in the mirror. With them it's
all your fault even if you don't do anything wrong. Me cansé. I got
tired of working for no money and for people who don't appreciate
me. You should see how La Señora Bixler loves me! Pobrecita, your
grandma Doña Trancha, she was a cruel old woman when she was
feeling good and meaner when she was out of sorts. One of my Americanas, she buys me Arby's every Tuesday, another gets me pizza.
There was food, Soveida, at your grandma's, that wasn't it, she just
didn't want to share it. Even with herself she was stingy and ate like a

bird. Your mother always complained that her mother was always telling her not to eat so much and now, because of that, she always has an icebox full of food. Now with the gringas I can eat. Ay it's the little things. And they give me rides to work and back home. One old woman I used to work for, she was a Mexicana, she made me walk to work and then back to my house with two cars sitting in her garage. And not only that, she gave me chiles for lunch each week with a single tortilla These were the same chiles we used to peel for her restaurant. No thank you, I said. Someone else hired me, I told her. Soveida Dosamantes, that's who. My new patrona. So do you want this old ice cream or not? I'm throwing it out and also these old tamales in the back. The aluminum came off and they're covered with ice. Hand me the pan with the soapy water. Like I always say, remember this: Never work for someone who won't feed you. What they want is a dumb animal not a person to help. If a person is stingy in their own home, imagine how they are out in the world. If they screw you in the kitchen, what will happen in the street? Just because you see their filth on the inside doesn't mean you are filth if you wipe it away. Just because I clean your toilet doesn't mean I'm not a woman and don't love to dance. So don't push me or I'll get mad. Watch out! Because if you're pushing me to get me mad I will. A clean house is a virtue. If you need a priestess, I'm the one. Call me, but softly. And then get out of my way unless you can keep up with me. Now *you* almost can keep up with me, Soveida! The others, if they get in my way, it'll be too late for them to say they're sorry unless they really mean it. I know. I was born with this extra body part most people don't have. I call it my other brain. It's this dark little nudo, this knot-like root in between my eyes that lets me know what's true and what's a lie. Sometimes I can feel it throbbing there in my head like a question mark or an exclamation point depending on what it feels, lies or truth. It's no bigger than the size of a frijol but very powerful. Not too many people have this extra body part. I never usually talk about it, but it just came up. My grandmother had one too. She called it the nudo. With it, I can read people. I've dealt with them enough. Just hand me the sponge, I'm going to mop up the spilt water. What do you say we have Chinese next time?"

Soveida loved these Mondays with Chata. Talking in Spanish and laughing in no particular language. Spanish, her grandmother Lupita's favorite language, her father's little-used language, he having grown up at a time when children were punished for speaking Spanish on the playground. Spanish, her mother Dolores' language of intimacy and need. Spanish, Doña Trancha's shrill invective language of complaint and horror without ceasing, sharp and hard as a fist and painful as flesh doubled over, words spat and splattered on the white walls of her tiny room at the Del Valle Nursing Home, walls covered with family photos hung by Dolores, the daughter who wasn't a daughter, no real daughter could put her own mother in a nursing home. Spanish. Laying with her lover Tirzio, him telling her thickly in the long darkness, "Te quiero, te quiero, te quiero." I want you. I want you. I want you. In Spanish. In Spanish. In Spanish.

Cleaning up in Spanish with Chata the remnants of her other worlds: work and the deceptively quiet and desperate living of a once-divorced, now-widowed pregnant woman who was in love with a married man with two children. Soveida was a waitress who knew what it was to serve others and a woman who knew what it was to work hard. She knew so well what it was to lift and clean up and mop and hose down that she had to stay home every third Monday to help her cleaning woman clean her house. She didn't want Chata to do it alone, although she was a woman who knew what it was to be alone, to work alone. Soveida worked just as hard as her cleaning lady because she wanted to, because she had to.

Soveida felt guilty when she handed Chata the Oven-Off with lye, because it was a job *no one* should have to do. When she could, Soveida always wore gloves. She owned three pair. Blue. Pink. Yellow. She didn't feel it was right for Chata to burn her hands cleaning the stove, but Chata only refused to use the gloves once again. "I can't feel with them on, girl. And I need to feel." Soveida felt she was no better, no less than Chata, she felt that they were equals. Except when it came to the stove. Or maybe because of the stove.

This was Monday's Chata. Chata on Mondays. The other Chata had a couple of children from a man named Candenacio "Candy" Limon. Chata worked every day of the week except Sundays. Soveida had only heard about this Sunday woman, she never knew her. This was the woman who met with Candy when his wife, Sidelia, was at Mass. Both Chatas had calloused hands that stroked and loved and offered lingering caresses, both had hands made no less beautiful by either scars or burns. Both Chatas had efficient bodies, whether working seemingly tirelessly for some Americana or making eternal, passionate love to her Candy.

Chata and Candy had loved each other, but he was married in the church. Eventually he died of cancer. He was much older than Chata and it was to be expected, she said. She'd gone to Candy's funeral but his grown children asked her to leave. His wife, a living saint riddled with tumors, stopped Chata on the way out and pulled her over to the casket. They sat side by side during the Mass, his two wives, holding hands like long lost sisters, each comforting the other. And when Sidelia, Candy's tumor-ridden widow, died that June, Chata was barred again by those middle-aged brats. She wept to herself, remembering both Candy and Sidelia at the same time, envying them their peace. Someday she thought, she would happily join them. But for now, she was "in her flesh" and there was work to be done.

Chata adjusted the radio that was tuned to XELO, a Juárez, Mexico, station and then threw out the dirty water she's collected from cleaning the freezer. "There, that's it, Soveida. What's next? Are we doing the cabinets this week, or walls?"

There was a peace in Chata's Mondays. All was ordered. Calm. Correct. As any polite Mexican will say with great courtesy befitting something that is natural, apt, appropriate, "Es propio." It's proper. It's as it should be.

Every third Mondays were a breaking of bread between two hard-working women who honored each other's work. A communion. A sacrament. "You're a good worker, Soveida," Chata once complimented her. Coming from Chata, this was the highest honor ever given to Soveida by a fellow worker. Soveida cherished that blessing all her life.

Chata lived in a tiny, two-room shack on Chiva Town, where once goats used to roam through the streets. This squatty woman with thick hands who lived crowded with her two children in a place with no kitchen, just a counter with a sink, a small stove and much-used refrigerator, taught Soveida what home really meant, what comfort really was. And it was because of Chata, who shared a living/sleeping room with her teenage daughter, the son sleeping in the alcove outside the main room, that Soveida eventually came to know what happiness could be. Chata taught Soveida what work was and how every woman should continue to work, even in the worst of times, day after day, week after week, year after year. Chata worked as a maid, a job no one would have ever really chosen if they'd had a choice, yet she managed to bestow upon it enormous dignity.

"Laughter is good and so are the tears," Chata said, as she reached for a clean rag, pulling out a pair of Luardo's softened Fruit of the Looms. "I had me my Candy and he had me. My kids know that I love them. Manuel is a freshman at State University and Leticia's in the band at the high school. She'll graduate next year. Their Daddy would be proud, Soveida. And you, when are you going to have children? It's never too late. Not for a woman like you, 'in your flesh,' a woman like you who knows what it is to work and to love. Because, girl, let me tell you, loving is work! Even if you have an extra body part like I do, the little root still can't stop suffering. Hand me the Pledge. We're almost out, Soveida. Get some for next time, don't forget. I'm moving into the living room."

Chata on Monday. The Order. The Calm. A woman in the state of grace.

Salvador Late or Early

Sandra Cisneros

SANDRA CISNEROS was born in Chicago, the daughter of a Mexican father and a Mexican-American mother. She is the author of *The House on Mango Street*, awarded the Before Columbus American Book Award in 1985, and *My Wicked Wicked Ways* that will be published in hardcover by Turtle Bay Books in 1992. Her short story collection, *Woman Hollering Creek*, was published in 1991 and received the Lannan Award for Fiction and the PEN Center West Award for Fiction. Her work has been translated into seven languages. She lives in San Antonio where she is at work on her novel, *Caramelo*.

Salvador with eyes the color of caterpillar, Salvador of the crooked hair and crooked teeth, Salvador whose name the teacher cannot remember, is a boy who is no one's friend, runs along somewhere in that vague direction where homes are the color of bad weather, lives behind a raw wood doorway, shakes the sleepy brothers awake, ties their shoes, combs their hair with water, feeds them milk and corn flakes from a tin cup in the dim dark of the morning.

Salvador, late or early, sooner or later arrives with the string of younger brothers ready. Helps his mama, who is busy with the business of the baby. Tugs the arms of Cecilio, Arturito, makes them hurry, because today, like yesterday, Arturito has dropped the cigar box of crayons, has let go the hundred little fingers of red, green, yellow, blue, and nub of black sticks that tumble and spill over and beyond the asphalt puddles until the crossing-guard lady holds back the blur of traffic for Salvador to collect them again.

Salvador inside that wrinkled shirt, inside the throat that must clear itself and apologize each time it speaks, inside that forty-pound body of boy with its geography of scars, its history of hurt, limbs stuffed with feathers and rags, in what part of the eyes, in what part of the heart, in that cage of the chest where something throbs with both fists and knows only what Salvador knows, inside that body too small to contain the hundred balloons of happiness, the single guitar of grief, is a boy like any other disappearing out the door, beside the schoolyard gate, where he has told his brothers they must wait. Collects the hands of Cecilio and Arturito, scuttles off dodging the many schoolyard colors, the elbows and wrists criss-crossing, the several shoes running. Grows small and smaller to the eye, dissolves into the bright horizon, flutters in the air before disappearing like a memory of kites.

Nellie

Roberto G. Fernandez

ROBERTO G. FERNANDEZ is a prose fiction writer and teacher. He belongs to the new generation of Cuban-American writers who grew up and were educated in the United States. His third novel, *Raining Backwards*, received high critical praise and was one of the first Cuban-American novels to be written in English and published in the United States. He is also the author of *Life Is On Special* (La Vida Es Un Especial) and *The Roller Coaster* (La Montaña Rusa). Presently he is working on *Nellie*, a novel about the ongoing tribulations of Cuban-Americans living in Cuba and in Miami. He lives and teaches in Tallahassee, Florida.

Nellie unplugged the sizzling iron, put the starch underneath the kitchen sink and began to fold the clothes she had just finished ironing. She was glad she hadn't burned herself this time and began to place the garments in the worn suitcases which were resting open-mouthed at the foot of the bed. The luggage was spotted with faded stickers, echoes of journeys taken long ago—an eyeless bullfighter battling half a bull, a Tower of Pisa which was no longer leaning, and a Buckingham Palace Royal Guard beheaded by time.

She began by positioning the underwear, then the blouses, followed by skirts, shirts and pants. Last of all, she carefully laid on top of everything her favorite and only remaining evening gown, a royal blue dress with brocades, pearls, and sequins, and covered it with moth balls, impregnating the house with the stench of time. Though the dress had not felt the warmth of human flesh or heard the music and laughter of a ballroom for some time, Nellie brought it out each time she ironed just to look at it for a moment. Then, with a suddenness born out of her small hope, she slammed the suitcases shut and

with a series of vigorous kicks made the luggage disappear underneath the bed.

Nellie licked her index finger and flicked the iron to make sure it
could be stored inside the closet without risking a fire. Delfina had
warned her when she was a young girl to be careful of fire. At the
time, Delfina had been trying to light a blaze under a kettle of water
to boil Nellie's father's soiled shirts while Nellie, always the observant
child, watched her and contentedly sucked on a mango.

"See the fire, child?" Delfina asked. "In your path there is an
embracing couple charred by flames. Beware of anything that burns!"

Even though the two years which Nellie and her family had spent
in the bungalow had seemed like twenty she still could not bring herself to unpack the family's bags. The daily routine of ironing the
clothes and putting them in suitcases helped to keep her faith from
being snuffed out altogether. She still hoped that all that had happened was not lasting, not permanent.

It was hot for January and Nellie took the cardboard fan she had
found at her doorstep and escaped from the bedroom to the cooler
porch. The front of the fan depicted a Scandinavian Christ resting by
a river bank surrounded by tall beech trees and holding a black sheep
in his lap. The back side proclaimed a holy message written in an
incipient Spanish: PESCADOR ARRE PIENTA DIOS ENOHADO CON USTED
BEN Y TIEMPLO PRIMERO VIVO LLAMAR REVEREND Y AMIGO AUGUSTUS B.
FENDER. OLE! SE HABLA PEQUEÑO ESPAÑOL. (FISHERMAN, REPENT! GOD
MAD WITH YOU. COME AND I SCREW FIRST LIVING. CALL REVEREND AND
FRIEND AUGUSTUS B. FENDER. OLE! A SMALL SPANISH IS SPOKEN.) Nellie
wiped the rocking chair with the rag that hung from her left pocket
and smelled of garlic and sat down. She started to fan and rock herself in perfect synchrony. Her gaze was lost in the cane fields that
stretched beyond the horizon surrounding the house. As usual, her
eyes became cloudy with the memory of Rigoletto, attired in a red
light sweater, who grew smaller and smaller until it became a tiny
glowing speck in the horizon of her mind.

Nellie remained on the porch with her gaze fixed on the fields
until she heard the clanking and whirring of old bicycles approaching. School was out for the day and her children, happy to be free,
were coming home. It sounded as if they were bringing home a few
friends.

"Clean your shoes before coming in. The rug is going to get dirty and we have no more maids. I'm the maid!"—shouted Nellie to the children from the porch.

"She sounds like my mom."

"Yeah. They always say the same thing."

"Did you really have maids?"

"That's what Mom says."

"Billy, did you bring your ball?" Nelson, Jr., shouted from his room.

"Yeah, it's in my backpack."

"Is it your brand new one with all the Dodgers' signatures?"

"Are you crazy or something?"

"Just kidding. But we need a catcher."

"We could ask that new kid."

"You mean Eloy?"

"I guess that's his name. He's in my social studies class."

"He's a sissy. He doesn't know how to catch. We might as well ask my little sister, Maria-Chiara!"

"That doesn't matter! We need one more guy for a team."

"Ok, but I ain't calling him."

"Big deal, where's your phone?"

"We don't have one yet. Do you want a Pepsi?"

"Yeah, but with lots of ice!"

Hearing the boys in the kitchen, Nellie hurried to supervise the cola refueling operation and lament her fate. After the kids had left, burping with satisfaction, she turned on the television, an old RCA whose picture faded in and out every five minutes, and began watching her favorite show, "Donna Reed." The set did its best to produce a vision of the family's life but the fuzzy picture soon became a downpour of tiny gray dots causing Nellie to rely on her ears to follow the plot. As best as Nellie could tell, Donna and Doctor Stone were planning a trip to Europe. Donna wanted to go to Paris and her husband to London. The theme music signaled that today's show was about over, the episode ending with the couple in the midst of a heated argument, and suddenly hushing because Jeff and Mary had come home from school. Donna dried her tears with her apron and Doctor Alex Stone welcomed the kids with a big smile. The conclusion to the episode was to be broadcast the following Wednesday. Nellie turned off the set thinking how Donna should best resolve her dilemma and practiced the new words she had learned. It was in this way, through

T.V. shows, that she was practicing the language she had learned as a child with her English governess.

Her husband Nelson would arrive about six. He worked as a stockroom man for Rosser and Dunlap Trucks and Rigs. It was the first real job he had found a few months after he arrived from Xawa and had remained happily stagnant in the same position despite having been a university graduate, the heir apparent to his father's business empire, which included the nation's biggest company, the Food Import of Xawa, Ltd., and the sole distributorship of Gold Medal flour and Canadian bacon. For Nelson, his new environment was like a labyrinth from which he did not want to escape. It seemed to have frozen him like a pre-Cambrian bug in a drop of amber. As opposed to Nelson, Pepe, previously a truckdriver for the Food Import Company, adapted better to his new surroundings. Though Pepe came three years later than the Guristains, he opened his own grocery store only a year after his arrival. The store was called "Pepe's Grocery" and was destined to later become the notorious "Pepe's Grocery-Bar" where the chic, rich, and famous would flock to be seen while shopping for yucca or sipping one of Pepe's papaya rums. Pepe had written his former boss from Union City, New Jersey: "I'm moving to Pahokee, a few miles from where you live. How would you like to be my partner? I'm opening a small stuffed-potato stand at the sugar mill entrance. What would you have to lose? We have to start anew somehow. We have all come here with one hand in front and one behind." Pepe had scribbled a small drawing of a naked man covering his parts with his hands on the school-ruled paper. The symbol would eventually become Pepe's business logo. Nelson crumpled the letter up and threw it into the wastepaper basket, leaving it unanswered.

Nellie, wearing her thongs, padded into the kitchen to prepare dinner. She walked as if facing a firing squad. A note from Nelson was trapped against the refrigerator door by a magnet in the shape of an angry green worm with an M-16 on his right shoulder and a tricolor flag with a lone star in his left hand. The note suggested: "After placing the pots, pans, and skillets on the burners make sure to turn the burners on." Nellie usually tended to forget that final detail. She opened her cookbook and started reading the instructions:

SAUTEES—Saute a la Criolla: $2/3$ cup olive oil, one diced pimiento, one chopped bell pepper, one teaspoon sugar, one teaspoon oregano, $^1/_2$ teaspoon cumin, one chicken broth cube, $1^1/_2$ cup thinly chopped onions, 5 garlic cloves, one can tomato sauce, $1^1/_2$ teaspoon of salt, and one teaspoon of vinegar. Nellie was overwhelmed by so much chopping, so many teaspoons, so many tiny slices. She closed her eyes and wished her fairy godmother would come to her rescue and turn the bell pepper into Delfina, the onion into Tomasa, and the garlic into Agripina. She closed her eyes again, but this time much tighter. Her godmother was obviously vacationing somewhere. She resigned herself to her fate and opened the kitchen closet and took out a can of Kirby's Black Beans and opened it. She poured the can's contents in the pot and turned the burner on low heat. She rinsed her hands and her eyes reviewed the large scar which marred her pale forearm, reminding her of the battles she had fought with the house. Nellie rubbed the iron-burned flesh, thinking that the imitation tortoise shell bracelet which she had seen at W. T. Grant might camouflage the scar. She dried her hands with the garlic rag and went to her room.

She pulled the suitcase with the bullfighter sticker from under the bed and dug around the clothes searching for her photo album. Nellie was reconstructing her old life with the pictures Delfina was sending in exchange for Gillette razor blades and flints which she could sell in the black market. Nellie enclosed these in each letter padded with toilet paper to avoid the letter censor back home. Delfina had found the old albums under a pile of trash by the curb a few days after Don Andres' mansion was confiscated. Nellie sat in front of her dresser and began combing her hair one hundred times, a ritual she had been following ever since she had battled tinea when she was almost ten. She flipped through her album with her free hand.

On the first page was her favorite picture: "1940 Yacht Club Dance—The Odalisques' Conga." The photo said on the back, "I also danced in the Ladies' Tennis Club, the Air Club, and the Doctors' club." Then "Xawa-on-Deep River" and in much fresher ink: "To remember is to live again, but I feel like dying when I remember. Belle Glade, Florida, 1963. (Still in exile)." The Odalisques' Conga was always composed of eight delightful damsels, society's best. They all wore red transparent linen veils, velvet cassocks embroidered with silver thread, and gold coins of different sizes to cover their convulsing navels. In the midst of the fictitious harem sat a sultan called Mario. He was a tall, dark gentleman with hairy arms which caused nightmares, insomnia, and premature ovulations in the unsuspecting harem. Nellie never realized that her attraction to "The Donna Reed Show" had its basis in the similar secondary characteristics shared between the sultan and Carl Betz. But, why tell her? It would only cause her anxiety to know that she was unfaithful to Nelson every Monday through Friday from two to three.

The days of the Big Band era were rolling. It was the time of American actors, of smoking Lucky Strike and dreaming yourself blonde, pale, and freckle-faced. From left to right, forming a bouquet enveloping Mario: Pituca, Maria, Rosa, Loly, Cuqin, Helen, Ignacia, and Nellie, though, among themselves, they went by Joan, Ginger, Hedy, Betty, Debbie, Lana, and Irene. The aroma of a nearby Kentucky Fried Chicken made Nellie recall Lana's premature death in '42. It was attributed to the chicken with which she slept. His name was Curly, and he was a gift from one of Irene's father's young farmhands who had fallen in love with Lana. The biped arrived in a show box with a note which said: "For Miss Ignacia. Now, you'll never be lonely. Truly, Juan Benson." This was the only way the poor farmhand could have gotten close to his beloved. In a few months Curly grew from a fuzzy yellow ball into a robust specimen with shiny feathers, fastly developing spurs and a firm comb.

He accompanied Lana to every rehearsal of the conga ensemble and perched in the first seat of the second row patiently waiting for the odalisques to finish their act. At night, Lana would dress him in flannel pajamas and cover his comb with a diminutive cotton hat. But Curly was very demanding. Many were the parties Lana couldn't attend because of the unyielding biped. He loved to go to bed early, seven at the latest, and he wouldn't sleep unless Lana was with him. Irene secretly envied Lana and wished Curly could be hers. She became so sad and Don Andres gave her a little pet of her own. Irene named him Rigoletto. One night after Curly was sound asleep, Lana left silently for a New Year's Eve party at the Yacht Club. When she returned the following year, Curly was nowhere to be found. He had flown through an open bedroom window to the chicken coop where he mixed himself with all sorts of low-life hens. Lana found him three days later almost featherless and with a bleeding comb damaged by violent pecking. In his frenzy Curly had made amorous advances toward a peahen without realizing that her peacock was perched directly above him.

It was that night that Curly was contaminated with lice that carried a deadly microbe. A week later, Lana woke up with a bleeding scalp from her nocturnal scratching. Irene had come to visit her to show her the new silk veils for the ball. Lana had greeted her with a big smile and a blonde wig that her father had bought for her on a trip to Key West. Three days after Irene's visit, Lana was found dead with a pool of dried blood under her wig, her brains exposed. A few days later, when Juan Benson found out about his love, in despair he cut his little and ring right fingers with his machete.

Facing Lana in an exotic Middle Eastern pose and with the biggest coin in her navel was Hedy. Hedy and Irene played the piano every afternoon at Fabre's Academy of Music. Hedy wanted to be a concert pianist and play with the national symphony. She was jovial and always wore shorts, a legacy of her days at Mobile's Finishing School and a scandal for her hometown. It was while in Alabama that she met her boyfriend Rudy Jones. He was attending Springhill College. Rudy died during the Normandy landing, but not before he had given Hedy the only passionate night she was ever to experience. One afternoon, when Irene was accompanying Hedy in her personal rendition of "Claire de Lune," Elvirita, the instructor, tried to imprison her hands, using the pretext of the lesson. Hedy and Irene escaped screaming from the ambush that Elvirita was launching from the island of Lesbos. Thus, Hedy abandoned a piano career that undoubtedly would have led to Carnegie Hall. When Hedy was forty and still raising her younger siblings she decided to stop mourning for Rudy and married Senator Zubizarreta, the owner of La Campana Hardware Store. The hardware man forbade her to use shorts and forced her to wear long heavy black stockings to the beach, until exile gave her enough courage to have her marriage annulled.

Though she saw them often at Pepe's Grocery, Nellie didn't care for the remaining four odalisques and in spite left them without a future. And the sultan? There was no need to create a future for him. He was born, grew up, and died in the same old town. He never married because the responsibility of the annual odalisques conga line didn't leave much time for love. He had hardly finished one year's conga when he immediately started laboring on the next year's theme variations—more veils, more tambourines, less gold. His choreographies propelled him into the national limelight. But he didn't allow fame to

cloud his world vision, never accepting the many bribes that were
offered by politicians and capitalists to have their daughters form
part of the seraglio. Mario continued selecting his girls from Xawa's
cream. He never suspected the many moments of secret joy he had
given to generations of dancing maidens, young girls whose fingers in
the midst of the night and the intimacy of their alcoves would go wild
and sink uncontrollably beneath their panties and dream of the hirsute sultan. When he died in a car accident, The Legion of Mary took
charge of the collection to build a monument to him that would per-
petuate his memory. The statue was sculpted from a single piece of
Carrara marble by the famous Gianni Galli. It bore the name, "The
surrendering of Odalisques." The inscription read: "To you who
filled our free time with the greatest of joys. We will not forget you,
The Legion of Mary and the Ladies' Tennis Club."

She turned the pages once more and time elapsed swiftly, skipping
the sleepless nights when she felt the vacuum of her mother's absence,
coming out party, her first cigarette, Nelson's first kiss through the
living room window, stopping at Nelson's graduation ceremonies. It
was 1944 and the Allies were bombing Dresden. This time Nellie was
in the center of the photo, elegantly dressed in a black silk gown
embroidered by her own hands. She had taken up embroidery to
occupy her time while Nelson was away finishing his degree. They
had been engaged for nine long years, years in which Nellie sewed
sixty-two blouses, knitted twenty-five sweaters for her Rigoletto,
embroidered thirty-two table cloths, and made all the Lent covers for
all the saints of all the churches, monasteries, and convents in her
diocese. When she had finished these tasks there were still two more
years before Nelson's return, so Nellie began the composition of five
hundred and four sonnets. All the poems were recorded in the Italian
manner as prescribed by the Dottore Marco F. Pietralunga Dell' Uni-
versita di Saluzzo in his *Viaggio All' Amore: The Muses Within Your
Reach*.

The tenth sonnet of the one hundred and four rhymed like this:

*Your divine eyes, Nelson
are not what submitted me to love's yoke;
nor your swollen lips, the blind cupid's sweet nest,
where nectar springs,
nor your olive cheeks,
nor your hair darker than a chestnut;*

nor your hands, which have conquered so many;
nor your voice, which seems more than human.
It was your soul, visible in your deeds,
which was able to subject mine,
so its captivity would last beyond death.
Thus, everything that has been mentioned can be
reduced simply to the power of your soul,
for by its commission each member performed its ministry.

Pressed against the paper on both sides of the tenth sonnet was a pair of seductive purplish lips.

As Nelson's commencement godmother, Nellie wore her hair loose in a cascade that started from her forehead and ran down her neck, finally coming to rest one half inch from her shoulders. Nellie had blossomed and she still thought of herself as Irene Dunne's twin. Her physical attributes could have been explained in terms of apples, two in front and half of one in the rear. She had used heavy make-up around her eyes to accentuate their almond shape. Nelson, with golden spectacles and sporting a cap and gown, held a diploma in his right hand as he tried to assume an air of sagacity. His business administration degree had cost him, more than sweat, a nervous stomach. Nelson's fear of having to head his father's enterprises after graduation was the source of the stomach spasms which caused him to shower his peers with pineapple chunks, black beans, and salami before each exam. He became known as the Black Vomit. That night, after the prescribed picture-taking under the loving arms of the Alma Mater, the radiant couple danced at the Montmartre. Rene Touzet's orchestra played "You Don't Need To Know," and Nelson held Nellie very tight against his chest. He murmured the lyrics in Nellie's ear while thinking of the squirrel's roomy hips. Like any other Saturday, she would surely be waiting for him until three o'clock, when the night was still young and her older clients would be heading home to their suspecting wives. Nelson always left her a generous tip and a few pieces of bubble gum. Nellie, her heart racing, was almost gasping for air as the song finished.

She was going to continue flipping the pages when someone unexpectedly knocked at the door. She immediately thought it was the wandering reverend with a new cardboard fan. She was amazed to see a woman dressed in tight pants and a sleeveless blouse. She strained her eye to observe her better through the peephole, recognizing the lady who had so diligently ordered around the Mayflower movers. She was obviously one of the people that had moved to the corner house, the one that had been vacant for so many years. Since no one answered, the tightly clad lady peeked through the Florida room window, shouting:

"Hello, hello. Any one home?"

"My husband is no here," answered Nellie uneasily.

"My name is Mrs. James B. Olsen," she said raising her voice.

"My husband is not here. He is working," Nellie answered.

"I ain't here to see your husband," a slightly irritated Mrs. James B. responded with a musical rhythm. "I'm your new neighbor. My name is Mrs. James B. Olsen II. May I come in?"

"Well, yes of course. Excuse me, I am even losing my manners. Please, come in."

"We've just moved to the white house. The one with the picket fence. We used to live in Tallahassee. Do you know where that is? Where are you from?"

"Oh, yes! The corner house. Do you have any children? We have a boy and a girl. The oldest is Nelson, Jr. and the youngest is the little Maria-Chiara. The boy goes to the junior high school." Nellie was feeling nervous and started scratching her head.

"Yeah! We've got ourselves a little couple, too. The boy's name is James B. Olsen III, and we call the little belle Missy, but she's really named after me. They're both in boarding school in Mississippi. James B. III goes to a military academy and Missy to pre-finishing school. You just can't send kids to public school no more, too many Negroes." She had lowered her voice to utter the last three words.

"That is very bad because the children could have played together. Maybe in the summer. May I offer to you anything to drink?"

"Yes, coffee. But no cream, please. I like it black. Where are you from?" Mrs. James B. raised her voice for the last question and carefully enunciated each syllable.

"Please make yourself at home. I am from Xawa, but I was meant to be born in Mondovi."

"Oh, is that so! Oh a picture album. I love albums! A picture is worth one thousand words." Mrs. James B. started flipping through the album without first asking if she could.

"You can open it if you want," said Nellie post facto.

"I could bring mine tomorrow. I have lovely family pictures. Actually they aren't pictures but photographs, and there's a difference! Photographs of my great-great-grandma's plantation, Fairview. It had a beautiful wrought iron fence. The Yankees sacked it and burned it to the ground. My great-great-grandma died trying to save the family heirlooms. But please, don't come to my house. If my husband knew I was here he would kill me. I've always been ahead of my time. Do you realize I was Leon High School's homecoming queen? There were lots of people that came to my crowning, even though it was the same weekend as the county fair. I had to compete with the Ubangi Woman, the Alligator Lady, the Bearded Lady, and the Quarter Man. I remember as if it was today. I was crowned inside a giant redwood log. Boy, did I cry that day! I felt special and fearful of the great responsibility I was about to assume. My ladies in waiting, those are the girls that tended to my every wish, were throwing rose petals at my feet. I was crowned by the football team captain, Captain James B. Olsen II. His jersey was number 24, and it was retired. In the school yearbook he was chosen most likely to succeed, most athletic, best personality, and best all around during his sophomore, junior, and senior years, something really unique in American history. He was really dying to place that shining crown on my head. The week before we played the Marianna Bulldogs. We made this huge bonfire and burned a bulldog in effigy. An effigy is something like a big dummy, except you can really be nasty to it. Before we threw him in the fire, the big dummy was really mauled by the ferocious teeth of our fighting Lions. James B. took the biggest bite and ripped off a flank. Do you want to know what we did next? We began pelting the smoky bulldog with marshmallows, and we shouted that he was no bulldog but a chihuahua, which is a small scrawny South American dog from Mexico. Then the Captain slowly climbed the steps to the podium and told my future subjects, 'It's surely nice for you to show up. Let me tell you that team made the trip here for nothing. Y'all gonna be eating hot dogs for breakfast tomorrow morning. We want to have our best game and we're trying our hardest to do it.' The Lions went wild and the band started pumping them up even higher by playing 'You Ain't Nothing But a Hound Dog.' And right when I was gonna lead them into an uproar of GOOOOOOOOOO BIGGGGGGGGGGG REDDDDDDDDDDDDDDDD BEAAAAAAA-AAAAAAAAAAAAAAAAAAT BULLDAAAAAAAAAAAAAWS a tiny figure made her way through the pack. It was Mrs. Cornelia Williamson, James B.'s grandma, who grabbed the microphone. She was wearing a red sweatshirt with the words MY GRANDSON supporting a white number 24. Then everybody heard her yell, 'Who's gonna win tonight?' The crowd didn't wait to answer her cracking voice, it roared L-E-O-N L-I-O-N-S. I never forgave her. It was the most important moment of my cheerleading career, and she ruined it for me. Her grandson carried her on his shoulders while the band played, 'Oh, When the Saints Go Marching In.' But let me tell you that he had fallen for me since the seventh grade. Do you know what he wrote in my eighth grade yearbook? He wrote: 'I wish I was a mosquito so I could bite you. But please don't squash me. Lots of love, JB II.' All those years he was longing for me and I only gave him tiny little bits of hope. Like when he invited me to go to the pig races in Georgia and I had him waiting for an answer for a whole month. Actually, I really wanted to go 'cause they're a lot of fun and Sugar, Uncle Blue's sow, was one of the contestants. James B. arrived early, driving his father's brand new pick-up. He had just gotten his restricted license. I made him wait for forty-five minutes even though I had been ready for over two hours. James B. had used Brylcream for the first time and had brushed his teeth at least fifteen times. He smelled of fluoride toothpaste and breath mint. He didn't even dare to hold my hand and at the end of our date he didn't know how to say good-bye. He leaned forward and said in a deep voice, 'I had a ball!' I'm lots of fun! O something smells, are you killing roaches or something? What is it?"

"Please, please make yourself comfortable. I will be right back with the coffee."

"And who are all these people?"

"Myself and a group of friends at a party," said Nellie from the kitchen.

"I just love your dresses. Ain't them adorable? Do you always dress like that in your country or just on Sundays? And who's the man wearing the turban? Are y'all his girlfriends?"

Nellie couldn't quite hear her since the water for the coffee was boiling so she nodded from afar.

"I couldn't have shared my Mr. James B. Olsen with no one. Did I tell you he was chosen most athletic? He's always been my cup of tea.

I was the captain of the cheerleading squad," she added while she wet her index finger to flip the page.

"The one with the toga is Nelson, my husband. That was the day he graduated from the university. And the man to his left is my father. He was the owner of many factories, including the one that made the best rum, and the national railroad.

"I hate trains. They always wake me up in the morning with that awful whistle. I was thinking maybe you would like to come with me to W. T. Grant. They're having a clearance sale. On the way, we could stop at the Dairy Queen for some ice cream. Have you ever had ice cream?"

"Well, thank you very much. I wanted to buy a bracelet, and the ice cream is okay, too.

"What about tomorrow before Mr. James B. returns from base-ball practice? If he catches you near our place he'll hunt you down like a wild deer. He ain't very broad-minded."

"It'll be a pleasure, Mrs. James B. Olsen."

"Well, I'd better go back to prepare Mr. James B.'s supper. I'm going to perfume myself. I'm his horse doovers, it's French for snack. When he sees me, I drive him wild. He runs after me throughout the house and when he finally catches me, he kisses me savagely while I scream go go go go big red. Before I forget, did you ever meet Talihu Medina?"

"No."

"How about that. She being Filipino and all that. Anyway, I'm sure you'd have loved her too. Many of my friends thought she was my maid. Can you imagine! When we went shopping I managed to always go a few steps ahead of her, you know how short their legs are. As I told you, all of my friends thought she was my servant. I never told them so, but I didn't deny it either. I just smiled. She left when her husband, Sergeant Bahama Joe, was transferred to Eglin. Don't you forget, I'll come fetch you tomorrow morning. Well, like y'all say, 'sayonara'."

Nellie was happy to have made a new friend after so many years. She went to the mail box and found a letter from Delfina. They always came with the same stamp, a white dove surrounded by the word "peace" in many languages. She opened the envelope and saw her wedding picture. She took it out and put it on top of the night stand so she could show it to Mrs. James B. first thing in the morning. She walked to the kitchen whistling "The Donna Reed Show" theme song and opened her recipe book. She looked under "desserts" and started getting the ingredients to make her new friend a coconut custard. While measuring out the wrong amount of sugar, she realized that she had forgotten to tell her that her name was Nellie.

Tito's Good-bye

Cristina Garcia

CRISTINA GARCIA was born in Havana, Cuba, in 1958 and grew up in New York City. She attended Barnard College and the Johns Hopkins University School of Advanced International Studies. Ms. Garcia has worked as a correspondent for *Time* magazine in San Francisco, Miami, and Los Angeles, where she currently lives with her husband, Scott Brown, and their English bulldog. Her first novel, *Dreaming in Cuban*, was published by Alfred A. Knopf in 1992. She is at work on a second novel.

Agustin "Tito" Ureña thought at first that the massive heart attack that would kill him in a matter of seconds was just a bad case of indigestion. He had eaten spareribs with pork fried rice, black beans, and a double side order of sweet plantains at a new Cuban-Chinese cafeteria on Amsterdam Avenue the night before and he hadn't felt quite right all day. "Okay, okay, I hear you!" he lamented aloud, rubbing his solar plexus and dropping his fourth pair of antacid tablets in the dirty glass of water on his desk. He remembered with longing the great spits of suckling pigs dripping with fragrant juices back in Cuba, the two inches of molten fat beneath their crispy skins.

"*Coño!*" Tito Ureña protested as a violent spasm seized his heart then squeezed it beyond endurance. He stood up, suddenly afraid, and with a terrible groan he slumped forward, his arms swimming furiously, and swept from his oversized metal desk a half-eaten bag of candy corn, the citizenship papers of a dozen Central American refugees, his Timex travel clock in its scuffed plastic case, and the stout black rotary telephone he tried in vain to reach.

It was late Friday afternoon and Tito told his secretary to leave after lunch because it had started to snow and she lived in Hoboken, but mostly because he could deduct the eighteen dollars from her weekly pay. His law office, a squalid room over a vegetable market in Little Italy, was convenient to the federal courts downtown, his prime hunting grounds for the illegal immigrants who made up the bulk of his clients. Tito's specialities were self-styled—forging employment records, doctoring birth certificates, securing sponsors, thwarting deportation, applying for political asylum. Only rarely did he achieve the ultimate, the most elusive victory: procuring a legitimate green card.

Tito worked with the poorest of New York City's immigrants, uneducated men and women from the Dominican Republic, Mexico, El Salvador, Peru, Guatemala, Panama. He impressed them with his deliberate, florid Spanish, with the meaningful pauses and throat clearing they had come to expect from important men. In reality Tito Ureña's qualifications, elaborately set out and framed on the wall behind his secondhand executive chair, came from a correspondence school in Muncie, Indiana. This did not deter him, however, from charging many thousands of dollars, payable in monthly installments ("I'm not an unreasonable man," he protested again and again, his arms outstretched, palms heavenward, when his clients balked or appeared uncertain), for his dubious efforts.

Occasionally Tito Ureña would come by small-time jobs for the mob, defending lowlifes fingered to take the rap for their bosses. These cases paid handsomely and required virtually no work. Tito only had to be careful that his "defense" went off without a hitch and the saps went directly to jail. It helped take the pressure off the mob's local operations. Last year, flush with cash from two such cases, Tito bought sixty seconds of air time on late-night Spanish television to advertise his legal services. With his thick mustache and broad reassuring smile, he received over four hundred calls on the toll-free hotline in less than a week. The only trouble was that his wife, who was something of a night owl, also saw him on TV. Haydée called his office, posing as a rich widow from Venezuela, and made an appointment with her husband the following day. It took Tito months to cover his tracks again.

Tito Ureña had been separated from Haydée for nearly sixteen years and in all that time she had steadfastly refused to divorce him. Whenever she located her husband, Haydée managed to wring from him considerable sums of money to maintain, she said, the lifestyle to which she had grown accustomed as a descendant of the Alarcón family, the greatest sugarcane dynasty in Trinidad, Cuba. Tito insisted that Haydée could smell his cash three miles away in her tiny apartment on Roosevelt Island, even on the hottest days of summer when the stench from the East River and all that was buried there would have stopped a bloodhound dead in its tracks with confusion.

For a while Tito skittered from place to place in the vast waterfront complexes of apartment buildings near Wall Street which, during a downturn in the economy, were offering three months' free rent with every two-year lease. Tito rented beige furniture, always beige (he preferred its soothing neutrality), and lived high above the river, face-to-face with the lights of the city in his glass box suites in the sky.

It snowed hard the night Tito Ureña died of a heart attack in his office in Little Italy. Nine inches fell in the space of twelve hours. It continued to snow the next day, blanketing the city's rooftops and fire escapes, its parks and delivery trucks, awnings and oak trees with a deceptive peacefulness, and it snowed the day after that. It snowed on the black veiled hat Haydée had stolen from Bloomingdale's that very afternoon and which she would later come to interpret as a premonition of her husband's death. It snowed on the sliver of concrete she called a balcony, decorated with a life-sized plastic statue of Cinderella. It snowed on Tito's daughter's brick Colonial house in western Connecticut, across from the country club with its own riding stable. Inés Ureña had married a Yale-trained cardiologist the year before and devoted her days to mastering the baroque recipes in *Gourmet* magazine. It snowed especially hard in Prospect Park, near where her older brother, Jaime, had rented a room and plastered his walls with posters of Gandhi, Beethoven, and Malcolm X.

Tito lay dead in his office all weekend as it snowed, well preserved by the freezing temperatures. His mistress, Beatrice Hunt, called him Saturday night from Antigua, where she had returned to visit her family for an extended holiday. She cut her trip short when a policeman, who had found her number in Tito's wallet, called her in St. Johns. Beatrice, dressed in her Sunday finery, went to claim her lover's body at the Manhattan city morgue. After four days, nobody else had come.

If Tito Ureña had had the chance, if he had known that only a few moments remained of his life and that it was neither indigestion nor an incipient ulcer that was causing his gastric discomfort, he might have permitted himself the brief luxury of nostalgia. He would have remembered the warmth of his mother's cheek, smelling faintly of milk, and her face the last time he saw her (Tito was only nine when she died), or the sight of his father's hands—enormous hands with stiff hairs sprouting near the knuckles—stroking the doves that roosted in his study. He would have remembered the girl he loved madly when he was seven years old and in a moment of melancholy would profess to love still.

And since these would be the very last moments of his life, Tito might even have permitted himself the memory of his first glimpse of Haydée at sixteen, riding her thoroughbred, English style, along the road which marked the southern boundary of her father's vast plantation. She was a magnificent sight—so small, so white, a china doll. How afraid he was of breaking her on their wedding night! He would have remembered, too, her belly, swelling with his child, and the pride he felt strolling with her through the Plaza Mayor. This was long before the problems began, long before they'd sent their son to the orphanage in Colorado to save him from the Communists, who, it was rumored, were planning to ship Cuba's children to boarding schools in the Ukraine. Jaime was still healthy and without rancor then, and Tito's daughter, Inés, danced to please him, clapping her dimpled hands.

It was that life that Tito Ureña would have remembered if he had had the opportunity, a life richly marred by ignorance.

But he had no time to reminisce when his heart attack came. No time to save the Salvadorans from deportation or to pick up the dry cleaning Beatrice Hunt had forgotten on Broadway and 74th Street. No time to call his brothers, whom he hadn't seen in five years, or his sister, Aurora, in New Jersey, who'd announced her determination to save his soul. No time to have dinner with his daughter, Inés, estranged from him in her brick Colonial house in western Connecticut (Tito had missed her fancy wedding and she never forgave him). No time to apologize to his son, if he could have even worked up the courage, or to earn enough money to finally keep Haydée happy. No time to visit his father in Cuba or to plant jonquils on his mother's sad grave. No, Tito no longer had time even to hope. When his hour came on that snowy winter afternoon in Little Italy, all Tito had time to do was say *coño*.

Frazer Avenue

Guy Garcia

GUY GARCIA was born in Los Angeles and graduated from the University of California, Berkeley, and Columbia University. A staff writer for *Time* magazine since 1980, his writing has also appeared in numerous other publications, including *Rolling Stone, Interview, Elle, San Francisco Review of Books,* and *American Film.* His first novel, *Skin Deep,* was published by Farrar, Straus & Giroux in 1989. Mr. Garcia lives in New York City with his wife, Cathleen.

Every Sunday morning you could hear them just down the street at Millie's Bar, still going strong from the night before. Somewhere between getting up and breakfast, the band would fizzle out and Millie's customers would stumble forth, sometimes crawling like dazed cockroaches, down our street and across Whittier Boulevard. The rays of the Lord's Day made them seem especially pale and somehow vulnerable to the disdainful stares of people on their way to Mass.

Later, after my father had mowed the lawn, the neighbors came over to drink beer and talk about the latest family of *marranos* to move in down the block, shaking their heads gravely to express their disgust. It was then that my parents announced their plans to move from the barrio. Jim Bossly, our neighbor for fifteen years, asked them why it was that only the good Mexicans moved out nowadays. At first there was no response, and then someone said it was because only the bad ones stayed. My mother said we should all think about that and shot me a furtive glance, but I was already thinking.

It all started so smoothly I must have slid, aware only of the rush, toward the outcome. Right after dinner when I had excused myself to go out, my father, as usual, shook his head in silent disapproval. Ducking into my room, I quickly changed into what my mother called "street clothes" and left quietly by the side door.

Outside, October's evening warmth was reassuring and I welcomed the darkness. On nights like these the short walk to John's house always seemed to sharpen my senses. Tracing the familiar route would send my mind racing ahead to the place where we met. This time, turning down the alley behind Gill's liquor store, I could see their outlines already perched on the fence.

"Hey," I yelled.

"Hey, Bear."

"Hey, Jackass."

Laughter. I hated nicknames and everyone there knew it. By now Al, the leader, had slid down off the block wall to tell me something while Steve, Robert, and Benny peered down, waiting for my reaction. I searched Al's brown features for a clue in the dim neon light.

His handsome face had not always worn the grimace that passed for others as a twisted smile. Perhaps even he had forgotten the wide grin that once mirrored his father's gift for mirth. In those days they were both clowns and they supported each other; surviving on Al's depthless humor and money his father made appearing in carnivals and local parades. Every September 16 we would zigzag through the crowd to sit on the curb on First Street—cheering for the horses that dropped their dung and whistling at the girls on the floats. But our loudest cries were reserved for Big Al who, loping down the street in full clown costume, never forgot to toss an extra bunch of balloons and candy our way. When this happened the rest of us would scramble in the gutter, while Al just beamed at his clown-dad, terribly proud. They were friends; partners in a cruel world. And on the evenings when Big Al would return from a parade with his greasepaint still on and sweep Al up in his arms, it was enough to make anyone there envious.

There were other times too, though. Times when the clown did not show and Al was left, eventually, to wander the streets alone. In the beginning, right after his mother had died, he would remain awake in his bed and wait for his father's unsteady gait, unsteady hand on door, unsteady voice:

"Al . . . ?"

In the interminable silence that always followed, Al would bite his tongue to not answer. He would wait instead until his father had stumbled to his own bed, fumbled with his clothes, and moaned his wife's name, before losing himself to sleep.

Al and his father had little besides each other, yet they were envied and admired by everyone they knew. The apartment where they lived together was on the backside of a small two-story complex. To get there, you had to walk down the driveway of the front house and then turn left onto a small cement courtyard, where a narrow wooden stairway led up to a small porch and their door. If you climbed the stairs to the porch you could look straight down onto the courtyard. And that's exactly where Al found him.

I wasn't there that night, but Jim Ortega from next door said they found Al sobbing over his father, who lay motionless in a pool of blood. Big Al never moved again, but others say that while they waited for the ambulance, tears had at first welled up and then flowed across the greasepaint. And that nothing could ever break your heart like seeing a clown cry through his smile.

"Man, have we got something lined up for tonight."

"Oh, yeah," I looked at Al's painful smirk, "what kind of thing?"

The first two went beautifully; each streetlight exploding away from an electric sputter in a shower of glass. The Sears .22 made relatively little noise and was easy to run with in the shadows. Knocking out streetlights was an easy task for five youths feigning guerrilla warfare. The targets were easy to spot, and the locals, if you found any, would run more often than not. It was simple.

"Let's do another one."

Al sensed that actually holding the gun had been too strenuous an exercise in daring for the rest of us, and now it became a dangerous symbol of his authority. I was scared and wanted to leave, but was afraid to.

"You this time," he held the gun out to me, and the pressure to accept it made my voice hoarse.

"No."

"He's chickenshit," again the grimace.

What is it about a dare that pinpoints peer pressure like a magnifying glass, igniting the irrational desire to perform against the norm and beyond the common sense? Something inside of me accepted that challenge as I stood my ground and watched them walk away. Rejected, I swore out loud at my growing dependence on their approval as they crossed the street. I watched the headlights of an approaching car, reflecting hard on their eyes and the gun, to illuminate them in my mind before I crouched down in the shadows. Thinking only of their betrayal and their stupidity, I grasped the truth that I was better and smarter in my right hand, and hurled it at them with all my contempt. And for a moment, as the small stone sailed through the air, I wanted to rejoin them, already regretful of my defiance and the enormous distance I had just put between us.

I didn't wait to see the rock crack the car window, or the look on Al's face as the men piled out from the car, because I was already running—running alone and afraid. The next morning, while I could still hear the gunshots in my head, my parents wordlessly read the newspaper account of what had happened. They understood, if only for their own reasons, that we would soon be leaving.

In those last weeks, before the moving van came to take our furniture, I had expected to see them again, and I did. I saw them hanging around the liquor store next to Millie's, and walking the streets at night with nothing better to do. Always with nothing better to do. It made me think of my grandmother describing a village in Mexico where young men passed the idle parts of the day playing checkers under whitewashed verandas. I tried to imagine the dry dusty hours and made a promise to myself. In those final days I often watched my former companions and wondered: What makes me so different? And by the time my father had checked the doors and windows for the very last time, I was impatient to leave the place. My only regret, as I watched Jim Bossly wave good-bye from his front lawn, was not our going, but the fact that I had to leave so much of me behind.

The police are everywhere. Scanning the boulevard as I drive past, looking for faces I'm sure they can't remember. Did I really once live here? Seeing glass on the street reminds me of a certain night and I look up—yes, the streetlights are broken. There's where the reporter was shot. How strange to see Millie's quiet on a Sunday, looking empty and sober with the windows boarded up and the doors locked.

For years now I've avoided anything that links me to these people and this place. It was not easy to forget where I came from and where my grandmother was born, but I did, making up stories when my new friends asked me where I had lived before. In high school, I remember dreading roll call in a new class because they'd call my name out loud; exposing me before I'd had a chance to prove I was different. It didn't even matter if my classmates were Chicanos, because I didn't want to be like all the rest. Always striving to clear my voice of an accent that didn't exist; it was important to show that my mind was clear and my English good. Branded in my mind was the image of the typical Mexican, whom I hated and loathed, making every effort to avoid his look and his mannerisms.

I knew how they thought and how they talked, standing on street corners in cocky stances, because I was almost one once. When people asked me if I spoke Spanish I always said no, even though I did fairly well. My cultural identity had been broken into little pieces and scattered about in a society that consumes little things. My past and present, a collection of scraps and discarded extras, never fitted in any one place.

I have returned to these streets as a stranger would; surveying the trash and debris in disbelief. My feeling for these people and their neighborhood was burned out with the storefronts, leaving a charred vacancy.

The day of the demonstration I watch from the fringes as the herd is moved on toward the park, pushed and prodded along a predetermined path by law enforcement ranch hands in black and white. Reaching the stage where the marchers can only huddle around it; corraled by its focal point in concealed intimidation. The police move their cars up on the grass and wait; the crowd reflects on their sunglasses for a while. Three officers spot a target and move in, they drag the boy back to their car against a hail of jeers and litter. A wine bottle flies through the air and shatters on the hood. A scuffle in the crowd while the onlookers stare, paralyzed in fear and growing in frustration. The predators cannot be allowed to take their prey without endangering the species; without assaulting the tribe; others join in. And then the crunching nightsticks that evoke a woman's bloody cry: "You dirty bastards!" And then running; the stampede that pushes the barriers into the hills and away from the slaughter. Shots in the distance echoed in nearby moans of terror. A girl stumbles in the dirt . . . no one stops until they're safe; no one is safe until they stop . . . running, running scared, running alone.

As I see Latinos banding together to gain power, I wonder if they can turn a shared weakness into strength. Will their common identity be enough to support them against the persecution and hatred it brings? Can it afford them a quiet place to take refuge that is not compelled and cramped by unemployment checks, welfare roles, and violence? Who could realize a vision of transcendent brotherhood under such sordid conditions?

That vision, in my tear-filled eyes, becomes blurred. I see it swept away in flash floods of dogma and frustration. I see it ultimately channeled and guided by a fierce determination to exist; by an animal anger; by sheer emotionality. And only that same emotionality could ever lead to the vicious defamation of the faithless onlooker; the non participant; the traitor.

We had won the game that night. John Velasco, a big tackle, had asked me to wait for him so we could walk home together. I sat outside the gym and talked with some friends while the crowd emptied out and the final pick-ups were made. Finally, they too departed, and then John came out wearing his letterman's jacket. We left by the side gate and crossed the wide lawn towards the nearest corner. When we reached the intersection a car stopped for us. I stared into its lights as we crossed. We had walked down the block for some time before I noticed that the car had not moved from the corner, and just then it turned down our street. John and I looked at each other in the darkness—I could not see his face. We stopped and waited in the deep shadows under a large oak. The car stopped, waited too, and just as the doors clicked open, we ran. We had started across the wet lawns with nowhere to run, and then I spotted an alley to our left. Both of us raced into it and cut left again into an unfamiliar maze of cement passageways and courtyards. The car had come after us and screeched to a halt, cutting off our exit. We ran blindly past trash cans and startled cats, until I saw one clinging to the top of a tall chain link fence and then bounding for the street beyond. I reached the fence before John did and fell against the concrete on the other side in time to hear them pull him off.

I stayed down for a moment, stunned by the fall and the realization of his capture. I saw John through the fence as though from a tremendous distance; my involvement as well as my emotions seemed to be held back by the wire mesh. My mind struggled to rejoin the reality of the brutal circumstances. It was as if a rational part of me were at odds with my body, fighting the pangs of alarm that gripped my stomach. The dark figures before me seemed locked in a humiliating struggle without purpose or justification and the cold uninvolvement I felt towards them made me shudder. Pinned there in the darkness, John flinched, piercing me with a soul-sickening scream that yanked me back into the hard certainty of fear. For a moment I still crouched there paralyzed, watching John's assailants mount the fence, and then I turned to run against a growing nausea of helplessness and grief.

My grandmother's house was exactly as I had remembered it; ten years had changed nothing. As familiar as the narrow streets that had led me there, it rested snugly behind a green curtain of ferns and potted plants. I walked slowly towards the dusty brown door, and it made me uneasy to find that no sign of time had passed; nothing to reflect my own changes since we had moved from this area. The house, it seemed, would greet me only on its own terms.

I stood there on the driveway surveying the dusty exterior with mixed emotions. A few years ago, the very thought of seeing the family again would have made me squirm; this was the cultural baggage within me that had gone for years unclaimed. Here were the people I had scraped off of my skin; the foreign-sounding voices I had taken out of my own. This is what I had learned to hate when taught that English was the only language of real Americans, and that the forefathers that mattered were from England. The family, pleased with my good grades, did not realize how well I was learning to be ashamed of them. If I could not hide from my own brown skin, I could at least hide from theirs. And now, years later, I was back, weary and exhausted from the flight.

The same free will that had led me against myself, and projections of myself, now led me to the door. There in the lines that so vividly spoke the years on her face, I saw my grandmother wait for three sons in the great war, the death of her first husband, and her frustrated love for a grandson who spurned her and the culture she represented. She pulled me to her and I almost stiffened against the embrace. Her slightly wheezing breath gasped out now:

"*Mihijito* . . . mihijito . . . "

"Happy birthday, Grandma." She had not expected me.

Over her bent shoulder I briefly glanced at my relatives who, it seemed to me, were watching too closely for healthy interest. Their eyes made me feel awkward, and my heart contracted against the stony silence. I detested their gawky stares. They had always looked on, with mouths slightly ajar, pressing their ears to my life; silently weighing; waiting with judgments. The burden of their standards and expectations chafed my spirit, now, as it always had. I felt numb and stupefied in my acute embarrassment; my eyes wanted to unfocus.

"Hey, Tiger!"

I looked up to see my tío's grin. His smile was a little too wide, as usual, almost a leer. I offered him my hand and he scowled at me.

"Is this the way you greet your uncle?" The handshake had been a subtle rebuff that he managed to turn on me. I smiled sheepishly and gave him the proper *abrazo*.

"That's better," he said.

Meeting his eyes again reminded me that I disliked this man. His ears offended the most, because they did not listen. We stared at each other now and exchanged facts with an amenity that went no deeper than the pointlessness of the conversation. And yet if he felt the chasm between us, he did not show it.

"Well, now that you're back, don't be such a stranger, O.K.?"

"Sure," I said, trying to focus between his eyes.

It was over. Hopefully, I could avoid him for the rest of the evening, but there were others. The room was full of familiar people whom I had grown out of and away from. Still, the smiles were met and the pleasantries exchanged—mostly questions about school.

College had been a very big place to begin with, and then it had narrowed down to two people and a few choices, and then only one.

"Why are you running again?"

Inwardly I winced at this betrayal of our intimacy. She had learned so much in so little time, and that question was the fulcrum of her leverage against me.

"I was running when we met. Remember?"

She did not reply. For the moment we were both lost to the memory of the riot; the shouting and screaming was recalled to me in silence.

I had passed her as she fell, and then I had stopped, turning back against the waves of panic and people. She was shaking badly when I helped her to her feet.

"Are you alright?"

She did not answer, but her body did as she clung to me crying and trembling convulsively.

Now, two years later, she had been watching my face from across the room in her apartment in a furious effort to read my thoughts: deciding where to strike next. And I looked back at her now with an understanding we could not share.

"You just couldn't hack it," she sneered. "All that bullshit you gave me about the movement isn't worth a damn to you now, is it? You only joined us to hide from your own personal hang-ups, and now you're leaving for the same reason."

"Then why should I stay?" Two years before I had taken the wrong path, it had begun to crack, and now as it crumbled beneath my feet a whole lifetime seemed to tumble away with it. My effort to find a place in the Chicano Left had been a failure.

"I'm fed up with demonstrations and pickets and rallies. It doesn't support my weight anymore. I don't need the crutch."

"Well, what will support your weight now?"

"Nothing."

"That's right. Because you've got nothing—you're too screwed up inside to see the value of anything. The only thing you'll ever find is what you've always found: nothing!"

We both knew that the last had been about us. Our relationship had been the lead-in to a new part of me that had existed from the beginning: my past. It was our love-lie that had drawn it out so long; keeping me involved until I had to break off, suddenly, painfully. I looked into her eyes and answered the last question that remained unasked.

"I've got nothing here." If we had been in that village together . . . maybe just dirt floors, maybe just love.

She had understood. I watched her a while, listening to her wretched sobs through the filtering numbness in my mind. My presence did not add up anymore, so I left. As I headed toward the dormitories, I was aware of putting a false start behind me. The girl was no longer a comfort and Chicano radicalism had long since ceased to be an answer.

Yet I had been determined to glean some final truth from my rejection of the girl and her strangled hopes. The breakaway had been clean and hard, in an effort to give my last two years in college a personal relevance. I saw now that my life as a Chicano activist had been painfully contrived. The noble world of oppression and struggle, if it existed, had never existed for me. But I still felt the terrible need to belong, so I had taken refuge in hopes, visions, and fears. And then, once again, the double-edged blade of identity and purpose had cut deep, and something in me snapped. I was alone.

There was music in the backyard. Wearily turning from the television set I looked over at my cousins who, despite the ruckus outside, were watching in the dark with rapt attention. I observed the erratic blue-gray flicker on their faces and imagined it going deeper, coloring their minds and then their souls in the same dull monochrome. These were the real inheritors of my generation, they would survive because they did not question. But the mutants, the non-comforming misfits, would not thrive. We were the vanguard which would fall for the rest, consumed by dangers that were not yet real. Those of us who survived, the few who could remain clinging to the sheer walls of the self, would continue the evolution. I stared at the unblinking sockets of my cousins' eyes and wondered if they would ever see where there was no light; breathe where there was no air. Because from the precipitous perch of my consciousness I would still look down and yearn for their security, knowing all the while that if I ever lost my grip I would come crashing down to their world and be swallowed, while they retained their identity.

Laughter and applause made its way into the room and I followed it out through the small cluttered kitchen. There in the spacious backyard, amid rosebuds and avocados on a large concrete slab, sat my relatives. I hung back for a while, admiring the bushy plants and fruit trees that flourished under my grandmother's expert attention. Everyone had been drinking heavily; and now, while two of my uncles played guitar, the elder one broke out in an old, lusty folk song. My grandmother, having joined earlier in the drinking, now joined in the singing. She sang with unusual abandon, and it made me angry to see the others stare glassy-eyed, with just the slightest amount of contempt in their smiles. Sick with embarrassment, I heard her voice strain in a pitiful attempt to harmonize. She was wearing the same dress that she had worn to my parents' wedding—even then it had been old-fashioned and reminiscent of her youth in Mexico. Tonight it was worn in poignant contrast to her faded beauty. The girlish good looks sagging behind the heavy makeup of an old woman. When she began to sway in her chair they did not try to dissuade her. Instead, they laughed and applauded, until she lost her balance and almost fell. I felt my face flush—she was much drunker than

I had thought. Hoping to make a final appearance and then excuse myself, I approached the concrete slab.

"*Mihijito*, mihijito . . ." She had seen me and motioned to the chair next to her. "*Mi amor . . .* " she said, cuddling me against her like a lover.

Everyone was singing now. I traced the large circle they formed with their patio chairs and watched them retreat into the song. Some were harmonizing, others listening, and a few, like my grandmother, barely moving their lips; returning to a long gone dream world still inhabited by moody silences. My grandmother's hands were turned upward in her lap, slightly apart from each other. I was noticing how brittle, how fragile they looked, when the delicate fingers suddenly, horribly, collapsed together into tiny white fists of pain. My heart contracted in fear when I saw her face; so terribly calm and unfixed. But it was the resignation in her smile, as I drew her hands and attention to me, that killed us both. The strumming had grown hard and vivacious again. It was dancing music and before I could refuse, she had dragged me to my feet with great effort. She was drunk and I did not know the dance; we stumbled together. I could not believe that this young girl whom I had fallen in love with, whom I had always loved, was my grandmother.

My family, thoroughly enjoying the show, began to hoot and clap their hands as we careened crazily on the concrete. With a coy smile she stepped back to spin like a farmer's daughter, when all at once her legs seemed to lose their strength. I caught her in my arms and staggered back. She held me tight.

"*Mihijito* . . . " Her fingers clawed my back. "*Mi amor . . .* "

"Grandma!"

Her body had gone rigid in a paroxysm of pain, and then limp and lifeless. The music had stopped. I looked up to see the whole family standing in a large circle around us, not knowing what to do or say. The older ladies were beginning to pray.

"God dammit, somebody call an ambulance!"

I stayed with her until it came. Then all of them rushed out to the ambulance or into the house. As I stared vacantly into my grandmother's garden I experienced a bittersweet pang of revelation. Her old hands, so much like withered roots, would be returning to the soil.

I felt as though we had died together on the concrete. I couldn't even cry anymore; there was nothing left. My thoughts were fixed on the stories she used to tell me. Stories of Mexico, of her youth, of her loves in the tiny village where she was born. "For years your grandfather was only one of many," she would say, as if revealing something. I wondered for a moment where her body would rest; I already knew about her spirit. If only I could rest with my grandmother. So tired of stances and counter-stances; so tired of rejections, yet even now I rejected my own grandmother's death. Could there be a place where one did not fight one's own reflections? Perhaps in the reflection of someone else.

I turned to leave, taking one last look at my grandmother's plants; my grandmother's life. In a daze I walked through the house toward the front door.

"Wait," someone touched my arm. "Where are you going?" I looked up at my uncle's tear-streaked face.

"South."

Confession

Lionel G. Garcia

(Photograph © 1992 by Becky Reiso)

LIONEL G. GARCIA was born in San Diego, Texas, in 1935. In 1983 he won the Discovery Prize from PEN/Southwest for his novel, *Leaving Home,* which was published by Arte Publico Press. He is also the author of *A Shroud in the Family* and *Hardscrub,* both novels. *Hardscrub* was named the novel of the year for 1990 by the Texas Institute of Letters. He had just finished a new novel and is at work on another, also a collection of stories and a collection of essays on Mexican-American life in a small rural South Texas town. By day he is a practicing veterinarian in Seabrook, Texas, a suburb south of Houston.

We were raised to believe that confession was the one sacrament of the Catholic Church that afforded us all an everlasting life in Heaven—if, my grandmother used to say, Father Zavala pardoned our sins. Father Zavala was no problem, despite the warning from my grandmother. He dispensed pardons and penance to everyone. We knew that as long as Father Zavala was alive we had nothing to worry about. No matter what sinful things we did, what horrible thoughts we had, Father Zavala would ask God to give him the power to forgive us and we were absolutely positive He did.

So we were sure to follow my mother's and grandmother's admonishment and every Friday night we would go to confession. In fact, we would arrive early, while the drone of the praying of the Rosary could be heard, so that we could play at the park across the street. We wrestled with each other, getting the itchy grass under our clothes while someone kept an eye on the church and the rectory for the priest. Soon the old women dressed in black would come out of the Rosary, like crows emerging from a heavy meal. They would linger outside, talk about the day, how things had been, who had died, who was sick, who had someone sick, dead. (Death was their common bond.) Their duties done, satisfied that the daily vital information of the little town had been passed around, they would disperse in all directions by ones and twos and threes and fours, my grandmother among them. She could not see us across the street. We would giggle behind the bushes to hear her talk so animatedly to the other women, as though that was a surprise to us and not the usual way in which she behaved. It was just that hearing her and seeing her from afar seemed to exaggerate her being.

After Rosary, at seven in the evening, Father Zavala would come out of the screened porch at the rear of the rectory in a great hurry, ready to hear confessions. We would watch him spring down the stairs, stride on the sidewalk under the grape vinery that connected the church to the rectory. As soon as he closed the church door we would run and meet him inside the church halfway down the center aisle. He would greet us by squeezing our ears in his fat fingers. It was impossible to get away from him, as stout as he was. He could stretch out his arms, herd us against the pews, and have us surrounded in his flesh. One or two at a time he would subject us to this ear torture. We allowed him this pleasure at our expense because my grandmother always reminded us that we were not to make Father Zavala angry if we wanted to go to Heaven.

We knew that he liked us—my uncles Juan and Matias, my aunts Cota, Maggie, and Frances, my sister Sylvia, my brother Richard, and me. We brought him some laughter in the drudging solitude that was his daily life.

Despite his loneliness, he acquired and kept a good sense of humor and a reddish complexion reinforced by wine. He hurried everywhere he went. Even the last rites to him was a race against time: lighting candles sloppily, rushing about the dying, trying to do all things at once. And yet, when he spoke inside the church, it was without feeling. His Masses, Rosaries, Stations of the Cross, everything, were in a lifeless monotone that showed us how tired he had become with the repetitive nature of his work. We often wondered how he could maintain his sanity living in the sameness of day after day. Not that he didn't love being a priest. Many times he would tell us that to love God and Jesus and the Holy Ghost was the ultimate love in the world. Privately, we could not believe it. To us, to love a ghost was not possible. We had seen the ghosts dancing on the wall at night by the lantern light at my uncle Merce's house, had been so scared of them that we could not sleep.

He had worn thin his gold band, twirling it while he prayed. He wore a small wooden cross around his neck which his mother had sent him.

Away from the church, a man freed of his trappings, Father Zavala took on a different air. His eyes danced when he spoke. He joked and laughed with the people. He bathed infrequently. My grandmother said that priests had no one to smell good for. The dandruff from his eyebrows floated occasionally from his brow like a white mold shaken off a dead limb. No matter his age, to us he was always old. He had come to town old and had remained old and gray-headed.

Usually we had no major sins to confess. So we would sit on the grass, between wrestling, trying to figure out what stories we could make up to tell Father Zavala in the confessional.

Once inside the church, we would stand as close to the confessional as he allowed, listening to other people's woes and poking each other in the ribs. Then Father Zavala would clear his throat in the near empty and darkened church (he had turned off most of the lights to save money), a sound so resonant and menacing that we would be quiet immediately.

That night, with the open windows, we could hear the sounds of the locusts coming from the creek. A dog barked just long enough to irritate the neighbors. We waited for the dog to resume his barking. A firefly floated in through the window, flew around the lighted votive candles, and then went to settle on the shoulder of one of the saints. It crawled around the saint's beard flickering its little tail light off and on. Being a Catholic I tried to attach some divine importance to this random act. What could God possibly be telling us? That the church was about to catch on fire? That we ought to deposit ten cents and light a candle in the saint's name? Were we going to receive money? (My grandmother's favorite.)

Cota pinched me and told me to pay attention to what the old lady in the confessional was saying. She was having trouble with her husband. He drank too much and worked too little, a familiar lament. To add insult to the injured woman, the man had another woman on the side. How could he afford her? She could not answer to an amazed Father Zavala's satisfaction.

The lady came out, saw us standing close enough to hear. She recognized us and we recognized her. She was one of the many ladies that liked to visit my grandmother, one of the many that my grandmother would hide from when 'she saw her coming toward the house. She gave us a disgusted look. She threw her head up in the air and rushed straight to the altar rail, crossed herself several times and began to pray, beating her chest gently.

My aunt Maggie went first and we heard her confess to killing a wren at the creek. What a surprise that was to us all! We had planned to confess to having had bad thoughts. Father Zavala, very serious, asked her how the death had occurred. Maggie had not expected Father Zavala to be so interested in the death of a little bird. Usually she was the first in and very fast to come out, pray one or two Hail Marys, Our Fathers, and an Act of Contrition and that would be it. Tonight, Father Zavala wanted to know how the bird had died.

Maggie stammered and delayed, lied some more, piled lies upon lies and finally began to cry. She confessed that she had not killed the bird. She confessed that she had lied. Her brother, Juan, she informed the priest, had killed the bird.

Father Zavala peeked out through the curtain that covered the confessional and he motioned for Juan to step in. He excused Maggie. Maggie came out and Juan went in. Father Zavala wanted Juan to explain the death of the wren. Juan began his story, making it long, adding dialogue, saying things that had never been said—all lies. Finally, he explained to the priest in the greatest detail, when he had the little bird in his sights and was about to shoot it with the slingshot, his brother Matias had gotten overly excited and had shot the bird. The bird crawled out from its nest, tried to fly, flapped its wings, and teetered on the limb. It lost its grip on the limb and clung with one foot, hanging upside down. Then the bird gave out a terrible squeal to alert her little babies in their nest that she had been mortally wounded. Not until then did the bird lose its grip, spiraled down like a kite without a tail, and fell with a horrible sound against a rock by the creek. Juan told Father Zavala that the wren had a hole on the side of its face where Matias had shot it. There was blood all over. It would be like Juan to complicate the story. By now Father Zavala was both confused and angry. He cleared his throat again, this time heavily, a sign of irritation. We heard him ask God if there was anyone in our family that ever told the truth?

Juan came out of the confessional with a load of prayers to offer throughout the church. He winked at Matias as Father Zavala angrily asked for Matias to step in. Matias was not three feet away.

Matias stepped in, knelt down, and began to tell Father Zavala his version of the lie. He claimed he had not killed the wren intentionally. He was trying to scare away a hawk that was trying to kill the wren and her babies. He was not good with the slingshot, he explained to the old man. He had aimed for the hawk and killed the wren. He felt so horrible about it that he had not been able to sleep. He was having nightmares over the episode. We heard Father Zavala give out a soft whistle of concern. Matias continued his lament. He had misfired in trying to do a good deed. Furthermore, Matias told the priest, very seriously, that that was what he got for trying to be good. That triggered a fit of rage. Father Zavala yanked open the curtain to the confessional, almost tearing it off its rings, reached across the perforated sheet metal that separated him from Matias and grabbed Matias by his thick hair. He escorted Matias to the center aisle and told him to go pray. He sentenced him to four Hail Marys, Our Fathers, and Acts of Contrition for killing the bird and four more of each for adding lies to the story. Matias complained to Father Zavala that he had lied a lot less than his brother Juan. Father Zavala told him to be quiet and go pray. Father Zavala looked around for Juan to add some more prayers to his penance but Juan and Maggie had left, having said only a few prayers of their sentence. They were at the park smoking a cigarette waiting for us.

My aunt Cota had been walking through the pews looking for coins that might have fallen out of the pockets of the women at the Rosary earlier that night. When Father Zavala called her in she knew nothing of what had been said. She had been too far away from the confessional to hear the lie that Maggie had started. Father Zavala asked her who had killed the bird? Cota was stunned. She was prepared to confess to having had bad thoughts. She was very resourceful, though, a great liar and an expert at exaggerated theatrics. She regained her composure very quickly. She had not heard of the bird, but she knew the others well enough that she had to do something bold. She confessed that she had killed the bird, whatever bird it might be. She confessed that she killed birds all the time—all sizes, colors, and shapes—using ricks, slingshots, guns. She killed horned toads all the time too, had made horned toads smoke cigarettes before she killed them. Father Zavala let out a sigh that filled the church. He got after her very sternly. He had never known this side of her. She had always seemed like a pleasant young girl. Did she know that it was a sin to kill God's creatures?

Frances then said out loud that we had seen Father Zavala's yardman kill a goat in the churchyard between the rectory and the church. We had seen him slit its throat. We were grumbling. Father Zavala stuck his head out again and put his finger up to his mouth to ask for quiet. He informed us that the killing of an animal for food was perfectly appropriate in God's eyes.

From the altar where he was saying his basketful of Hail Marys and Our Fathers and Acts of Contrition, Matias stood up and said that we had eaten the wren. It had been our food.

We all agreed to that. It was true. One time, when we had killed a wren we had pulled the feathers and roasted the wren on an open fire like we had seen the cowboys do in the movies.

Father Zavala proclaimed our innocence then. We had not sinned. He seemed relieved to get that out of the way.

He pointed at my sister Sylvia and she went into the confessional. We crept up close to hear. For some reason Maggie had started out the evening in a lie and everyone seemed not to be able to confess to having had bad thoughts. Sylvia confessed to being disrespectful to our grandmother. Father Zavala wanted to know what she had said and Sylvia made something up quickly, saying that she had told our grandmother that she was a witch. When we heard Sylvia say "witch" we started to giggle. That was a new one on us. Father Zavala got after her enough to make the confession worthwhile. For her sentence she received two Our Fathers and two Acts of Contrition and a promise from Sylvia that she would never again call our grandmother a witch. Later, Sylvia said to our grandmother that she could call her a witch one time without having to go to confession. She had already done penance ahead of time. It was like having money in the bank.

My brother Richard confessed to saying bad words and there Father Zavala drew the line. He didn't want to hear what my brother had said. He had made the mistake with Matias one time and Matias had been glad to repeat the bad words. My brother received, for punishment, one Our Father and one Act of Contrition.

At that age, Frances was the timid one in the family, and trying to get her to make up a sin to confess was hard. Tonight she was stubborn. She knelt inside the darkness of the confessional while Father Zavala tried to get her to confess to something, anything. He asked her questions upon questions and Frances kept answering "No." Then, when Father Zavala could go no further, Frances blurted out that she had once seen a man and a woman kissing in the belfry at the back of the church. We had confessed this lie to Father Zavala several years ago. He became angry. Apparently he had forgotten. Father Zavala wanted to know who the couple was. Could Frances identify the couple? Frances said no. It was too dark and she had run as soon as she saw the couple. Had they been doing anything besides kissing? Frances wouldn't know. She had seen them kissing, an old man and a woman. Father Zavala remained quiet for a time, not knowing whether to believe this story or not. He proclaimed that Frances had not sinned. She had inadvertently seen something that she should not have. In the future, if she saw the couple again, she was to try to identify them and contact him immediately. Father Zavala stuck his head out and informed us all that it was our responsibility to watch out for this couple so that he could punish them. Finally, the priest gave Frances one Our Father and an Act of Contrition in case she had forgotten some vague sin in her past that she had never confessed to.

Since no one else had confessed to having had bad thoughts, I figured it was up to me. I confessed to having had bad thoughts and when Father Zavala asked me what those thoughts were I didn't know what to say. Cota leaned in and whispered into my ear. I repeated what Cota had told me. I had thought of a naked girl. Father Zavala admonished me about such thoughts, thoughts that led to corruption and degradation of the human spirit. I should be chaste. I agreed and accepted the harshest sentence so far that Friday night: ten Our Fathers, ten Hail Marys, ten Acts of Contrition, and the Stations of the Cross—all for being what he called a degenerate, whatever that meant.

I could hear the rest of my family playing at the park while I was inside saying my penance under the watchful eye of Father Zavala while he was shutting down the church for the night.

Later on, after the church was locked, he would sit on one of the concrete benches at the park and smoke his cigarettes. We would join him, sit around while he told us stories about Spain.

For some demented reason, he loved to distract us by pointing at a star and while our gaze was turned upward he would try to burn us with his cigarette. He never could, though. We were much too fast for the old man.

In 1945 Father Zavala was transferred by the Bishop to a nearby town. We would see him once in a while when we hitched a ride to see a movie. He would greet us, ask us how we were doing, and at the same time gather us around him to pull on our ears. He remained in the area until his transfer to Mexico in 1950. He came back in 1957 and added an electric motor and fan to the organ. He played with so much volume that he could be heard in the center of town. He retired in 1960 and left to spend his last years in Spain, his native land. Word reached us that he had died in Guipazcoa on July 10, 1974.

The Useless Servants

Rolando Hinojosa-Smith

ROLANDO HINOJOSA-SMITH is the winner of the National Award for Chicano Literature (Quinto Sol), and is considered, along with Mr. Anaya and Mr. Villarreal, to be among the foremost Chicano novelists. A master of satire, humor, and understatement, Mr. Hinojosa-Smith has nurtured his characters through generations in the history of his fictional Rio Grande valley town, Klail City, in the novels *Rites & Witnesses*, *The Valley*, *Dear Rafa*, and *Becky and Her Friends*. He is a senior professor in the English department at the University of Texas at Austin.

July 17. Spend day resting, setting up howitzers, loading, and stacking ammo crates: high explosives (H.E.), plus armor piercing and white phosphorous shells.

Report on Lt. Edwards is that he is among the evacuated.

Talk about going home (Japan) for Christmas is crazy acc. to Old Guys.

"Just get that out of your head," Frazier here. "This is a *war*, and we're in it."

Just learned that we still have troops north of the river Kum. (Runners bring word to HQ, but we also get news from them. A tough job being a runner. I thank God I wasn't picked for that job. I'd crack for sure.)

Runners say fighting still going on here and there north of the river Kum. Also, that at least two of our bird colonels captured by NKPA.

Some cannon and small arms fire to our right and left.

"Has to do with the defense of the rear guard set up north of the Kum. All along the meanders of the river." This acc. to Lt. Billy

Waller. Meanders are the same as bends of the river, and *bends* I know because of the Rio Grande.

The youngest-looking runner I've ever seen came and went straight to HQ. Left a few minutes later in direction different from the one he came; told us many of our troops giving in, giving up the fight, and running.

Soon after, Frazier and Dumas took us aside. In five minutes they explain why *we* hadn't run at Osan fighting: pride. Pride in the outfit and ourselves? That's part of it. Mostly pride in each other and so on.

I know why *I* don't run. Joey and Charlie and I were all born in Klail City, Tx., we enlisted together, and how would it *look* if I ran? Everybody back home would know of it. I'd die here first before I'd face *that*.

Joey asked John Dumas how can we have pride in the unit if we don't belong to anybody. Good question. Dumas said it's too early in the war for us to belong to a division since we came here as orphans (part of Task Force Smith). But we'll join something big; so, for now, we belong to a small unit, the battery. As soon as war settles down and bigger fighting begins, will prob. be assigned to a Div.

Frazier cut in to say that it always boils down to the smallest unit anyway: the soldier. From there to the squad, platoon, etc. In our case, the gun crew and battery and each other. A pep talk.

Hat. came up and said Lt. Edwards is out of the war for now; may lose his voice, but too soon to tell. Hat. now battery commander (although he's still a five-stripe sgt.).

Loaded up and driven outside city of Taejon. Due to move inside the city in $1\frac{1}{2}$ hrs.

We wait. Told that 24th Div's 34th Inf. Regt. is *inside* Taejon making a fight of it. Can't fire inside city because of troops. We wait; C-ration: lima beans and ham, ugh.

July 18. Early this a.m., drove to outskirts of Taejon and told, almost as soon as we got there, to get going again: further east this time. Away from the city.

Communication bad all around; radios don't work most of the time, and you need a Guglielmo Marconi to get them to operate.

Still much fighting inside Taejon. Disorganized; house to house; street to street. City fighting.

Runner came by: NKPA dressing up in white robes which is what Korean farmers wear. Runner got shot at by snipers, but he made it to give HQ order to go east again. Runner hitched ride with us; his name, Petey Sturmer (Donora, Pa.). Running *is* the worst job. Got to be.

July 19. On way eastward yesterday, rear element of our convoy ambushed. NKPA let us go through and they thought we'd leave our guys behind. Well, tough luck, NKPA. We stopped and fought that off: our 105s fired at 200 yard ranges at NKPA. Drove up to a knoll and blasted away.

Continued east as a unit, stopped at designated point, the first Y on road east, and set up roadblock. We're to serve as cover for Gen. Dean (24th Div, commanding) when he and his troops pull out of Taejon.

Runners say 24th Div's 34th Inf. Regt. has a new C.O. A Col. (maybe a Light Col.) named Pappy Carrington. He with Dean inside Taejon. Hat. served with Col. Carr. in Europe. A Maj.-Inf., then. Good man, acc. to Hat.

The radios stink! Nothing works, and the hills don't help. Much, much firing inside Taejon. Disorganized groups passing through our roadblock (mostly service troops, but armed).

July 20. Taejon is no more. Gen. Dean among missing. Col. Carrington walking with his men out of Taejon. Looks too old to be fighting, but there he was, passing through our roadblock: walking. No rides for him. Hasn't changed, says Hat.

We marked targets on hills east of us; pre-selected sites just in case we have to fire there. Roadblock strengthened and ready; if more troops on the way to safety, NKPA sure to follow.

Waiting for another part of 24th: division artillery (Divarty) to pass through us from Taejon. Our roadblock opened the way and held door open for retreat. (Called a retrograde movement, but it all amounts to the same thing: we give up ground, real estate.)

Air Force flew over troops as cover part of the way.

July 21. Making a stand at roadblock; still east of Taejon. 24th Div guys still passing through; to reorganize, I guess. 24th Div lost much equipment. Plus: no less than 2400 GIs missing in action inside Taejon. Many Os dead and many Old Guys dead too. These last important to hold *us* together.

All kinds of reports: high, very high, heroism, and a lot of low lifes running away and abandoning their units.

Old Guys say heroism and cowardice (panic) part of war; trouble is that individual heroism is just that: individual. Army doesn't operate individually say Old Guys.

Our Old Guys lost more friends in Taejon. These guys are *regulars*, like Dumas who lied about his age—he was 15—and enlisted in 1930; and here he is with 20 yrs. in 1950.

Fighting in/out of Taejon sporadic. We fired guns off and on for 3 hours with help of light liaison plane spotting for us. Gave protective and cover fire for remnants of 24th Div still dribbling in from Taejon.

Charlie rushed out of roadblock and gave pack of cigarettes to guys of 24th Div still passing through.

You can see it in the way they walk, look. These guys have had the war for now.

July 22. 0930 hrs. We're leaving Yongdong, the village outside Taejon. Replaced by two new divisions just in from Japan. 24th Div gave up much real estate but delayed NKPA and we need the time. A delaying action.

Replaced at roadblock and got to work loading up and ready to move. Ate, packed and ready to go when word came in: unload, we're staying in Yongdong. Lt. Brodkey set up his forward observer's hole. We're up on a ridge. Signal Corps guys relaid wire and phone contact on again.

The 24th Div happy to leave; few guys still going through roadblock.

We being assigned to 1st Cavalry Div which is really an Inf. div. The 1st just in from Japan via Pusan.

24th Div being reorganized; given new guys as replacements. Moved out by noon and our Old Guys went to see old buddies from 1st Cav. Their Old Guys are cadre, just like ours.

Charlie, Joey and I along with Stang and Skinner helped the relieving division set up. (What we wanted was a look.) Looking at them, and they looking at *us*, we must look like bums to those guys. We'll see how they do. We'll help, but they're the ones who must hold Yongdong.

(One of their medics spotted my eye, looked at the bone ridge and the eyebrow and then pulled out 2 bits of black thread. Stitches rotting off but no danger of infection, he said.)

Hot food. 1st Cav has 3 kitchen trucks! Standing in chow line and spotted 60 to 80 GIs from 24th Div that just straggled in. The last bunch to walk out of Taejon. Not wounded; exhausted and looking like death. These have to be the guys that fought 30-hours straight. One fell in with us and asked if we part of unit leaving with 24th who we're with. Told him we held the roadblock. Asked if we part of unit leaving with 24th. We said no and he said:

"Lucky you."

We laughed and so did he. 1st Cav guys didn't find it so funny. They'll learn to laugh.

Still July 22. 1st Cav held Yongdong briefly then gave way. Couldn't hold it. Yongdong lost and we rode south again. Ride hot, humid. Helped Lt. Brodkey with phone and wire; he rode with us. Quiet, college guy.

War almost a month old, and a far cry from Task Force Smith days; men and equipment coming in including a new division, the 25th.

It's supposed to be southeast of us. Old Japanese maps call the place Sanju; an area, a region, not a town or place.

Loss of Yongdong *serious*, acc. to Lt. Waller. We are between two rivers, the Kum and a bigger (longer? deeper?) river called the Naktong. No idea what Naktong means in Korean; no idea what *anything* means in Korean.

July 23. No fighting for our unit yesterday after loss of Yongdong. Got some time to look around the area; Ellie Cohen was right: this place smells bad. Rank, as Lt. Brodkey calls it. Glad I'm not a full-time infantryman. I'd be throwing up 24-hrs. a day.

K farmers use human fertilizer on rice paddies. Big, blue flies can cover parts of sun; I swear this on my Government Issue missal. Had not noticed stink before. Here, *one* day off and now *this*! Who can eat chow line food? I'm sticking to C-rations; I'm not standing on any line.

We have the Naktong River to our backs; walked up to higher ridge to try to see it; couldn't. It's some 15 mi. behind us, I'd say. We are officially (for now) a part of 1st Cav which is part of 8th Army. Place nearest to us called Kumchon; we're here because we lost Yongdong.

July 24–25. Reorganization.

July 26. Lines not stable or stabilizing. NKPA has initiative Os say. An hour of heavy fighting near Hadong Pass. Don't know, but GIs must have set up roadblock; hill and mountain passes good for that.

Told by Os and Old Guys we have only two places to go: south and east. (We're still here and holding.)

Still July 26. Noon. Boiling hot. Where's the rain? Hot here up on hill; you can forget the valleys and the rice paddies; like BBQ grills down there and with that stinking rice paddy smell. Like a house made of muck.

Much truck movement. Inf. trucked here, trucked there. Little walking, but how long can anyone walk in 110 degrees? Well, the Old Guys say: the NKPA does it. True enough.

Some Air Force about. A big help for Inf., but you still need Inf. and Arty. Talked about strafing.

Frazier showed how one can beat strafing. What usually happens, why strafing is effective, is because 1) troops are pinned by ground fire or 2) people are caught and don't know what to do.

Here's what Frazier says—and he's lived through it in Europe. If on a road or field, and not pinned down, spot the plane and move *sideways*. Run like a scared rabbit, of course, but do it R to L of plane. Planes travel at high speeds, got to go straight; they can't maneuver. Pretty gutsy, but it works. Will keep this for future reference. Like everything else here: don't panic.

Worst things here are the hills and the heat; and K is one hilly, hot, smelly country.

See units below; on road and pulling back. We're holding. Air Force bombing hills, ridges and roads. We in no too little danger; like watching a movie.

July 27, 28, and 29. Moving south; our backs still to Naktong River, and we're due to cross it soon. NKPA on offensive, maybe hard probing.

Fighting reports regarding Taejon: many individual acts of heroism, but reports also of others who did not perform. Once again, a good-sized number of guys quit; dropped weapons, canteens, ammo, etc. Patrols and Battle Police units brought stragglers in wearing nothing but their shorts: no uniforms, no rifles, most without helmets. Worse: they threw away their canteens and they drank from rice paddies! No idea if they'll die drinking from there but that's what they get for abandoning their canteens and equipment.

Some Os too exhausted to go on acc. to runners. Os doing too much. Too much fighting too, and then to see guys dropping everything and running away.

Word is NKPA Os and Noncoms won't hesitate to drop one of their own if act cowardly. Don't know this for a fact, though. I wonder if our Os would ever shoot someone who deserts or runs?

Heard mortar fire, but we not engaged. Stand by the guns; four runners came in: was told some units pulling back but still engaging NKPA. Retreating part of plan but keeping NKPA engaged and in sight. Gives NKPA something to think about.

Some Inf. units not engaged or firing their weapons. This creates trouble since orderly retreat by units saves lives. If Inf. not engaged in fighting, NKPA has a free ride.

July 31. Sad day, but first things first: Registered the hills, preselected sites: when NKPA comes by, we'll have them cold. Fired most of the afternoon. A long fire; we assigned to rearguard; 1st Cav moving to east bank of Naktong River. One of our gun crews caught a direct hit; no survivors.

Aug. 1 & 2. Main body of 1st Cav across bridge and we covering some 1st Cav units as rearguard.

Refugees. As soon as we get off ridge and onto roads to move somewhere, we bump into refugees. Happens all the time and part of war say Os and Old Guys. They're a bother and Battle Police have hard time with them. *We* can't do anything about it. We've got the guns, etc. And so, Battle Pol.'s job is to clear and rid the roads for us to get through.

Refugees not to blame; who wants to stay here with the NKPA on your back?

But this is the point:

We're on rearguard. We're to be last or next to last unit to cross the Naktong. The Naktong is *it*; the last stand. No place to go.

So, here we are: rearguard and only one bridge to cross and can't cross because of refugees. Air Force holding back NKPA larger units and no danger there. Hundreds of refugees (maybe 2/3,000). Like a town full of people. Much crying, screaming, yelling, and Battle Police pulling and pushing, shoving, cursing to get *us* across.

It's an old bridge, too, and mobbed with refugees. Entire families.

Finally bridge cleared: Battle Pol. makes room for us. We turn guns west and drive east, and we get out of there, fast; we cross bridge and try to reorganize on beach. Refugees rush to bridge again.

We reorganize and watch B. Pol. holding bridge and pushing back the refugees. We're standing on hoods of vehicles. We can see columns of refugees (must be thousands; people, carts, oxen, etc) running to bridge which is *already* full of people, but bridge must be destroyed. This is last operable bridge in our area on the long Naktong.

Battle Pol. fighting over control of bridge since not all of Cav guys have crossed yet (our inf. guard). They the *last* unit and picking up stragglers and two NKPA prisoners (in their mustard-yellow uniforms). Finally, the 1st Cav guys and our inf. guards make it across, but the bridge is still full of refugees and more on the way, and the B. Police telling them to go back, back.

The order is given, relayed, and passed on three times. Get those people off the bridge.

The Gen. (don't have his name) gave the order himself. And *then*, the bridge was destroyed. Blown up. Hundreds of Ks. died on it: kids, families, animals.

Joey and I turned our backs to avoid seeing the bodies. Bridge blown up in all kinds of pieces. A roar, a geyser of water, and who knows what else went up in the air. All the time, our vehicles revving the motors and we can't hear the screaming and the crying. The engineers had set up the charges and were waiting for us to get across.

This is worse than hand-to-hand fighting we had in Chuchiwon. The Os and the Old Guys ordered us off the hoods and to mount up. Drove to site cleared for us by engineers.

Still Aug. 2, after late chow. In 1st Cav sector (it now our division). Below us and along Naktong is the unlucky 21st Inf. Regt. of 24th Div; to the south of us, the 25th Div. 24th Div's 19th Inf. Regt. prob. in reserve, but Old Guys say most likely not, most likely on line to hold NKPA at Naktong River.

The word: no more retreating. No place to go.

The US Army and its ROK friends are to hold. We hold or we're run out of Korea. (For once Brother Leo's Greek translations lessons at St. Boniface come through: Possession for all time. Thucydides, Pelop. Wars.) Joey laughed when I told him, and he said he always knew a Cath. education was worth something.

Don't know which 1st Cav unit in front of us, but told that ROK divisions are now to N, to E, and to S of us; don't know how many, though.

Aug 4. Chaplains and doctors made the rounds; spoke to groups of us. Explaining actions and destruction of bridge. (And the refugees? No mention.)

Old Guys had a better and a truer version of the *why* of the destruction of the bridge: it's *war*.

Once you say *war* and accept it for what it is, that explains it all. You don't have to like the explanation or even understand it. But once you see it as war, that's it. It becomes very, very clear. NKPA dressed as farmers, dressed as GIs, shooting our guys in the head: it's *war*. It's crazy and no, it isn't right, and yes, it's cruel (un-Christian our Cath. chaplain said), but it's nothing of the kind. It's war.

As for the people on the bridge, that was war. I don't imagine the Gen. was smiling when he gave the order, but he gave the order: what choice did *he* have?

Would I have given the order? That's a question I didn't have to face, but I'll face others acc. to the Old Guys, and then *war* will be brought even closer. Closer because *we*, down here, the enlisted men, will have to decide.

Lt. Waller said he'd never give the order to murder NKPA, and so we wouldn't have to face that decision. But he then said:

"All right. Would you throw a grenade at a truck full of wounded NKPA?" The answer (from him) was:

"You damned better 'cause I fail to see the difference between a truck of NKPA and a trench full of wounded Americans."

All of this to help us accept the bridge. But the Old Guys still say it best: it's *war* and nothing short.

Doesn't mean one has to like it; all we have to do is understand it and to see war for what it is: Death. (And yet, I, and am sure the rest of the guys, think we'll survive.)

After the pep talk, back to work. The business at hand: we registered every inch of ground, hill, ridge in our sector. NKPA goes into those places, they die.

Lt. Brodkey sounded like a parrot during registering: hit, hit, hit, hit.

No more retreating is what Gen. Walker says. As our Os say, "We have no place to go. This spot is it."

For breakfast, Frazier and Dumas brought us a case of beer and each one of us got a GI razor. Gifts from 1st Cav 'cause we look like tramps.

A shave, a beer, and a bridge full of people all in 24-hours.

City for Sale

Wasabi Kanastoga

WASABI KANASTOGA (a.k.a. Luis E. Lopez) was born in Santiago de Cuba in 1962. Living in California since 1970, he is one of the few tri-cultural Latino-American writers. He is a poet and a fiction writer whose poems and stories deal with the absurdities of the day-to-day life of Mexicans and Cubans living and dying in Los Angeles. Currently, he is at work on a novel, *City for Sale*, about the real estate business. He lives and works in Chino Hills, California.

Entering Huntington Park, you get the feeling something has gone wrong.

The rectangular circling moving sign stretches into the sky and in block letters welcomes everyone to the city, "PROUD TO BE GANG AND DRUG FREE."

Standing tall, this fiberglass monster, erect on its steel base, like an oversize Century 21 for sale sign, overlooks Salt Lake Park and most of the city itself.

Dividing Huntington Park from its neighboring townships is Randolph Avenue. Also known as factory row, Randolph Avenue runs parallel to the railroad tracks, which extend across the city.

Early morning, as the golden rays from the sun mix with the milk-white fog, locomotives rumble across vibrating glass windows and the sharp whistle awakens like a steaming tea kettle.

The hollow roar from the locomotives and its tag-alongs remind Loui of late night cowboy movies, where stampedes of buffaloes with foam exiting their nostrils brave across the barren hills, followed by screaming Indians.

"Hey, Benny, how come these Indians are always chasing some-thing?" Loui's khaki cut-offs dancing below his chopstick knees. "Why can't they leave things be? When they're not chasing buf-faloes," he continues, his white gym sox, stretched just below the kneecaps, leaving bare an inch or so of his brown skin, "they're chas-ing cowboys to scalp."

Benny, wearing red corduroys, green converse hightops, and a white, below the hip, baggy t-shirt, hooks the basketball across the rails, which is fumbled and dropped with a surprised look.

"I guess that's just the way the ball bounces," he says looking across at Loui and smiling. "You see, Carnai, John Wayne kills the Indians, the Indians kill the buffaloes and the buffaloes kill . . . ah. What the fuck do buffaloes kill, Loui?" Benny asks, a bit puzzled.

"They don't kill jack shit, man. They don't even eat meat. All they eat is grass and all they want's to be left alone."

Benny, who's heavier than most kids his age and whose nickname is Wolfy, sports his dirty-blond hair straight back, held immobile by tres flores brillantine. The way his hair forms a V-shape at the top of his forehead and the roundness of his babyface are reasons for his nickname.

On each side of the tracks, rocks the size of chicken eggs cover the distance. Being the last day of summer vacation, Benny and Loui's early morning walks to the park will have to end.

"Loui," Benny says and looks across at his friend, who was ready to surprise him with a behind the back pass, "you know what my old man would do when he was living in San Felipe?"

"What's that, Homie?" Loui answers while attempting to twirl the ball on his index finger.

"He'd get up before the roosters, walk a mile to the railroad tracks, lower his pants, open his buns and sit on the chilling rail for as long as he could."

"I guess he's been a wino all his life," Loui says, then breaks into hysterical laughter, spraying part of the ball with saliva.

"No man, he didn't drink in those days."

"Then why the fuck do that, Ese?" Loui asks, while wiping the ball with his t-shirt.

"Hemorroids, Homes. The pain was so fucken bad, one early morning he decided to try it out for the hell of it. After a while, he started feeling so much better, it became a daily thing for him."

The morning sun, by now, has cut through the thick fog and the surrounding area becomes more familiar. The factories in the background begin blowing waste into the air and blowing their whistles. The bright lights from within, yellowish-blue, reach out through the broken glass windows.

At the corner of Randolph Avenue and State Street, a short man, stretching as far as he can, uses a roller with white paint so as to cover last night's street art. Jim's Liquor is the place to get your cigarettes and six packs without having to prove your age.

Directly above Jim's Liquor is a large billboard advertising a human-like camel dressed in a blue tuxedo, sporting dark shades. With a long round nose that resembles a penis, the camel leans against a sports car surrounded by slim, glamorous women.

As Loui and Benny enter the store, Jim follows.

"Let me have a pack of Marlboros," Loui tells Jim.

"Hey Loui," Benny interrupts, "why don't we get Camels instead, so we can become Smooth Characters?"

They laugh hard. Benny's face turns red, matching his corduroys. Jim stares confused.

"If that ugly camel can get to those chicks," Benny continues, noticing he's on a roll, "then we should be able to score."

"You kids know who's been painting my walls?" Jim cuts in, attempting to gain control.

"No," Loui answers.

"You didn't give us time to read it, Ese," Benny adds.

"Ese, your mother, you little sons of bitches," Jim murmurs behind his thick, blond mustache, while searching for loose change.

The smooth characters leave the store, leaving behind smoke and laughter. "You cock suckers and I are like oil and water," Jim says. "Like oil and water," he adds, shaking his head. After a couple of cigarettes, more street art and endless factories, they arrive at the park.

The name Salt Lake Park is deceiving. Yes, it is a park, but the salty lake is nowhere in sight. There is a pool, though, but it's been dry and waiting for repair.

The wolfpack is out early, five or six, similar in appearance and with similar objectives. As cars approach the parking lot, they outrun each other, while nervously glancing from side to side. Marijuana and

Crack are in high demand, but the ones who've been at it for a while now carry Smack and Ice. The city's fire station, across from the park, has become easy access for the boys. Working the late night shift, as well as the firemen, looking for an outlet to their boredom.

Loui and Benny commence their one-on-one game. The outside courts have always brought Benny bad luck. The vast, open space surrounding the basket gives him a feeling of insecurity and imbalance.

As if overlooking a scene from a high-rise while standing barefoot on ice, he feels a tickling sensation between his legs whenever he goes up for a lay-up.

The small, intertwined chains serving as nets rattle and dance whenever the ball hits the rim. Sometimes, when a jump shot falls in perfectly and hits nothing but steel net, the ball jumps back out. The arguements which follow are endless.

"Loui, you're the greatest, man," Benny says, gasping for air. "I've never seen such moves, Ese."

Out of breath for sometime now, Benny convinces Loui of his greatness as they walk off the pavement court to sit underneath a shady tree.

Benny's face has transformed from pale white, to pink, to red, his nose sprinkled with sweat droplets. His soaked t-shirt, wet against his skin, moves up and down, while he lays flat on his back and tries to catch his breath.

"How about a smoke, Wolfy?" Loui asks with a weak smile, which exposes a chipped front tooth. From his rear pocket, he takes out a ziploc bag.

"Where you get that from, Homes?"

"One of the homeboys from the parking lot gave it to me."

"He gave you a dime-bag for free?" Benny asks in a tone of disbelief.

"Yeah man, he's gonna be one of the vatos jumping me in," Loui answers confidently, while with the tip of his tongue adds a bit of spit to the almost ready to burn joint.

"Which gang's gonna jump you?" Benny asks, while watching Loui hold the joint to his lips and deeply inhale 'til the tip flares red.

"The Little Termites," Loui answers. "They're like the little vatos from Florencia Trece." He glances at Benny, proudly.

The joint, now between Benny's lips, fizzes and crackles as he takes in a long drag.

"There must be some seeds in this fucker," Benny blurts between coughs, with eyes squinting.

The properties, which at one point surrounded the west side of the park, have been leveled and cleared. Much like an acne-plagued teenager, with fingers pressing down and squeezing tight against virgin skin, condominiums have burst from the soil. These oversized pigeon coops with frail bones have taken over the region around the park. Not yet fully constructed, the dark halls have become temporary homes for transients in need of shelter, prostitutes with clients unable to pay for a room, and junkies in search of a shooting gallery, or room to get sick in.

"My father says this city's gonna be the next Beverly Hills," Benny says, looking at Loui glossy-eyed.

"Yeah, and he's probably going to be the Mayor, right?" Loui answers, almost burning his fingertips, as he takes the last drag.

"I'm serious, Ese. He says the state just gave a lot of money to this city. He says they found this place to be the worst, so they ditched out some money for a facelift."

"Listen, Wolfy, the fucken mayor and councilmen of this city don't even live here. How the fuck you think they're gonna give a shit? Besides, dress a monkey in silk and a monkey's still a monkey."

"You calling us monkeys, Homes?"

"No, you asshole. I'm calling this shit-town a monkey." Loui flicks what's left of the joint and lets out a deep breath.

The boys look at each other and begin to laugh.

The rectangular for-sale sign in the sky fans the clouds with its circular motion. The steel nets cease to rattle and dance. The afternoon grows cold.

Swats and Bombardment.

Welcome to Henry T. Gage Junior High. The six-foot-tall, chain-link fence with rust creeping like ivy surrounds the school. Like a lack-luster clown, made of concrete, old and lifeless with colors numb, the faded gray buildings with white patches covering the daily graffiti stand impotent and victimized by the passage of time.

From a two story building overlooking the asphalt track and field come the shotgun blasts echoing and vibrating through walls and windows. Rubber sole tennis shoes, burning the hardwood, squeaking like a thousand rats being stepped on.

"Get that fat fuckhead," screams a blond, long haired boy.

"Aim for his head," yells another on the opposite side.

"Smash his ass!"

"Pop that eye, baby!"

"Oooh, right on his ear."

Leather volleyballs flying from opposing sides. The brave ones, standing close to the dividing line, risk being hit and eliminated, but increase their chances of destroying the enemy. The more brutal the hit, the louder the cheers coming from those who've been retired and must adorn the gym's bleachers. The more timid remain in the background, hoping the bell will ring and class will be dismissed.

Loui, who was caught early in the game by a line drive to the right side of the face, sits burning red. Benny, hoping for the bell to ring and shielding himself in the background, has suddenly become the sole survivor of the shirtless team.

On the opposite side stands a boy he recognizes from the wolf-pack. The boy is tall and elastic and has the name Joker tattooed on the left side of his neck.

Joker, with his quickness and bullet-sharp left arm, has almost singlehandedly retired the opposition. He's the mightiest of the Termites, and has done time in Juvi for stabbing a teacher in the gut after being caught cheating on a Math test.

Losing to anyone else would suit Benny just fine, but losing to Joker and his penetrating line drive meant excruciating pain. To defeat him could be deadly.

The screams from the bleachers intensify. Louder and louder words criss-cross in this blender of emotions.

From the upper rows, some begin spitting high into the air, green and white paste landing like bird droppings on heads and shoulders. Scuffles break out.

The Physical Education coaches stand on the sidelines. Arms crossed. Smiling.

Thumbs down is the verdict. Each gladiator holding a ball, Joker smiles from across. First time Benny has seen this happen. Benny begins to feel that tickling sensation, like going for a lay-up.

Joker rushes at full speed. Benny is frozen.

A Christian in a lion-filled arena. A guinea pig in a rattler's cage. His pink face has turned pale. His shorts are on too tight. His volley-ball slowly leaves his sweaty palm.

As Joker nears the dividing line, the veins on his forehead thick as worms, his right ankle twists. He hits the hardwood, grimacing.

This is it. It's action or shame. Benny's jellyfish stomach and water balloon chest wiggle as he charges, his right arm cocked, his eyes closed. The ball, in slow motion, lands on Joker's head.

Laughter spreads. The bell rings.

"Assume the position," Mr. Vincentino shouts, his candy-apple-red mustache covering his whole upper lip, serving as a filter for his spit.

"But I don't need to take a shower," Freddy Fudge yells back. "I didn't even sweat, you idiot."

This last burst of frustration brings silence to an entire locker room. By a metal trash can on the pavement floor, a greasy hair boy ceases scraping the black dirt lines between his toes.

Mr. Vincentino's cheeks and ears have become red. The tension is as thick as the hot water steam crawling over the pavement.

To be called an idiot by unquestionably the brightest kid in school was an act of subversion which had to be dealt with quickly and severely. Mr. Vincentino's reign of terror had been tested before, but never in front of so many and never by such a person.

"Listen, you little jerkoff," Mr. Vincentino whispers, grinding his teeth. With his right hand, he numbly grips a perforated wooden pad-dle, "if you don't bend your ass over, I'm going to have you sus-pended for the next two weeks. If you want to make me look bad in front of these little punks, you go right ahead. I'll make life miserable for you."

Missing the first two weeks of class would be a serious setback. For now, the cards were in Mr. Vincentino's favor.

There are moments when the most insignificant things appear to possess significance beyond belief. The drunken journey of ants. A spider floating in midair. A fly rubbing its front legs, as if waiting for a Genie to steam out of a lamp. For Freddy Fudge, with his plastic, black-frame bifocals, this was one of those moments. His loose-fitting Fruit of the Loom underpants, clashing against his black skin, stretching as he doubles. His eyes moist. His head within the confines of his locker.

Every breath taken echoes. He thinks of the wooden paddle and its aerodynamic holes. He thinks of the wood greeting his flesh. How the impact would sound like someone doing a belly flop on a still pool of water. How, at this moment his mother is packing door knobs in a factory line at Westlock, Inc.

SWUSSSH!

"Uhmmm . . ." groaning with eyes tightly closed. One million needles inserting themselves on each side of his face.

"Why you do that for, man?"

The cold, still morning silence is suddenly broken.

"What are you talking about?" A shaky voice answers.

The sound of flesh striking flesh and bodies bouncing off metal comes from the most distant locker room corner. Within seconds, a circle forms around the next event.

Like a couple of fighting cocks, Loui and Benny face each other, while Joker makes sure there is no interference.

"I didn't like the way you made my homeboy look bad, Ese," Loui, with clinched fists, yells at Benny.

Benny can feel the blood tickling his upper lip. He runs the back of his hand underneath his nose and sees the red streak.

"Look at this." Benny looks down at his bloodied hand, then up at Loui in shock. "I thought we were friends."

"Hey man," Loui answers, "not when it comes to my homeboy. He's my homeboy now. You can't fuck with my homeboys." Benny stares at Loui, who proudly exhibits his swollen eyes and lips, his proof of loyalty to The Little Termites.

Benny is speechless. He looks around the circle and sees nothing but expressionless faces.

With his head hung low, Benny struggles his way out of the circle and heads toward the showers.

"Asshole," Joker adds, while the rest of the crowd dismantles in laughter.

At the opposite end, Mr. Vincentino is looking down at yet another boy. Saliva spraying. His face not as red.

Freddy Fudge, gingerly buckles his pants, and the greasy hair boy on the pavement floor slips his socks on.

The after-school crowd lingers under a cloudy afternoon sky. Like patches, unevenly sewn, they separate themselves into clusters, each regarding the others with disdain.

By the handball courts, a group plays their usual after-school soccer. They wear their raggedy second-hand clothes and speak only in Spanish, the language which classifies them as T.J.'s.

Behind the horticulture building, the lizard-like Surfers lounge, with their bright blue, red and green Hawaiian shirts; their Levis, dangling half-way down their asses; their hair shoulder length, blond.

On the asphalt basketball court, the Hollywooders chat. Wearing neatly ironed pants and shirts, they sport the latest fashions and compare earrings. The freshest style, always.

The Chicano gang members, or Cholos, kneel by and lean against the chainlink fence. Some wear their bandanas in their rear pockets, while others strap them on their foreheads, just above their eyes. Baggy pants, baggy shirts, shiny shoes, hands behind their backs and feet parted, duck-like.

As Benny exits the school ground and walks toward Randolph Avenue, he catches a glimpse of Loui.

Loui is squatting on the cracked pavement, holding his breath, while passing a joint. He's wearing a white bandana, which brings to life his dark-brown, mousy features.

The railroad tracks curve into the horizon, interminably extending. Each rail independent of the other, disfunctional on its own.

Benny, doing a high wire act on one of them, loses his balance and continues to walk on the egg-shaped rocks.

The fiberglass sign continues to fan the sky with its circular motion.

"I think I'll call and put this city up for sale," Benny says, while looking up with a smile.

In the South

Jack Lopez

(Photograph © 1992 by Pat Geary)

JACK LOPEZ is a former first-place winner of the Chicano Literary Contest sponsored by the Department of Spanish and Portuguese at the University of California, Irvine. He has a Master's of Fine Arts in Creative Writing from the University of Arizona in Tucson. His short stories have been widely published in both national and literary magazines throughout the country. He resides in Costa Mesa, California.

When Raymond married Jill more than four years ago, they had both agreed that should things go badly between them, that should the relationship be at risk, they would spend a weekend together, away from everything.

Reluctantly, but remembering his promise and keeping his word—he *always* kept his word—Raymond had suggested a resort on the Baja Peninsula, a place he remembered from his youth, one that was sufficiently far from accessible roads yet was easy to get to by plane. For things had indeed gone sour. So they had taken the "San Diegan" to the border and then a cab to the airport, where they had caught their flight.

It was a warm spring afternoon and Raymond, actually Ramón but for business reasons he'd added the y and d to his name, which made people feel more comfortable in their dealings with him, and made him more comfortable in his dealings with them, watched the surf roll in from his vantage point on the cliff. The bathing beach was far below, littered with sunbathers and vendors, and a few people had ventured into the rough surf to escape the heat. Raymond, swathed in the gathering breeze, looked back toward the resort. Jill was in the bungalow. He'd tired of arguing with her, had tired of the long, unbroken silences in between each argument, so he'd begun his walk along the cliff.

One of the swimmers caught Raymond's eye. The bather, far out beyond other swimmers, thrashed about. Something didn't look quite right to Raymond, but he figured that in his present state of mind he was probably imagining things. Yet he couldn't take his eyes off the bather. As he looked out to sea, he saw a pile-up of waves, larger than any of the previous, approaching. And now watching the swimmer in earnest, he really did sense danger, for the image of the swimmer had faded under water.

Raymond ran along the cliff until he was directly over a group of sunbathers. He yelled down to them, pointing to the sea. They waved back. Raymond flapped his arms above his head, trying to mimic the movement of swimming, and yelled as loudly as he could, finally realizing that the breeze was blowing every word back in his face where the sunbathers couldn't hear them. The people below soon lost interest in Raymond's antics and turned away.

The resort consisted of a large Mediterranean style building, white with a red tile roof, surrounded by smaller white, red-tile cottages. The resort was built on a cliff; the only path to the beach was in front; Raymond ran for it.

The first wave of the set completely engulfed the small swimming bay in a white explosion. Raymond, as he ran, felt just the slightest bit of movement in the ground from the breaking waves. He was scared, and he ran, his heart racing, and he could no longer see the swimmer thrashing about. Yet giant combers still pounded the bay, which was a maelstrom of silver, pristine white, and diamond-like reflections.

By the time he reached the sand the bay was calm, still swirling with angry water, some of it milky green, some of it dark and sandy colored. Raymond discarded his sandals so he could run faster. His feet made loud squeaks in the dry sand each time they hit, and except for the roar of the sea, everything was silent, almost cold. He tried to envision the last place he had seen the swimmer, running until he felt satisfied with his point of reference in relation to the cliff. But you can never be sure.

Raymond told two children making sand sculptures to get the lifeguard (the resort employed two full-time lifeguards, or so it said on the brochure), told them what he'd seen. The children didn't react until Raymond removed his Guatemalan shirt and waded into the ocean, searching for any sign of the swimmer. After his short pants were wet and he had somewhat adjusted to the temperature of the surf, he dove in, swimming out to where he had last seen the bather. Almost immediately he felt himself in the grip of a tremendous rip tide, moving sideways much more rapidly than he moved out to sea. So he relaxed, waiting for the breakers, and soon he was back in shallow water, but much farther south.

He stood ankle deep in wavelets, his hands shielding his eyes, trying to see movement in the shimmering, roiling ocean before him. But he couldn't. Hearing the siren of the lifeguards' jeep, he moved up to dry sand.

The lifeguards questioned Raymond, and he answered them as capably as he could. Soon, every sunbather was involved in the search. They spread themselves along the shore, walking in and out of shallow water. One of the lifeguards went up on the cliff with binoculars.

At last in the evening, just before dark, Raymond saw his swimmer. She wore a dress. A festive red floral print one. How could he have known the swimmer was a woman? Two teenaged boys dragged her from the surf, at the south point of the bay.

The boys handled her like baggage, dropping her in the sand, out of the water. Already a sand crab scurried over her neck. And her dress was hiked up above her thighs so that you could see her pubic hair contrasted with her white underwear. Even though she was indigenous, from Baja California, her skin had a lighter tone to it, one that seemed strangely off. Her eyes were half-open, her gaze to the sky. Raymond wanted to close her eyes, wanted to pull down her dress, but instead he turned away. It would be much too familiar for him to touch this drowned stranger. Instead, someone draped a beach towel over her so that she was lost from sight, a bump on the sand, a tourist body hiding.

The resort manager was now on the beach, and he assured Raymond that "things" would be placed in order. He spoke to Raymond in Spanish, and he used the familiar *tu*. Raymond turned away from the manager and away from the small crowd and away from the woman's body and stared out to sea. Even though the sun was gone, a few textured white clouds on the horizon held pink on their edges.

"You did everything that you possibly could," Jill said. She leaned on her elbow, lying on the bed, covered by a white spread. Her eyes were puffy.

The curtains flapped in the evening wind. Raymond felt as if his eyes too should have been swollen, as if he should have cried, but he couldn't. He only felt emptiness. "But I didn't," he almost whispered. His throat ached. From yelling when he was on the cliff, he supposed.

Someone knocked at the door. Raymond stood up from the love seat at the side of the bed and slowly walked into the small sitting room. Each step he took felt heavy, felt leaden. He opened the door. A young waiter entered and set a tray with drinks on the wicker coffee table. Raymond signed the tab, tipped the waiter, then took the drinks into the bedroom. He gave the gin and tonic to Jill; he kept the double scotch, knowing that he needed something strong for this day.

Jill had removed the spread and sat huddled against the headboard with her legs drawn up underneath her. She wore one of those long, extra large T-shirts with an emblem on the front, but Raymond couldn't make out exactly what the emblem was because only part of it was stretched across her knees.

"Do we drink to ends, then?" Raymond asked. He was thinking of the drowned woman as well as his nearly failed marriage to Jill.

"Of course not! We drink to trying."

Raymond stood at the side of the bed. They clinked their glasses together. He took a gulp and then sighed. "I just feel like shit."

"I know," she said. "I know."

Raymond took another drink, this time a large one. He set his glass on the nightstand while sitting on the bed. Jill leaned forward, and they held each other. Off in the distance Raymond heard the sound of breaking waves, but he thought of the faraway look he'd seen in the swimmer's eyes, the look that seemed to be searching for what?

As they hugged, Raymond felt Jill's strong back. He ran his hands over her smooth legs, kissing her neck. She pulled him tightly into her.

Then suddenly remembering her infidelity, Raymond backed

away. He reached for his drink, slugged the entire contents down, and said, "I better shower."

Jill exhaled hard, a hurt look crossing her face as she turned away from him, but he moved into the bathroom anyway.

He tried to cry while showering yet was unable. His eyes clouded while he shaved but that was the extent of it. Sometimes you don't have anything left—he'd done his crying long before this last ditch effort to save the relationship, but never once in front of Jill.

As Raymond re-entered the bedroom after bathing, he saw that Jill was already dressed for dinner. She wore her black Yohji Yamamoto suit, the one that was cut unevenly so that it looked like a huge, hip mistake. But on Jill it was no mistake. She knew how to wear it. She had the right body, a model's, except with weight in the right places, which was a contradiction because of course she wasn't really model-like. Had Raymond been able to choose what models would look like, Jill would be his ideal. No little boy/girl stuff. Women. Women with big thighs and women with real bodies. Jill had green eyes that contrasted wonderfully with her light hair. She thought her neck too long, her mouth too large, but Raymond thought these things all added up to true beauty, as nothing was predictable.

From the walk-in closet he took his black pinstripe suit because black was, after all, really the right shade for the state of things as they now existed.

After Raymond dressed, he and Jill walked among the bungalows to the resort restaurant. They didn't speak and they walked amid palm trees and climbing bougainvillea and even fir trees, the entire setting reminding Raymond of their honeymoon in Rome. A large moon, not full, highlighted the transplanted flora.

At the entrance to the restaurant Jill took hold of Raymond's hand. She held it firmly, exciting him, but he stuck to his stubborn facade of indifference toward her. She finally let it go, following the maître d' to their table.

"Pretend we're on a date," Jill said, sitting. "I know it's not festive, but we can still like each other."

Raymond pushed the chair in for her, waving off the maître d'. Sitting in his own chair, he said, "That's the big problem." He felt much, much more than "like" for her.

"It doesn't have to be a problem."

Raymond looked around the restaurant at the clusters of guests arranged strategically so that one had a feeling of people, of crowd, even though there were only four other parties. It was still too early in the season to be crowded, though in a week or two it probably would be. He thought he recognized a few people from the beach, but they were going about their business, eating and drinking as if nothing out of the ordinary had occurred. Weren't you supposed to be affected by big events? By death. By the breakup of your marriage? He somehow couldn't get into the spirit to act out his role in this evening's entertainment.

"Sometimes it's a big problem."

"But it doesn't have to be."

Jill stared in toward the lounge. A band was setting up. She liked to dance, Raymond didn't particularly. He knew that the root of their problems lay in the fact that she was able to exist in the "now." Raymond was always either fretting about the past or worrying about the future. And that was his problem: he wasn't able to forget the past.

But how could he not like Jill? She was everything he needed. She was sexy at the right times, elegantly sexy. She was intelligent. She didn't bore him. That had been his problem in all his past relationships. He'd ultimately become bored.

Had she been sexy in her affair? Other than saying that it had been with someone Raymond didn't know, that it was over, that it had started because this man had taken an interest in her at a time when Raymond hadn't, she would give no concrete details, even under the most exacting interrogation by Raymond.

The phone machine had given it all away. The message much too familiar, much too chancy. When Raymond had asked who'd left it, Jill hadn't hesitated telling him.

His energy had been violent for a time, and he'd stayed in a motel until he'd cooled. Jill said she wanted the marriage to work. Raymond still loved her.

"I want lobster." She stared at him.

Raymond couldn't take her gaze, so he looked for a *mesero*. Instead the wine steward approached, took their order, leaving them once again in solitude.

The band began tuning their instruments. Jill raised her eyebrows suggestively to Raymond, and he couldn't help smiling at her.

"Was that so difficult?"

He nodded his head.

The wine steward returned, did his ritual with the corkscrew, cork, and let Raymond taste, then filled their glasses. To coincide with the wine ritual, the *mesero* materialized and took their order.

"Don't make it so hard," Jill said after the waiter disappeared. "We're not enemies."

Raymond answered: "I don't trust you." Then, "I keep thinking of the drowned woman."

"Think of *me*. I'm here. I'm alive. We're married."

Raymond snickered. Was this how *gabachas* conducted their marriages? In his own culture it was okay for the male to stray. Not really okay, but it was done. He'd never known anyone in his position. He'd never known anyone who had to deal with their wife cheating on them. Raymond himself had had many opportunities to be with other women had he so desired, but he hadn't. He hadn't wanted to hurt Jill. He had kept his word.

"You broke your promise," he answered.

"So did you. Where were you? Where?"

That was a silly question. He was working, becoming a success, assimilating, becoming a positive role model. "You know where I was."

"You weren't there for me."

They had drunk about half the bottle of wine by the time their dinner arrived. Raymond had trouble eating his food because he kept thinking of lobsters as living in the ocean, and when he thought of the ocean, he was reminded of the surf, and when he thought of the surf, he saw the drowned woman. He couldn't figure out why she wore a dress. Such a festive one. He even speculated to himself that she had worked at the resort. She was gone now, so the speculation was really quite worthless. But it wouldn't stop. He kept seeing her face, her skin almost glowing in the gathering darkness, the white sand sticking to her wet legs. Finally, he pushed his plate forward.

Feeling very hot, unable to catch his breath, he said, "I've got to get out of here."

Jill looked at him with concern and anger. "Thanks a lot."

"Finish your dinner. Listen to the music."

"You coming back?"

"I don't know. I don't know. I don't know!" The few people in the restaurant looked their way. Raymond, lowering his voice, said, "I need to walk."

"What about my needs. Our needs?"

Raymond was out of the restaurant, almost gasping for air. The sea breeze was stronger now, heavy with the smell of salt and ocean mist. He walked to the edge of the cliff and bent over, taking very deep and slow breaths. Soon, his mind cleared somewhat.

He passed along the cliff top, away from the resort, to the place where he had first seen the swimmer. He gazed out over the bumpy, tinsel ocean, searching for her. He wanted a replay, another chance. He wanted to leap down the face of the cliff, dive into the sea, and power stroke to the rescue. Or better yet, he tried to will himself flight. Fly to where she thrashed, pluck her out of the water, and make things right.

He wanted to will her back, but of course he couldn't. He knew this. Yet he wondered if her spirit were still close, hovering over the waves, for when death is this palpable, you're supposed to feel something, aren't you?

All Raymond saw were phosphorescent explosions as the waves broke in rhythmic, cosmic beat. Over and over the breakers hit the beach. Over and over Raymond saw the woman, her dress, her color.

Losing track of time, but after staring at the black ocean for what seemed eternity, Raymond turned and began moving inland. He brushed and scraped through the chaparral, skirting the edge of the resort, walking all the way to the road that led out of town. He'd always been fascinated by those stories in which people simple wander off and assume new identities.

The road was steep, heading south, a great, gradual incline. All around Raymond were hills and the natural brush of Baja California. Way off in the distance he saw headlights approaching the upgrade. As the lights neared, Raymond discerned that they were from a truck, because he heard the heavy grinding of gears as it downshifted, making the climb. It moved slowly and carried a strange cargo. A cargo that glowed. Raymond knew that the moon cast an unpredictable light on things, but this truck actually glowed. The trailer gave off a blue light. He instinctively backed away from the road.

All of a sudden the truck was upon him, rattling, swirling the dirt on the shoulder, creaking and groaning and roaring with mechanized fury. As the truck passed, Raymond saw the halo surrounding the truck was created by ice. Tons of ice in the wood-slatted trailer. And fish. Huge tuna with heads sticking up, dorsal and pectoral fins darting through the slats, all commingling with the ice.

In an instant the truck, the glow, the fish were all past Raymond. Everything smelled dry. The stars seemed clearer, seemed to fill the sky so much that it might become overweighed and fall. But it didn't.

Even though he wasn't cold, Raymond shivered hard as goose bumps formed on his shoulders, traveling his spine to his lower back. He looked at his shoes. They were covered with dust. His suit slacks had burrs on them.

For some unknown reason he thought back to another time when he'd been far down in Baja California. He'd been a senior in high school and had come down with friends, surfing. They had explored many coves, driving for hours on dirt roads that opened onto the bluest sea that you could ever imagine, diamonds glistening off the swells. And they found one cove that offered almost perfect waves. They surfed all day, but when they returned to shore in late afternoon, there was a Volkswagen camper parked on the beach, something they hadn't expected—other people in their secret place.

The new arrivals were a couple, older than Raymond and his friends, though not by much. The couple spent most of the afternoon in the van, which inspired quite a bit of envy by Raymond because he just knew they were making love.

In the early evening Raymond approached the couple's campsite to offer them lobster that he'd bought earlier at a fishing village. The Volkswagen camper had an awning sticking out from it. A young woman sat under the awning on a camp stool, sipping hot chocolate and brandy (he saw the bottle of brandy and the chocolate on the camp table next to the fire), crying softly. "He won't come back," she said to Raymond.

Raymond looked to the surf, barely making out a shape entering the water.

"I dreamt it," the young woman said. She wore bathing suit bottoms and a white muslin peasant shirt. "He's not coming back."

Not knowing how to respond to the woman's statement, Raymond said, "We have some extra lobster."

"He got his draft notice and I dreamt his death and things will never be like this again."

Raymond felt extremely embarrassed for having intruded upon this couple's private anguish. There was a small war going, and Raymond himself would soon enough be subject to the very same draft. But that was something he would contend with later. Then, he was a senior in high school on a surfing trip, trespassing on lovers.

He had set the lobster on their camp table. On his way back to his own campsite Raymond had passed the young woman's lover, returning from the sea. The man had nodded at Raymond in a serious yet knowing way.

Now, way up on a hill, in another galaxy, the glowing truck rounded a curve and was lost from view. Raymond was in motion, once again, yet this time he was going back to Jill. He walked past his rented bungalow, all the way to the restaurant, quickening his pace as he neared. Inside, he searched for Jill, but she was no longer at their table. From the lounge he heard the band playing, so he entered. And there he saw Jill sitting in a large booth, alone. She gazed over the empty dance floor like a mariner watching for beacon lights in a fog, and her mouth was set, the breeze from the open window at her back wiggling her hair.

Without realizing, Raymond was leaning against the bar. Nobody else sat at it, and only a few people occupied other booths in the lounge. The bartender asked Raymond what he wanted to drink. In spite of the fact that he'd barely eaten, he ordered amaretto. And he sat at the bar, watching Jill through the reflection in the mirror.

The band punched out a quickly paced *ranchera*, but there were no dancers to revel in the music. From a side door two men, American, entered the lounge, stopping before Jill. They smiled and spoke to her, yet she remained impassive, sort of staring onto the dance floor. The bartender set Raymond's liqueur down. Jill shook her head in the mirror.

She had claimed that Raymond hadn't been there when she'd needed him. Maybe she was right. Where had he been? How had Jill felt through all this? How much had she suffered? Was it possible that Raymond had been unfaithful, though not in the sexual connotation. If all this was about betrayal, then it was certainly possible that Raymond had been a participant in some sort of fraud. He struggled, trying to make the right connections.

He watched her reflection in the mirror, saw the backs of two men who continued to speak with her in spite of no encouragement, and saw too the drowned woman, the ice-filled truck, the young surfer who'd dreamt her lover's death.

He downed his drink, grimacing at the sweet heat that passed down his throat, swirled on his bar stool, and quickly strode to the stage. Astonishingly, the entire band stopped playing. Raymond made his request to the singer. Then he pushed between the two men before Jill's booth.

"Dance with me?"

"Did you commune with her dead spirit?"

"Don't be mean."

"I guess this was a mistake."

"No, it wasn't."

"You can't even eat with me. You can't stand the sight of me."

"You're important. Dance with me."

"I don't trust *you*."

"Just a dance."

"What for?"

"Because we agreed."

Jill looked to the bar. Did she now see both herself and Raymond? After a moment she stood up, taking Raymond's extended hand. Raymond led her to the dance floor, placed his arm around her waist, and began slow dancing. He could feel tension in her back, stiffness in her legs as she involuntarily followed him.

"You lead," he said.

She stopped for a moment and almost smiled. But she showed no hesitation at trying this new way to dance. In a moment they were moving around the floor, but in a reverse mirror image of how they'd danced only seconds earlier.

Yet all of a sudden Raymond was no longer dancing with Jill. He was instead chasing her down the stairs that led to the beach. She was ahead of him, running for the south point. The tide was in high, water lapping at the bottom step. He carefully picked his way on the stairs until he hit sand, which had a sudden spring to it because of a piece of driftwood that lay at the bottom.

Raymond lost his balance as a result of stepping on the jetsam. He fell into the shallow, cold sea. His shoes were immediately filled with gritty wetness, his legs as heavy as two cement posts. The wave that had hit the steps pulled back with the tidal surge, colliding with a new incoming wave, which made a loud clap and shot a geyser-like line of spray along the shore as far as Raymond could see. He pushed himself to his feet.

The wet sand before him glowed in the stark light from above. Now almost at the south point he saw the lightest movement from a dark form. He knew the form was a wife, a woman, a person.

Running toward the form, and feeling lightheaded, he felt Jill's grip tighten on his hand, felt her pull him hard into her body, felt her pelvis bump against his own as he went the wrong way on the dance floor. And as he began relaxing he heard the sudden and distinct cacophony of sounds around him. The restaurant curtains flapping in the steady night breeze. The bass guitar, lead guitar, snare drums, and even the words the singer told. But loudest of all he heard the unseen and truculent ocean scraping the beach, always scraping the beach.

The Ingredient

Julio Marzan

JULIO MARZAN is a graduate of Columbia University's Graduate Writing Program. He is a poet, writer, editor and translator. He recently completed *Unforgettable Tangos, Indelible Pagodas*, a collection of stories. In 1990, he was a resident at both the MacDowell Colony and the Edna St. Vincent Millay Colony, where he has been at work on a novel.

When Vincent finally looked down from the roof across from his grandmother's building, he realized how crazily he was behaving. Why had he come up here? Just to catch a glimpse of Robert and confirm with his own eyes that his friend was fucking Magda? The idea of coming up, now executed, seemed stupid—even dangerous, but there was a kind of beauty to the view. The setting October sun behind him reflected golden in rows of windows. In every building an assortment of old people, teenagers, housewives leaned out, one or two talking to people below. On the sidewalks children jumped rope or chased a rubber ball or simply each other. From the far end of the street rose the shouting voices of a stickball game in progress. At the nearest corner, a steady trickle of men and women, returning from work, turned and paraded to their respective buildings. From up here a kind of peace indeed washed over everything. Unlike the baked street, the gray and black rooftops had a breeze blowing over them. The moment made him think of lines he had underlined in Wordsworth's "The Prelude" the day before, as his professor lectured:

Whate'er mission, the soft breeze can come
To none more grateful than to me; excaped
From the vast city, where I long had pined
A discontented sojourner . . .

But he was in the city and he noticed just then that a faint cross-current of salsa and merengue danced in the dusk air. Louder still was the rap music from below, from a suitcase-sized boom box beside a guy sitting on the top step of his grandmother's stoop. He was gesturing to Vincent's side of the street, to a one-legged guy seated on a car fender. That had to be Rafy the Vietnam Vet, who hadn't been there when Vincent entered the building. Contemplating those two characters prompted Vincent to ask himself how it could have occurred to him to show up in this shit neighborhood to stupidly surprise Magda with a visit, especially since he should have seen the signs that she had no interest in him. Slam! A metal door had shut loudly behind him. On the roof of the building to his right walked a man and little boy whose entire body was shielded by a white plastic kite. The man took the kite from the boy and walked toward the roof wall. Raising the kite with one hand, he waved off the kid, who took backward steps as he unspooled the cord. The kite wafted briefly before teetering-tottering back down. The man picked it up and ordered the kid to run holding up the cord. It was aloft. Blown away . . . like him, as if Magda had just puckered her lips and exhaled a gust that set him sailing up on this roof, with no hope of having her and without a best friend.

Robert had been like his second brother at Fieldston. This year they entered Columbia together. They both signed up for Intermediate Spanish, although Vincent needed it more than Robert, who only took the course to boost his average. Robert spoke Spanish fluently. His diplomat father had been stationed throughout the Americas, where Robert grew up. If he hadn't taken the initiative to join the Spanish Club, Vincent wouldn't have joined because, to begin with, he didn't speak Spanish fluently and it was going to be a chore. At Fieldston he took French. Now he would have given anything to be fluent in Spanish, just to be able to defend himself against the Spanish Club snobs who expected that, because his father was Puerto Rican, he should speak it. Robert didn't have those problems. The Spanish club welcomed him. He even possessed the confidence to try to join the more militant Latin Students Association, although he was let known straight out he wasn't wanted. The L.S.A. students were the type who used their campus roles to fantasize having the power they were denied in the real world, which Vincent had always assumed was more his domain. He hadn't planned to join the L.S.A. until he learned that Magda, the president of the Spanish Club, was also a leader of the L.S.A.

Vincent picked up his backpack by the straps. Inside were books, syringes and insulin, his mother's only apparent legacy, and hard candy because chocolate melted in summer. He heard the boy complaining as the man spooled the cord. Before turning to depart, Vincent noticed that in the low sun lost behind buildings, the lighted apartments were sharply visible through their windows. His grandmother was in the kitchen, stirring something in a pot. He had eaten her food only a few times, never forgetting the roasted pork loin one Christmas. As they grew up, his father stopped taking his sons to visit her, and they never felt compelled to visit on their own. He couldn't recall ever looking directly at her, studying her, as he was doing now. What irony. Magda had told Robert about Rafy the Vietnam Vet, the one-legged drug dealer who hung out on the stoop two doors from her building. Robert passed it on to Vincent that this street was where they could score some pot. Vincent kept to himself that that street was his grandmothers's.

Slam! The man and kid were gone. Vincent looked around the tar-coated roof. Anything could happen up here in the dark. He had to get back to his real world, after an hour's subway ride to the West Side. He took a last look at his grandmother's window. Behind the sofa, she had dinner with a younger, heavier woman. What must they be talking about? What was the world of that gray-haired dark-skinned woman whose blood ran in him and whom he hardly knew? Of her two grandsons only he was burdened with her brown complexion. Vincent's father was fair-skinned, like his father, who had died before Vincent was born. He had only seen his grandfather in an old wedding photograph. In its yellowing sepia, his grandmother looked as blond as his grandfather. It was difficult for him to imagine that the young woman in the photograph and the old woman in the window contained a past connected to his present. He could cite no folklore or bedtime stories passed on by her. Neither he nor his brother ever called her. Nor she them. Because she and his Irish mother disliked each other, his father never forced her on the family.

Vincent last saw her when he was in the ninth grade. She was supposed to be very sick and his father insisted the boys come with him. She didn't appear that sick and wasn't very loving or grateful. Their coming down from nice Riverdale to this part of the Bronx was a psychological chore and a half, but she never displayed an ounce of sympathy for the difficulty of their coming down to her. Instead she looked at them with a kind of shame, exhibiting no sense of being the source of so much embarrassment to them in their world, in which her blood line elicited from others a look that enveloped them in an isolating cellophane. Afterwards he complained about her attitude to his mother, who considered herself "an American, just that," and whose only past, to speak of, was embodied in a brother in Philadelphia, whom she rarely saw. She thought Vincent's identity concerns were a waste of time. She got impatient with him. "You don't have to identify with her because you and she have nothing in common," she advised him. Then what was he supposed to say his father's last name was? "Tell them you're French, that's all, Beauchamp is French."

Magda had looked shocked to find him standing at her door. As usual her eyes refused to meet his. He had always thought the gap between them was cultural. She was the president of the Spanish Club, member of the Latin Students Association governing board, organizer of protest marches in favor of every cause, Latin Women's Rights, Puerto Rican Independence and the Ad-Hoc Committee on Fairness in Admission Practices. In every respect she embodied the single motivation for his and Robert's moving in on the Latin scene: to meet Latin women. Robert thought they were the sexiest-looking and Vincent couldn't agree more. Everything else about the Latin students he and Robert mocked in private. They felt above the few José's, Manuel's and Tito's—studying on minority scholarships, which his mother turned down—with their sleazy mustached-look, their ghetto English that always just sounded black. Robert theorized that their hot ladies were also hot for social mobility and a better class of man.

Caught up in his friend's sexual agenda, Vincent shared Robert's fair-haired confidence, forgetting his being different. Additionally, Magda's magnetism further inspired him to overcome his insecurity among Latins. She always wore a dress or skirt that revealed her full, proportioned legs. Her long ash blonde hair, half way down her back, bounced with her constant exuberance. Her every gesture excited him. In pursuit of her he made every effort to bridge the cultural distance between them. He plowed into Spanish, practicing for hours in the language lab. He signed up for every elective on Latin American culture and literature that fit his schedule. He wouldn't have minded at all coming to these streets to take her home. He had gone as far as to think about a way of breaking the news to his mother.

At that very second Robert had to be sitting in Magda's living room, holding her hand. Maybe her mother was about to serve fried green plantains and pan-fried steaks with sautéed onions and white rice with red beans, a dish his grandmother once prepared so deliciously. After dinner they might discuss his future career plans, with Robert giving an Oscar performance. Vincent's jealousy inflamed his mind. He had to wipe his soul clean of the whole episode, begin a new chapter. He contemplated the twin peaks of the Triboro Bridge outlined in blue lights, the blackness of the surrounding night, and heaved a deep breath. Another girl, what the fuck, just another girl. He turned, frightened of the intense dark, finally come to his senses that he had to get back.

When he opened the steel door, a hard-bassed rap music resonated in the stairwell, a flight or two below. He shut the door and listened to the music become louder. He ran to the darkest spot, behind the chimney base, and squatted there, wedged between the chimney and the roof wall. The metal door opened. The guy who had been standing in front of his grandmother's building with the boom box stepped out on the roof and leaned his back against the open door. In the triangular light from the stairwell, out came Rafy, who had climbed, incredibly, five flights on crutches. His skin was smooth brown and his hair wavy black, combed straight back. He wore baggy jeans with one leg rolled up and an Army fatigue shirt with the sleeves torn at the wriggling biceps. He hopped out in front of the stairwell door as Boombox turned off the boom box and placed it in the center of the light. Rafy leaned against the door while Boombox tied it open from behind, then disappeared behind the stairwell to bring out a milk crate that he placed at the edge of the light. Rafy sat on it, laying his crutches beside the crate, and immediately pulled on the velcro strip that held together his rolled-up pants leg.

Boombox kneeled beside the leg and unrolled it flat. Out of pockets sewn along the inside of the leg, he removed an inventory of small manila and plasticine envelopes and an assortment of vials. He

straightened his torso and took out of his side pocket a wad of bills
and a small note pad. He counted the bills, wrote in the pad, then
returned both into his pocket. Out of his back pocket he took out a
folded knife and whipped out its blade. Tilting back the boom box,
he wedged open the right lower speaker. The grid, covering no
speaker, popped off. From that cavity, he removed merchandise that
he stuffed into the appropriate flap-covered compartment in Rafy's
pants leg.

Vincent's sugar level dropped. He needed to suck on a candy but
was afraid to move. It occurred to him that these two guys represented all he knew about that half of his past that the world had
thrust upon him. Robert knew a better kind, that's why he had no
problem with getting close to them. He tried to keep poised, resisting
the dizziness and lethargy from his need for sugar. He thought of his
father, who near the end looked at the entire family as if from a distance, the way Vincent was observing Rafy and Boombox. His successful father, a chemist and later a pharmaceutical's representative,
had risen far away from this street. Even though he felt oddly left out
of the mainstream in which his father had left him, he always thought
that that was where he belonged. What gene caused him to gravitate
to this neighborhood and these broken people? His hands pressed
against the roof wall and the chimney, holding him up as his head
seemed to spin in a low-blood-sugar vertigo.

Boombox commented to Rafy about the white guy who had been
scoring some pot. Boombox had made the sale, then gave a sign to
Rafy who, across the street, went into the hallway to get the stuff
from his pants leg. He came out and as usual leaned against a car to
drop the envelope on the curb beside a tire. This time a patrol car was
coming up the street. Boombox whistled. Rafy hobbled into his hallway and Boombox vanished into his. The white guy panicked and
yelled into Boombox's hallway that he'd come back for it later.
Boombox was laughing because that guy, Bob, thought the street was
some K-Mart with a layaway plan. "He left his shit on the street, man
he fucking gave it away," as far as Boombox was concerned.

Their restocking done, now they were sharing a joint. Boombox
sucked fervently on the roach as looked down from the roof wall. He
was fat and wore a white T-shirt over a pair of baggy, pink knee-
length shorts. His high-necked sneakers were loosely tied. He looked

up and down the length of the street. Then, bursting out in laughter, he pointed down and looked back to Rafy because that white guy was back, coming up the block. "One unique dumb motherfucker coming back to K-Mart." They both laughed wildly at that. Boom-box described Bob's motions in front of the building across the street. Bob went into the hallway. He came out and looked around. He crossed the street and looked along the curb. "Guess what? He didn't find nothing." They cackled. Now Bob was going back down the block. Boombox returned to Rafy. "We better go downstairs and do some business." Boombox held the crutches upright for Rafy, who mounted his armpits over the pads. Boombox put away the milk crate, picked up his boom box and untied the door. The metal door sounded like a shot, leaving the roof totally black. Rap music resounded in the hall.

Drenched with sweat, Vincent came out of the fetal position he had assumed to hide in the shadow. He sat against the roof wall and felt in the dark through his backpack for the cellophane-covered candies. He sucked and bit into one desperately. He waited for the sugar to kick in. As he relaxed, relieved of his discomfort, the only thing he could think about was the name Bob.

. . . Over her loud stereo playing Rubén Blades, one of the few Latin singers whose music he knew, Vincent had had to identify himself three times. Magda's repeating "Who?" to herself cut mortally into his confidence. When she finally opened, instead of inviting him in she had demanded to know why he was there. He asked to be let in. She warned him that she was waiting for Bob. Bob who? "Your friend." Vincent had always known Robert as Robert. He hadn't expected to be turned down, not in a million years. Robert knew how he felt about Magda. Nevertheless, Vincent kept to his script. He needed to talk to her, could she lower the volume. No, she wouldn't. He sat on her sofa, sensing the need to talk fast. He explained that he was brought up very differently from her, but that because of her he had taken Spanish and joined the Latin American Students Association. Magda cut him off. "What are you getting at?"

"Because of your commitment and sense of identity. You're like the star of everything Latin, Magda, you know that."

"Well, so what?"

"I just thought you saw me as some assimilated guy from Riverdale and I wanted to get close to you. I was ashamed I couldn't speak Spanish fluently, for instance."

"And what if you could?"

"Then you would pay some attention to me. I like you a lot, Magda."

Magda rolled her eyes upward and went to get her pocketbook. She took out a pack of cigarettes. Shaking her head, she opened the pack and lit up. She started to speak but paused. When she found the right words, she spoke looking at her lap, as if speaking to herself, the red-tipped cigarette punctuating every word, "I just told you I'm waiting for Bob. Wasn't that enough of a hint?"

"I didn't know that when I worked up the courage to come here. And, right now, I don't care."

"I'm going to tell you something, Vinny. I'm going to be frank with you." She took a deep drag, dispelling the smoke hard, her eyes toward the window. Her long hair wore the afternoon light coming in from the window. Her blue eyes were Bermudan coves in travel posters. She began the next sentice with "I . . . ," then looked into his eyes for the first time. "I don't go out with Rican guys. Okay?"

His words flowed out thickly: "Bob only likes Latin girls because he thinks they all look like sluts. Those are his words, Magda."

"Well, I'm no slut and he knows it. So I think it's just better if you get out."

Downstairs Rafy and Boombox were back at work. The asphalt looked smoother and cleaner in the yellow street lights. Some kids still played in the dark. A mother leaning out a lighted window hollered out a name. A kid answered her from the sidewalk. Vincent's grandmother sat in a sofa facing the window. The younger, heavy-set woman sat in a chair. They watched TV as he watched them, a portrait framed by the window. Suddenly his mind came up with an answer to a question he hadn't consciously asked: he hadn't joined the Latin Students Association or his Spanish classes because of Magda. He had joined because of the inevitable "What are you?" after he was told he looked "Spanish" and he responded he wasn't that he was born in the Bronx and he was half-Irish. Nobody believed the Irish part and the other half stuck in his throat. In high school this identity crap seemed like a stupid game, but in college it had become all-important. Until that afternoon, Magda was the one person who could help him. She was the solution to his solitude. Magda, he realized that very second, reminded him of his grandmother in his father's old photograph.

The streets below looked fathoms deep. The city's lights formed a labyrinth he was seeing for the first time. Robert's path in it started at any point in this country and led to Riverdale, the West Side, the South Bronx and to wherever on the planet he wanted. Rafy and Boombox had only one, this street to their island and back. On the same path belonged his grandmother and also Magda, who coveted Robert's, on which she would find Vincent's mother and blond brother. But what was his father's path? Did he have one of his own or was that why he married his mother? The thought was cruel, but he felt angry. Nobody ever told him he would grow up deprived of a path. Now, losing Robert, he had lost the path on which he had been a guest. *What dwelling shall receive me? in what vale/ Shall be my harbour? underneath what grove/ Shall I take up my home?* And that afternoon Magda had shoved him out into nowhere, alone with his father's treacherous gene and his mother's diabetes. Maybe that's why he had come up to this roof: because he was walking in a maze he had intuited and not yet acknowledged. Or maybe to observe in his grandmother the ingredient that caused Magda to reject him, that thread bonding him to even Rafy and Boombox. This defect for his entire life was, after all, inherited from his grandmother, who would vibrate in his bones like Boombox's music behind the metal roof door, which he had just opened. The chipped-beige halls around him were identical to those he remembered in his grandmother's building. In the naked-bulb light, he descended to what borrowed path would get him to Columbia.

Spider's Bite

Pablo Medina

PABLO MEDINA was born in Cuba and has lived in the United States since 1960. His poetry, prose, and translations have appeared in many periodicals and anthologies. He has published a book of poems, *Pork Rind & Cuban Songs*; a collection of essays, *Exiled Memories: A Cuban Childhood*; and has translated the poetry of Tania Diaz Castro. Mr. Medina is assistant professor of English and Spanish at Mercer County Community College in Trenton, New Jersey. He is also the Jenny McKean Moore Writer in Residence at George Washington University, Washington, D.C.

Ruperto's death was a surprise to everyone but his sister. For a month Felicia had noticed his normally erect posture sag in the rocking chair where he rested after dinner and his electric green eyes flatten in long stares through the afternoon. The doctor, the same one who used to make incognito visits to the house years before, had declared Ruperto to be in excellent health. But she knew that her brother was dying.

The night before it happened, Ruperto called the funeral home where he worked and said he wasn't feeling well; but there were three wakes scheduled and the director pressed him to go. When Ruperto returned in the morning, he had lost his shadow and the eye sockets had deepened to the point where no light came out of them. He sat at the rocker and asked for his coffee, and when she brought it, she saw him, chin to chest, hands clenched on his lap, and without touching him or checking his pulse, she knew his moment had arrived. She called the doctor and Ricardo; she called Ruperto's wife Areli, who responded with tiny whimpers but refused to come to Miami to claim the body. It was the last time Felicia would speak to her.

He was buried in a less than dignified manner. While the legal complications as to who was responsible for the body were straightened out, the corpse lay in a morgue freezer for eight days. As a result, the few friends he had remaining and the family members who stayed in Miami waiting for Ruperto to be released into the hands of the embalmers grew weary of keeping their mourning in check and turned what should have been a somber week into a festival of card-playing, drinking and jokes.

The wake was a ramshackle affair, lasting only an afternoon, for the hall in which he was laid out had already been assigned for the evening, and the funeral home director was unwilling to move the later wake into another room, no matter that Ruperto had been his faithful evening facilitator for upwards of four years. It was enough, he told Fernando, that he was giving the family the usual employee discount. The burial was quick and efficient without a priest to lengthen the proceedings with a homily. Even unto death, Felicia felt bound to accommodate the prejudices of those close to her.

The only tears shed were those of María Antonieta, Ruperto's seventeen-year-old daughter, and of Lucho, who grieved more for himself—death now an arm's-length away—than for the cousin with whom he had shared the oranges of youth.

After the symbolic shovels full of dirt were thrown on the casket and the small group dispersed to their cars, Felicia saw her grandson Antón standing over the open grave, a question furrowing his brow, his pale cheeks drawn against bone. To her he was still the child she had seen walk away from her in the dark morning seventeen years ago.

Back in the house, while the guests feasted on food Eduardo had brought, Felicia pulled Antón aside and admonished him that if he kept going the way he was, he would wind up like Simeon Stylites.

"St. Simeon, you know. He lived atop a pillar. As the years passed he had it heightened. The day came when he was so high off the ground the faithful could barely hear him preach. His only company was his own feces. He was too good for his own good."

Waving her finger before his nose, she added, "You don't know what you have until you lose it."

Alone that following morning she realized she could have told them all the same thing. Her brother's death had crystallized the possibility she had fought against since the death of her husband, that the family, her hope and her support, was splintering. Her two sons were busy enough making their way in the new world, and the other grandchildren were too young still to be anything other than pesky distractions. The process of elimination led to Antón, in whom she saw the faint seed of posterity, or imagined such.

Felicia trusted her instincts more than her intellect, more than her sentimentality, and certainly more than her guilt. Life went on and she received her guests—fewer now that her brother was gone—as she had in the past, with a pot of beans or stew and freshly perked coffee. More and more time she spent in funeral homes paying her respects to friends and relatives she had known from her youth. Some months she went to as many as six wakes, but her average was two, enough to have her generation decimated in a few years. It was in Arístides Berza's funeral, as she looked at his waxen face before the casket was closed for the last time, that a voice at her ear, a voice that sounded as if it came out of an ancient mist, told her she had five years to settle her affairs. That same night she called her old friend Marina for advice on the matter.

Nothing, not even the blindness that had come upon her as a result of advanced diabetes, kept the old seer from coming to her friend's aid. Marina was married again, not to the wealthy Presbyterian she had mused about before leaving the island, but to a butcher twenty years her junior who doted on her and brought her elephantine roasts and red, juicy sirloins fresh from the block. Marina had taken to wearing dark glasses to cover her sugar-bleared eyes; her skin, once tight against layers of fat, now hung loosely round her neck and down her arms. Her hair was still dyed red, and her presence, preceded by the jingle of her jewelry, was as mesmerizing as it had been twenty years ago when her career was at its height.

She gave Felicia the name and phone number of her cemetery's agent. There was a nice plot left next to hers, shaded by a royal poinciana not far from the service road. They spent the rest of the visit comparing funerals they had attended and exchanging the bland gossip of the old, which limits itself to the diseases, conditions and operations to which friends in common are prey. Toward the end Felicia brought up her grandson's aimlessness.

"This is the land of confusion," Marina said.

"He had so much promise as a child. He might have been somebody."

"Today he is nobody. Tomorrow he will be a different man, and the day after that a different one still, and none of these men will have anything to do with you. We will be dead soon. Nothing on this earth will matter after that."

"But the family!"

There was a note of desperation under the exclamation. She was the one holding up the roof. Without a successor the future would crumble.

"He is too much the child," said Marina with the weariness of someone tired of language. "Too full of himself, and he has too few responsibilities, other than making himself miserable."

"He is lost."

"He is not. There are no accidents in this life. He is teaching himself a lesson."

"What?"

"That he can only be fulfilled in blood. But you won't see him freed of the weight of your control."

"My control?"

Marina did not reply. The answer blossomed on Felicia's forehead like a black flower, and she remembered Antón at birth, the little aardvark she had so disdained and for whom she'd shed so much of herself.

The lady took to her preparations with a zeal that, while unsettling the younger family members, nevertheless made her age gracefully in their eyes and kept from them the unspoken but ever present sense of dread that burdens families when one of them teeters at the edge of darkness. Much needed straightening; words had to be said, hurts healed, friendships renewed and concluded, angers explained, secrets unveiled, God graced, mercy confirmed, illness borne honorably and her memory assured. Death, in short, became the purpose of her life.

Felicia put a down payment on the burial plot, just as her friend suggested, and started saving money so that her children would not be burdened with the cost of the funeral she had planned for herself. She wanted a lavish affair that would last the full two days and not a moment less, replete with foods and liquor for the guests and gifts for the children. She wrote that white was to be the color of her death, white the limousines and white her burial dress; that any mourner showing up in black should be sent home to change; that none of the

relatives should work that day; that the children should in no way be
reprimanded and should be allowed to do as they pleased. And that
there should be no rain, but that the sun should shine, the sky blue as
the love of the angels and the earth smooth as a baby's thigh.

Over the next five years she wrote farewell letters to all her relatives and closest friends. She put the sheets of onionskin paper in the
same cigar box where she saved the funeral money until the box was
stuffed and she had to get another.

Fifty-seven years of smoking began to manifest themselves. Her
voice grew rough and gravelly, and she became afflicted with a quick
dry cough that never went away. Her sons urged her to give up
tobacco and the doctor issued the usual ultimatums, but she saw no
reason to stop. Cigarettes were her companions and allowed her
mind to drift upward with the smoke; besides, other more immediate
ailments occupied her—a weakened stomach, rotting teeth and a
rheumatism that stiffened her joints and kept her awake nights with a
pulsating, fluid pain in her extremities like the motions of the seas,
that she took as the persistent messages from the other world. The
casing of her life was wearing out. To forgo smoking at this point
would only forestall the process.

When not accommodating herself to the unavoidable and thereby
helping others do so as well, she sat on the rocker with her cigarettes
and her handkerchief, looking back not with nostalgia or regret, but
rather as one rereading a favorite book, in full knowledge of the basic
plot and thus better able to appreciate the nuances of the author's
style.

Once, after a particularly virulent attack of rheumatism that
made the joints of her hands feel like they had been dipped in molten
lead, she remembered the last time she saw her mother. The mother's
eyes were fixed on the flickering oil lamp at the foot of the bed and
her mouth was frozen in a soundless scream. Her cheeks, injected
with the yellow venom of death, had repelled the daughter to the
point where she had to make a superhuman effort to keep from gagging when she kissed them. Felicia vowed then, at the age of thirteen,
never to let death tyrannize her like that.

She remembered too the verbenas at the Lyceum in Corral Falso
and how all the town would turn up and the music wouldn't stop
until the sun came up the next morning. At one of these dances she'd
met Napoleón Silva, the famous general who'd risen up against the

dictatorship of Inocencio Fuentes. He was then a young lieutenant visiting his family on leave. Dressed in full uniform as he was, all the girls had made eyes at him, hoping to get at least one dance for their efforts. But he had ignored them and danced only with Felicia. They saw each other daily after that, until it was time for him to return to the regiment; then he turned from her and went to his ambitions like a man possessed. When he returned to town a year later, Felicia heard that he was engaged to the daughter of an oligarch from the capital.

Her disappointment lasted until the next verbena. By that point she had already met Luis García, one of several eager young men who hovered round her at the parties. He was a serious, formal fellow with vivid amber eyes and a nervous way about him. He was still in his father's shadow, and everyone expected him to carry on the family's export business. At the time she had no way of knowing of the worms that would invade his personality years into their marriage and lead him to bankruptcy, drink and the beds of countless women.

Sometimes she thought of recent events—Ruperto's death or a talk with Marina or a funeral service where she'd met up with someone she hadn't seen since better days—but more often than not, her mind stretched to the foggy past, focusing on the flash of light through a milk-streaked glass, or the smell of leather and horse sweat in the old farm's tack room, or the feel of the sun on her skin and the sound of early morning waves outside a window where once she'd spent a holiday, or her wedding night, the first time she made love.

She remembered her fear, which increased through the night to a giddy terror, and her longing that swirled in her like a wind becoming storm, the two emotions growing together until they became one white-hot ball. And when the time had come, after the celebrations and the dancing and the guests, she waited in bed for her husband, who slipped under the covers naked. They kissed and his hands groped all about her body, reaching places none had before. She felt his manhood, hard like no flesh, slithering up her thighs, then his entry into her and the painful thrusts, his smell like a wild animal loose in the night, a sabre slicing her organs, arc of release, head on fire, the world at her throat, and love, love like a fruit split open bursting with a thousand seeds. She remembered as if it were yesterday, and she still loved him—Luis, Luisito—who had given her so much pleasure and so much pain.

* * *

Her grandson Antón stayed away for three years. She saw him only once during that time, at his wedding, and to bridge the distance she wrote him long letters of advice and support, which he answered telegraphically, if at all, compelling her to fill the void with news she got from his parents. She learned that he'd taken to writing when teaching became too leaden; that his successes were always short of his ambitions, his publications meager and limited to translations and articles on technological subjects, and of late, a do-it-yourself manual on the installation and upkeep of sump-pumps, of which she'd demanded and received a reluctantly signed copy.

When Antón finally visited, he looked as if the black pachyderms of the African apocalypse had stampeded over him. His hair was tousled and streaked with gray; his forehead, that had offered Felicia so much promise of light, was blemished and swollen over the eyebrows; his cheeks, colorless and glassy, lay flat against the bone and his ears protruded outward as if they'd been cut and reattached without concern for balance or design; the nose loomed over his thin lips and overwhelmed his diminutive chin. It occurred to the grandmother that he was once again the rat-like creature that had so disturbed her over thirty years ago. Still, her immediate reaction was to embrace him, and as she did so she could feel through the damp jacket and unironed shirt, not the meat life ought to put on a man, but the sharp jags and heavy matter of bone. His wife stayed behind, he explained, too busy to leave her job, but it was what remained unsaid that was significant to Felicia.

It was a Saturday and the living room was crowded with guests. The blind Marina was there with her ruddy husband Bill, and Lucho too, smiling like a man about to enter Paradise. Eduardo and his wife Lidiana rounded out the company.

Antón sat in Felicia's rocker. Eduardo handed him a drink and Lidiana brought him a plate of food which he ate, not voraciously as he would have in better days, but judiciously, as if each forkful carried the whole weight of existence. As he finished the food and started on his third scotch, he noticed the figure of a girl flash out of the bathroom and enter one of the rear bedrooms.

"Who's that?" he asked his grandmother.

"María Antonieta."

"Ruperto's daughter?" he asked stupefied. "She's beautiful."

Her appearance in the living room a few minutes later further jarred Antón's leaden mood. From her spread the sweet scent of flowers and virginity. She kissed everyone present but only shook hands with Antón who would have worn out his lips kissing that angel.

"What a waste!" said Eduardo.

Antón looked at his uncle and Eduardo repeated his exclamation.

"Stop it!" said Lidiana, materializing out of the shadows of the kitchen. "The girl has made up her mind. If she wants to be a nun, then so be it. At least she won't have to put up with the likes of you."

"That," responded Eduardo extending his arm and pointing a shaky finger at Lidiana, "is my wife."

"María Antonieta will make a very good nun," Marina spoke up in her sibylline voice. "She will be blessed by God and all the saints, but she is destined for secular greatness."

María Antonieta did not take Eduardo's complaint seriously, nor did she acknowledge the seer's prophecy. A few minutes later a car drove onto the gravel shoulder in front of the house and she was gone.

"What a thing," said Eduardo. "She's going out on a date!"

"So what?" Lidiana broke in, working to aggravate her husband.

"If she's going into the monastery . . ."

"Seminary," Lidiana corrected him.

"Convent," Marina corrected her.

"Monastery, convent, seminary," Eduardo protested. "If you people were not so intent on showing me up, I'd be able to finish a sentence."

"If you weren't so drunk, there wouldn't be any need to correct you," said his wife, ignoring that she herself had been corrected.

"Carajo!" yelled Eduardo. "I know better than anyone when I'm drunk. And let me tell you something else."

He was wiggling his finger at his wife, but he meant it for everyone.

He did not get to continue. Felicia, aware that the gathering was about to deteriorate and eager to send her visitors away on an up note, addressed the one person who had been silent throughout.

"What do you think, Antón?"

The whiskey made his thoughts float to the surface and bob on the waves of his consciousness like the flotsam of coherence. He focused his concentration on the muscles of his mouth and spoke.

"Ma-ri-an-to-nie-ta."

Lucidity was a bird taunting him through amber light.

His grandmother stared at him through the plume of cigarette smoke. She remembered how difficult language could be when it turned to gravel in the mouth.

"Is-a-luf-ly-air. A luffly gull."

"Yes. She is lovely."

"And . . . viv-a-shusss."

Later, after the guests had left, he raised his head and asked clearly, as if the cobwebs of drunkenness had temporarily lifted, if María Antonieta was happy because she was young or because she was certain of what she wanted. Or was it that she was simple-minded?

"At twenty-one it is easy to be full of cheer. The only consolation is that tomorrow will come."

"What if tomorrow doesn't come?"

Almost immediately his eyes closed and his jaw dropped open. Out of his mouth came a pestilential odor that made her bowels shiver. She arranged cushions around him as best she could and spread a bedsheet over him that he might not catch the evening chill.

Then she sat in the dining room to play a game of solitaire. It was another one of her many habits, acquired as a young wife to allay the anxieties brought on by her husband's increasingly late arrivals. She was too old for anxieties now, but the habit had stayed with her and become one more companion for her solitude. María Antonieta would be home soon.

She was three cards from the end of her hand when she heard Antonio's greeting, *vaca vieja*, old phrase from the distant past. She stopped, looked around, wondered if she was asleep or awake, alive or dead, or whether someone was playing tricks through the window.

Vaca vieja!

It wasn't coming from outside but from the seat directly across from her. She felt a shiver down her arms, and her chest tightened with held breath.

Red jack to black queen.

She turned to the living room and saw Antón lying sideways on the couch, his back to her. Behind her the kitchen was dark and empty.

Red jack to black queen.

She uncovered a red jack and placed it under the queen of spades in the sixth position.

Ace of diamonds.

She flipped the next three cards and the last was the ace of diamonds. She moved it to the top and waited for Antonio to speak again.

"Antonio," she whispered after a long silence. "Antonio, where are you?"

I am dead. Muertecito. Deader than you could ever think the dead could be. And if you ask the dead what the dead are like, they'll point to me and say "like him, like him." Antonio is the deadest dead of all the dead who are truly dead.

"I can't see you."

Then you can see the dead. All the dead are one and all around you like a soup of nothing.

"Why did you come?"

Red jack to black queen.

The lock on the front door moved and car lights shot across the room, followed by the crunch of wheels on stone. María Antonieta flew into the living room the same way she had left, bringing with her the gusts of reality. She smiled at her aunt, who was strange and troubled, but more than relieved at her niece's appearance.

"Do you feel all right, tía?"

"Yes, yes," answered Felicia, unblinking. "I'm gathering the cards. Would you like some milk?"

The girl declined and went to the bedroom.

That night, sleepless and long almost beyond endurance, Felicia spent trying to call back her brother, and when that failed, remembering him as a young man coming home in the middle of the night weary and morose, reeking of bordellos, or else nervous and jumpy and smelling of gunpowder after one of his battles with the police.

Dawn was the usual blessing. It came in grayness, not brilliant as she would have preferred, but cloud light was better than none. She sat up and looked at her toes, mangled from rheumatism, nails brittle and cracked. It was the first time since she'd given up vanity on her fiftieth birthday that she realized how far from birth she was: eighty-three. Long life, long life indeed, and not a day had she been bored, not a day when she had doubted that everything was not for the good. She thought of this as she wiggled her toes, pleased this morning that there was no pain and she would be limber enough to wash the kitchen floor, mow the lawn, transplant a rosebush.

Felicia kept Antonio's apparition to herself until María Antonieta left to become a member of the Seraglio of Christ, as Eduardo put it, and Antón went back to sloshing through the bayou of self-doubt. Then, when quiet returned to the house and the long afternoon hours were hers to prove to herself, and, she expected with increasing confidence, to God, that she deserved whatever it was He had prepared for her, she resorted to the one person whose authority in matters supernatural was unsurpassed in the glimmering city. Marina la Ciega had honed her gift to such sharpness and accuracy that she knew, well in advance of Felicia's call, what Antonio's apparition meant.

"He is calling you," Marina told her friend. "He will come two more times, and on the last you will have to go. He will take His time. You mustn't tell anyone else, unless you want to die sooner than your appointed hour.

"Above all, keep your ears open to Him, and you must clear your heart of earthly hopes. Disentangle yourself from the tendrils that bind you and when you are called, dive into the murky waters. Bring nothing with you. It will be hard at first and you will be tempted to hold on to your glasses, but your eyes will soon grow used to the silt. Don't be afraid to reach bottom. That is best. Underneath the mud are the bones of your parents and brothers, and all of the dead. If you can slip through the bones—few can on the first attempt and some try for the eternity of time—then you will reach the rose of all existence."

Felicia waited six months for her brother's reappearance. She was at the stove preparing the bland food the doctor had ordered to keep her blood pressure in check—boiled potatoes and turnips, broiled fish without sauce, a cup of tea, and in defiance of the diet (for what was a diet if it wasn't violated?), French toast with plenty of syrup, when she heard Antonio's peripatetic voice greeting her—*vaca vieja, vaca vieja*—like a metallic ghost speaking through a fan. For the first time since her exile she broke into a sweat, no matter that it was winter and the day was cool.

Enjoy, gorge yourself

"Did you come to Ruperto?" she asked, beside herself.

Every day for four years.

"Marina said three times."

Every day for four years.

He said nothing more and just as Felicia reached for the cigarettes on the counter next to the stove, she heard, *Stop smoking*, this time from outside fading away. She looked through the window and thought she saw an angel disappearing into the crystal blue Florida sky.

Stop she did, and in a short time she gained weight and her cheeks acquired a youthful hue that few people alive had had the fortune of beholding. Her voice too changed, losing the smoker's rasp and turning soft and mellifluous. All who saw her maintained that she looked not a day over seventy, although, she liked to point out, at her age that was hardly a significant consolation. The last thing she wanted at this stage, after all her preparations had been dutifully accomplished, was to grow younger and retard death.

Antonio's third and final visit came just as she was sitting in the living room to have her breakfast orange. Without a greeting, or a kind word, or a sentiment of commiseration, he said *Today*.

She wanted to argue that it was a bad day, that she was being taken to lunch by her children, but at that moment her daughter-in-law walked in through the front door.

They found her in the tub with the shower spurting water on her chest and new rounded belly. Her face was drained of expression and her lids dropped halfway down the balls of her eyes. Small sounds, between moans and whimpers, bubbled softly out of her mouth.

It was an aneurysm—ripe berry that birth had planted on the crown of the circle of Willis—that burst and let the blood stream down the sides of her brain, taking what paths the gray mass allowed, a subarachnoid spider grasping its fat prey with long, graceful, coagulating legs. In short, Felicia's brain was being strangled by the slim fingers of fluid that contained her past and her hope, what she was and what she could be. In half an hour her pupils were the size of pinheads; in half an hour the doctor was advising the family that the hemorrhage was massive, that there was nothing to be done, that it was just a matter of time.

Felicia Turner, widow of Luis García Yanes, daughter of Gabriel Turner and Rosaura Fontana. Granddaughter of Wellington Turner and Magaly Noriega, passionate lover and eager wife, dutiful mother, indomitable grandmother, faithful friend, pillar of the family, fountain of patience, interlocutor between generations, planter and reaper of roses, scourge of despair; Felicia, boss of all bosses, patron of posterity, Queen of Canasta, lay silent and supple in a hospital room attached to machines measuring the progress of her egress from time and into memory. Nothing needed to be done. Her sons announced the circumstance to those who had known her well and those who had known her little and those who hadn't known her at all: Felicia Turner Fontana de García had been stung by the spider of death.

The Coast Is Clear

Ed Morales

(Photograph © 1992 by Elizabeth Ho)

ED MORALES is a freelance journalist, short story writer, and poet. He graduated from Brandeis University with a BA in Sociology and Philosophy, and worked toward a Master's Degree in Economics from the graduate faculty at the New School for Social Research in New York. His writing has appeared in *The Village Voice*, *Vista*, New York *Newsday*, and in many other national publications. He is currently the curator of a poetry reading series at the Nuyorican Poets Cafe on the Lower East Side.

When the heat came up from the boiler into Angel Luis Cabrera's apartment on East 11th Street, a cacophony of whistling, hissing and clattering sounds drowned out the television so completely that he moved it from the kitchen into the living room so he could watch the midday news. Angel Luis, who had just passed his 71st birthday, struggled unsuccessfully with the wheeled contraption that supported the television and decided to turn up the volume instead. He realized that water was boiling for a cup of instant Bustelo and that the kettle on the stove was contributing to the din. His fingers trembled slightly as he turned off the flame. The television newscaster smiled as he read his notes, recounting something about a scandal in the White House. The word *Contragate* appeared in the form of an action-logo behind the announcer. Pictures flashed which showed a map with arrows drawn from the Middle East to Central America.

Angel Luis was only vaguely interested in the use of the word *contra* in the news over the last few years. The sudden use of Spanish words in the American news media perplexed him, and this particular one was the source of confusion, since contra meant *against*. Almost every night they had been mentioning this *contra*, and Angel Luis would wonder, "Against? against what?" One day the President said "I am a contra." Angel Luis waited in vain for him to say who or what he was against. A week later, he thought he had figured it out. A billboard on his block advertised a device to be used for controlling household roaches which read "Combat Contra Las Cucarachas." So the President was against roaches, Angel Luis thought, so who wasn't? Los Americanos, especially the ones on television, had a tendency to overstate the obvious.

Angel Luis poured the boiling water into his coffee cup, spilling some on the table near the Christmas cards he displayed under a small tree he'd bought at Woolworth for $5. He quickly reached for a towel to wipe up the spill, which threatened to douse the card from his only daughter, who was driving in from Long Island to see him tomorrow night. Her name was Carmen Luz, she had a son, Bobby, who was ten and loved model airplanes and a daughter, Julia, who was thirty-six months old and had only seen her grandfather twice. Carmen's husband, Joe Acevedo, had struggled long and hard to become a lawyer and move to the suburbs. He was not anxious to make the trip to the Lower East Side, a neighborhood which had swallowed his two brothers in gun battles over drug money.

The newscaster frowned as he introduced footage of undercover policemen raiding a store on Canal Street that was warehousing thousands of fake Rolex watches. Angel Luis smiled in satisfaction over never having been taken in by these phonies and knockoffs. He preferred not to own a watch, yearning for the slower pace of Peñuelas, his hometown in the south of Puerto Rico—a place he had left so long ago. On 11th Street, he kept the time by the "ta-tos" he heard coming in through the window.

The papos who steered potential drug buyers to their transactions just outside Angel Luis's window regularly shouted codewords for the block's current security status. "Ta-to!" they earnestly cried out, "ta-to *bien*!" characteristically slurring the Spanish words *esta todo* (which means "everything is") *bien*, or well. The coast is clear.

The organization which handled the drug dealership on the block regularly shouted codewords to announce the block's security status. The "ta-tos" would start in the late afternoon during the winter, as soon as the sun went down, forming a rhythmic consistency that would blend in easily with the street sounds. Only when the lookouts urgently yelped "*bajando*!" would this rhythm be disturbed. *Bajando*, literally *coming down*, meant that the police were approaching. Sometimes this would be qualified by "*de pies*" or "*en carro*," to warn of their approach by foot or a patrol car. One afternoon, after spotting a cruiser, an imaginative lookout came up with "*feo, feo*," which in its sharpness of tone assumed an onomatopoeic quality, for its literal meaning was *ugly*.

The coffee cup was almost drained and the news was almost over. Angel Luis was absentmindedly stirring what was left, murmuring *tato* in unison with the lookout. He decided to look up Doña Flores from the second floor, due inside after an afternoon of stoop sitting. She had just come inside after spending the afternoon digesting first-hand accounts of neighborhood news. Obviously distracted, she was impatient with Angel's complaints about the Anglo television news. "Why don't you watch the Spanish news on Canal 41?" she said, mildly annoyed. "Ay, *yo no los creo a esos Mexicanos*," Angel Luis said as if it were common wisdom that Mexicans were liars.

But Doña Flores was more concerned with the young neighbors from down the hall. "Do you know what I saw those disgraceful ones do the other day?" she had told him this morning. "They were taking pictures of each other with their clothes off! What kind of respect is that?"

"You're just jealous of their youth," grunted Angel, swatting at a fruit fly hovering over a bunch of bananas that sat on top of the refrigerator. "That kind of thing makes no difference to me."

Doña Flores fumed, forced to invoke the specter of economic reality. "You know how much rent they are paying, Angel? $600, my love. $600 for the same little rat hole that you and I live in. $500 more than what we send to that bastard in Queens every month. How long do you think he's going to let us stay here? Juana Reyes, remember her? She can't get any hot water. Sixto and Mercedes went back to Puerto Rico last month when their landlord gave them a couple of thousand. Where does that leave us, Angel? Where are we going to move?"

Felito was a skinny, withdrawn thirteen-year-old living through the most awkward part of his adolescence, not sure what to do about the hair that was appearing on his upper lip, a little unsteady about how to approach the girls in the neighborhood. He spent his days on 11th

Street racing up and down the sidewalk on the same bike he'd gotten on his ninth birthday, playing with a group of younger boys. While most of the adults on the block castigated him for his apparent immaturity, he had always gotten along with Angel Luis, who often gave him a quarter for helping him carry his groceries into the building. Today Angel Luis was waiting on a stoop for the mail to be delivered, knowing it was too early for his check, but waiting nonetheless, since the day had turned out nicely, bathing the block in unseasonable warmth. Junkies raced past with painfully contorted strides, engaging in their routine body scratching, and depositing their phlegm into the gutter with awful sounding rasps and gargles. The gutter was brimming with the used syringes and transmission fluid that flowed down the gutter as a mighty river of waste.

Angel noticed that the young neighbor from down the hall was coming toward him, newspaper in hand, feeling at his back pocket as he approached their building with a wary nervousness. Behind his sunglasses was more evidence of distrust, a look of indifference poorly feigned, an uptight stare radiating in all directions, attempting to ward off what he most feared—a possible assault. Angel was all smiles, however, as he greeted him on the stoop, wanting to engage in a round of small talk. Doña Flores's fear of eviction was an old woman's paranoia; young and decent sorts like his new neighbor would only make things better, bringing more police to chase the junkies and their suppliers. He smiled as he imagined those nasty photo sessions she bemoaned—ah, the resilience of young flesh!

"Nice day, my friend. You have a day off from school, I guess?"

"No. I'm done with school. Graduated in '84."

"A day off from work, then?"

"Well. You could say that. Work part time, you know, temporary."

"Why not work a government job, like I did. It's secure. You get taken care of when you're old, like me."

Bill was his name, Angel remembered. "Right, Bill?"

"I don't exactly have that in mind. I have to have time to work out my ideas for my movie."

"Movie?" Angel wondered how serious he could be.

"Tara and I are putting all our money into it. We're selling almost everything we own."

"Right here?" Angel's eyes lit up, imagining the presence of all the trappings that go with a film shoot. Appearing in this movie would set up a stylish grand return to Puerto Rico.

"Well, not really. That's a ways off right now, anyway. I just hope I can save enough money to buy some equipment, but I don't always get enough work. Who wants to spend your whole life in a nine to five, ay, buddy?" His eyes were open as wide as they could be behind the sunglasses.

A deranged looking man in his late fifties was coming down the block on the other sidewalk screaming at the top of his lungs in singsong fashion. His face was red and his hair was turning white; he wore a denim jacket, black jeans and sneakers. He looked exasperated but not exactly drunk, and he addressed the block like a broken heir to Paul Revere:

"El Housing no es tan lindo! No tan lindo como yo creia! En el Housing estan pendiente de todos que estan viviendo en su casa y si estan trabajando y entonces suben la renta hasta que ya no tiene ni bastante dinero para comprar la comida! El Housing no es tan lindo! No como yo creia!"

Angel Luis and a couple of women who were walking nearby shook their heads in nervous laughter. That fool hillbilly is drunk and shooting his mouth off again. If he stayed off the booze, he'd be able to pay his rent and not blame everybody else for his problems.

"What's that? What's he saying?" Bill asked, half-concerned and half-threatened.

"Oh, just complaining about the government again, you know, too much papers, too much lines."

"Really?" Bill gulped, tightening his grip on the bottle of beer he carried in a brown paper bag and making his way around Angel Luis to the door. "It sounded pretty hairy."

Angel Luis laughed facetiously as he let Bill pass, but the creases in his face faded as he spied Felito down the block pushing a younger boy into the rubble in the vacant lot and pedaling off toward Avenue B with a freshly stolen radio.

Emerging from his afternoon shower, Angel Luis was thinking better of turning on the news again as he watched big drops of water fall from the tired squiggly hairs on his chest and stomach. He put on a pair of slippers and went to sit by the phone, in case his daughter and son-in-law called. He imagined them to be somewhere on the Long

Island Expressway, maybe even as close as the Brooklyn-Queens
Expressway, which made a long arc pointing to the Williamsburg
Bridge. He could hear the sound of the wheels of commerce spinning
over the steel grating, a groaning sound of worker bees in a Naked
City hive. He was in the back seat of a green station wagon, the kind
with the fake wood paneling on the sides, on his way to Sunset Park
to visit distant relatives. His brother Agustin was doing up capfuls of
whiskey and singing old time ballads from the forties, Jose Luis Mon-
ero and his orchestra.

"This Bill and his *puta* are going to have us all tossed out of
here!" shouted Doña Flores, who was suddenly standing next to
Angel Luis, holding his shirt and trousers. "Are you going to go
around the house naked like them? Here, put them on!"

"Beatriz! *Por favor*, don't get so excited. It's Christmastime. Do
you want some soup? I'll heat some up for you." Angel Luis shuffled
over to the stove running his hand through the lonely strands of hair
that remained on his scalp. He lit a match and thrust it into the
burner, saying a Hail Mary silently, looking at the ceiling. There was
a knock on the door.

It was Liviano, that old Cuban bachelor whose skin was so white
he could pass for an Anglo. He had a job at Citibank that paid pretty
well and could have afforded to move out, but stayed on the block to
save money, and, he says, because he's nostalgic about the area. "*Qué
tu quieres, flaco?*" Angel Luis groaned impatiently, "I'm making
some soup for—eh, I'm making some soup, I have company."

"And who is there with you?" Liviano whispered with hardly a
trace of an accent, even though he was very fluent in Spanish. "Doña
Flores? When are you going to accept the fact that it wasn't your
fault she was killed?" When Angel Luis became very angry he spoke
quickly and in a hoarse, crackling voice—sounding like he did when
he was a working man. "You don't know anything about that! You
weren't there!"

"I would have opened the door to those *tecatos* just like anyone
else would have. How did you know they were going to pull a knife?
Listen, Angel, it hurt me just as much as it did you, I adored Beatriz,
she was the funniest, friendliest, most daring woman in the neighborhood. This place died with her. If I could go back to Cuba, I would."

"Then why don't you, you miserable idiot! Why don't you get out
of my apartment and leave me in peace. My daughter and son-in-law

are coming tonight and I don't need the likes of you around." Angel Luis was clutching at Liviano's shoulder now and pushing him through the doorway.

"Get out."

"I just wanted to see if you needed anything," Liviano moped.

"Get out!"

"I can help you move out of here," Liviano pleaded.

"*Aquí me muero*!" insisted Angel Luis. Here I will die.

Sometime around 7:30, they finally arrived. The little girl had a cold and Joe was solemn as usual, retreating to the living room to read. "Ai papi," lamented Carmen Luz as she wiped the kitchen cabinets clean, "you need someone to help you clean up around here. It's so dirty. Why not come and live with us? We'll take care of you."

"That's no good," Angel Luis stammered, shaking his head, "your house is in the middle of nowhere, I can't even go to the store to get coffee." He took a long, noisy slurp of the fresh brew Carmen Luz had just poured him. "I'm the kind of guy who likes to get out on the streets, you know, bullshit for a while with those *pendejos* who play dominoes on Avenue A."

"Hah, *esos sin verguenzas*? Those good-for-nothings? Mixed up in the numbers and stolen bicycles and who knows what? Cockfights? You know and I know that you don't have anything to do with them." Carmen Luz thought better of pressing the point. She caressed her father's shoulder and tried to reflect on the better days of her youth, before she even thought of wearing make-up and stockings. The days she spent on the fire escape peeking through the iron casting at the street below, drawing the people who walked by with a set of crayons she had gotten for school. Sixty-four colors, the most diverse palette she had ever been blessed with.

"You miss mom, right?" Carmen Luz asked softly. "I can hardly remember her, papi. I was so young."

Angel Luis bit his lip and looked up at the ceiling unhappily, as if to say that he would rather not be drawn into the subject of his late wife, Carmen Luz's mother. An overwhelming sense of failure creased his brow as he took a long breath and uttered, "Your mother—yes, I . . . would rather . . . stay here . . . with her."

Carmen Luz and then her husband Joe were becoming increasingly distracted by strange noises that seemed to be coming from down the hallway in another apartment, the one that faced the back way. They were violent-sounding ones, shouting followed by screams. Someone was in pain—you could hear the crack of a broom handle, or was it a baseball bat?

Joe stepped out into the hallway about the same time that Felito came staggering out of the back apartment, followed by those new kids, Bill and Tara, *los artistas*, swinging a tripod and calling for someone to call the police. Felito was holding his head trying to stem the surge of blood that flowed fitfully from his forehead, groping along the hallway and leaving a trail of stains that led back to the apartment.

"He crawled in through the bedroom window," they growled like mountain cats, "we caught him taking our things." The young couple was in a frenzied state, protecting the nest, so to speak, striking out at Felito with the vengeance of a mother in the wild.

It was all Joe could do to choke back anguish as he held onto one of the new breed of his block, of which he was once the latest model. The torment of the situation had slowed the passage of time enough to allow him to examine the contorted looks of fear and rage on the faces of everyone in that hallway, and at that moment theirs was a unity not unlike that of the victims of a great war. Felito had been reduced to a sobbing infant, and his tormentors' faces began to soften, for the first time beginning to feel remorse for their part in the episode.

The door to Angel Luis's apartment swung open and the old man's head popped into view, the youngest child scanning the scene wide-eyed, her hands resting on either one of her grandfather's squat, hillbilly legs.

"That's my son, Bill," he said slowly, clearing his throat.

"Let him go."

Walking in the heavy snowfall, Angel Luis finally felt at peace with the northern climate that once seemed so hostile when he had first arrived in New York City forty-five years ago. The snow brought solitude to the street, freed him of nosy neighbors and the drunken fools on the corner, and covered the uncollected garbage and the forbidding gray of the sidewalks that had all but erased his memory of the fertile fields that bore the endless green stalks from the pineapple plants of his hometown.

It was also a relief that Christmas was over and that no one would be bothering him with any forced displays of emotion or religious proselytizing. And that Carmen Luz wouldn't be suggesting that he move to Long Island and spend his time watching television, babysitting, and acting as a buffer between her and that insufferably serious husband of hers.

At the corner of Avenue B, Doña Flores was waiting as usual, with a quart of milk and a can of vegetable soup, drawing a scarf around her neck.

"What would you have me do, Beatriz? Eh? Tell Carmen Luz that I never really loved her mother, that she was so obsessed with that suffocating church she used to go to that I began to lose the desire to work, to feed my family, to be a man?" Doña Flores could only give him a look of unusually deep sympathy, as if she had been softened by the snow that was still falling.

"No, of course not. Not me. There are some things, Beatriz, there are some things in a man's life that he can't even tell his own family, not even his daughter."

The snow began to swirl and fall in bigger flakes, making Angel Luis uncomfortable, giving him a bit of a chill. He took Doña Flores's hand and they turned around, making their way back to their building.

"You know what, Beatriz?" he said pensively, "You were right about those kids. Liviano sounds like he wants to move out, and one by one, before you know it, those kids will have us all out in the streets, Beatriz. And where in hell do you think we're supposed to go, eh? Where are we going to go?"

The amber lights that stood guard to the broken and decaying tenements of East 11th Street began to flicker on now, the sun was setting as strangely early as it would during the winter months. The drug lieutenants began to bark out their signals as the customers formed nervous, haggard lines that wrapped around the abandoned buildings on the corner. "Ta-to *bien*," the lieutenant announced. The coast is clear.

The Movie Maker

Elías Miguel Muñoz

ELÍAS MIGUEL MUÑOZ is a widely published Cuban-American poet, fiction author and literary critic. His published works include two works of criticism, *El Discurso Utopico de la Sexualidad en Manuel Puig* and *Desde Esta Orilla: Poesia Cubana del Exilio*; two novels, *Los Viajes de Orlando Cachumbambé* and *Crazy Love*; as well as two collections of his poetry, *En Estas Tierras (In This Land)* and *No Fue Posible el Sol*. His musical theater adaptation of *Crazy Love*, titled *The L.A. Scene*, had a successful run Off-Broadway in New York in 1990. His new novel, *The Greatest Performance*, was published by Arte Publico Press. He is at work on a new novel titled *Alive & Kicking*.

I saw a woman dressed in gray, grief-stricken, provincial clothes. Is that her? My *abuela*? Is that who I really saw that June night, seconds before the phone rang? Her doughy countenance. Her bulging body bouncing. I saw a pallid woman who looked wan and cold. A woman turning into the witch's ghost. White Lady.

But what about the emblematic dress? Breezy, impeccable white cotton doused with rainbow embroidery. Or, weren't you supposed to be mourning someone's death, *Abuela*? Yes, I saw you in black, *de luto*. And I caught the whiff of cheap cosmetics on dead flesh. And then I saw myself, oh God, putting up with your incantations, just the way it happened in *Cult People*; with the smell of rotting food and burning wax that came from your bedroom, just the way it was described in the book *Santería*; listening to your singing in the middle of the night, in a strange language; to the cawing sound of your prayers. Oh God.

Instants later I heard the phone ring and Daddy shouting "*Mamá*!" (Yes. It was only seconds later.) I picked up the receiver in my room and Daddy's voice blasted me away. I coughed gently.

"Gina, what are you waiting for? Greet your *Abuela*!" Daddy told me immediately, empowered by his joy, playfully authoritative. I said "Hello, *señora*," and my grandmother laughed. "I'm coming to visit you, Ginita," she said then. "Happy birthday!" Gagging, groping for words I came back with, "Thank you, *Abuela*. But my birthday was last month."

"We'll celebrate it when I get there!" she hollered.

"Yes. Sure. Of course," I stammered.

I wished her the obligatory *buen viaje* and I hung up, hurrying to my folks' bedroom to join the celebration. An unexpected spectacle was awaiting me there. I peered through the door, before going in, and saw my mother sitting at her dresser, talking to herself; or rather, talking to her mirror reflection.

"It's been such a long time, *mi niño*, I've missed you so!" she wailed. "We're finally going to be together," she cried out, as if she had become an older version of herself. "Reunited!"

I saw my mother getting up and glaring at Daddy, who was still on the phone, with her sinister French-Cuban eyes; sitting back down in front of the mirror and, wiping away fake tears with her robe, resuming her incredible act with: "Oh, my son, how are you? Are you well?" My mother laughing. "Yes, yes, I'm fine. No, I don't need anything." My mother staring at her own face as if she couldn't recognize it. "Time is up, *mi niño*, we have to hang up. Gotta go and march with the troops! The Revolution calls! Gotta go and stand in line. They're selling something-or-other-and-whatever at the store . . . Stand in line! Stand in line! Gotta go, *mi niño*. But I'll be with you soon!"

Daddy was finally saying good-bye to his mother and hanging up. I went in. Maman walked back to bed. "When is she coming?" she asked Daddy. "In one . . . one week," he mumbled. "Not enough time to fix a room for her," stated my mother. "But I will try."

There were tears in Daddy's eyes. "One week!" he kept saying. "Yes, Daddy," I hugged him, "and seven days go by real fast!"

Back in my room, trying to go to sleep, I was going crazy thinking, *What if she doesn't like me? What if I can't understand her?* I was wide awake for hours, exhausted from thinking, *You don't start loving a person overnight, know what I mean? Even if that person is your grandma and you have read all her letters* . . .

In my dreams, that night, I saw my *abuela* mumbling prayers and putting spells all over the house, throwing holy water in the corners, hanging red ribbons from the windows, digging up Maman's plants and hiding secret ancestral messages inside the pots.

In my dreams, that night, I ran to Daddy. "Daddy, talk to me about grandma, will you?" I implored him. "Well," he muttered, "what do you want to know exactly?" Yeah. What *did* I want to know? "Tell me, Daddy . . ." My father's face was suddenly vanishing. "Tell me . . ." Tenebrous depths of a fade-out. "Tell me about my grandma's rituals." Blackout. Dead of night. "Whenever," he murmured, "whenever there was a full moon . . . she'd have me save my urine for her potions . . ."

He gasped for air as he went on, "One time she cut off a big wad of my hair while I was asleep . . . She made a charm out of it in the shape of *Changó* and asked me . . . to wear it inside my undershorts for five consecutive days." *Changó* again?! "She also asked me once . . . to take down my pants . . . so she could paint the sign of the cross with chicken blood . . . on both my testicles." Daddy, please! Don't get obscene! "And then . . . then there were those times when she would act . . . when she would act like she was possessed . . . "

"Possessed," I cried, that night, in my dreams.

"Your grandmother is on her way," announced Maman the next morning. "I know," I responded, playing the smart mature American teenager in *Follow Me*; the kid who leads his friends into a thrilling and forbidden adventure. "I was there when she called, remember? I even talked to her."

"You will have to put up with her for a while," said Maman, cunning and ruthless. She had obviously chosen to be Lady Juliette in *Monarchy*.

"Maybe she'll be cool."

"Very unlikely, Gina. She's not like us."

"What do you mean she's not 'like us'?"

Lady Juliette vacillated, giving this last inquiry serious consideration. She selected a low, slow voice, and slyly she answered, "Your grandmother spent her life on a farm, surrounded by animals."

I would now impersonate the apathetic-empty-headed teenager in the hit sitcom *Growing Up Is A Pain*. "That's kinda kicked," I stated.

"'Kicked'?" Lady Juliette approached her subject swiftly and royally melodramatic. "It is rather apparent that you don't know what you're talking about," she said.

No Pinos Verdes teenager would ever take such loaded grown-up statements seriously. "It'll be OK, Maman," I came back, smiling. "Don't worry about a thing. Be happy."

"The problem is, Gina . . . "

"Always a problem. You're such a drip."

Lady Juliette didn't know what "a drip" meant exactly, but she was able to detect her subject's condescending tone.

"Don't patronize me, Gina Domingo!"

"Don't do what?"

"I don't know where you're getting that attitude of yours, but let me tell you, *jeune fille*, it won't work with me!"

"Attitude? Yeah, I've got lots of that."

"Will you listen to me for a moment?"

"OK." I pulled at my ears, making a funny face.

"The Cuban government has given your grandmother Estela permission to come to the United States."

"Yes, I know that already."

"She's going to be staying with us . . . "

"Neat."

"No so 'neat'."

"Why not?"

"Our lifestyle will seem strange to her, Gina."

"So what?"

"You've got to be prepared."

Prepared for what? I wondered. For fighting a poltergeist or something?

"I have given your father my consent to bring her."

"Cool of you, Maman." (She didn't catch my sarcasm.)

"But under certain conditions."

"Conditions?"

"That's right."

"Like what?"

"She must stay out of the kitchen."

"Oh."

"She must never engage in domestic activities."

"Ah."

"And most importantly . . . "

"Yes?"

"She must never do any of her Santería rituals in the house."

A very kind, warm welcome, I thought. In order to live with her family for a measly couple of months, my grandmother had to stick her Santos up her ass. That is, if she actually did bring her Santos with her.

I was no longer curious but furious, ready to skip the Teaser, Act Two, and jump right into the tag of my little Cuban-American sitcom. Ready to tell Maman to take a hike and shove her Lady Juliette routine down her French throat. Which I didn't, of course. (Chicken!)

"Thanks for the advice, Maman," I said. "I'll try to be prepared for Abuela." (Whatever that meant.)

"Social Events" was a strange category, I thought. It could encompass anything from Homecoming to the principal's flu. Everything could be considered social, really, as long as it involved people.

As Social Events reporter for "All Saints Bulletin," I had been granted the honor of writing an article on Sister Martha's mystical experience, which I described as the nun's "near-encounter of the blessed kind with the Pope, when the latter almost paid a visit to the South Bay." I had also provided information on Mrs. Tate's acute appendicitis; thanks to which—I wanted to say in my essay but didn't—many happy students were saved from the Witch's claws in algebra for several weeks.

My report on Miss White's wedding was a hit, deserving one entire front page and three long, juicy columns. My personal view of the event—which I didn't dare express in my article—was that the religion teacher had finally found a pious Ramosan hunk to read her body words and help her bear her heavy cross-cross-cross.

I had produced a piece on Homecoming, narrating how the glorious evening began with the traditional parade into the ASHS Stadium, as handsomely decorated vehicles and banner-carrying groups representing classes and clubs led the cars bearing the members of the Court.

And I had published an entertaining compilation of the latest and trendiest expressions used by most All Saints High School students. The editor advised me to exclude "cacus," "dude," "bagged-up," "barfed-up," "hot dig," and "cork head," for fear of insulting the faculty. Among the most popular and presumably less offensive terms

I'd cited "obdurate" and "kicked," which happened to be two of the synonyms for *cool* that I had appropriated for my own hip discursive practices.

My grandmother's visit was the first exciting news I would be able to report. At last I'd be hitting home by writing about my abuela's saga and the Cuban "thing." I consulted with the faculty editor and two other "All Saints Bulletin" staff writers, finding resistance at first. "Most students won't know where Cuba is," said one of the staff writers. "Your idea has nothing to do with our school," said the other writer. "It's too political," added the faculty editor.

"We'll publish a map of the Tropical Sea with all its islands!" I said. "We'll include a geographical introduction! I won't say a word about Communism!"

This was going to be the article of the year, a media masterpiece, I promised. "And what do you mean it has nothing to do with our school? I'm a student here, aren't I?" I definitely had a point there: CUBAN GRANDMOTHER ALLOWED TO LEAVE HER COUNTRY SO SHE CAN VISIT HER GRANDDAUGHTER WHO HAPPENS TO BE AN ASHS STUDENT!

I'd write it up as a touching, triumph-of-the-human-spirit type of story, a sentimental journey, a tearjerker in good taste: GRANDMOTHER WROTE MANY LETTERS THAT GRANDDAUGHTER NEVER GOT BUT GRAND-MOTHER AND GRANDDAUGHTER ARE FINALLY UNITED IN SPITE OF A SINIS-TER DESTINY SCHEME.

So, I managed to persuade the editor to let me run the piece. Remembering this experience months later, I would admit to myself the wisdom implicit in one of my grandmother's Cuban axioms. It is true after all—I'd tell myself—that a baby who doesn't cry doesn't get to suck her mother's breast.

I slaved over the questionnaire until the questions were perfectly clear and poignant. *Número uno*: "Señora Ruiz de Domingo, tell us please, what impressions do you have of Pinos Verdes, the South Bay and Ramosa Beach?" *Número dos*: "Do you see any major differences between life here and life in Cuba? *Número tres*: "In what circumstances—and I mean the *real circumstances*—do old people like yourself live on the island of Cuba?" Fourth and final question, *número cuatro*: "Tell us, please, Señora Ruiz de Domingo, anything you can tell us about *Cuba today*, the real scoop if you'd be so kind."

Then I searched for a fresh and original form to tell my story. Suddenly, the words MOVIE SCRIPT flashed before my eyes in tubular, pastel-colored neons. Yes! I'd write the piece as a script! I'd film my grandmother's arrival and describe the video clip in my article. (Wow!)

I decided not to wait for the glorious event to take place; I was too excited. I picked up *How To Write a Movie In Seven Hours* again, to review the technical jargon, and I wrote, in delirious and delicious frenzy:

Los Angeles Airport. INT. DAY. This woman hugs and kisses me, calling me "*Muchachita*!" (Little lady!) Close-up of Daddy lifting this woman up and shouting "*Mamá*!" ("Mother!") turning her around and around, "*Mamá*!"

My camera pans the waiting area, a crowd staring at the Cuban family. Zoom in on Maman in the crowd, looking barfed-up.

A song is heard: Gloria de Miami's "The Day I Left You, Baby, Seems Like Today."

Gina's point of view: We pick up this woman's luggage—one piece, fifties-style—and drive to the mansion, and during the ride the Visiting Woman and Daddy are talking (in Spanish) about their relatives back home, about how grown-up and intelligent Gina's cousins are, etc.

Woman: *Gina se parece tanto a su primo Nelson*! (Gina looks so much like her cousin Nelson!)

Gina: Wow!

Daddy and Visiting Woman telling each other stories and crying like babies.

Woman: *Ay, mijo. Ay, mi Benitín*! (Oh, my son. Oh, my little Benito!)

Daddy: *Mamá mamá mamá*!

My mother's point of view: Gina holding the Visiting Woman's hand. Maman's voiceover: "*Garce garce garce*!" ("Bitch bitch bitch!")

Zoom in on woman: In her late sixties; tall; clad in a blue cotton dress, no jewelry; her face hardly wrinkled; short brown hair.

Cut to: Pinos Verdes hill. A splendid, smog-free summer day. Panning of pine trees and the beach; a deco building down below, expanding over an entire block. Zoom in on sign on edifice: GALA MALL.

Cut to: Our Mercedes parked in front of a mansion which resembles a plantation house, tall white columns, etc. (That's our home.)

Close-up on Estela Ruiz de Domingo, smiling. Her son Benitín carrying her suitcase. Her daughter-in-law Elisa coming out of the car, looking totally bagged-up.

Benito and Estela walking hand in hand.

And Gina filming.

Fade out.

Following my plan to the letter, I interviewed Estela Ruiz de Domingo as soon as Family with Guest got home from the airport. But the responses my grandmother proffered were not up to par, I thought, definitely not ASHS journalistic material.

Pinos Verdes, the South Bay and Ramosa Beach for Estela were simply *muy bonitos*—very nice—although she wasn't sure about that since "I haven't seen much of anything yet."

Yes, she was certain that there were major differences between life here and there, but it was too soon for her to make any statements about such differences.

(C'mon, Cuban grandma! Make a statement! I've got a deadline to meet!)

About the topic of old people, Cuban grandma related what she'd heard in her country, that in the United States old folks were not wanted, that they were put in retirement homes where they vegetated and wilted away. But she hadn't visited such places so she couldn't attest to the truth of those rumors.

(The deadline! The article of the year!)

"Old people in Cuba? Well, they work very hard," she said, "just like the young ones . . .

"Cuba today? Well, it is a beautiful island. As beautiful today as the day it was discovered by Columbus."

By the time Estela Ruiz de Domingo became knowledgeable about life in Pinos Verdes, I had lost interest in the heart-rending article and had missed the deadline. By the time she was willing to open up and speak the naked truth, I was more interested in hiding the truthful data in my computer files than in displaying it for the entire ASHS student body.

Oh well—I said to myself, slightly disturbed by the fact that I had missed an opportunity for journalistic stardom—guess it was meant to be.

* * *

I haven't seen or talked to anyone for weeks. Months? But I don't feel ashamed of my seclusion anymore. I know now why I'm doing what I'm doing. I knew all along, but was afraid to turn my knowledge into words. Afraid, as always, to face up to the facts: my writing is an act of self-defense and survival. Not just flight. Not simply self-indulgence.

Years of professional success (making forgettable summer flicks and prime time sitcoms about Pinos Verdes teenagers) have instilled in me a puerile fear of failure. The next project *has got to get* higher ratings and/or revenues than the last one. Whatever it takes. And what it takes is paralysis, obliteration. Phobia.

Young Gina had the seed in her, the potential for "making things happen" (remember the phrase?). And she did. She *made it*. She's one big profitable, marketable, one-woman media spectacle. A gringa with no past but with an enviable present. (With a future?) The facts: this successful "gringa" took an honest stand only once, fifteen years ago. And she hasn't contested anything or anybody since then. Until this day of May of 2007, the New Century. Until this instance of remembrance.

The phrase seems spent, anachronistic: *remembrance*. Today its utterance is a criminal act. They have forbidden it. They: the ones who invented our Turn-of-the-Century Crux, the clangorous knelling of doomsday, *the end*. The ones who prescribed and enforced our "collective and official effort" to integrate ourselves into a (moribund) whole.

Movie, Dollar, Constitution, Motherland, Dream, Prison, America, Home, Family, Flag, Image, Oblivion, White, Word, War. This fabricated and desired whole is our last hope for union, they claimed. The first and only goal our citizens *must* share.

That's why I'm here, remembering my grandmother Estela. Ready to fight with my bare hands; prepared to start somewhere (yes: somewhere in time) and remake us.

The off-white walls of the mansion bore too many paintings—all by very famous artists, Maman explained. Colorful pictures of circles and squares and distorted faces were hanging next to yellowing Romantic landscapes and portraits of queens and kings. "You live in a museum!" exclaimed Abuela. Each room had been carefully furnished in a different style, my mother informed her. The living room was done in genuine Louis Quatorze. "We make an effort to spend as little time as possible in here," said Maman. "That furniture cost us a fortune and we wouldn't want to ruin it through daily use."

Abuela looked up at the high, barrel-vaulted ceiling, discovering there the source of the dim bluish-green light that invaded the room: four round, shell-shaped structures, one in each corner, which resembled overgrown bullfrogs. "The light effect is uncanny, is it not?" said my mother. "The idea is to penetrate space completely but subtly," she added, as if describing a monument to a crowd of bedazzled bystanders, "letting the luminous artificial rays caress each furniture piece and each painting. A masterpiece of post-modern visual design, wouldn't you say?"

The den was dowdy and too cluttered with oddities, admitted Maman, apologetically. This was the one part of the house she favored the least. Because it was done in comfortable, practical post-Pilgrim American, it lacked an aesthetically conceived design. Its only advantageous feature was the wall-size window overlooking the bay and featuring French-style awnings. "You'll get to see breathtaking sunsets from the den," said Maman.

The breakfast nook was Paris-Deco. "Here's where we consume most of our meals," she explained, as she caressed one of three gray chairs—the garden type—and a round pink table. "Don't you just *love* these colors?" she asked her guest, receiving only a shrug in return.

Contemporary was the name my mother used to describe the kitchen; which contained, she claimed, the most advanced, state-of-the-cooking-art technology: "You will find appliances here that are not available to the general public yet."

Estela was then shown a large patio covered with artificial grass, a lush garden of tall and unusually shaped flowers, a greenhouse full of exotic plants, a quasi-Olympic swimming pool, a sauna, a Jacuzzi, a four-car garage, a powerful radar which was probably used—Abuela must've thought—for contacting flying saucers; and other features of the house that Abuela would never be able to describe to her family back in Cuba.

When the interminable tour was completed, Estela was taken to her "assigned quarters." Daddy had filled up his mother's bedroom with daisies, her favorite flower. She doused her son's face with kisses. "Benitín," her voice drowned by the tears, "what a nice gesture." Then she smiled, "But you expect me to live here? This looks like a cemetery!"

"It's actually a very spacious room," remarked Maman, taking umbrage at my grandmother's blatant honesty. "One of the largest in the house."

Daddy moved some of the floral arrangements out of the way and made space for his mother to sit. She sat and called me to her side, "Yes. An entire family could live in here," she said, and she kissed me. "Such a big house for just three people. What a waste of space!"

"We can afford it," said Maman.

"It's still a waste," said Abuela, and she got up. "This is a very nice room. *Muy bonito*," she added, as she inspected the place. "But I don't need it."

"What?"

"That's right, *mijo*. I don't need it because . . . I'm going to sleep in my granddaughter's room."

"What?!" asked Maman.

"Yes, Elisa. You heard me correctly. I want to share Ginita's bedroom."

My first reaction was, No Way! Why would I want to give up the comfort and privacy of Laika's shed? Why would I let anyone in on my nocturnal howling? A princess' throne is never shared! But then I thought, hell, I do have the biggest room in the house, and it's only for a while. It would certainly make Abuela feel unwelcome if I said no. So I said, "Yes. Great idea!" And Maman turned to me with lethal French eyes. She was hyperventilating.

"Please try to understand," pleaded Abuela, "I have sixteen years to make up for."

My mother stormed out of Estela's *muy bonito* room in near hysteria, dragging Daddy with her. Poor Grandma, I thought, she hasn't been around for an hour yet and she's already having to put up with Maman's cacus. We heard her calling Abuela "insane" and Daddy trying to shut her up. But Maman obviously *wanted* to be heard. "I won't have it! *No se lo permito!*" she said in crisp Cubanglish. "I go out of my way to accommodate her and she asks to be given a bed in Gina's room! Talk some sense into her, Benito!"

But Daddy didn't talk any sense into Abuela because Maman's request simply made no sense. Or I should say it did only to her.

Motivated by jealousy, propriety, or a royal complex, she was acting as if Abuela had asked me to have a slumber party at the Mall. (Not a bad idea, actually.) Daddy settled the argument with a short and punchy phrase, "Gina said great."

Suddenly, I thought of the Terrible Santera. When would she turn up? At the stroke of midnight, during a full moon? Would there be thunder and a howling wind?

Once her few things were arranged in my room, Abuela took a color print of Jesus Christ out of her suitcase and displayed it on the night table next to her bed. It was a pleasant image of the Messiah looking swarthy and hirsute, with curly black hair and beard, and glinting gray-green eyes; a non-suffering *Jesucristo* without a cross.

Later, as Abuela grew accustomed to her new environment, she would light a candle to the image now and then, a regular candle, not a red one, and she would quietly mumble a prayer before going to bed.

Was this to be the extent of her powerful magic, of her demonic "rituals"? I wondered. Where were the long, elaborate spells she supposedly concocted; the long, exhausting prayers, the symbolic offerings?

None of it would ever happen.

I guided her to my rose-colored bedroom and there, before we went in, she hugged me. The warmest, most comforting embrace I'd ever experienced. "You live like a princess, Ginita," she said as she stepped into my palace.

"Yes," I responded, "this is my little castle. Yours, too, now. Our castle, Abuela." And I went through my *castillo* playing tour guide the way I had once before, with someone else. "Look, Abuela, a tiny flag of Cuba! And my gold chain has The Island on it, look, have you noticed? The golden island. And this cool radio is a birthday present from my boyfriend Robby . . . Yes . . . I have a boyfriend . . . "

I turned on the radio and a strident neo-sixties song came on. I had imagined this scene. I had seen my grandmother dancing with me, a stout old woman trying hard to keep up with my pace, with my adolescent craze. And in my fantasy she would give up, a blob of inert Cuban flesh collapsing on my bed, her hands gnarled, her hippo mouth begging for rest and silence. "I can't handle this! Get me back to Cuba!" And thus the beginning-and-end of a friendship that never had a chance would take its fatal course. Who ever heard of an aging

Caribbean *campesina* and a sophisticated cosmopolitan American teenager being friends? Who would buy such a farfetched premise? As a back story for a sitcom it hadn't the most minimal chance for production. As a plot for a box office smash it wouldn't even make it past the talking stage.

And yet we danced. We held each other and we turned and swirled and we laughed. There was no halting or collapsing. Only vertigo at our intrepid turns. Our girlish prattle. Our bodies reeling. The din of our words, boisterous and Cuban, merging with the music. "I wanted to be here for your birthday, Gina! I'm sorry I missed it!" Phrases muttered and phrases hollered. "You didn't miss much!" And the feeling of safety. "I want to meet your boyfriend!" The sense that I was truly alive. "You will!" That I was breathing for the first time.

American History

Judith Ortiz-Cofer

(Photograph © 1992 by John Cofer)

JUDITH ORTIZ-COFER is the author of the first original novel published by the University of Georgia Press, *The Line of the Sun*; a collection of personal essays and poems, *Silent Dancing*; two poetry collections, *Terms of Survival* and *Reaching for the Mainland*; and *Peregrina*, a chapbook which won the 1985 Riverstone Press International Poetry Competition. Her novel was listed as one of the "25 Books to Remember" of 1989 by the New York City Library System. She is on the associate teaching staff at the Bread Loaf Writers' Conference. Judith Ortiz-Cofer is a native of Puerto Rico, now living in Georgia with her family.

I once read in a "Ripley's Believe It or Not" column that Paterson, New Jersey, is the place where the Straight and Narrow (streets) intersect. The Puerto Rican tenement known as *El Building* was one block up from Straight. It was, in fact, the corner of Straight and Market; not "at" the corner, but *the* corner. At almost any hour of the day, El Building was like a monstrous jukebox, blasting out *salsas* from open windows as the residents, mostly new immigrants just up from the island, tried to drown out whatever they were currently enduring with loud music. But the day President Kennedy was shot there was a profound silence in El Building; even the abusive tongues of viragoes, the cursing of the unemployed, and the screeching of small children had been somehow muted. President Kennedy was a saint to these people. In fact, soon his photograph would be hung alongside the Sacred Heart and over the spiritist altars that many women kept in their apartments. He would become part of the hierarchy of martyrs they prayed to for favors that only one who had died for a cause would understand.

On the day that President Kennedy was shot, my ninth grade

class had been out in the fenced playground of Public School Number
13. We had been given "free" exercise time and had been ordered by
our P.E. teacher, Mr. DePalma, to "keep moving." That meant that
the girls should jump rope and the boys toss basketballs through a
hoop at the far end of the yard. He in the meantime would "keep an
eye" on us from just inside the building.

It was a cold gray day in Paterson. The kind that warns of early
snow. I was miserable, since I had forgotten my gloves, and my
knuckles were turning red and raw from the jump rope. I was also
taking a lot of abuse from the black girls for not turning the rope
hard and fast enough for them.

"Hey, Skinny Bones, pump it, girl. Ain't you got no energy
today?" Gail, the biggest of the black girls had the other end of the
rope, yelled, "Didn't you eat your rice and beans and pork chops for
breakfast today?"

The other girls picked up the "pork chop" and made it into a
refrain: "pork chop, pork chop, did you eat your pork chop?" They
entered the double ropes in pairs and exited without tripping or missing a beat. I felt a burning on my cheeks and then my glasses fogged
up so that I could not manage to coordinate the jump rope with Gail.
The chill was doing to me what it always did; entering my bones,
making me cry, humiliating me. I hated the city, especially in winter. I
hated Public School Number 13. I hated my skinny flatchested body,
and I envied the black girls who could jump rope so fast that their
legs became a blur. They always seemed to be warm while I froze.

There was only one source of beauty and light for me that school
year. The only thing I had anticipated at the start of the semester.
That was seeing Eugene. In August, Eugene and his family had moved
into the only house on the block that had a yard and trees. I could see
his place from my window in El Building. In fact, if I sat on the fire
escape I was literally suspended above Eugene's backyard. It was my
favorite spot to read my library books in the summer. Until that
August the house had been occupied by an old Jewish couple. Over
the years I had become part of their family, without their knowing it,
of course. I had a view of their kitchen and their backyard, and
though I could not hear what they said, I knew when they were arguing, when one of them was sick, and many other things. I knew all
this by watching them at mealtimes. I could see their kitchen table,

the sink, and the stove. During good times, he sat at the table and read his newspapers while she fixed the meals. If they argued, he would leave and the old woman would sit and stare at nothing for a long time. When one of them was sick, the other would come and get things from the kitchen and carry them out on a tray. The old man had died in June. The last week of school I had not seen him at the table at all. Then one day I saw that there was a crowd in the kitchen. The old woman had finally emerged from the house on the arm of a stocky, middle-aged woman, whom I had seen there a few times before, maybe her daughter. Then a man had carried out suitcases. The house had stood empty for weeks. I had had to resist the temptation to climb down into the yard and water the flowers the old lady had taken such good care of.

By the time Eugene's family moved in, the yard was a tangled mass of weeds. The father had spent several days mowing, and when he finished, from where I sat, I didn't see the red, yellow, and purple clusters that meant flowers to me. I didn't see this family sit down at the kitchen table together. It was just the mother, a red-headed tall woman who wore a white uniform—a nurse's, I guessed it was; the father was gone before I got up in the morning and was never there at dinner time. I only saw him on weekends when they sometimes sat on lawn-chairs under the oak tree, each hidden behind a section of the newspaper; and there was Eugene. He was tall and blond, and he wore glasses. I liked him right away because he sat at the kitchen table and read books for hours. That summer, before we had even spoken one word to each other, I kept him company on my fire escape.

Once school started I looked for him in all my classes, but P.S. 13 was a huge, over-populated place and it took me days and many discreet questions to discover that Eugene was in honors classes for all his subjects; classes that were not open to me because English was not my first language, though I was a straight A student. After much maneuvering I managed "to run into him" in the hallway where his locker was—on the other side of the building from mine—and in study hall at the library where he first seemed to notice me, but did not speak; and finally, on the way home after school one day when I decided to approach him directly, though my stomach was doing somersaults.

I was ready for rejection, snobbery, the worst. But when I came up to him, practically panting in my nervousness, and blurted out: "You're Eugene. Right?" he smiled, pushed his glasses up on his nose, and nodded. I saw then that he was blushing deeply. Eugene liked me, but he was shy. I did most of the talking that day. He nodded and smiled a lot. In the weeks that followed, we walked home together. He would linger at the corner of El Building for a few minutes then walk down to his two-story house. It was not until Eugene moved into that house that I noticed that El Building blocked most of the sun, and that the only spot that got a little sunlight during the day was the tiny square of earth the old woman had planted with flowers.

I did not tell Eugene that I could see inside his kitchen from my bedroom. I felt dishonest, but I liked my secret sharing of his evenings, especially now that I knew what he was reading since we chose our books together at the school library.

One day my mother came into my room as I was sitting on the window sill staring out. In her abrupt way she said: "Elena, you are acting 'moony'." *Enamorada* was what she really said, that is—like a girl stupidly infatuated. Since I had turned fourteen and started menstruating my mother had been more vigilant than ever. She acted as if I was going to go crazy or explode or something if she didn't watch me and nag me all the time about being a *señorita* now. She kept talking about virtue, morality, and other subjects that did not interest me in the least. My mother was unhappy in Paterson, but my father had a good job at the bluejeans factory in Passaic and soon, he kept assuring us, we would be moving to our own house there. Every Sunday we drove out to the suburbs of Paterson, Clifton, and Passaic, out to where people mowed grass on Sundays in the summer, and where children made snowmen in the winter from pure white snow, not like the gray slush of Paterson which seemed to fall from the sky in that hue. I had learned to listen to my parents' dreams, which were spoken in Spanish, as fairy tales, like the stories about life in the island paradise of Puerto Rico before I was born. I had been to the island once as a little girl, to grandmother's funeral, and all I remembered was wailing women in black, my mother becoming hysterical and being given a pill that made her sleep two days, and me feeling lost in a crowd of strangers all claiming to be my aunts, uncles, and cousins. I had actually been glad to return to the city. We had not been back there since then, though my parents talked constantly about buying a house on the beach someday, retiring on the island—that was a common topic among the residents of El Building. As for me, I was going to go to college and become a teacher.

But after meeting Eugene I began to think of the present more than of the future. What I wanted now was to enter that house I had watched for so many years. I wanted to see the other rooms where the old people had lived, and where the boy spent his time. Most of all, I wanted to sit at the kitchen table with Eugene like two adults, like the old man and his wife had done, maybe drink some coffee and talk about books. I had started reading *Gone With the Wind*. I was enthralled by it, with the daring and the passion of the beautiful girl living in a mansion, and with her devoted parents and the slaves who did everything for them. I didn't believe such a world had ever really existed, and I wanted to ask Eugene some questions since he and his parents, he had told me, had come up from Georgia, the same place where the novel was set. His father worked for a company that had transferred him to Paterson. His mother was very unhappy, Eugene said, in his beautiful voice that rose and fell over words in a strange, lilting way. The kids at school called him "the hick" and made fun of the way he talked. I knew I was his only friend so far, and I liked that, though I felt sad for him sometimes. "Skinny Bones" and the "Hick" was what they called us at school when we were seen together.

The day Mr. DePalma came out into the cold and asked us to line up in front of him was the day that President Kennedy was shot. Mr. DePalma, a short, muscular man with slicked-down black hair, was the science teacher, P.E. coach, and disciplinarian at P.S. 13. He was the teacher to whose homeroom you got assigned if you were a troublemaker, and the man called out to break up playground fights, and to escort violently angry teen-agers to the office. And Mr. DePalma was the man who called your parents in for "a conference."

That day, he stood in front of two rows of mostly black and Puerto Rican kids, brittle from their efforts to "keep moving" on a November day that was turning bitter cold. Mr. DePalma, to our complete shock, was crying. Not just silent adult tears, but really sobbing. There were a few titters from the back of the line where I stood shivering.

"Listen," Mr. DePalma raised his arms over his head as if he were about to conduct an orchestra. His voice broke, and he covered his face with his hands. His barrel chest was heaving. Someone giggled behind me.

"Listen," he repeated, "something awful has happened." A strange gurgling came from his throat, and he turned around and spat on the cement behind him.

"Gross," someone said, and there was a lot of laughter.

"The President is dead, you idiots. I should have known that wouldn't mean anything to a bunch of losers like you kids. Go home." He was shrieking now. No one moved for a minute or two, but then a big girl let out a "Yeah!" and ran to get her books piled up with the others against the brick wall of the school building. The others followed in a mad scramble to get to their things before somebody caught on. It was still an hour to the dismissal bell.

A little scared, I headed for El Building. There was an eerie feeling on the streets. I looked into Mario's drugstore, a favorite hangout for the high school crowd, but there were only a couple of old Jewish men at the soda-bar talking with the short order cook in tones that sounded almost angry, but they were keeping their voices low. Even the traffic on one of the busiest intersections in Paterson—Straight Street and Park Avenue—seemed to be moving slower. There were no horns blasting that day. At El Building, the usual little group of unemployed men were not hanging out on the front stoop making it difficult for women to enter the front door. No music spilled out from open doors in the hallway. When I walked into our apartment, I found my mother sitting in front of the grainy picture of the television set.

She looked up at me with a tear-streaked face and just said: "Dios mio," turning back to the set as if it were pulling at her eyes. I went into my room.

Though I wanted to feel the right thing about President Kennedy's death, I could not fight the feeling of elation that stirred in my chest. Today was the day I was to visit Eugene in his house. He had asked me to come over after school to study for an American History test with him. We had also planned to walk to the public library together. I looked down into his yard. The oak tree was bare of leaves and the ground looked gray with ice. The light through the large kitchen window of his house told me that El Building blocked the sun to such an extent that they had to turn lights on in the middle of the day. I felt ashamed about it. But the white kitchen table with the lamp hanging just above it looked cozy and inviting. I would soon sit there, across from Eugene, and I would tell him about my perch just above his house. Maybe I should.

In the next thirty minutes I changed clothes, put on a little pink lipstick, and got my books together. Then I went in to tell my mother that I was going to a friend's house to study. I did not expect her reaction.

"You are going out *today*?" The way she said "today" sounded as if a storm warning had been issued. It was said in utter disbelief. Before I could answer, she came toward me and held my elbows as I clutched my books.

"*Hija*, the President has been killed. We must show respect. He was a great man. Come to church with me tonight."

She tried to embrace me, but my books were in the way. My first impulse was to comfort her, she seemed so distraught, but I had to meet Eugene in fifteen minutes.

"I have a test to study for, Mama. I will be home by eight."

"You are forgetting who you are, *Niña*. I have seen you staring down at that boy's house. You are heading for humiliation and pain." My mother said this in Spanish and in a resigned tone that surprised me, as if she had no intention of stopping me from "heading for humiliation and pain." I started for the door. She sat in front of the TV holding a white handkerchief to her face.

I walked out to the street and around the chain-link fence that separated El Building from Eugene's house. The yard was neatly edged around the little walk that led to the door. It always amazed me how Paterson, the inner core of the city, had no apparent logic to its architecture. Small, neat, single residences like this one could be found right next to huge, dilapidated apartment buildings like El Building. My guess was that the little houses had been there first, then the immigrants had come in droves, and the monstrosities had been raised for them—the Italians, the Irish, the Jews, and now us, the Puerto Ricans and the blacks. The door was painted a deep green: *verde*, the color of hope, I had heard my mother say it: *Verde-Esperanza*.

I knocked softly. A few suspenseful moments later the door opened just a crack. The red, swollen face of a woman appeared. She had a halo of red hair floating over a delicate ivory face—the face of a doll—with freckles on the nose. Her smudged eye make-up made her look unreal to me, like a mannequin seen through a warped store window.

"What do you want?" Her voice was tiny and sweet-sounding, like a little girl's, but her tone was not friendly.

"I'm Eugene's friend. He asked me over. To study." I thrust out my books, a silly gesture that embarrassed me almost immediately.

"You live there?" She pointed up to El Building, which looked particularly ugly, like a gray prison with its many dirty windows and rusty fire escapes. The woman had stepped halfway out and I could see that she wore a white nurse's uniform with St. Joseph's Hospital on the name tag.

"Yes. I do."

She looked intently at me for a couple of heartbeats, then said as if to herself, "I don't know how you people do it." Then directly to me: "Listen. Honey. Eugene doesn't want to study with you. He is a smart boy. Doesn't need help. You understand me. I am truly sorry if he told you you could come over. He cannot study with you. It's nothing personal. You understand? We won't be in this place much longer, no need for him to get close to people—it'll just make it harder for him later. Run back home now."

I couldn't move. I just stood there in shock at hearing these things said to me in such a honey-drenched voice. I had never heard an accent like hers, except for Eugene's softer version. It was as if she were singing me a little song.

"What's wrong? Didn't you hear what I said?" She seemed very angry, and I finally snapped out of my trance. I turned away from the green door, and heard her close it gently.

Our apartment was empty when I got home. My mother was in someone else's kitchen, seeking the solace she needed. Father would come in from his late shift at midnight. I would hear them talking softly in the kitchen for hours that night. They would not discuss their dreams for the future, or life in Puerto Rico, as they often did; that night they would talk sadly about the young widow and her two children, as if they were family. For the next few days, we would observe *luto* in our apartment; that is, we would practice restraint and silence—no loud music or laughter. Some of the women of El Building would wear black for weeks.

That night, I lay in my bed trying to feel the right thing for our dead President. But the tears that came up from a deep source inside me were strictly for me. When my mother came to the door, I pretended to be sleeping. Sometime during the night, I saw from my bed the streetlight come on. It had a pink halo around it. I went to my window and pressed my face to the cool glass. Looking up at the light I could see the white snow falling like a lace veil over its face. I did not look down to see it turning gray as it touched the ground below.

Martes

Ricardo Pau-Llosa

RICARDO PAU-LLOSA was born in Havana in 1954, but he has lived in the United States since 1960. In 1983, his book, *Sorting Metaphors*, won the national competition for the first Anhinga Prize, judged that year by William Stafford. His second book, *Bread of the Imagined,* was published by Bilingual Press, Arizona State University, in the fall of 1991. Currently he makes his home in Miami, where he is also an art critic and curator, specializing in twentieth century Latin-American art. His essays, poetry, and fiction have appeared in numerous publications throughout the continent.

Ever since he was six, when his parents brought him into exile in Miami, José Martes had been imagining Clarita, the cow his father left behind in Cuba. There she stood, in a dream edged by cinematic fogs, deep in tobacco leaves, chewing on sugar cane leaves. Or walking down the Malecón in Havana, slump-striding traffic and knowing when to turn so as not to trample the peanut vendor or the *negritos* fighting a kite war after a hard day of begging. Martes would call out her name and Clarita would turn to him with a lumpy smile, her pink udder swaying as the dream dissolved and the world presented its vulgar credentials. To school, and eventually to his hardware store, to a wife and three children, to debts and dominos, to the inevitable wonderings about what it is about exile that reveals a facet of life to him that it could not possibly reveal to the Americanos.

He had contemplated studying farming, or later simply buying some land on the outskirts of Miami, even though it would mean that the Clarita image would have to live as a Florida cow, stop chewing cane leaves and strutting down the Malecón. Cow facts would have to replace cow dreams, and José, at first welcoming the prospect, abandoned it for reasons he never spelled out to himself, as he might have at the misty end of one of his Clarita episodes, right after the turn and the smile when the udder bounced into emptiness to leave his vacuous eyes lasering the tasseled cushion of a sofa. At the north end of the sofa was a golden fiberglass pedestal where Venus struggled between modesty and herself, caged by strings from which droplets of oil continually descended equally spaced before vanishing into the jaws of plastic fern leaves. At the south end of the sofa was a shrine to Santa Barbara, the catholic mask of Changó who is the thundering orisha of war and could appear as either man or woman. He remembered his mother frantically covering the mirrors of their little apartment in Hialeah whenever she heard thunder. "If Changó sees himself in a mirror, it will shatter," she would pronounce with reverential fear, stretching impossibly out of her high-heel house slippers to drape the sheet over the gilt frame as her florid breasts flattened on the glass.

That little Americanita girlfriend he had in high school, and without whom he might have nurtured his virginity until who knows, told him, long after their love cooled and they became star twins, that Clarita was, she suspected, more than a cow for him. Yes and no, thought José, but he thought yes and no about most things. "Maybe Clarita is Cuba," he said to Jill that night on the phone, and she said no, no, it's not that simple. He did not hear her say no, no, because a plane was passing and he became distracted by his mother's false alarm shuffle for the sheets.

What Clarita had become in his mind was never entirely clear to him. Fidel had finally fallen, and José owed it to his dead mother and his senile father to return to Cuba where Clarita in some way still lived. More than thirty years had passed and José, caught in the cross life between youth and middle age, never really felt different because, after all, he had been in the middle of everything forever. Between cultures, between languages, between allegiances, between Changó and Santa Barbara, between Jill and the oily Venus, between Clarita and reality. Havana, the city of his birth and the capital of his fantasies, was completely alien to him, although he had memorized a map of the place down to the last detail, a map his tío Juanín had given to him on his thirteenth birthday. The mapped city was circa 1932 when Juanín was a young university rebel shooting it out with Machado's thugs and other rebel groups on the tiny streets with the romantic names, all except one whose name was obscured by a smudge. He imagined many names for this street, except one. That night he thought the street might be named Clarita and he awoke in a drenched fear. It was his first sleepless night, and in truth one of the very few such nights he would ever have. José, the seller of this and that, was always a sound sleeper.

And he was proud of this because tales of Fidel's sleeplessness comforted him. He would think, *As I snore away, Fidel must be stalking the streets of Havana, pondering where the next assassin might lurk, where the next conspiracy might blossom. I can sleep in Miami, even if I forget all my dreams except those of Clarita.* One other night was particularly bad for José, after he had read somewhere that Fidel was in love with a cow name Ubre Blanca—White Udder. Fidel stroked the beast, who broke countless milk-producing records, in a press conference called to witness his insemination of Ubrecita. That night José dreamt Fidel sinking his bull-semened fist into Ubre Blanca, the cameras clicking away as the milk mother of the Revolution swooned almost inaudibly. Surely Fidel must have caught her long, mute, bi-labial swoon when he pulled his fist out.

Soon afterward, and quite by surprise, Ubrecita died and Fidel ordered a monument be built to her. A noble gesture, José thought, until it suddenly hit him. Maybe Ubre Blanca was Clarita! Hadn't Fidel stolen everything in Cuba, and couldn't this be Clarita with a communist name? No, no, he thought, Clarita's udder is pink. Clarita is safe in her field of tobacco leaves, chewing sugar cane leaves, and foretelling the arrival of hurricanes. José's father had told him that when hair started to fall out of a brown patch on her left side it was a sure thing that a hurricane would hit that year.

He had just checked into a hotel in liberated Havana, free to ignore the ruins of the revolution and concentrate on finding Clarita. He called cousins on his father's side of the family who lived in Havana. They would tell him how to get to his father's farm. They might even take him there since so much had changed. José repeated his father's stories to them—there was this brook and five trees next to a *caminito* where someone had made a wooden Martí and planted it among some rocks. The *campesinos* would come and leave flowers there for Martí, and Clarita herself would go there once in a while and lick Martí's ear. All this was near *fincas* of rich people, although his father's was a small farm. All these details, José thought, and his cousins—made even more stupid by the revolution than they already were—couldn't direct him. He called one of his mother's cousins, Mario Miguel, and they agreed to meet on the steps of the science museum which had once been the capitol of the republic.

José walked from the hotel to the *Capitolio*. All around him former exiles and *habaneros* were embracing. There were tears, but less than one might expect, and many strange silences. A former exile would be walking down a street in the heart of Havana, map in hand, and she would suddenly freeze gazing upon a tattered building where perhaps she had been born, where a mother died, where a father once had a store. Or an aging man wearing a Miami guayabera would point this way and that and explain to his doctor son, who could still understand spoken Spanish, the cherished if forgettable anecdotes of petty corners and dirty doorways. The wordless miracles through which the past makes peace with the present swirled all around the oblivious José who hadn't had a Clarita dream since Fidel had fallen three months ago, and who was entirely focused on making his appointment with Mario Miguel at the Capitolio. Tío Juanín's 1932 map filled José's mind and turned him here, then there, until the Capitolio raised its renaissance head above the tattered roofs and branches of the capital.

José spotted a thin man on the steps, hands clasped behind his back, face turned to the golds and blood of a Havana sunset. "Mario, Mario Miguel!?" and the man began a slow turn toward José, already at the foot of the steps and accelerating. "Mario!" "Yes, I heard you, *primo*." The turn was completed. Mario's hands come undone and to his sides; he wore the necessary smile. They hugged, then talked as they descended across Prado toward La Habana Vieja.

Deeper into the old district, where the once elegant colonial houses had been punished into squalor by power and weather, they walked, the silences between the periods of conversation growing longer and more awkward. Finally Mario Miguel stopped at the corner of Zayas and San Ignacio. Above his cousin's head José could glimpse the old cathedral. "*Jose, hijo mío*, I don't remember where the farm was and it's probably not a farm any longer, part of an UMAP perhaps." José wasn't sure what the acronym stood for. "Labor camps, José, where Fidel put '*elementos anti-sociales*' like the *maricones* and the *disidentes* to work for the state. And Clarita, it's *sabroso* to dream about these things, but *querido* José, I don't know what to tell you."

They parted but José lingered in the old sector, walking to the Plaza de la Catedral, then north toward the Malecón. He looked intensely, for the first time, at everything around him. It was hot, as usual, but this was a heat whose differences from those of Miami José began to savor. "*Sabroso*," he said to himself, "the delights of this old place." The Malecón seemed like the perfect place to let go of a dream, and he stood there in the early night painted the color of his father's good *azul noche* suit and tasted the salt air. Then it happened, he saw them, the ankle boots. The woman's dress was Miami, no question. She was walking with a purposeful speed west on the Malecón past José. *Her boots, my God, those boots are Clarita!*

Indeed, they were made of hairy cowhide, and the right side of the left foot was covered by a bald brown spot. *The spot that foretold hurricanes*, José thought to himself. He imagined the soft inside of the boots pink like Clarita's udder. "Not like," he corrected himself, "I must be brave and face this squarely, like a *plantado*. Those boots are all that's left of Clarita. If the inside is pink and soft, I'll know for sure—it's her udder, and the white heels must be made from her bones." As he began to follow her, José noticed every detail of the boots. They were new so she must have bought them in Havana. More evidence. "Poor Clarita."

José noticed little else about the red-headed, discreetly voluptuous woman in her early thirties. He had again lost his sense of the open world and had focused his sight and soul on the dialectical rhythm of the boots that suddenly stopped at the curb, pondered the empty oceanside boulevard and crossed into the city at El Parque Maceo. She rounded the park and resumed her course west on San Lázaro, with José half a block behind her. *She was from Miami, alright. An habanera, trained to watch for secret police trailing her, would have noticed long ago that I was following her,* he thought, comforting himself with the obvious advantage that predator has over unsuspecting prey. Again she stopped, this time at one of the few kept-up buildings left in Havana, and she began searching her Italian leather bag for the keys. Actually, she pretended to fumble, then, unexpectedly and calmly, she closed the bag while staring at the door for a few seconds as if it were a mirror. She fixed her glasses and turned to José, calling out to him half a block away, staring now directly into her eyes, even at this distance.

"*Oyé tú*, if you want to talk to me, now's your chance, but I'm tired of being followed, so make up your mind. *Atrévete*, right now!" José waved to her to wait for him and walked toward her.

"Could I invite you to a drink or some café?"

"Bueno," she said, "I know a place which will seat us in no time, at the corner."

She was unusually loquacious, thought José, especially with a man she didn't know. He said little on the way to the café, only his name and that he was from Miami. She motioned needlessly to the headwaiter who knew, just glancing at her come in, how to respond. Her table, quite literally, was waiting.

"It's been a while since a man did something as romantic and Latin as what you did, chasing me down the Malecón like that, and I really liked it. So, José, are you here to see family? No, let me guess. You are scouting for cheap investment opportunities. No, no. O, I know, you are one of those *gusanos* who has come back to reclaim a house or something like that. Of course, you believed what your parents told you—*el central de la familia*, miles of sugar plantation and healthy cheerful *negros* cutting all that cane while the family lived in luxury in El Vedado. O, I can hardly believe it, I am actually looking at one of you." José kept staring at her as she talked endlessly. Fidel, he mused, was not the only one who thought that breathing between torrents of language was a shameful waste of time.

"O, I'll sleep with you, José, don't worry. And you wouldn't be my first *gusano*, either." She hadn't ordered but the waiter knew what to bring, *café con leche* with assorted pastries. José was surprised, "There aren't any things like this anywhere else in Havana, this is quite a well stocked place."

"Ay, don't be stupid, *niño*. This place only serves bad soup and old crackers, but I'm from the Party. And I'm also the head *caderista* in this sector so I control this block. They always have nice things for me. Tell me, did you bring American condoms? *Mira*, this SIDA thing has everyone crazy in Cuba too, you know."

Putting his *café con leche* down, José interrupted her. "All I really wanted to speak with you about is your boots." He smiled. "And what is your name, anyway?"

"Migdalia, and I can't believe you're serious. During the revolution very few men flirted with me because I was the chief of the neighborhood committee and they were afraid to disappoint me in bed. *Las terribles consecuencias*, you know. Except of course the ones I approached directly. *Y bueno, hijo mio, no estoy tan mala hembra, después de todo!*" Migdalia said this spreading her fingers with bright red nail polish across her breasts and traveling both hands slowly toward her waist while cocking her head to one side as if catching a glimpse of another male. José agreed, she was definitely a very screwable *buena hembra*, "But those boots, Migdalia, where did you get them and, even more importantly, where were they made?"

"*Y dale con las botas*. Okay. I bought them at a *diplotienda*—a store for diplomats or tourists with hard currency, I forget that many *gusanos* don't know about these things. *Dirigentes del partido* also got to buy, or sometimes just get for free, all sorts of things at the *diplotienda*. *Esos días divinos no volverán, sabes gusanito*." José wanted to ask her to stop using the fidelista "gusano" which designated exiles as "worms," but the boots were the important matter at hand. "I think they're from Bulgaria. Let me see." Migdalia took off one of the boots to look inside. As she turned one side out to read, José turned pale. It was pink, udder pink. Poor Clarita.

"It doesn't say the country, but I'm sure this leather came from us, you know. We sold a lot of leather to Italy, Spain. Bulgaria and Russia bought some. No, no, these can't be Russian because they are comfortable. Italian, I'll bet, or Spanish. Although the outside is too harsh. I have lots of Italian shoes, no, no, I think these might be Bulgarian after all. And what on earth am I doing reading my shoes in my café with a crazy *gusano*, anyway?" Migdalia was getting angry, but José's sudden hand on her arm stopped her from putting the boot back on. "Please, let me hold it. I mean, let me see it, the boot, please, Migdalia." She handed it over, passing her other hand nervously through her dyed hair. He ran his finger along the delicate pink insides and across the brown spot on the side, and for a second he thought of holding the boot to his ear but figured Migdalia would call the police.

But he could contain his anger no longer. José stood up spilling the *café con leche* cups, and threw the boot at Migdalia. "*Asesinos!* You killed my Clarita and turned her into a pair of boots! *Asesinos!*" He ran out of the café toward the Malecón, and Migdalia ran after him. "*Gusano hijo de puta*, I haven't killed anyone since 1980 when all those other *gusanos* ran to the Peruvian embassy and then to Mariel! We were under orders to club anyone who wanted asylum. If you think you can accuse me of killing anyone now, you're really crazy! You have to *prove* things now in court, it's not like before when my word could have you in jail in two seconds. Do you hear me, *gusano hijo de puta!*" José kept running and Migdalia too, screaming at him all the way. Finally the sea. He bent over the veranda at the Malecón. His mind was torn with perishing dreams. It was one thing to accept Clarita's death, perhaps dream her collapsing in a hot tobacco field. Maybe she was slaughtered to feed hungry *campesinos* and that, in its own way, would have been fine. But to have Clarita turned into a pair of Bulgarian boots for someone like Migdalia to strut in, what dream could reconcile him to that?

José looked back but didn't see Migdalia anywhere and began walking west. It was early Wednesday and it didn't matter which day it was, or which night. He recalled an exiled uncle who wrote books telling him how different Havana was from Miami. "Havana, at least the Havana I knew, had a night culture which was very different from its day culture." José threw his eyes and ears around him to absorb that night culture, anything to get his mind off Clarita's terrible fate and that monster at the café. What night culture Havana had once had was dead. The streets were still gray and empty months after the new revolution had destroyed the dictatorship. "In the old days, all the *gente linda* came out only at night—apart from the *puticas*, the *chulos*, and the *transvestis*—the poets and the painters, the *bongoseros* and the *trompetistas*. The dreamers, Joseito, the dreamers claimed the nights of Havana for themselves and would not live under any other light but that of the *lámparas* in the old plazas." There were no old lights left. There was the sea, howling like an angry woman who has no reason to be angry. There was the sky, burning with stars and learning little by little to hum again the distant melodies of a stranger's joy. And if he shut his eyes, José could muster vague forms and smells, the moist curl of a tongue—fragments of Clarita, pieces of a being wise enough to stay in the place it was once loved.

My Life as a Redneck

Gustavo Pérez-Firmat

GUSTAVO PÉREZ-FIRMAT was born in Havana, Cuba, and raised in Miami, Florida. He attended Miami-Dade Community College, the University of Miami, and the University of Michigan, earning more degrees than he cares to remember. Currently he teaches at Duke University and lives in Chapel Hill, North Carolina. He is the author of several books of literary criticism, including *The Cuban Condition* and *The Cuban-American Way*, as well as of two volumes of poetry, *Carolina Cuban* and *Equivocaciones*. His story in this collection is excerpted from a novel in progress, *My Life as a Redneck*.

The more I know, the less I understand.

I had been Cuban for forty years and I'd just about had it. Cuba is a body of land, smaller than a continent, surrounded by mothers on all sides. Big mothers. Mean mothers. Total mothers. No Cuban is an island because we're all caught and connected in the great chain of maternal being. Some years ago, when my sister was about to leave her husband (but she didn't leave him after all), Mami counseled her: "*Cuando yo me casé, deje de ser mujer para ser madre.*" Which in English would be something like, "When I married your father, I stopped being a woman and became a mother." Truer words were never spoken. A mother she was, a real mother. Lovely and lethal and overweight.

So I had had it with mothers, the kind you visit, feed, and sit silently in front of as well as the kind you marry, sleep with, and sit silently in front of. I had been Cuban long enough.

But unmooring myself from Mami wasn't easy. My theory is that if you're male and born in the Caribbean, you have a complicated relationship to water; and if you also happen to be Pisces, which I am

(March 2, like Desi Arnaz), the relation is complicated to the point of unintelligibility. Geography has a gender: Cuba is a feeble phallic epiphenomenon awash in the endless mothering ocean. And you better not forget it. That's why we have hurricanes, to remind you. They swoop down on those poor uppity islands like so many watery spankings administered to wayward children. It's no wonder Cuba suffers from tropical depressions.

All my life strange things happened during hurricane season. When I was a cute and self-conscious kid in Cuba, the slightest hint of a disturbance was enough to send the men in my family into a frenzy. Windows were taped, maps were brought out, courses were charted, barometers were fawned over.

Ah, yes: barometers. Someday perhaps I'll write about the secret Cuban rituals of barometer worship. Forget about *santería*, it's barometers we're really into. Suffice it for now to say that each year, for several months, the barometer in our living room became the center of the house, a cosmic navel that I beheld with uncomprehending awe. Night after night the men gathered around the circular dial with the undecipherable markings. They argued endlessly about readings, about the time and place of landfall, about which streets would be flooded and what to do with boats and automobiles. Sometimes it seemed that in Cuba history was measured not by revolutions but by hurricanes. Things happened either before or after or during the *ciclón* of '26, or of '42, or of '54. The feverish binge of drinking and eating and planning and memorializing ended only when the storm had passed us and was on its way to Yucatán or Bermuda.

But if a hurricane turned my placid father into a manic man, my mother remained calm as an ocean. Taking whatever precautions she deemed necessary, but untouched by the sense of urgency that gripped the men, she went about her business. When a hurricane struck, my mother was in her element. The heavy weather that threw my father out of whack only made her more herself, as if the wind and rain enhanced and ratified her most inward being. Hurricanes did not faze her in the slightest.

It has always been thus in my family. In times of crisis, women reign. One morning, in September of 1972, toward the end of hurricane season, Mami had a heart attack. But it was Papi who collapsed on the bed. As they waited for the rescue squad to arrive, my mother held and hugged my father, who couldn't stop himself from whimpering,

"You're having a heart attack, you're having a heart attack."

"*No, chino, no es nada, no es nada*," she replied, holding steady on the fast track to martyrdom. She did not stop consoling him until the paramedics whisked her away. When she recovered, it was not her illness but my father's crying that I would have nightmares about.

But this was all years ago and now that I was grown up (though in my family this is still a matter of some controversy) and safely landlocked, hurricanes were the least of my worries. I had graduated to other terrors.

It was the Fall of 1989. I had been married for fifteen years but I had fallen in love, probably for the first time, only a couple of months earlier. Catherine was my ideal date of 1968—twenty years later. I used to tell her (but she didn't understand) that she was not just a *tipa* but an *archetipa*; in English I might have said that she was not just a pair of legs but a paradigm. But the Spanish was better. Catherine was the *Americanita* of my dreams, the girl I should have married had I become American when I was supposed to, back in the sixties, when everybody else was doing it. Catherine was slim and hard and elastic and, best of all, earthy. No *agua*-anguish here, no question of getting water-logged or drowning in her effluvia. When we finally made love one night in the office, I felt I was settling, not sinking.

It did not take me long to go head over heels over a paradigm. In September we began working together; by January we were living together. My colleagues were scandalized, my family was aghast, my wife was in therapy. The courtship was a weird blend of cold feet and bravado. I was feeling pretty good about myself at the time and so wasn't afraid to take a few chances. Catherine, for her part, is not the type to play games. Several times during those blessed and cursed months we called it off (think of our children, think of our spouses, think of our families), but each time the reprieve lasted only hours or days. Sometime in early November we started meeting after hours; soon after we began getting intimate.

I went into a frenzy. The way I felt, she might as well have been the only woman I had ever seen or touched. The afternoon she took her clothes off for the first time, I was in a trance. She was so beautiful. I was so scared. This was the week before Thanksgiving and we had decided that it was time to put a stop to the adolescent groping and simply screw. But it wasn't simple. I had a four o'clock meeting and Catherine was going to wait for me in the office. The meeting ended late and I ran all the way back across campus, thinking she would go home. When I got there, Catherine was sitting behind her desk, smoking a cigarette. She snuffed it and we went into my office. I tried to catch my breath. We clutched, fell back on the new purple sofa, and began kissing. After a few minutes she said, "Let me make it easier." She got up and began to undress. I was stunned. There she was, my paradigm, my American dream, my ideal date of 1968, taking off her clothes in front of me, her hard, flat belly only inches away from my nose. When she stripped to her garters, I couldn't believe my eyes. I was used to panty hose and girdles. Garters! White and lacy and complicated. Garters! Loose ends everywhere. Garters! How did she get her panties off? Garters! Garters! Garters! My head was swimming, my heart was racing, I trembled. Catherine's Cinnabar permeated the room. To say I was scared stiff would be misleading: I was scared flaccid. To say I lost my cool would be misleading: I wasn't even warm. I put on an awkward show of passion, but it didn't work, for her or for me. Finally Catherine told me to stop because I was hurting her. I waxed philosophical,

"The woman I don't love, I make love to all the time; the woman I love, I can't make love to."

This wasn't really true, since in fact I hardly ever touched my wife, but Catherine said she understood.

Catherine was my Typhoon, my tornado, my twister. Her luminous body, offered without ruse or ceremony, bent me out of shape. For weeks I didn't know what to do with myself. I was antic. I was frantic. I was romantic. I attached sexy postscripts to memos. I bought silk underwear at Victoria's Secret. I wrote her poems. I circled her house. I stashed condoms in the tenure files. I got sick. I grew a beard. I ranted. I raved. I even made love to my wife.

Those puddles of libido that I thought had dried up were suddenly seeping through my pores. I was wired for sex, redolent with late-flowering lust. My days were spent peeking into her blouse, or catching a glimpse of her garters, or daydreaming about her thighs. When she walked away, I was transfixed: her ass became my barometer. At meetings, as she took notes, I played footsies under the table. This was a real office romance. I played the Boss; the Secretary was played by a sexy Cat—forty years old, married to her high school sweetheart, and with two grown kids, blonde and beautiful and unambitious. Every morning, as I walked up the stairs and down the hall, I could smell her Cinnabar, the scent of sin.

In Spanish there are two types of desire, but only one of them has a name. You have your regular, everyday, get-up-in-the-morning-with-a-hard-on kind, which Americans call horniness but which Cubans don't call anything at all, perhaps because it goes without saying. This type of desire is ephemeral, a hydraulic imbalance relieved by solitary exercises in one-handed gratification. What does have a name in Spanish, and a good one, is protracted abstinence, the long-term, in-the-marrow-of-your-bones frustration that, unlike horniness, is only exacerbated by masturbation. The name for this is *atraso*. *Atraso* is as much a spiritual state as a physical condition. It may begin with hormones, but it eventually spreads to your soul. It may begin as lust, but it ends up as longing. The word itself means "lateness" or "backwardness," the idea being that a person with an *atraso*, rather than plain horniness, breeds civilization. It is *atraso*, rather than plain horniness, that sublimates into art or philosophy. It is *atraso*, rather than plain horniness, that is responsible for the prose and the poetry of the world. You can always tell an *atrasado* by the sad soulful languor in his eyes (*his* eyes: women do not get *atraso*). If love makes the world go around, *atraso* keeps it in orbit.

My *atraso* was monumental. I had a lot of boning up to do. I married my wife for many good and bad reasons, but sex was not one of them. Our marriage was a meteorologist's nightmare: instead of tempests of passion, doldrums of indifference. Marta was my shelter from the storm, a sandbagged sanctuary against uncertainty. She did not arouse passion, she forestalled it. We had completed connubial calm, and I thought our marriage was the better for it. But I was dumb beyond my years then. In fifteen years Marta and I had intercourse a few times, enough to produce two children and a case of herpes, but we never actually made love, much less fucked. Many and artful were the excuses we devised to let ourselves off the screwing hook. Besides the usual ones—fatigue, offspring, and menstruation—we had: intestinal gas, dizziness, glaucoma, "Fantasy Island," "The Love Boat," masturbation (hers or mine), Monopoly, Trivial Pursuit, Domino, and getting tenure. So it's understandable when Catherine's garters snapped, I did too.

Catherine's explanation of my reluctant behavior was that I felt guilty about cheating on my wife. Not true: my pangs of conscience were puny in comparison to my fear of failure. The truth is that I was scared shitless. Even if I could have gotten it up, I wouldn't have known what to do. My first fumbling attempts to fondle her breasts were a tempest in a C-cup. Whereas Marta's nipples were erection-proof, Catherine's all you had to do was breathe on them and they leapt to attention. It was scary. I was getting a crash course in the school of hard-knockers. Do I squeeze? Do I pull? Do I bite? Do I pretend not to notice? Mostly I stared. Paradigms are hard to please.

Had I been able to, I probably would have avoided sex altogether, but I didn't think she would go along. "Richard and I have always been good lovers," she said once, speaking of her husband. Just my luck. It was not until after New Year's that I finally resigned myself to the inevitable.

The first few times it was Catherine who made love to me. I was still in a trance, but once we started, I caught on fast. I also caught up fast. My *atraso* disappeared in a fierce, feverish hurry. Everything fit, everything felt good. Our bodies meshed and grooved and flowed. I was triumphant. My pants bulged. My pecs grew. I began to strut. In my eyes Catherine and I became the protagonists of the great Cuban-American love story, a Lucy and Ricky for the nineties. Sleeping with her was like making cross-over dreams come true. I was bewitched, bewildered, and bicultural. I loved the daily details of her body, the way she shuddered when she came, how she held me when I did. Each time was the first time. Each time, after it was over, I babbled unintelligibly in English and Spanish. Catherine thought it was funny.

It was around this time—in January or February—that I first had my Gary Morton dream. Gary Morton, you may remember, was Lucille Ball's second husband—the guy on whom Lucille, no longer Lucy, took revenge for all Desi, no longer Ricky, made her go through. In my dream it's Gary Morton except he's not Jewish and he looks somewhat different, but still has the perfect blow-dried gray hair, the pleasant smile, and amiable disposition. Catherine and I are married, but there's a vacancy in our family, a slot that needs to be filled. What the family needs, I say to myself in the dream, is a hus-band. I know Catherine already has a husband, me, but Gary would have a different role. He would be a symbolic father, a steadying pres-ence, a square peg in the hole of our family structure. All this seems self-evident, and after some convincing Catherine also goes along. Catherine and Gary get married. Suddenly I wake up (as it were) to the fact that, if he's her husband, I won't be sleeping in her bed or sit-ting at the head of the table. I go bonkers. I throw a fit. I scream. The wedding is annulled.

Once Catherine and I began sleeping together, I had to leave my wife. Our last weeks were sheer adulterous hell. I couldn't stand the sight of her. Marta's body, to which I had been indifferent for nearly two decades, started to repel me. Marta thought it was one of my things, another bout of *neura*, my family's catch-all term for everything from PMS to schizophrenia. According to my mother, my grandfather had had *neura*, so I was a logical candidate. But when I got *neura* before, I used to hide under my desk or bang my head against the wall. As she waited for my self-destructive fury to abate, Marta fed me Valium, Librax, Transene, Atarax, Equanil, Ruvert, Antivert, Trazodone, or whatever else she had handy. Coping is something she's always been good at. It's no wonder, she has the sea inside her. But this *neura* was different. I kicked and I screamed, but not at myself. Our normal bickering blossomed into full-blown battles. The bedroom, formerly the sea of tranquility, became a theater of war. We locked the door and went at it endlessly. The children sat outside, watching TV or playing Nintendo. They took turns knocking on the door and asking when we were coming out. Although we tried to shield them, when Marta stormed out of the bedroom one Saturday afternoon screaming, "I'm going to kill myself, I'm going to kill myself," they probably realized something was wrong. After a while, each time Marta and I would head for the bedroom, Sarah, who was five at the time, would say, "Oh no, Mami and Papi are at it again."

"Mami and Papi are only going to talk," Marta would reply.

"No, you're not," Danny chimed in. "You guys have been fighting all morning."

"We're not fighting, Daniel, we're talking."

"No you're not, Mami, you're fighting, I know you're fighting."

By the time the discussion got this far, I was already in the bedroom, priming myself for another bout. Marta soon followed and off we went. I probably won more than I lost. Marta screamed with the best of them, but lacked stamina. A fast starter, she faded in the later rounds, just when I was hitting my stride. At some point she usually broke down and conceded. I won on a TKO.

Coming down with herpes didn't help any. At first we didn't know what it was. I thought my face was breaking out, as it had so many times before. (I was a pimply kid who had grown up into a pimply adult.) Marta thought she had a vaginal infection, as she had so many times before. (One of the first and most beautiful words I ever learned from her was "trachymonads.") I grew a beard and stayed home from the office for a week, until my face cleared up a bit. Catherine brought me my mail. She was there when Marta came back from her gynecologist, who confirmed our diagnosis, gave her some literature, and wrote a prescription for Xovirax. Marta was upset, but not as upset as I was that she had butted in on me and Catherine. If there is a gene for compassion, I must have been born without it. Catherine quickly left. Marta and I got into another row. I thought she had not been very polite to my secretary.

For Christmas we went to Miami. Mami and Miami: for thirty years these two little words had ruled my emotional life. But not this year. I couldn't stand to be away from sexy Cat. After a couple of days I packed my bags and went home. Before I left, I sat down with Danny on the roll-away bed in my mother's house, where we always stayed. As Marta stood by ("you talk, you're the one who's leaving"), I told him that Mami and Papi were not getting along and that we wanted ("you want," Marta corrected) to spend some time apart. He crawled under the bed and started to scream, "No, no, no, no, no." This was bad enough, but when my mother heard him, she ran to the door of the room and began banging on it. "Stop it, stop it, the poor little angel, the poor little angel, what are you doing to him, stop it." I do not remember this day fondly. It was not a pretty sight. There was my son, whom I had just scarred for life, hiding under the bed and screaming, and there was my mother, who had scarred me for life, banging on the door and screaming. And there was Marta, sitting on the bed next to me, with a self-satisfied smirk on her face. And there was Catherine, with her plush thighs, waiting for me in North Carolina.

What would you have done? I got out as fast as I could. I didn't leave: I fled.

Back in North Carolina, school was out and I kept a watch on Catherine's house. My routine was to circle her house about a dozen times in each direction; then I went to the mall and walked up and down a couple of times, got back in my car, and went back to Catherine's house to circle some more. A couple of times I thought I saw her through the kitchen window, but I'm not sure. The most difficult part was when I went by late at night and the lights were all out. I thought of her in bed with her husband. "Richard and I have always been lovers," she had said. I wondered what that meant.

Catherine made me a Billy Joel tape, and that's what I played in the car—"Innocent Man," "The Stranger," "This Night." I was living in 1968. As my new Integra circled and circled her house, it turned into a time machine. I had skipped the sixties and this was my chance to get them back. Catherine was my passport to the past. I was transported. It was no longer 1990. It was no longer North Carolina. I was a no-longer pimply teenager and Catherine was my date. She was glowingly beautiful. We went to a dance. She let me hold her hand. We necked in the car. (I had a car!) The night lasted forever.

New Year's Eve I cooked myself filet mignon, got drunk on champagne, and wrote Catherine a long desperate letter, which I still have. It's not half-bad. At midnight Marta called. A few minutes later Catherine called from a friend's house. She and Richard had greeted the new decade by playing Pictionary. Americans have strange customs sometimes. She told Richard she was phoning her sister.

Marta got back with the children and a week later I moved out. By then she knew about Catherine. I had told her on the phone the same night Catherine and I made love for the first time. "I knew it, I knew it," Marta said. "Rebeca told me there had to be another woman." Rebeca, the least evil of her two sisters, spoke from experience. There had been any number of other women in her life; she herself had been an other woman. But when I told Marta who the other woman actually was, she was relieved. The way she figured it, I'd be crazy to leave her for someone like Catherine. What was in it for me? A few wild oats, the thrill of mischief, a little night music. Not much, really. Or at least not enough. The whole thing didn't add up. Marta was sure I would come to my senses.

I understood the logic, but even now I think she had it wrong. Anyone can leave his wife for a twenty-five-year-old. Nothing remarkable about that. But it's different when the other woman and your wife are contemporaries. More wrinkles, as it were.

I know that Cuban husbands always come back. Their mothers wouldn't have it any other way. After each of his affairs an uncle of mine routinely throws himself on the floor of the kitchen and begs his wife to take him back. She always does. She's a real mother. Still, my point is that when the competition is a shiny new body-by-Fisher, it's apples and pears, and the apples usually win. But when the competition is as old as you are, it's apples and apples, so it may be a toss-up. And Catherine was a real McIntosh: firm and tart and tasty. Marta's plump be-girdled mealiness didn't stand a chance.

The same weekend I moved out Catherine left Richard and got her own place. After about a week of going back and forth we moved in together into the two-bedroom apartment I had rented. Soon after we gave a party to celebrate our union. The invitation said, "Fête accompli." I found out later some people thought that was in bad taste. Fuck them. The party was great. It made up for New Year's. I drank and I danced till I dropped. Some who came to dinner stayed for breakfast. Nobody played Pictionary.

Catherine and I spent our days together in the office and our nights together in bed. Danny and Sarah were allowed to come for dinner on Wednesdays and Saturdays. When some of my fallow feminist colleagues complained that they felt uncomfortable around the Department, I quit the chairmanship. Fucking and feminism make uneasy bedfellows, and I have to admit that my plan to hold a beauty pageant and pick Miss Literary Theory of 1990 may have been a bit too much. The throne might have gone vacant anyway. My legacy to the Department was a three-year subscription to *GQ*.

But it was nice while it lasted. For several months, pheromones suffused the rarefied air around Cultural and Literary Studies (CLit Studies for short). I had finally understood what the pleasure of the text was all about. My life in theory devolved into the most frenetic kind of praxis. This was my hour of power in the ivory tower. And although I tried to act cool and collected, I'm sure I didn't succeed. My *atraso* howled for restitution, like the unquiet ghost of a wronged *cubano* forebear. Like my father, I had become a manic man. I worked my ass off in the office and I worked my ass off in bed. All things considered, my ass did better in bed.

For Spring Break, Catherine and I went to Cedar Key. By then we had been together for three months; our radiant half-life was coming to an end. We found out about Cedar Key from the travel section of the *New York Times*, where it was touted as the redneck Riviera. The Beachboys' "Kokomo" had been a hit that year, it had sort of become our song, and we regarded Cedar Key as our Kokomo hide-away. On the way we stopped at Lanier's Oak, at St. Augustine's, and at a bookstore in Gainesville where they had multiple copies of all of Harry Crews' books, even the good ones. For the first time ever, I got on I-95 and didn't go to Miami.

I spent most of our twelve hours in the car interrogating Catherine about her sex life. I already knew the general outlines, but I wanted details. What. Where. How. With Whom. How Many Times. And How Big. All the usual questions any Cuban man would ask. The *Americanita* of my dreams had been homecoming queen in New Jersey, dated a lot, and had her pick of the boys. She said she had a reputation for being a tough date, but I didn't believe her. As a teenager she probably was a downsized version of what we used to call *un caballo Americano*, which contrary to what it sounds is a term of respect, even awe. When she was sixteen, she had been raped by her next-door neighbor, a family friend. A few years later, Dominic Piglia (his name) was one of the guests at her wedding. I've seen pictures of him sitting in the front row at the church. Otherwise she had an unexceptional life (though she did live in a trailer for several years).

Cedar Key was the wetlands that time forgot, a Key West without Hemingway or Jimmy Buffett. We stayed at the Paradise Inn, a decrepit wooden hotel that I suppose Americans consider quaint. Our bed had posts and a mosquito net, but only for decoration, since the room had been air-conditioned. When we made love, I measured our pleasure. I mean, I kept a tally of orgasms. We began Friday night and by Saturday morning I knew it was going to be a rout. By Sunday evening the score was 27 to 8. I stopped counting.

Since there are no beaches in Cedar Key, when we weren't in bed we spent time at a seafood place owned by a gay woman whom everybody called Fred. At night we went to what seemed to be the local hangout, the L&M, a bar on the ground floor of another old wooden building that was probably a hotel in its prime. One large room contained the bar and pool tables; another large room in the back had a small stage, tables with chairs, and a huge inflated bottle of Smirnoff's hanging from the ceiling. The first night we were there, Friday, the streets were lined with pick-ups. The nearest town, Chiefland, is about twenty miles away, and a lot of them must have come from there. As we walked in, it was like the Red Sea parting and letting us through. Gordon and the Red Clay Rockers played rockabilly, which somehow I liked. When they covered "Betty Lou's Getting Out Tonight" (which they changed to "Betty Lou's Going Down Tonight"), I became a Bob Seger fan on the spot. Then Gordon and crew sang happy birthday to a man they identified only as "The Imperial Wizard of Chiefland." Good thing I didn't open my mouth all evening except to order drinks. But since I don't look particularly

Cuban and since Catherine looks especially American, I felt anonymous rather than out of place. It was wonderful. We were happy that night, Catherine and I, a spic and his paradigm dancing the night away in the redneck Riviera. For several hours the L&M bar was the center of our universe. We were two diminutive stars in a veritable galaxy of bare midriffs, bleached blonde hair, and jeans. I drank Myer's on the rocks, which I'm not sure is a redneck drink, but it didn't make any difference. Catherine drank beer.

When we weren't at the L&M or at the oyster bar, we fucked. I'm not sure if we made love, but boy did we fuck. The last night we sat on the wooden porch outside our bedroom, drank Amaretto, watched people drift in and out of the L&M, and talked endlessly about sex. It was a way of not talking about anything else. Sex was the one unique thing we had, our distinctive form of achievement. Everything else flowed from it and we both knew it. On the porch, gently swaying next to me, Catherine seemed to me infinitely desirable and intolerably foreign. I knew I was going to leave her. Something about cultural differences, intact families, new wrinkles. Or perhaps it was just fear. Transitions have never been my strong suit. I spent ten months in my mother's womb (*atraso*, even then); were it not for forceps, I might still be there, softly boiling in Mami's ooze. Trying to make a life with Catherine taught me that forty years hadn't changed me that much. I was intrepid enough to ditch my old life but too fainthearted to start a new one. Hot head and cold feet, that's me. Our time together was a stormy interlude, a kind of *tiempo loco*. Like hurricane season, it came and it went.

We got back from Cedar Key on Tuesday evening, after a bitter and desolate car trip. Early the next morning I took the first flight to Miami, where Marta received me with open arms, like the sea retrieving a piece of driftwood.

Blizzard!!!

Mary Helen Ponce

MARY HELEN PONCE is the author of *Taking Control*, a collection of stories, and *The Wedding*, a novel published by Arte Publico Press. Her stories have been widely published in literary reviews and magazines. She is currently working on a new novel.

The sky is gloomy and dark. The gray clouds that loom overhead remind me of an umbrella that at any moment will collapse—and send rivers of water dashing down, down. The weatherman says we can expect a blizzard, which in my handy dictionary is defined as snow combined with rain. The storm is coming from the east, as do most storms that hit Albuquerque. It should reach us by mid-afternoon.

From behind the heavy screen door, I stare at the darkening sky and breathe the crisp, cold air that swirls round my comfy adobe house. Toward the east the sky appears a bit lighter, white almost, with touches of gray near the Sandia Mountains. Near University Heights however, dark clouds gather.

Across the way I see my neighbor Mrs. Smithers taking a reading from the barometer that hangs on the wall of her enclosed porch. She does this each morning, sniffs the air, then announces to the entire block her weather predictions. She waves, steps outside. I join her near her newly painted house gate and prepare for a five-minute lecture on New Mexico weather. "It's at least in the 20s," claims this eighty-year old authority on Albuquerque weather. "Coming from the northeast this time. All the makings of a storm!" "A blizzard?" I lean against the fence to allow for her detailed answer.

"A blizzard is a storm," she corrects, her faded eyes staring up to the sky. She explains the particulars: how when snow and wind combine they wreak havoc on the town. "It takes cold, cold wind, and snow," she smugly concludes.

"I've never been in a blizzard," I say, pulling tight my light sweater. "What should I wear?"

Her blue eyes open wide; her wrinkled lips purse in a frown. She looks me up and down, appalled at how blasé California can be, then walks into her house, all the while shaking her white head. She mumbles at Chastity, her cat, who stares back with greenish eyes, then tiptoes to her basket near the kitchen stove.

A blizzard is on its way, I write in my journal, excited at this new experience, one to be discussed with friends and family in California. I rush to pack classnotes, Blue Books, and worn texts inside the plastic bag used in place of a briefcase. I squeeze into my pink jacket with leather trim bought at the Los Angeles garment district. It's 100 percent wool, cut close to the body, and fully lined in pink brocade. It's my favorite piece of clothing, and although a bit snug, when worn with my white silk blouse looks really sharp. Academic even! I slip on short alligator boots that barely cover my chilled ankles, grab a silk scarf off a chair, check my silver hoop earrings, and get ready to leave.

It's getting colder by the minute! The trees that line Princeton Street sway back and forth, the bare branches hanging on for dear life. Mrs. Smithers has got to be right!, I conclude as I bolt the door and prepare to move. I adjust my pretty jacket, shift the plastic bag, then stare at my hands.

Damn! I forgot my mittens. And heavy scarf! I fumble for the keys and re-enter the warm house. Once I relocate the detested mittens and hideous maroon scarf I reluctantly put them on. The mittens are so bulky! I can barely lock the door after that.

I walk into a howling wind that is icy cold. I'm not ready for a blizzard, I grumble at Chastity sitting by the windowsill. "This was not on my calendar!" Still, I know the neighborhood sage—plus the local weatherman must be right.

To date Mrs. Smithers has correctly predicted just when the

garbage men will come (late), the time it takes the gardener to cut the front grass—then split—(8 minutes)! She was right too, in saying the spring flowers: zinnias, cosmos, and shasta daisies, planted late, would freeze, although each night I religiously covered them with plastic.

The street is nearly empty: shiny-wet cars creep by Central Avenue, the main street that crosses Princeton. Here and there people swaddled in hugh puffy jackets go by, faces pressed against chests, heads covered in woolen caps and huge scarves that flap back and forth in the chilly wind. It's impossible to tell if it's a man or woman. But it's clear they too are heading for the University of New Mexico.

Once at UNM I head for my small office and go through the mundane tasks that will ensure my literature class will go smoothly. I xerox class handouts, file or trash papers into the metal wastebasket, and arrange my notes. In the hallway I spot our office secretary on her way to make coffee. I'm tempted to wait for a cup, but she makes it too damn strong, more like coffee pudding. Sometimes I beat her to the job, then quickly gulp the weak brew before she gets back.

At Mitchell Hall I go through the motions of teaching to a half-empty room. The few students present are restless, eager to get home, their eyes glued to the window that faces the Science Library and the solitary eucalyptus tree that braves the oncoming wind. It's the last of seven trees in the square that, according to "The Lobo," will become a parking lot. The others were cut down earlier: the trunks that for generations were embedded in the New Mexico soil wrenched out by a yellow caterpillar. Their remains: twisted branches, woody stumps, are sprawled across the wet dirt, waiting to be carted away.

From afar, the wet branches dangling from the lone tree resemble a spaghetti mop. They dance back and forth, in tune with the howling wind. I watch them swirl, trying to gauge the wind's velocity. The students, many from small towns—Nambe, Tesuque, Galisteo—are nervous, worried about the effects of the storm on ancestral adobes built by grandparents. And about elderly folks who no longer weather well the winter storms. They're less concerned about cattle and horses, animals with inherent survival instincts. In a last-ditch effort to hold their attention, I cite certain passages in *We Fed Them Cactus*, the assigned reading in which blizzards are mentioned. Alas! Nothing helps. All my students want is to go home. I sigh, close the book, and excuse the class.

I scurry to the Sub, dodge between students muffled to the Max!, eager to get out of the cold to enjoy the hot chocolate sold here. It never ceases to amaze me that after four PM this heady drink sells for a dime! A whole dime!! Students *are* notoriously poor. It's comforting to know someone cares about their meager budgets. This would never happen at UCLA. But then, this is New Mexico, my adopted home-state, said to be poor and backward, yet rich enough to give away hot chocolate.

I drink up, wipe my mouth with the thick mittens, wipe the mitten on a slightly damp napkin, then prepare to exit. My favorite jacket is lightly damp, the tucks along the sleeves beginning to pucker. There appears to be a veneer of ice along each arm of the jacket that took me three weeks to find! I re-adjust the scarf that is scratching my neck and walk out a chilly glass door.

There is tension in the air. A mail clerk dashes by, his thick glasses frosted over, the fur of his heavy jacket pulled up to his thick neck. On one shoulder hangs a canvas bag chock full of mail. He stops to wipe his nose with a hankie that sticks to his mittens. *Pobrecito.* His job is to ensure the mail gets out. By the time he's done he'll be sopping wet. He walks behind me towards Mesa Vista Hall, then pushes his way up the stairs. His heavy boots slither across the wet hall.

"The blizzard is headin' down," cries our office secretary, a young Navajo woman who each weekend drives home to Grants to care for her elderly mother—and her sheep. She owns a hogan inherited from her grandmother. She has often invited me to visit her hogan, but is being polite, and probably glad I have not yet showed up on her doorstep.

She looks worried, her dark eyes glued to the window shift from the wall clock to the stormy sky. She's anxious to get going, I know. Often on Fridays the secretaries or Administrative Assistants, as they prefer to be called, sneak off early. They first transfer incoming calls to another office, then head for the back stairs that lead to the parking lot. But today the second floor of Mesa Vista is almost empty; the hallway deserted, offices and phones silenced.

She covers the typewriter, a sign that all typing has come to a screeching halt, gathers her heavy coat, thick wool scarf, knitted cap, furry gloves, and prepares to leave. From past experience—and from watching her—I know it takes her at least fifteen minutes to layer on an assortment of clothes to help her brave the storm. As a single parent of school-aged children she is especially nervous about getting them home too. "I have to get to the market before it hits!" she sighs, then winds a scarf around her round face. Only her brown eyes are now visible, and a tiny part of her nose. She grabs her purse and disappears around the hallway.

Around me, those left move at a fast clip, taking care of business while time allows. The wind has picked up, but the phone lines are still up. Now and then the lights dim, and appear to be going out, then come back on with new intensity. My office-mate, fearful of getting caught in the clutches of the cold stinging wind that blows across the campus, is also taking off early. She is from the East, I think, where it snows all the time, and like a Girl Scout, is always prepared. She carries Band-Aids, aspirin, tissues, lip balm, and beef jerky in her backpack. In her half of our closet she keeps an assortment of sweaters, raincoats, torn umbrellas, galoshes, and a pair of hiking boots. Now and then she litters the office with her jogging stuff: smelly sweats and an equally smelly pair of hightops bought at Sports Chalet.

"I have to get going," she grumbles, as she prepares to exit. Her stubby body is encased in what resembles a quilted astronaut suit; her blue eyes peep out from a hood lined in early opossum. On her feet are sturdy shoes with rubber soles thick as bicycle tires. Her hands are encased in thick pink mittens that from afar look like giant hams. Around her neck are two scarves: one red, the other a pink plaid. She read where during snowstorms, folks wearing bright colors are easy to spot. She dashes to the door; her thick body weaves from side to side. I can hear her tire shoes go plunk, plunk, plunk. From the upstairs window I watch as a strong wind blows the red scarf into her eyes. She comes to a screeching stop, yanks the scarf from her face, then heads toward Lot 3, hoping to beat the blizzard, which from all indications, is almost here.

From my perch inside the warm building I look out at the adobe buildings that make up much of the University of New Mexico. They huddle together to await the storm, except for Ortega Hall, an odd building that sticks out like a sore thumb. In the semi-desert environment this edifice is out of place. The adobes are feminine. They reminded me of Mexican sculptor Francisco Zuñiga's women; round, resilient, with wide backs, thick arms, and broad faces. Unlike the square buildings that buck the elements, the adobe-like structures blend into the earth from where they will survive this blizzard.

"This is my first blizzard," I explain to Marie, a part-time instructor who teaches evenings. She dashes by, her startled eyes glued to the Sandias now barely visible. "I want to enjoy it to the fullest," I add to her retreating back. She gapes at me with alarm, rattles off statistics on past storms, in particular those she experienced in her home state of Michigan.

I thank her for the unsolicited information, then peek out towards Johnson gym and points west. Everything looks deserted. The space around the fountain, normally crowded with sellers and their wares, is empty. The makeshift tables on which they exhibit turquoise earrings, hand-carved *santos* and organic weavings long gone. I am probably the only person left in our building, but will stay on campus till the last minute, then walk the short two blocks home.

The cottonwoods near the Sub, visible from a back window, reel from the strong wind, their branches lightly flecked with snow. Across the way in International Studies, which each Monday offers ethnic foods for a modest price, lies a branch split from a tree now listing to the left. Across the way, next to Student Services, smaller trees hang on for dear life, while the Chinese elms that line the path to Johnson Gym stoop and sway as if doing the Maypole dance.

In summer these same trees are home to cicadas, called *chicharras* in Spanish. The fat bugs screech and screech, as if going mad from the New Mexico sun, then fall dead. Cicadas, I'm told, are indigenous to the Southwest although I never heard them sing when in California. In some Chicana poetry cicadas are a metaphor for seasonal workers that each year cross the U.S.–Texas border to work in agriculture. Like the cicadas, they arrive at the beginning of summer. I find the bugs interesting—but noisy.

In winter the elms give shelter to blackbirds who defecate all over the trees and sidewalk. The blackbirds, like the eucalyptus trees, have been uprooted. They circle campus in search of tall trees. *Pobrecitos.* Ever since the trees on the far side of campus were cut, the birds have had to find a new habitat. They like it here and keep coming back, much to the disdain of the maintenance men who hate their seasonal mess. By spring the Sub courtyard is encrusted with bird shit, droppings that must be scraped with a shovel, then washed off with thick hoses that snake across the sidewalk and create a hazard for students rushing by to class. Still, the cicadas are part of New Mexico, and while not the national bug, come close to it.

The blizzard is coming closer! Outside the air is a light pink, translucent almost. The Sandia mountains that literally blow into the jogging field adjacent to the parking lot and send shivers up the spines of early-morning joggers, are no longer visible. On Central, across the way, traffic has screeched to a halt.

From the security of my office I stare out at a sky that reminds me of a movie. Not quite *Doctor Zhivago*, but almost. Just then the wail of sirens, heavy rains, and Saturday night fills the air. The sudden changes in New Mexico weather, flash floods in particular, bring out municipal loud sirens on the way to excavate stuck drivers.

"The phones are down," shouts someone on the floor below. Clearly this is a serious storm!

I struggle into my designer jacket, run my hands over the leather trim which I have come to equate with high couture. I check my lipstick, chosen to blend with the pink of my jacket, then retouch my eyebrows. My mother always cautioned us to look our best, especially during hard times! I can't remember whether I'm wearing my best undies, but at least my lipstick is the right shade. I slam student papers into the trusty plastic, pull down the cuffs of my light pants, and lightly buff my elegant boots. Once the windows are secured, I snap off lights, then creep down the dark hall and prepare to greet my first blizzard.

The cold wind blasts me back into the building. I struggle with the door, push out with all my might, but end up inside. Designer jacket askew, fashion earrings about to fall, I push and push. Slowly the door opens. Just then my plastic-briefcase slides to the floor, spewing papers left and right. A bottle of white-out rolls near my feet: large papers splatter the walk. Shit! I yank off mittens, gather the papers within reach and quickly stuff them back in the bag, trying not to notice those flying towards the Sandias. Students, I have found, can be very understanding. I slide inside once more. On go the mittens. I lean on the door, bend my knees, and push hard. Slowly the door opens, then closes in my face. Once more I'm blown in. What gives, I grumble? Will I be forced to spend the night here? How in hell will I make it home?

The parking lot, visible through a small window next to the

stairs, is empty of cars. No one is about. Even the designated area where busloads of handicapped folks are dropped off each morning and retrieved at night, is empty of cars.

I think back to a Women and Nature class, of female explorers and mountain climbers. I now identify with the brave women, North Americans mostly, who in the 1970s scaled Anapurna, a mountain in the Himalayas. I know how they felt upon leaving the safety of their tents to make a stab at the 12,000-foot summit. Each day they advanced a few feet, only to be driven back. In the end a blizzard killed three of the climbers, although the others made it to the peak, and lived to recount this adventure. But this is not Anapurna, I grumble, as I brace against the door. It swings open! Then just as quickly slams shut behind me.

Far away I spot a stray body struggling with a car door; another hugs the walls of Johnson Gym. I take comfort in knowing I am not alone. The "buddy system" that served me so well in Scouts comes to mind, but will they hear my frantic shouts? I yank the scarf off my face, take a deep breath—and swallow cold rain.

My glasses mist over; my nose is runny and cold. Still, I must keep moving. Statistics show that in extreme cold it is important to keep up the body temperature by moving around. If I stand still I'll freeze to death. Unlike Lot's wife, *I'll* turn to ice. I think back to an old Western story where, during a blizzard, a farmer walked a short distance from his house to the barn and became disoriented. He was found the next day, feed pail frozen in his hand. I keep my eyes glued to the lights and sounds coming from Central Avenue and pray a lot.

The wind is like no other. Loaded with snow it feels thick, heavy. It neither glides nor sweeps, but slams into me. I think fondly of the Santa Ana winds, tame by comparison. I think too of my home town in southern California, where in 1972 it snowed for about ten minutes. Newscasters had a field day, and cautioned listeners on how to drive on snow! A local K-Mart sold snow chains at discount. A wedding was almost canceled; football games postponed. Formerly distant neighbors shared hot toddies on icy lawns while kids begged for shiny sleds.

I pull my pink jacket close, and curse my luck at not having brought a heavy coat. The coats were ugly! Ugly colors, ugly styles, and weighed a ton. I thought of buying a ski jacket, but they add pounds to my hefty frame. I push on. The plastic bag does a St.

Vitus dance, and slams against my fashion boots with a vengeance.

The icy wind penetrates my jacket. I've never been this cold, not even when in Scouts I camped out at Big Bear. I take a tiny step, shuffle-off to nowhere. The sidewalk is encrusted with ice; the asphalt teems with slush. I hunch my damp shoulders, chew on the scarf stuck to my mouth, and push on.

Slowly I move to the safety of Johnson Gym. Ahead of me a yellow van crawls away. It's a service vehicle, sent to repair telephones—or something. I wave the plastic, yell with all my might, then stop to think. If I throw myself in front of it—will it stop? Will the driver take pity on me, my flimsy jacket? Take me home? I thrust my legs forward, as if cross-country skiing, then wham! I hit the ground.

The blizzard, now at full tilt, has brought fresh snow. It mixes with the oil in the parking lot. I have slipped on an oil slick—and can't get up. I slump to a sitting position, as when doing squats—trying not to cry. But, if I squat across the lot I just could make it!

I feel my jacket scrape on the building, but no longer care. My leather boots are sopping wet. As did the women at Anapurna, I can wait—or keep truckin'. I try again. I clutch my jacket, smash the plastic bag to my chest, and slowly squat to the next building. I reach the safety of the wall, bend over, then lift myself upright. Elated at having traveled this far in an hour, I take a deep breath—and gag on the cold air.

It is cold. Terribly cold. I have never in my life felt such cold. Across the baseball and track field I see bent bodies moving towards the dorms; to the safety of cars. The screech of sirens fills the air; from my perch I see an ambulance inching across Central. I wonder if the Frontier Restaurant is still open and serving the breakfast rolls they're famous for. I salivate; images of hot cider and warm rolls fill my frozen head. Just then a garbage can, unhinged by the storm, flies by, and reminds me of the task at hand.

The wind has shifted! Or so it seems. My hair is stuck to my face. My jacket is sopping wet. Unmindful of the seams now coming apart, I bend over and slowly inch towards the parking lot adjacent to Central, and the street lights that, like a beacon, will guide me home. I lift my head in time to see a tow truck going by the lot to my left, past the adobe buildings huddled tight. Slowly the truck turns around. They've seen me? I'm saved! I'm going to make it!! I slide forward, grab a parking meter, and hang on for dear life.

La Yerba Sin Raiz
(The Weed Without a Root)

Leroy V. Quintana

LEROY V. QUINTANA was born in Albuquerque, New Mexico, where he went to school and received an M.A. in English and an M.A. in Counseling. He is a licensed marriage, family and child counselor, and a Vietnam veteran. In 1978 he received a grant from the National Endowment for the Arts in Creative Writing. He is the author of *Sangre* and *Interrogations*, the latter a collection of poetry on Vietnam forthcoming from Pratt Press. In 1992, the Bilingual Review/Press will publish *Now and Then, Often, Today*, another book of poetry.

As I have not proved capable of doing much else in life except tell stories, I have no choice but to relate this one. You will be outraged by the end (I will tell it so that you have no choice but to read all, or most, or enough to figure out the outcome), but you will also be amused because nowhere will you find, nowhere, a story as unusual, odd and outlandish. Nowhere. You will also, I assure you, exclaim that I should be ashamed of myself for writing such an unutterable and unsuccessful, and yes, unsophisticated tale, and I am, and so should you for reading as far as you will.

Let me begin by saying that in the sheep camp the most important position is that of camptender. In the morning he drives the wagon to the spot where the sheep are watered and rested for several hours at midday, and in the afternoon to the site where the herder will spend a restless night jumping out of bed at the distant tinkling of bells to prevent any sheep from drifting, as well as lighting sagebrush fires at the perimeter to frighten off predators.

The camptender was Calisto Garcia, a man with the eyes and nose of a buzzard and a wagging tongue. A detestable man, I assure you, who bragged about pissing in the coffeepot and then brewing the contents for breakfast. Once we found him bathing—and singing a song about ripe mountain girls—in the large barrel where our drinking water was stored. And it was no secret that when he rolled the masa for the tortillas or biscuits he would wipe the sweat from his brow, maybe his underarms too (and his crotch, he once admitted when questioned), and go right back to kneading the dough. Then too there was the issue of his fingernails which he said always seemed to come clean during the preparation of a meal. But I assure you that by the time we got the sheep to the spring pasture up in the mountains, Calisto had been taught a lesson, humiliated like no man in any story you've ever heard.

Juan Marquez was the herder, and all that is important to know about him is that he ate with his mouth open, burped all day long, ate sardines as often as possible and took a shit (as they say in the sheep camps) every day, be it spring, summer, winter or fall, national or religious holiday, leap year or not, at exactly seven o'clock in the evening. You could (and we often did) set your watch by it.

Myself? I was fifteen when I first hired out as a young herder for old man Johnson. Times were bad and I went to work for half-pay so I could support myself and not be a burden to my parents, who had ten other children to tend to. The sheep camps were my classroom. I assure you I never looked back that last day of my contract as I headed for the highway, thumbing down anything that was headed for Albuquerque. Three years of lonely, cold winters, blazing summers, rocky trails, coyotes, viboras, of lambing, shearing; three years of dust clogging my lungs; a year of Calisto's wagging tongue.

Oh yes, something else about Calisto that is important to know: every evening come quarter after seven he would lie down, cross his arms over his chest, yawn a couple of times, scratch his ass for a little over a minute and then drift off to sleep the sleep of the innocent.

As I said before, the camptender is by far the most important person in the sheepherder's life, in more ways than one his only friend out in the range. He is the tie to the outside world. He brings in provisions (cans upon cans of sardines), the precious mail, new boots when the old ones have worn out, as well as being the cook. In short, a best friend who can revive the lowest spirit of a homesick herder with a kind word or gesture, or with a pleasant meal.

For all of October, November and most of December of my last year (including Christmas day), we went without salt. There wasn't a

grain of salt in the entire state, Calisto informed us. Not until the salt
war was over, when the strikers got a decent wage and returned to
work. And of course, there had been precious little left before the salt
war. There it was. Front page news, but no settlement in sight (and
who else in the camp knew (or dared claim he knew how to read,
besides Calisto?). For some strange reason I can no longer recall, even
sardines and salted crackers were unavailable. I assure you that going
without salt for even a month can drive a person crazy. You start lick-
ing rocks, salting your meals with sand simply to keep from going
mad. And then one day Calisto spat out a huge glob of frijoles complaining that they were too salty and I had to bulldog Juan by the
ankles in order to keep him from butchering the taunting Calisto.
Like I said, the herder's best friend is the camptender.

I suppose the trouble really started (although we were not really
aware of it at the time) when Calisto learned that Juan was married,
that first time Calisto drove in with the mail, a month or so after he
replaced a man by the name of Lazaro Padilla, I believe. Lucky for
him that Juan and myself were entering the last year of our contracts.
I assure you that I would be writing this in prison, instead of at my
corner table in the La Golondrina in San Luis with a beer arriving on
schedule every half hour on the half hour (as I have not proved capable of doing much else in life except tell stories), if I would have had
to spend any more time with that disgusting . . . but he paid, oh yes,
he paid dearly, I assure you.

As you shall shortly see.

Immediately after handing over the soiled envelopes Calisto stuck
his big buzzard nose over Juan's broad shoulder (you could tell also
by the wrinkles and folds he had fooled with the mail, trying desperately to discover the contents, as if he could read), and the first thing
out of his mouth when he saw the picture of Juan's wife was, "I knew
a woman like her once!" "In Las Animas," he continued, "or was it
in Puerto de Luna, or maybe in Bueyeros . . ."

Juan very quietly slid the photo back inside the envelope and
patiently dropped the letter into the pack that he carried full of *Yerba
de la Vibora*, which he brewed for whatever ailed him, stood up and
treaded off slowly to check the band.

But it was too late. Calisto had persuaded the postmaster in San
Luis (we got it out of Calisto later) to read him the name of the
sender. You see, in those days the postmaster would write and

address a letter for you if you didn't know how to write. "Laura," he said, "was her name, or was it Rosa?" (Knowing full well it was.) Juan stiffened in midstep, and that's when Calisto's gray eyes brightened and a broad smile spread across his mottled face.

And so it went for the rest of that year. Calisto loading the morning *huevos rancheros* with pepper (there was no pepper war that year, I assure you), on payday slamming his money down and betting Juan he could steal his wife away, sardines, pebbles in our beans, "now, was her name Concha, or was it Laura? Laura, I think it was! *Si*, Laura. No. No. Rosa. *Rosa, la mas hermosa . . . en Mosquero?* La Jara? . . . " (As he stroked his cleft chin in mock puzzlement, sour coffee, Juan burping all day long, sour tortillas, vinegary biscuits, curdled desserts, Juan as dependable as the town clock—even more so!), pebbles in our beans, ". . . Laura? No, Rosa. Rosa! . . . " Tattered mail, Calisto lying down at quarter after seven, crossing his arms over his chest, yawning twice, rolling over, scratching his ass for a minute or more, ". . . fifty dollars says she'll never answer another letter of yours if I write her . . . "

And then spring came and with that the thaw and then the hundred-and-fifty-mile-walk north from the desert valley where we had passed the winter (fortunately and unfortunately it had been a good winter: no blizzards, we lost no sheep, and Calisto came and went for supplies regularly), to the spring pasture in the mountains where they would graze all summer. Along the way we would run the band through the shearing camp and then to the lambing grounds, where the ewes would drop one, two and sometimes three lambs apiece. With spring came so much work: two thousand sheep, most of them bred ewes to keep track of; no more short winter days, checking the sheep at our leisure; now it was going to be two weeks of little or no sleep all the way to the sweet mountain pasture. Even Calisto would be kept busy, advancing the camp twice a day. And with spring came *viboras*. And with *viboras* Calisto's collapse.

One day, at the shearing camp (a Friday it was), towards nightfall, from Calisto's wagon came the rattle and clatter of pots, pans, and shattering of glass and suddenly Calisto running as fast as his spindly legs would allow yelling "*Vibora! Vibora!*" ("Snake! Snake!").

"*La yerba sin raiz*," Juan said, an odd, twisted smile beginning to spread across his heavy face. "*La yerba sin raiz*," he said to himself again. His eyes had that look the holy rollers get just before they begin yelling "Praise Jesus!" and they fall trembling to the floor. "*La yerba sin raiz*," he said again, completely and totally convinced. When I asked him what kind of weed that was, a weed without a root, he said, matter of factly, an odd smile I had never seen before frozen on his face, "A weed for snakebite. And headaches."

"Better than *Yerba de la Vibora?*" I asked.

"*Mucho mas.*"

"And common?"

"*Si*," he said, "*muy comun.*"

"*La yerba sin raiz*," Juan said to Calisto, the first words he had spoken to him in months, other than those necessary for business. Calisto, frazzled, asked what *la yerba sin raiz* was. "What's it good for?"

"The best medicine there is for snakebite. And a big headache."

"Never heard of it," Calisto said as he circled the wagon, in slow, hesitant steps, as if maneuvering through an obstacle course sowed with fresh cowpies.

The next day I noticed Juan walking from the shearing camp with a burlap bag, a bounce in his stride that I hadn't seen for quite some time. He returned in an hour or so, holding the bag carefully. When I asked him what was in it he said it was part of the *remedio* for a headache. He had also cut a *nopal*, a piece of cactus the size of a steer's tongue, and began peeling it with his pen knife. All I had ever seen him use was *Yerba de la Vibora*, so I couldn't understand what he was planning to brew.

Seven o'clock came and I noticed that Juan was a regular as ever, but what struck me as peculiar was that he had made his pile so usually close by, especially since he had loaded up on sardines the night before. Afterwards he got a stick about the length of his arm, mounted a pair of cactus needles at the tip and secured them by winding some thread around them.

At this point some of you probably feel you don't want (some, or perhaps many, came to this conclusion quite a while ago) or need to continue, having figured out the end. Very well then. If indeed you figured out the end sometime ago, perhaps it is you who should be ashamed of him or herself.

At a quarter after seven Calisto stretched out, crossed his arms over his chest, yawned twice, rolled over, scratched his ass for a minute or more, and muttered something about Rosa. He was about to tumble into the contented sleep of the unerring when Juan tiptoed up to him carefully, aimed the cactus needles and then jammed them quickly into Calisto's ass, and just as quickly dumped the buzzing vibora on top of Calisto.

Well, I've never heard a more pained and loud "Aiiieeee!" in my life. "*Por el amor de Dios*," he pleaded, "help me! Help me!" By this time the shearers who had been playing *monte* had dropped their cards and walked over (a little too slowly, I thought; Juan had revealed his plan to everyone but me; he had put a lot of money on himself) and circled around nonchalantly. Calisto cried out for Juan and began pleading for him to give him something, anything. "I don't want to die!" he shouted over and over. "Help me, Juan. And forgive me. Please forgive me!" "*Pues* for snakebite, *la yerba sin raiz*," Juan advised, patiently, "unless somebody wants to suck out the poison." He looked around. The shearers stuffed their hands in their pockets, pulled down their hats, drew lines in the dirt with the tips of their boots, picked their noses, spat out tobacco, some muttered "*Que coma mierda*," under their breath. "*Por el amor de Dios!*" Calisto pleaded.

When he saw that no one was going to volunteer he asked for *la yerba sin raiz*. But Juan cautioned him that, even though it was the most effective, it was also the most . . . the most . . . " "The most what?" Calisto demanded. "Well, the most . . . but if taken immediately after bitten . . . " Calisto, no longer feeling comforted, and terribly confused, and sensing he had run out of bullshit (as they say in Albuquerque) for the first time since reporting to work as the camptender, asked Juan just exactly what this *yerba sin raiz* was, and Juan twisted his lips in the direction of the pile he had dropped. Calisto's eyes widened in horror, disgust and then horror again. " . . . Absorbs the poison like nothing else," explained Juan, "but only if taken immediately." Horror, disgust, horror. "On a piece of nopal," Juan explained, "it goes down quickly, absorbs the poison . . . " Horror, disgust, the inevitable. "*Bueno*," Calisto agreed, gasping.

It wasn't until the second desperate bite, with the shearers bursting into thundering laughter, that Calisto realized Juan had gotten the best of him. By then *la yerba sin raiz* had stuck in his gullet and he could neither swallow it nor cough it up. He retched so hard they had to load him onto a wagon and drive him into San Albuquerque, first to a throat then quickly to a stomach specialist.

Saturnino el Magnífico

Alberto Alvaro Ríos

(Photograph © 1992 by Hal Martin Fogel)

ALBERTO ALVARO RÍOS is the author of *Teodoro Luna's Two Kisses*, *The Lime Orchard Woman*, *The Warrington Poems*, *Five Indiscretions*, *The Iguana Killer*, and *Whispering to Fool the Wind*. His honors include the 1991 Governor's Arts Award, fellowships from the Guggenheim Foundation and the National Endowment for the Arts, the Walt Whitman Award, the Western States Book Award for Fiction, and three Pushcart Prizes. Currently, he is a professor of English at Arizona State University.

The entire circus train fell in the manner of a child's toy into the ravine just outside of town, its cars folding up in the fall so that from a distance they looked like the rough-angled line of teeth on a saw. The regular engineers from the federal railroad all knew the bank of the wide turn, and gave their trains some speed, but the circus came to this place only once every four years, and their engineer this time was new.

Moving out of town, the train came to such a point of angle, such a crookedness, the floor no longer a floor, that everyone and everything on the train moved or was moved to the left side to look. And when they did look, they saw themselves, falling into the dirt and the dark, falling and being jerked, so that their shouts did not go forward from their mouths, were not fast enough. For the length of the moment it seemed their voices came from the backs of their heads.

The circus train crashed a crash of spectacle, which, everyone later agreed, so showed the honesty of these performers that the townspeople felt better about having attended and paid good money for what had seemed a suspect affair the night before, even though they had enjoyed themselves.

* * *

The elephant Saturnino only half stood, or was only half fallen, at half-height on his knees when the two boys saw him.

They looked at him and said, it cannot be. The great elephant in this moment was a little boy himself, again kneeling at a game of marbles, reaching as if he were a cheater with his great arm into the game's circle.

Or else with his trump the elephant in comic pantomime was making fun of the caboose man's arm as he had made desperate signs to the engineer just a few minutes ago, that arm shaking to be understood, furious in its shake, furious failing of words in whose stead this shaking arm now found itself.

The elephant Saturnino looked half as tall as the truth, and helpless on the painful knees of his unsure legs even with all his strength, his capacious trunk moving back and around.

And then his trunk did begin to talk, that caboose man's flailing arm, with what looked like a mouth stolen from a man's face on its end. The elephant Saturnino's trunk began making all the noise it had made from all the years of his life all at once, the noise a drowning man's arm would make if it had a voice.

The scene evoked the picture of a performing trombonist, of a vacuum cleaner hose gone wild, in that particular depiction of action which cartoons in theaters all use sooner or later. But this was a mighty hose, upon which no story book face would have been convincing.

That this scene was further filled with the rest of the circus train and the rest of the animals and the rest of the clowns and tight-rope walkers and fire-eaters, revved an engine of color and noise and excitement more than equal to the best moments of this circus' long history.

This was the wreck of a circus train. This was what the sad boy Tavito Cano, who had been by chance walking along the tracks at this very moment, came into town yelling about, happy almost to bring news this big. It filled him so much he thought he had grown.

Animals, loose feathers, smoke, humidity, night and small fires, a noise from the insides of things, from the insides of bright oranges and yellows, a moan from the purple that would not stop, a red all pain, all noise but not for ears.

In trying to get someone to come to the train's wreck, Tavito

Cano's loud yelling and gestures could not properly give over to the townspeople gathered the true spectrum of occurrence. He could not adequately compare it to anything anyone here had seen, so many whirrings of wheels still, so many of the smallest pieces of universe still in the air, so that they almost did not believe him.

José and Lázaro ran quickly to the train, understanding something about the gravity of Tavito's words more quickly than the rest because they were boys as well.

"Quickly, a hand!"

The circus man with the long moustaches, moustaches which were themselves advertisement for his place in the world, moustaches which were themselves arms so folded as to flex muscles of their own—this circus man called to the two boys. Or at least they thought he was calling to them, so loud were his words and so much did they fit into the ears of these two boys, eager.

He was the man, after all, who with his real arms only just last night had held thousands of pounds of iron and stone and flesh. He was the man who had held three women borrowed from the trapeze acts on each of his arms, with a seventh in high heel shoes standing backward to the audience, her heels on his brows and the balls of her feet on his skull in that way he said he did not mind.

"A hand!"

Who would have thought that he could not by himself control the simpleness of a single wild elephant, could not grab hold of that trunk, whirl the elephant into a dizzied spin and stupor, then rubbing his hands together finish his natural business of saving the day.

The boys had thought the advertising posters for the circus to have said as much, and so they hesitated at his call. It smacked of the way in which some performers call for volunteers from the audience and then hypnotize them into biting off their own arms, the way they had heard, the way José said his mother had said that his one-armed uncle had been so foolish.

"You there!" he called again, and with greater urgency.

José and Lázaro looked at each other and shrugged their shoulders. They started in his direction, but could not get over the fact of their having to help, so experienced were they now as dazzled members of the audience from the night before, as dazzled members of the audience who had given themselves over to this man, who had taken such good care of them. How could it be that he was asking for their help: this is what the shrugging of their shoulders said.

"Over here, quickly," he said, gesturing to the right with the full egg of his head.

But then again, of course he would call on them. Had they not believed this all their short lives? That, as this man was superhuman, so were they also superhuman, that this was the proper and clear domain of two boys in a wild world: to be masters of everything, to have under their clothes their own large initials in red, that law of membership in the world of champions they had learned well from the comic books.

If he were not in fact singling them out with his words and the movements of his hands, they nonetheless believed themselves, at that moment, unquestionably chosen.

He could have called on any of the others in the crowd, on the men. But José and Lázaro knew what was what. They recognized the call to action—at last—as heroes on behalf of the Forces of Good in this World.

These boys threw themselves into the task of helping him untangle and calm the elephant Saturnino, but not without saying to each other with their eyes that this might still be some trick, some even more breath-taking part of the singular performance from the evening previous still lingering. It had cost enough money, after all, so that to think of this as still part of the show was not beyond the limits of the already-prodded imagination.

José and Lázaro could not have been more in agreement that the elephant Saturnino el Magnífico had won this battle of wills between himself and the strongman, whose true name was given by the owner of the circus as the Black Sheep Don Noé, but whose last name he would say to no one.

The elephant would not bow his great head on command, which was certainly an occasion for sadness, inasmuch as from the battle the strong man would not be returning. This was what happened to strongmen, the boys later said. Nobody after all ever sees an old one.

Through what seemed to the boys as hours of struggle with the beast, this Don Noé did more than his share, as was his way. But the elephant had its memory, the way they say elephants do not forget, which also presumably means they do not, as well, forgive.

With that memory it remembered whatever there was to remember about all of its years with the circus. The involuntary performances done as a favor to this man. The silly hats and the cumbersome saddle. The cartwheels and the anthem-singing, and the clean-up afterward, the rolling of circus tent-poles onto the train, the lifting of steamer trunks into the hoisted nettings of the docks.

The work, and the work again, and for not much, almost nothing, since an elephant after the show in the company of performers is so big no one sees it—this elephant, angry for so many years, angry and with wounds, finally took from this Don Noé more than his life. A life, after all, is simple. But a friendship at a moment of anger, this is something else, something more, and big.

The final manner in which the struggle was lost for control of the elephant was not something repeatable in conversation, and in the face of what the elephant did next, José and Lázaro had to stand back. Their small arms and puny pushes had effected no purchase of the grand master bull elephant's soul.

They had been no help, this much was clear. For a moment the two boys looked at each other, and saw only two boys and nothing more. Perhaps he had been calling to the men after all. But the men had seen they could make no difference, and so no man had stepped forward.

In that night's extraordinary moment the elephant Saturnino el Magnífico took the life both from Don Noé's body and from the memories of the boys. They did not want to remember. They were told not to. They could not: something so big did not fit onto a place so small as their tongues. There were no words.

Like the caboose man and like Saturnino himself, there were no words for Don Noé at the very end, and so he took a bow. That was all, but it was everything against which words must always fail.

That he took a bow in thanks at the end of his life, that he took a bow at the singular moment before everything happened, this was too big for José and Lázaro to hold inside.

But it was not the bow itself. Instead, it was the risk of such an act that mattered. It was not a risk in that there was danger; rather, the risk was in what people would think, and then say, in response to a true moment of simple and profound grace.

That was the risk finally: to give away something of the self, and hope that people would take it away with them, a little for each but plenty to go around.

Noé's was a most composed and methodical gesture of body at the end. His bones moved into position with a slowness and a balance, a perfect weariness, something in which his body was practiced.

At that moment, the circus was, after all, the most remarkable entertainment of the near-middle of the twentieth century, and he was, as promised, its star, whose fame would outlive the moon itself.

The bad joke of this all, of course, Lázaro would think later, is that, while the circus muscleman kept yelling for the two boys to give him a hand, finally it was his very own hand they saw as it flew through the air, not trapeze-like at all. They saw it taken from the stem of his arm and thrown like a rose flower to the floor of the bull-ring by what seemed to be the lady's hand of the elephant's trunk, that pink thing part inside of the gray glove.

Lázaro would remember how then it was as if the whole roar of the crowd, perhaps the roars of all the crowds Don Noé had ever heard through his ears, upon having his hand taken from him, suddenly came out through his mouth, as a scream.

That it was a hand and not an arm, this was the gesture of friendship, the terrible delicacy, the small detail conveyed in a whisper late at night when everyone else has gone home. A hand and not an arm. Only a friend takes that much.

At first, Lázaro would think, the sound had seemed borrowed, as if Noé had not himself ever had need of such a sound. But then it filled out, and became his to the end.

That night and the next day after the accident, there was of course an investigation.

Don Noé the Black Sheep, the owner called him, having heard it of someone who had once claimed to be a member of Noé's family. His people had lived for the most part farther north than the small towns in the jungles wherein the circus had traveled.

Neither would the owner give the last name of this Don Noé the Black Sheep, even after he died a little later from the bleeding, still in the arm of his elephant, who was sorry, and who wanted to help him—his only recourse being to keep everyone else away, to still be a wild and monstrous beast all around, but not at its center, not where it held Don Noé. It was wrong, but it was all the elephant could do, hold the man who had held him.

It was wrong for Don Noé because nobody could save him, and it was wrong for the elephant, who soon enough, because he would no longer eat, and no longer lift himself in song, shrank to the size of a large, hunched rabbit. It was wrong, but it was all he could do.

For some months, the new managers of the circus showed the elephant off that way, as much a marvel in this body as he was in the other.

But Saturnino died too, or rather, more disappeared than died, worn down like a stain on pants that at first seems like such a tragedy but which through use and washings begins to go away.

The actual night of the billed circus performance had been an affair of Byzantine triangles, between humans, between animals, sometimes with machines, and with glitter dust. There had been the obligatory wondrous throwing of impossible numbers of objects and children through the air. All the performers' hands in the air moved fast. White-gloved in the bad lighting, their hands seemed to make the bright lines of a campfire brand wave, quickly, through the air.

One expected the hands with their trailing lights to spell something, and they did, from childhood, from the practicing of penmanship, the many-o line, the o over and over, until the o took flight up into the stands, up into the crowds, onto the line of their mouths.

It was as if the hands of these performers were so fast in their movement that the movement itself was something of substance, so that with the flick of the wrist one of the white-faced harlequins spun an o out like a gentle bullet, like a moth, onto the mouths of the audience.

And the o took hold, like sugar from a doughnut, and followed into the throat, and therein lay the source of the sound of the room, so many o's, as if someone finally read all the lines from the penmanship books, read them as if they were lines from a play, oooo. It is the audience's part in the script, and the job was done well.

The night of the performance and the night subsequent, this was the circus after all, always fresh from the inhuman jungles of Chiapas and Tabasco, fresh from farther South still. After the erasure of Saturnino el Magnífico, the circus took on part of his elephant's great

back, some keepsake of his work, of his absolute pleasure and dis-
pleasure, and became *El Circo Magnífico* whose very name made
noise on the page.

They later added as a subtitle, *El Espectaculo de los Siglos*, and
later, *No Discounts*, but they had it right the first time.

This was the circus, and for the old strongman Don Noé there
was a new strongman, who did not yet have even a first name. But a
strongman, and soon, so as to fill in the need for a name, people
began to refer to this new man again as Don Noé, as if it were more
than a name for a man. As if it were a name for the job as well. A
level of rank. First the people called him in this way, and then the
other performers.

Don Noé was not, after all, there to object. He had never been
there to do anything but lift and move slowly, to heave and to groan.
To be at one with the object he was moving, almost as if it were
instead moving him. And here he was, his sounds sorted out once
more. Here he was, young and true again.

In later years Lázaro lost track of his friend José, who was with
him that night. But if he did not lose Don Noé, neither did he lose his
friend José. Nobody gets lost finally, he thought. And Lázaro would
find him, by walking backward in his sleep to that place. Lázaro like
José that way, a boy with the circus in town. It was a way to look at
himself. They are always good friends there.

There, there was popcorn and peanuts, and fried plantains rolled
in sugar, and *churros*, always something local, plum ices and God's-
beard. These things, and sadness.

A whole line of people came along the path to where the train had
derailed. A whole line of people who had gathered to watch this man
the night before stood in front of him once again. The men of the
town tried to help, but there was no opening. José and Lázaro had
gotten there first, and they were doing what could be done.

The men standing were carpenters and sweepers, a banker, the
twins who owned the clothing shop. No Tarzan leapt from beneath
their clothes, no surprise man in loincloth and leopard-skin hiding all
these years in the soul of a townsman who could sweep José or
Lázaro away and take care of this business as if it were something
simply bothersome, a nuisance of time.

And for the women as well there was no place. No mother of a mad bull elephant who knew its language, no orderer of a day's ingredients who could have made this, and so also know its remedy, its tea of mint for the stomach or mustard plaster for the dull fish-hooks of the raspy voice and the drowned chest.

Nor for those in between, who were something of a man and a woman both, and a child and a beast: those who were the capillaries of this town like all towns, those who allowed for the real and smooth interchange of words between the sexes, those who, as with the dances and sugar in coffee, had brought the circus in the first place.

Lázaro would remember being told later that no one had liked the Black Sheep Don Noé very much, who was rumored never to have slept since his arrival, not even at night. Don Noé, who almost never raised his eyes, as if that act in his life were the most difficult feat of all.

That was all the more a bargain, Lázaro later thought. Knowing they would get to go home, and that the stakes this night would be high, but not too high because they did not like him very much: Pure, simple, this life to death moment of Noé's wrestling with the Magnífico was a show, and everyone once again was in his audience, thrilled to the edge of disbelief, without harness.

Roaches

Abraham Rodriguez, Jr.

ABRAHAM RODRIGUEZ, JR. is a Puerto Rican-American who lives in the same Bronx neighborhood that he writes about. When he is not writing, he is a rock guitarist with his punk band named Urgent Fury. He attended City College of New York where he won first prize in the Goodman Fund Short Story Award three years in a row. He has been published in *Best Stories From New Writers* (Writers Digest Books, 1989) and his work has appeared in *Story Quarterly*. His collection of short stories, *The Boy Without a Flag: Tales of the South Bronx*, was published in June of 1992 by Milkweed Editions. He is currently working on a novel.

Annette was walking down the street when they grabbed her. She had gone to the cuchifritero's on the corner to get a pernil sandwich. She was walking back down the block to her building when this blue van pulled up. Its side door was open. Two guys jumped out and grabbed her. There wasn't much of a struggle, just a pathetic half-scream. All they left was the bag spinning on the sidewalk. The van sped away with a snarl of its tires.

Old Man Benitez saw the whole thing. He was sitting on a plastic milk crate right outside the bodega, as always.

"Incredible," he told his friend Quique, a local drunk. "I just sit here everyday. Can you believe the things I see? I tell you, it's better than television. Can you believe people pay to go see these things? And yet I can sit here and live the excitement. Remember last week, that shootout? The cars speeding by, the gun flashes like lightning from the windows, the screeching tires . . . I feel so fortunate to live in a time like this."

Joey was in the pool hall on Brook Avenue when he heard about it. The party was just getting started. He had been playing against one of the Ramos brothers, for the ass of Yolanda, who was sitting at the head of the pool table by the window, wearing jewelry belonging to both of them. Joey was two balls down when Smiley ran in and told him his wife had been grabbed.

Joey froze, his face framed by blue cigarette smoke squiggles. He smashed his pool cue against the side of the table, turning to stare at all the other posse boys in the house. There were Ramirez Brothers, there were Nasty Boy Crew members, there were TTG and FNB members, all along the wall, over by the bar, where the security man stood hawking beers to all the minors.

"Fucken shit," Joey screamed, "who fucken nabbed my wife."

There was silence. Louis, the Ramos brother he had been playing, grinned and shrugged. He was a short, nasty motherfucker, rumored to have blown down three mushrooms.

"If you need a excuse to stop playin', bro, thass cool," he said in his raspy beer voice, "Seein' as how you losin'. I'll jus' take care a' Yolanda for you."

"You hold it, man, it ain't through wif' us," Joey said, turning back to the others. "Now I wanna know who's in the house wants a shootin' war wif' my boys?"

"Maan, cut the shit," Leonard from FNB said, moving towards him. "You know there ain't nobody hea' would do that kinda shit."

The girls, sitting in a cluster near the back, began to chatter, then one of them says, "Damn Joey, you sure didn't take care a' yuh wife."

Joey swung towards the girls. "Yo," he yelled, "you guys ought teach yuh women t' know they place!"

"Lay off, man," Leonard said, handing him another pool cue. "Finish the fucken game. We got bets ridin' on this."

Joey snatched the stick. Twenty minutes later, Louis had buried him completely. There was cheering and yelling as Louis grabbed Yolanda and took her into the back room where there were cushions and stuff and they could be alone.

Then Joey went downstairs with Bobo, his lieutenant. Bobo handed him a joint.

"Anybody see anything?"

Bobo shook his head. "Nah. A van. Thass all."

They toked on the jay, staring at the traffic as it slowly made its way towards 138th Street. There was honking and voices yelling, people slowly browsing through the tables lining the streets outside the tiny storefronts, piled high with shoes, sneakers and clothes.

"This is bad," Bobo said. He had eyes like a beagle, sad and a little nervous. "I got David by the phone, jus' in case. He'll beep us if he gets word."

"We gotta keep the cops outta this right now," Joey said. "I'm gonna go talk t' huh parents."

"Man, she was pregnant, too," Bobo said, looking sorry.

Her parents lived in a tiny cluttered apartment on Southern Boulevard. They looked surprised to see Joey because he never visited them. The father was short and bald, with eyes that always squinted. The mother had wrinkled hands and a golden face that seemed molded by the mountains of Bayamon. Her hair was streaked with gray and resembled steel wool.

"What is it?" Annette's father asked as they led him into the living room, where he sat in a flower-pattern armchair that smelled like babies.

"It's about Annette," he said, clasping his hands, looking grave. "She's been kidnapped."

The mother let out a tiny scream, sitting on the sofa that was the same flower pattern as the armchair.

"What do you mean?"

Joey cursed. His Spanish wasn't so good. "They grabbed her is what I mean. But I know who did it and she's gonna be okay."

Annette's father stared at him, his eyes glistening. "Did you tell the police?"

"No. An' don't tell 'um," he said in English, his finger in the old man's face. "This is a posse matta'. Business. It's gonna be okay."

"My poor baby," the mother wailed, "she's with child!"

Joey got up. "Jus' don't call the cops."

Annette's father shut the door behind him. Then he picked up the phone. He dialed 911 and stood there with the phone to his ear, unable to talk. He slowly hung up the phone.

"I can't talk," he said, his voice breaking. "We have to find Maribel so she can call."

The cops came later. There were two of them, a white one and a Hispanic one. They were in plain clothes. Shaw was a big man, with a quick snappy voice, words spat out in staccato bursts. He had light green eyes that blazed with so many fires that they could be unsettling. He sometimes chomped on an old cigar, but that was just an affectation. He had quit smoking three months ago. He had six large packs of Juicy Fruit in his sports jacket.

Sanchez was smaller in stature, his voice soft, his skin dark, hair like a plush rug on the top of his head. He was wearing a gray double-breasted suit with a vest. He looked nice, but Shaw thought he was crazy. Shaw left his jacket in the car and was only in his rolled-up shirtsleeves. He already looked tired and sweaty. He stepped out of that car and walked up and down the block like he was going to hurt somebody, Sanchez writing notes into his flip pad. They both talked to the people in the cuchifritero's, the auto shop, the bodega. Finally they both stood in front of Old Man Benitez, Quique hovering nearby.

"I don't believe this shit," Shaw was saying, mostly to himself. He had his huge hands on his hips as he looked down on Old Man Benitez, sitting there on his milk crate. "So old man, compadre, tell me what you saw here."

Old Man Benitez blinked uncomprehendingly, leaning forward a little.

Sanchez translated. "Can you tell us if you saw anything?"

Old Man Benitez sat up. "I see everything on this street, do you know that? I sit here every day. At least in the summer I do. And some of the fall. Spring maybe. You know it has been getting warmer all around, so I can spend more time sitting here. Also, I have stolen these 3-D glasses from my nephew," he said, taking them out of his shirt pocket, "so as to add to the effect."

"Sure. But did you see anything here today?"

Shaw was fanning himself with a flip pad.

"Oh, is this about this shootout the other day? I tell you, that was amazing. The young boy came racing down Fox Street. He had an automatic rifle. He fired in my direction. The 3-D glasses made it look as if the bullets were coming straight for me."

"A girl was kidnapped from this very sidewalk today," Sanchez said patiently, his voice therapeutic, as if talking to a child. "Did you happen to see that?"

"A girl? Kidnapped? Here? Today?" Old Man Benitez scratched his oily head. "I don't think so, no. I didn't see a thing. I'm sorry. Perhaps I was having a sandwich at that moment."

Sanchez looked at Quique, who shrugged. "No see nothen," he said.

"You don't gotta fucken translate," Shaw said angrily, whapping Sanchez on the head with his flip pad. "We been gettin' the same shit all along this damn street. You tellin' me that a little after noon, with all these people out hea', nobody saw anything?" His voice was rising.

"Take it easy, Shaw," Sanchez said.

"Take it easy?" he bellowed. He looked down the street and saw three posse boys approaching. His nostrils flared. Something in his eyes started burning. "This is a pregnant sixteen-year-old girl we're talking about. Don't any of these people have any sense of outrage?"

"You stop. The way you shoot off your mouth, I can see why they haven't let you out from behind the desk for two years."

Shaw looked at him. "Did you read my file?"

"No. But everybody in Missing Persons thinks you're insane. When I got tagged with you, they said good-bye to me. They give me condolence cards. Becky, that pretty blond from statistics? She sent me flowers."

Shaw shook his head. "You ever work in narcotics?" There was a challenge flashing in his eyes.

"No."

"Then you stop criticizing. Pick up some pointers. Now can you tell me why everybody says they don't know anything?"

"I guess it's a fear kind of thing, man."

"Very good. Now you see why I was pulled off the streets, right? I don't accept any of this shit. Sometimes I think people are born with elm trees stuck up their asses."

"No. There is a definite someone shoving these elm trees up people's asses. That is why there is fear."

The three posse boys stood in front of them like some kind of committee. It was strange, to see these three boys in their baggy clothes, their baseball caps and gold chains, squaring off like gunfighters. Sanchez looked at Shaw because he felt a little nervous, somehow, but Shaw was smiling. He was holding the tiny photo of Annette that her father had given him when they had first talked to the parents, just a preliminary invest' talk. He held up the picture, flicking it so the posse boys could see it.

"Now ain't that pretty?" he asked, his voice thick. "I was just about to ask you young men if any of you knew this sweet girl."

"She's my wife," Joey said. He was standing in the middle, flanked by Bobo and this guy called Cleveland, because his family moved here from Cleveland.

Shaw suddenly pounced. It even caught Sanchez unaware.

"Shaw!" But Shaw couldn't hear him.

He pushed Joey back up against the brick wall by the bodega, one hand curled around his neck. The two posse boys started yelling, but Shaw pointed a finger at them. "Now you boys just step back and gimme some room," he said. "I need to talk to your master craftsman for a second."

Joey was making gurgling sounds, his face contorted. "Assho'," he said, "eitha' choke me o' shoo' me but make up yuh mine, yuh wrinklin' m' Raiders shirt."

Shaw showed his teeth like he was about to take a spit. "Little Joey. Don't I got you scoped out? My little drug dealer, we got us a lot to talk about. What, you think I'm from Missing Persons? Baby, I'm from Narcotics. I got you all checked out on my radio. Don't think I won't bash the brains out of your head right now, you little fuck. You're just a two-bit wet-nose punk."

"Shaw!" Sanchez pulled on his shoulder, made him back off. Joey stood there, straightening his shirt. "You feel betta'?" he asked, his eyes showing no emotion, just blank dots on a face that looked like someone used it for a hockey puck.

"Okay, Joey," Shaw said, like he was hosting Romper Room, flipping open his pad. "How old are you?"

Joey shrugged. "I'm older than you know."

"Smart kid. Fresh mouth. I like that in a police brutality victim. You're seventeen. Got nabbed six times. Petty theft, possession, resisting arrest, concealed weapon . . . a screwdriver. Now what are you doing with a screwdriver, ah? Haven't got your Uzi yet?"

"Jus' 'cause I wasn't caught wif' one don't mean I don't got one."

Shaw turned to Sanchez, grinning. "See that? They always talk back. Lis'sen, you dirty punk. I know you're dealing. I know what you're doing. The more we stand here and chat, the more familiar you're starting to seem."

"You gonna fin' my wife, or bore me t' death?"

"Your wife. Jesus Christ." He laughed, poked Sanchez on the chest. "He gets some baby broad, shuts her up in an apartment, calls her his wife. She's in there having babies while he's out fucking around with other babes. That's a good set-up, I like it, man, you got this shit licked. Now you shut your trap with the wise-ass remarks and tell me who you think did this."

"I don't know who did it," Joey said angrily. "I don't got so many enemies."

Shaw laughed out loud, coming up close to him. "Maybe you recently made a big drug deal. Maybe somebody didn't like it. Does that jar any memories loose? I mean, could that be a possibility?"

Joey looked over Shaw's shoulder, at Sanchez. "Hey, brotha'," he said, "you should get this white cop to calm down wif' this shit."

"Shut up and answer his question," Sanchez said.

"I tol' ju, I don't know."

"Yeah, you look like an idiot. How about your posse boys? Huh? You had your wife out here and nobody was out to protect her?"

"We were playing pool," Bobo said, his face cringing.

Shaw took out his cigar stub and put it in his mouth. There was a stain on the shirt pocket from it. "I want you," he said, holding up two fingers, "to stay right here. You don't move from here 'til we get back."

Joey scowled as they walked off towards Southern Boulevard.

"Man, this is bullshit," Bobo said, but Joey didn't seem to hear him. His eyes were glassy and distant, his lips moving as if he were doing math in his head.

"Are we in trouble?" Cleveland asked, tugging on Joey's sleeve. Joey smirked, looking at him like he was an idiot. "You kiddin'? We the joint now, man. The joint."

Old Man Benitez slapped his thighs with his wrinkled hands, his 3-D glasses almost sliding off his thin nose. "Man! The plot thickens. Kidnappings, plots, cops, police brutality. This is better than Kojak!"

"I may never watch TV again," Quique said, though with less conviction.

They climbed the three flights of stairs back to Annette's parents. The first time they saw them, the parents seemed too shaken to really talk. They sat on the couch like tiny kewpie dolls, clutching each other. Now they seemed a little better, as if seeing the cops doing their thing gave them hope. This time too, their other daughter Maribel was there. She was a short, long-haired girl covered in huge baggy clothes.

The first thing Shaw did when he came in was stare at Maribel, smiling a little. He took the wallet-size photo of Annette out and looked at it. It was a pretty face on there, the skin smooth and dark like tapioca pudding, the hazel eyes jumping out as if three-dimensional, sparkling with a kind of happiness. It was all innocence and charm, the smile making her look a little vulnerable. "Pretty," he said, feeling something sad, and then he looked at Maribel. "You look a lot like your sister."

"Thank you," she said without feeling.

"How do you feel about your sister getting nabbed?"

"Bad," Maribel said, her eyes not really looking at him. Shaw immediately picked up on it. He came closer.

"You're younger," he said. "How much younger?"

"I'm thirteen," she said, her eyes darting around, one sneakered foot resting on top of the other. Her limbs seemed listless and bored.

"Do you know what your sister was into?" Shaw's voice was getting a little hard. They were all watching him now, the parents looking uncomfortable.

Maribel shrugged.

"I said, do you know what your sister was into?"

"I don't know," she said, starting to back away a little. Shaw came right up to her and grabbed her by the wrist, holding it up so that the three gold bracelets slid down to her elbow, clattering and clanging.

"Oh yeah," he whispered, "I think you know what your sister was into. I think you know pretty well. Who got you the jewelry, honey?" He was still holding her wrist. Sanchez, across from her parents, stared at Shaw with large eyes.

"A friend," she said, not looking at him.

"This jewelry tells me you're somebody's property. I hope you're gonna think about this." Shaw's eyes were big and nervous, his lip quivering. "Unless you wanna end up like your sister." He let go of her wrist. When she turned up her eyes to look at him, they were ugly, twisted eyes, belonging on the face of a veteran of foreign wars.

"Necks time why don'chu put a lamp in my face an' interrogate me," she sneered, leaving the room, slamming a door hard.

Sanchez was sitting in the armchair, the parents staring at him.

"You ask them," Shaw said, whipping around to face them, "if they know their daughter is involved with a crack dealer who is seventeen years old."

Sanchez asked. "Yes," he answered for them, continuing to translate.

"Did your daughter tell you?"

"No," the father said, looking helpless as he massaged his hands, veins showing. "At first he was just a boy. The change came when she decided to live with him. By this time she was already pregnant."

"And you just let her live with him?" Shaw's voice was a mixture of scorn and anger. Sanchez looked at him disapprovingly for a moment before he translated.

"There was nothing we could do," the father said, face wrinkling up. "We didn't want her to go. But her mind was made up. She was going to live with him. We felt, well, at least the boy wants to live up to his responsibilities. So she moved. Three months ago."

"Did you see much of her?" Sanchez asked softly while Shaw flicked his tongue over his lips.

"I saw her a few times," the mother said, her voice cracked into chunks. "I would go over and see her." She fought the tears, but she was losing, the sobs sneaking up on her. "I would bring her food."

The father looked at Shaw, and said in English, "She no good cooken."

"So I would bring her food and blankets and things. They didn't have anything in that apartment. A mattress on the floor. Milk crates. The only big thing was the video game in living room, a big one. It was a Ms. Pac Man. She loved that game. He got her a big one. She never had to put quarters in."

Shaw was standing there, his hand wrinkling up his lips as he thought.

"Last time you talked to her?"

The mother wiped her eyes carefully. "Last Tuesday. She called to say she was bored and lonely. That she missed us." The sobs came now, and she wailed, falling into her husband's arms. Shaw's face was a mixture of anger and compassion. Sanchez had never seen anything like it.

"Did she ever," Shaw said softly, kneeling down beside them, "say that she was in any danger?"

"No."

"He was sometimes," the mother said. "Sometimes he would be missing for days and days. She would tell me, be all worried and crying, crying. Then she'd go look for him, and find him drunk at the pool hall."

Shaw rose up, his face disgusted. He touched both of them, the father on the shoulder, the mother on her arm. "We will try our best," and that was it.

They went to the apartment Annette lived in, Joey letting them in. It was a three room job, spacious in its own way, yet the walls looked weak and about to collapse. There was no ceiling in the bathroom, pipes and wooden beams showing like the ribs on a corpse. There was indeed an arcade game in the living room, surrounded by couch cushions (but no couch) and bean bags. Shaw hit the button, began playing a game, his tongue poking out of one side of his face as he wrestled with the joy stick.

"Damn, I always hated this shit," he said, his face seeming to glisten from the screen. "You're quite a man, getting your girlfriend a game so she could play."

"What the hell," Joey shrugged. He too was looking around the apartment like he hadn't been in it for months.

"Why didn't you get her some fucking furniture?" The little meanies trapped his Ms. Pac Man for the last time. She wilted, and Shaw smacked the machine.

"It wasn't gonna be permanent," Joey said.

In the bedroom, a mattress on the floor, cheap curtains in the windows, tied with girlish ribbons. A few stuffed animals sat on the mattress, looking forlorn and a little scared.

Shaw came up to Joey. "Gimme your beeper," he said, moving in on him like an oncoming truck. Joey backed up some.

"How come, man—"

"Gimme your beeper."

Joey lifted his shirt, unclipped it, handed it over. Shaw looked at it, smiled and then he bashed it against the wall, bits and pieces of it clattering down everywhere. He handed Joey what was left.

"I don't think it's going to be business as usual for you," he said, now pointing to Sanchez. "You give him a place I can reach you twenty-four hours a day, you little punk, or I'll show up at the pool hall you go to and stick a stungun up your ass."

They were sitting in their car with the air conditioner on full blast.

They were outside the restaurant on Hunt's Point with the golden
arches. Shaw ordered three plain cheeseburgers and was methodically
shoving them into his mouth as though trying to keep his mouth full
so he wouldn't have to talk. Sanchez, sitting behind the wheel, took
two bites of his quarter-pounder, then sat there staring at it.

"Do you know that this restaurant owns eighty percent of the
arable land in Honduras? They keep it from the people so they can
feed their cows so they can kill them so we can eat them. Half the
country is starving, and we—"

"Shut up with that," Shaw said, his voice muffled by burger.

"But don't it bother you that we make half the world starve so we
can eat this shit?"

Shaw put down a half-munched burger. "I'll tell you what fucken
bothers me. It bothers me that parents sit there like victims, letting
their kids run off with other kids, saying they couldn't help it. Letting
their daughters get pregnant at sixteen so they can live in a hole with
some teen monster. Does that bother you? Is there something special
about you people I don't understand?"

Sanchez sighed. "I really don't like the way you talk. Why don't
you try growing up here on these streets?"

"Tell me a parent can't discipline a kid, can't teach them right or
wrong!"

"Don't you talk about that!" Sanchez suddenly screamed. "There
are plenty of hard working parents out there bringing up their kids
despite this. And some of those kids even become cops."

Shaw sighed. He didn't know this guy Sanchez too good. They
never worked together. He was Missing Persons, Shaw was Narcotics. The nature of the crime—the drug connection—brought them
together. Shaw had never hung out with Sanchez. The closest they
ever came to that was that time when Shaw was drunk and hanging
out on Junction Boulevard and he happened to remember Sanchez
lived near there. He looked the guy up, got to meet his wife, got to sit
in the cellar, where Sanchez showed him his dozens of shoeboxes
filled with old baseball cards. That was the only real human thing
about Sanchez Shaw could relate to. So far.

"I'm sorry," Shaw said, breathing heavy. He watched the people
moving down the boulevard, black kids under a sports store awning
sharing a joint, two lovers sharing a slice and kisses by the flashing
neon sign screaming PIZZA PIZZA. "Look, man, I shouldn't be out on

the street. You know that. It's been the talk for a long time, hasn't it?"

"No."

"Come on."

"I'm saying no, man, I was joking. Nobody thinks you're nuts. I don't know you. I only heard little things here and there."

"Like what?"

"Like that Shaw, man, he's a hard working cop."

Shaw sucked on his milk shake. It was vanilla. It made a funny gurgling sound.

"I shouldn't be out here, Sanchez. You should. All the time. You're calm. You can take it in. Me, I'm losing my head. I can't accept it, I just can't. A pretty little girl like that. And her sister, did you see her? She's headed down the same road."

"You're a good cop, Shaw. That went right past me, man. You know your job. You should be out here."

"No, you're wrong," Shaw said, pointing his shake at him. "You're fucken wrong. I can't even look at this. My guts get all twisted. These people, they . . . that face on that kid, Joey. Did you look at him? Seventeen years old, he looks like he fought in Korea. My pop fought in Korea, he didn't look like that. They don't got no feeling. Numb. They act like they're alive, but they're not. Can't get feelings out of these kids. They're like insects. You ever see roaches, when you squash them? No screams, nothing. They look up at you as if they don't see you."

"It's the conditions they grow up in."

"Aw man, why ain't you shell-shocked then? You grow up in the South Bronx?"

"Right on Cypress Avenue. But man, I had great parents. Actually, I still do, they're on the island."

Shaw didn't say anything. Sanchez put the remainder of his quarter-pounder back into its Styrofoam container.

"You know why I was pulled off the street?" Shaw suddenly asked.

"No." Sanchez finished his soda, making slurping noises, the ice clattering around. "Was it maybe your temper?"

Shaw laughed softly. "Yeah," he whispered.

There was a silence. They watched a bus pick up passengers down the block.

"You'll be all right," Sanchez said.

"I bashed a kid's head against the wall. I bashed it and I bashed it. Chased that little fuck for ten blocks. He had my name on his back, no way I was gonna let him get away. I grabbed him and I pounded him against the wall. Almost cracked his head open like a walnut." He licked his lips. "He was a black kid. They made it this racist thing. But you know what? Those black people on the street should've thanked me for cracking his head open. They should've thanked me. That kid was selling junk to their children in grade school." He looked at Sanchez, his face a mixture of scorn and tragedy. Sanchez pressed his lips together with his fingers as if trying to twist them off his face.

"That Joey boy gets under my nuts," he said, cracking his knuckles.

"Let's find this girl," Sanchez said, starting the car.

Three days later they found Annette. She was lying in a trash bag in an empty lot on Fox Street. She was cut up real bad. Shaw and Sanchez had driven right over there, but when they saw her, their faces changed. They had both seen dead bodies before. This was just their first teenage girl. And she was pregnant, too.

"Those bastids had a real field day with her tummy," Shaw said, looking up and down the street, squinting at the sunlight. Around them were police officers, sealing off the area, carefully combing the area around the body. A man with plastic gloves on was removing stuff off the ground with tweezers and putting it in a plastic baggy. Cops kept pulling the garbage bag down so they could look. Shaw kept catching glimpses of her flowing brown hair, all squiggles and coils.

"Who called it in?" Shaw asked a police officer standing next to him, a tall man with pink skin and a bushy mustache.

"This woman there, she was walking her dog along here. She let him loose. The dog found it."

Shaw was munching three sticks of gum at once. He was thinking of going over there, but he couldn't move. He felt really tired. The woman was standing by the curb, clutching the leash on her dog, a brown mutt with gorgeous hazel eyes, who sat there watching everything with a pleased dog smile. Shaw could already imagine her fractured English: "I no see nothen." Nobody saw anything. He walked over and petted the dog, who flattened its ears to accommodate his hand, its nose sniffing up his cuff. Sanchez began to question her, his Spanish a gentle poetic sound. From the way she was shaking her head, Shaw already knew. He walked up to one of the police officers.

"Sergeant, can I have a cigarette?" The sergeant nodded and handed him a pack. Shaw held it for a minute, looking at it. He tapped its side and one nice smooth cigarette slid out, almost right into his hand.

"Is that a cigarette, lieutenant?" Sanchez was standing right beside him. Shaw looked at him and muttered something Sanchez didn't hear.

"Thank you, sergeant," Shaw said, handing back the cigarettes.

"I wonder what Joey boy's gonna think now," Sanchez said, offering Shaw a Starburst. It was a green one.

"I only like orange," Shaw said. Sanchez riffled through the pack, ripping it. He handed him an orange one. "Yeah," Shaw said, making smacking sounds as the candy landed in his mouth, already full of flavorless gum. "I can't wait to see that little bastid's face."

By law, Joey shouldn't be the one to identify Annette, because you always shoot for next of kin. This means the parents. Shaw didn't care about that. He would've spared them if he could, but he couldn't. There was no way he'd spare Joey. He wanted him in there, wanted to see his face slide, melt, disintegrate into pieces. He even wanted Maribel there, to show her what was waiting for her, but he couldn't do that. So he stood there by the slab where they had put Annette, wrapped in some kind of plastic bag. He had looked at her for a long time under the harsh blue light, cigarette smoke climbing up past his face, the graying hair around his temples. He stood there like a miniature volcano, exhaling blue smoke.

"Noooo, Dio' mio, noooo!" Annette's mother screamed, falling into her husband's arms. He too seemed on the verge of falling, Sanchez standing beside them like a strong Doric column. Her cries echoed and echoed forever. Shaw's face showed no emotion, his eyes glinting as if watery, probably from the cigarette smoke which swirled around his face.

"You bring that little bastid in now," Shaw said, amidst the dying echoes of a mother's pain. He tossed one flaming cigarette away and lit another just as Sanchez escorted Joey in, the boy clad in loose-fitting clothes, his walk a kind of strut that was arrogant and haughty. He came right up to where Annette was, and then he stopped to look at Shaw standing there surrounded by cigarette smoke.

"Yo mo," he said, as if greeting someone he knew.

"You didn't come here to see me. You take a good look at your wife." He stepped forward, the light harsher as he lifted back the plastic with a loud crackle. "Congratulations, big man."

Joey looked down at Annette. Shaw could imagine the stages now: first, the searching, bewildered eyes, then the sudden flash of recognition, the horror, the searching, bewildered eyes, then the horror spreading, disintegrating that rock-hard face. He was waiting for it, but Joey's face didn't register a thing. It remained unmoved, the eyes blank. It was like he was looking down on some squashed roach.

"That's it?" Shaw screamed. "This is your wife, you fuck! Don't you even feel anything?"

"Shaw," Sanchez said softly, coming around the table.

"Business is business," Joey said, looking right at him.

Shaw felt those waves hit him, the ones that made him want to grab that thin pulsing throat and squeeze the life from it, rid the world of one more empty shell. He felt nauseous. It could've been all those cigarettes. Sanchez was suddenly squeezing his arm.

"Let me put it to you this way," Sanchez said, his voice softly reverberating in the large cool room. "This guy I know gets into a heavy deal with some heavy dudes. Other heavy dudes hear about it. They warn him. They say either you drop that shit or something's gonna happen. This guy I know, he tells them to fuck off. Maybe you know this guy?" Sanchez stepped closer to the table, replacing the crackling plastic. "So these dudes come back and they tell him, Yo, you put that deal through, we'll kill your wife."

Joey smirked. He buried his hands in his pockets.

"This guy I know," Sanchez continued, working his way around the table to come face to face, "he told them, Fuck you man, you can't hurt me. He put through the deal. He made about sixty thousand dollars. From this one deal, man. That's a pretty good trade, isn't it?"

Shaw stared at Sanchez like he was crazy. Joey's eyes darted from Shaw to Sanchez, a strange grin twitching on his lips.

"You kiddin', right? Thass a crazy story."

"Well, maybe your friend Bobo is a good writer," Sanchez said, now so close he could smell the kid's morning mouth.

"Bobo? Get the fuck. You fulla shit."

"He liked Annette. I had a good talk with him."

"Bullshit. Bobo's always wif' me!" His eyes darted about uncertainly. He stepped back, then his face changed again, back to a hard consistency. "You can't make somethin' up like that. Thass crazy. Tha' won't stick."

"We'll see about that," Shaw said, "when we go visit your pals in the FNB and the TTG. And those Ramos Brothers, I'm sure they just love you."

"Sink or swim, motherfucker. You make me ashamed to be a Hispanic. Get your ass out of here. I think we'll be seeing more of each other as the weeks progress. I think I'll get a room ready for you and your friends at Riker's Hilton." Sanchez' voice took on a hard viciousness that Shaw hadn't heard before.

Joey grinned. "Yeah. Right. Dream on." He turned and walked out with the hopping street gait which made him look like he was going to do a dance.

"Damn, you're something else," Shaw said to Sanchez, who tried to grin but couldn't seem to.

"Let's get this poor girl put away now," he said.

Shaw took that wallet-sized photo and put it up on the bulletin board by his desk. It was still there two weeks later, half-buried by memos and stat sheets. By that time, thanks to an anonymous tip, they had found the car that had delivered her body to the lot. The car had been stolen. It was traced to an auto shop on Bruckner Boulevard, a fencing operation for stolen cars. Six arrests. That led to a lot of bargaining, and some information about where the car came from. Three boys from a well known posse down Prospect Avenue were nabbed. Shaw stood in front of them the day they were brought in, snatching their hats, pulling off their gold chains.

"You been demoted, boys," he told them, hating them. "We're looking for your prints. As soon as we find them on Annette, we'll start to play some real hardball." But there was never a connection to the boys, the link with the car grew dubious when it became clear people were yapping just to save their asses. Soon, the suspects evaporated again. Every night for a month after that, Sanchez had to pull Shaw away from his desk.

"Closing time," he would tell him.

"But I'm not finished," he would say, his head heavy, his eyes red.

And Sanchez would buy him a drink and call him, "My compai'." A compai' is almost more than a brother.

Joey elected himself another wife. She was a skinny girl named Vicki. She was already wearing some of his jewelry, but this other girl named Edie had jewelry too. She didn't like being a runner-up, so she waited for him outside the building on Prospect where Annette used to live. (He gave Vickie the same apartment.) When he showed up one night, she pulled a .22 on him, but she was too dramatic about it and shot herself in the thigh.

"Oh shit," she said, the shock draining color from her tanned face, "I shot myself."

The gun clattered to the sidewilk. Ramon picked it up and belted her in the face with it several times, just to remind her who he was. She was lying there rolling on the sidewalk, and the rest of the posse was kicking her, all except Bobo, whose face looked jagged and broken. He shook his head and walked off down the street.

"Wow!" Old Man Benitez yelled in English. He turned to Quique, who stood beside him, cringing a little, his face shocked. Old Man Benitez leaned forward on his crate, adjusting his 3-D glasses. "I don't believe it! Look at them beat her! Carajo man, they would never show this on TV! Ouch! That was a good one!"

"I'm calling the police," Quique said in a quivering voice, no longer drunk.

"Yes, call them! Sex, women, shootings, beatings, police . . . Holy Mother, I can't believe this country! I'm the luckiest man in the world!"

Abuela Marielita

Cecilia Rodríguez-Milanés

CECILIA RODRÍGUEZ-MILANÉS was born in Jersey City, New Jersey, to Cuban parents. In 1982 she received a B.A. in Creative Writing at the University of Miami, with an MA in English at Barry University in 1985. Most recently she has earned a Doctor of Arts degree from the State University of New York at Albany. She has published her fiction and poetry in many literary magazines and reviews. Her most recent fiction is a collection of short stories based on Marielitos in Miami entitled *Exiles and Outcasts*.

My daughter doesn't want people to know that I came through the port of Mariel so she tells them that I came by way of Spain in January 1980, four months before I actually arrived en los cayos. In the beginning, Gertrudes and Miguel didn't care, the first year it was fine to say that I came on a boat not a jet, something I've never done. I used to like to tell people about the nice young man who took me and the others on his speedboat, such an enchanting boy, so happy that the guards had found his aunt and uncle, his only family left in Cuba. He said he didn't care that we others weren't parientes of his, as long as Chelita y Tatín were on the boat, although he had tried to find a sister of one of his neighbor's, her name was Ester Ramirez, but that's all, just three people were on his list. Ah, que muchacho más bueno. He had been in Mariel Harbor waiting four days when his tíos were brought to the pier, imagine, not knowing if they would be able to go and all. I rode on the bus with them though I didn't know them at the time, of course. I was staying with my cousin's son and his wife in a section of the house I used to own before the revolution, and Jorgito, that's my prima's son, was making arrangements to get on the list to leave. Well, if they were leaving I wasn't going to be of any use to anyone. My mother died when I was pregnant and her only living brother went to Santiago with his wife's family. I didn't have any parientes left in La Habana, so what did I have to stay for? My daughter was in Miami and my son José Angel died as a young man in Playa Girón, I had no reason to stay in Cuba at all. Oh, I wanted to be with my daughter so much, pobrecita, after so many years, she didn't have anyone in Miami. It's true that Miguel's family is very large but that day Jorgito said that I had to decide right away and I did. I slept on it and prayed to the Virgins (both la Caridad del Cobre and Nuestra Señora de las Mercedes—one of my namesakes) to help me and they did. In three days some guards came to the house to get me, by then Jorgito y Lola were gone, poor things, God knows where they ended up. I gave him my daughter's address, but I've never heard anything from him. I believe his wife had some family in Tampa but Gertrudes says that's very far from Miami, although I know it's still in Florida because I found it in one of my granddaughter's books when I was cleaning her room. Well, anyway, after the first year or so, there were so many of us here and it was not popular to help Marielitos anymore. Things got very bad. One day I was darning some of my son-in-law's socks in the Florida room towards the rear of the house and I heard a big boom! My heart almost stopped; I thought it was a bomb but it was the front door that was knocked down. Right in the middle of broad daylight, there was this big empty moving truck parked right on the lawn and two men standing there ready to steal everything in the house. Que descarados! I yelled at them and they just calmly got back into their truck and drove away. Of course, I was very frightened. That's when Gertrudes and Miguel decided to move from La Pequeña Habana out to Westchester. That's also when they told me not to say anything about being an exile from Mariel. My daughter won't even let me speak about it in front of my grandchildren Marcos y Graciela either, though I'm sure la niña knows something, because she was already talking when I arrived, but even she doesn't say anything. She speaks non-stop English anyway; I can't hardly understand her sometimes. The little one, Marcos, has no idea of course; he'll be six soon.

My yerno, Miguel, owns a glass store on Flagler Street, the Cristalería Siboney, and Gertrudes works in an office for the county—a very good job with benefits for her, Miguel and the children. I go to the Cuban clinic for the doctor because her insurance doesn't cover me but I don't mind because I see so many of my friends there, especially now when I go every week for my terápia—my wrist feels much better. I twisted it while pulling Marcos away from the American man's dog next door. The dog had the ball Marcos threw over the fence in its mouth and the child was trying to pull it out and through the fence. Well, the dog wanted to play too, but children can be so bad sometimes, thanks to God, the boy is fine. After that, Miguel put up a wooden fence that blocks the view of the other neighbors' yards, a shame because Josefina and her husband have such lovely gardenia bushes and the neighbors's patio to the rear of us, the Lópezes, has banana and papaya plants that remind me of my own patio in Cuba. When I was newly married and my mother was still alive, I used to grow jazmínes and dahlias in the courtyard, I haven't seen any dahlias here though.

The new house my daughter and son-in-law bought has an apartment in the back; actually it's a little room, but I guess for one person it's fine. A few months after we had moved here and all the neighbors got to know us (and not know too much about me, of course) the room was rented to an older señora. She kept me company sometimes during the day, while I took care of the children, and Lord knows I could use Ofelia's, that's her name, help. Ese Marcos es un ciclón! Gracielita is no saint, either. Pobrecita Ofelia, what a kind soul, she couldn't take care of herself after a while, kept falling down and not being able to get back up, so her sons, God forgive them, put her in one of those hospitals where they are supposed to take care of old folks. She was only six or seven years older than me and I'm 72. She was such a good listener too.

I meant to talk about Yamile and maybe I steered away from the subject at times but forgive me because I'm an old woman. Yamile came through Mariel also and moved into the cuartico behind the house after Ofelia left. She was very fat for such a young woman, so my daughter didn't notice that she was pregnant although I could tell by her look almost immediately; it was the look of a woman with child. Miguel wanted to evict her when he found out, but when Luz came, the baby, she slept almost all night, so he could not complain too much; besides with the windows closed, you can't hear a thing anyway. Gertrudes doesn't like Yamile and treats her very rudely, something I lament very much because I have come to care for her and the baby, poor things. At first, Gertrudes did not mind that I was talking to Yamile, although sometimes she made little comments about Yamile and her being on welfare and only working part-time at the farmacia near us. But then again, she couldn't say too much because Yamile always pays her rent on time and in full. She doesn't know, of course, that I give her a little hand with my food stamps ever since they gave me more. I never told my daughter that I get $60 and not $40—I'm always here when la cartera comes; we have a woman to deliver the mail, isn't that something? Nice girl. Plus, whenever they give out cheese or powdered milk, I always give Yamile some. She needs it much more than we do and my grandchildren don't eat that cheese. They like the store-bought wrapped squares better. Anyway, Miguel has his own business which is doing well and my daughter makes a good salary. I shouldn't even be taking the stamps but my daughter says they pay taxes for them and we might as well take them. I don't say anything about it anymore.

Yamile has been living here almost a year now and Luz is just a little doll. I spend a lot of time with her now that both of the children are going to San Bernardo's. To me, Luz is like my own grandchild because I've been with her since birth. Yamile leaves her with me in the mornings when she goes to work. Most of the time the baby just sits and plays in the crib while I prepare the dinner or fold the clothes. She doesn't talk yet so we haven't cut her hair; it's long in the back but kind of thin on top, angelita, she'll look better when it all grows in. In the morning when it's still not so hot, after everyone's gone, Luz and I go to the patio to hang up the clothes. She watches from that baby swing Marcos used to love so much. My daughter was throwing it out before I stopped her. I hang the clothes because I really don't like to use the clothes dryer. It's so much better to sun the things and let them blow in the breeze; they smell so much nicer too. Gertrudes finally stopped fussing about it when Miguel said that they would save on the electricity. They spend so much already with the air conditioners on from the time they walk in the door until they leave the next day. I always turn them off (they have five!) when they're gone and open all the windows; I don't even sleep with the one in my room on though my daughter can't understand. The fan is really just fine for me; I tell her that the air conditioner gives me a sore throat. The children know how to turn them on and it's the second thing they do, after they turn on the television, the minute that bus drops them off and they run through the door. I only like to watch my novella in the evening; it's the same one my daughter watches so I can watch it on the big screen. I'd really rather listen to the radio during the day though. It seems that the television is on almost as much as the air conditioner sometimes and of course, la niña has her own little color t.v. in her room. Marcos is starting to ask for another one, so my son-in-law promised him a color set for his birthday if he brings home a good report card this term, I don't understand, but I don't say anything, because he is their father and I don't want him to say that I meddle, like I heard him say one time when I was going to bed. Anyway, Luz and me, we hang the clothes together and sometimes I'll sing to her, she's such a happy baby. I'm enjoying her much more than I did Marcos because I was always worrying about what Gracielita was doing the minute I turned away, what a child, that one, always into everything. I'm sure half my gray hairs belong to her.

It was a very hard thing for me to find Yamile in the condition she was in when I went to take her a plate of food from Marcos' fifth birthday party. They had set up the patio with rented chairs and tables and there were trays and trays of pasteles Cubanos filled with guayaba, queso y carne; sandwichitos of sweet ham with jelly and cheese or a creamy meat paste—I love those. And they ordered a huge blue and white sheet cake with those little robots, the cartoon ones that Marcos watches all the time; he has them all over the house. His parents got him a piñata in the shape of one of them, oh, what does he call them? Something of el universo, I don't remember now, but he even had a costume for that fiesta the North Americans have in October. Bueno, I'll remember it later. There was music and all of the neighbor families were invited; even the man from next door, Miguel said we had better invite him or he would call the police about the music which was way too loud because Gracielita and her amiguitas would change to an American station and turn up the volume whenever they got the chance, though they never did dance to it anyway.

There were so many people there besides the neighbors' children and kids from San Bernardo's. There was Miguel's family from Hialeah, all of them. Even a first cousin of his that came via Mariel, but he didn't say anything to her, imagine, not even hello. There were a couple more North Americans too from my daughter's job, though they left right away after we cut the cake. Probably got bored talking to themselves; the neighbor man left early too. It was already in the evening when people were serving themselves more arroz con pollo. By then it had cooled off and oh, there were tamales too and I made a big aluminum tray of potato and chicken salad. I spelled Marcos' name on top with pimento slices but he never saw it. He was too busy riding around all afternoon on the bicycle that Miguel bought him or running in and out of the house showing friends the new game tapes he got for his t.v. even though Gertrudes told him not to bring kids into the house. They didn't stop until they broke one of her Lladro figurines, she has a whole vitrina filled with them. It took me three pots of café to serve everyone, it's a good thing Ofelia left me hers, so I only had to wash one right away to make more for the last two people. Everyone seemed satisfied, either rubbing their bellies, sipping espresso or going back for more food, so I thought I'd check in on Yamile and Luz.

The music was still too loud but I could hear the baby. Luz was very little then, maybe three months, I could hear her crying above all the noise. Gertrudes was talking with Estrella from across the way, poor woman, her son killed himself with drugs, only sixteen years old, a sad thing, really. Hemm, ah sí. I think Miguel went for more ice or beer or both, though I can't imagine what was taking him so long; he slips away a lot lately but I've learned to bite my tongue about it. Marcos was playing computador with his friends and Gracielita was shut up in her room with two or three girls. They were talking on the phone when I checked in on them; I don't like it when she locks that door like that. Anyway, she did something that upset me very much. She's gotten such a mouth since starting school at San Bernardo's. I asked las muchachitas if they wanted any more soda, in Spanish of course, but Gracielita answered me in English with that face she puts on whenever she's acting up, and they all laughed. All I could understand her saying was something about me being a Marielita, but I'm sure it was worse than that. I would have slapped her right then and there but my daughter doesn't believe in that, so I called her a fresh and shameless girl, and they kept right on laughing. Such disrespect! I was so angry, I just wanted to shake her but the only thing I could do was close the door hard behind me. Marcos saw me in the hall and called out for more soda so I brought some back for him and his friends. None of them said thank you. Gertrudes asked me if the children were all right when I walked past the living room. I said yes and went to my room to get my fan; my face was on fire! I took an extra tranquilizer from my drawer and remembered Yamile and the baby; her room shares a wall with my bedroom.

Well, when I passed the living room to go to the kitchen, Gertrudes asked me for more café and I told her I would get it in a few minutes. She said she wanted some now with the cake she was eating and I told her to make it herself or wait for me, and walked right on by to the kitchen for the chicken and rice I left in the oven for Yamile and then back to the table in the yard and got some salad and a few pastelitos. Of course, Gertrudes would wait but I could see through the sliding door that she was raising some fuss about it with that conceited Hortensia; she's always talking about Spain, trying to catch me up in the lie but I always say I can't remember the names of places in Madrid. Anyway I got together a nice heaping serving for Yamile and I decided to put a big piece of cake on a separate plate because there was so much of it left. It had much too much meringue—even for me—and the children didn't like the pineapple filling, so more than half the cake was left even though there must have been close to a hundred people there at one point or another. I figured I'd bring Yamile cake later so I took the plate which had those universo robots printed on it—the napkins, cups and paper table-cloths all matched too. I managed to save one of the cake decorations for Luz, I felt it in my pocket against my waist, then, hands full, I walked around to Yamile's little room behind the utility shed where the washer and dryer are.

Angel of God, to remember that poor girl with that whimpering baby, ay, it just breaks my heart. It's always very hot in that part of the house and there wasn't a single breeze. Pobrecita, she only has two windows in that little room and facing the east so all she gets is hot air. She was drenched and fanning herself and the baby with a piece of cardboard. Luz was kicking around and bright red. I could tell that her sheets were all sticky too. I noticed that there was a plate of bread and I think mayonesa on the table next to the crib. But that's all! Yamile got up right away and told me to sit but I put the food before her and made her stay put. She always calls me Doña Soledad; she's the only one who's ever called me by my first name. Most everyone calls me Mercedes, but I have always liked Soledad because it was my mother's name and it reminds me of her; my full name's Soledad de las Mercedes Pérez y Pérez, not including my husband's name—Aguirre. Yamile's eyes were full of veins and she was in tears when she asked me what more she could do with Luz. I asked her how much she had fed her already, poor thing couldn't nurse because of the gland medicine she takes. She showed me two bottles that were still dirty with milk. I reached over and picked Luz up feeling the dampness of the mattress and the baby clothes and realized that I had never seen her drinking water. I turned right around bouncing Luz on my hip and called out, What that baby needs is water! Yamile's thin eyebrows arched up while I went on. You young people never ask the old ones anything, because you know it all already. She was smiling and crying at the same time and then tears fell from my eyes, too while I prepared a fresh bottle of water. I held Luz close to my bosom as she drank while Yamile was eating the food from the party and watching us.

Settlements

Virgil Suarez

VIRGIL SUAREZ was born in Cuba in 1962, left the island in 1970, and lived in Madrid, Spain, until 1974. In 1980 he graduated from high school in Los Angeles and matriculated at California State University, Long Beach, where he received a BA in English. In 1987 he graduated with an MFA in Creative Writing from Louisiana State University. His novels include *The Cutter* and *Latin Jazz*. He is also the author of *Welcome to the Oasis*, a novella and collection of short stories. Currently he teaches at Louisiana State University in Baton Rouge, where he also lives and writes.

B

E IT KNOWN:

I. I stole shoes and cash out of the register from the department store where I worked as a shoe salesman.

II. On a Friday, a week before inventory, I quit, took a girl from Lingerie and spent the evening with her in my one-bedroom apartment.

III. Later, after she left, I smoked a joint and called my mother to tell her I was leaving Los Angeles.

IV. My mother the lawyer blamed my father for my "aimlessness" in life (two years out of high school and I didn't want to go to college) and hung up.

The last time I saw my father was during lunch and he was drunk. I often wondered if the people who bought houses from him ever smelled the stink of alcohol in his breath. Between swigs (I drank beer, he cognac straight up) I told him I was leaving L.A.

"Oh," he said, "why?"

"Got to get away," I said. "Can't stand the bumper-to-bumper course my life's taking. My painting's going nowhere."

"Your mother's got nothing to do with this, does she?" he asked, giving me one of his you're-full-of-shit stares from behind his thick-framed glasses. My father had divorced my mother five years ago.

"I want to prove to her that I'm headed in the right direction."

"What direction's that, son?"

"Southeast," I said, "I want to go to the desert. Fill up the gas tank and ride, ride, ride."

"That'll only get you to Blithe," he said and smiled.

"Blithe's desert, isn't it," I said.

"Coyote and Gila Monster territory," he said.

Later that same day, I packed my clothes, sleeping bag, portfolio and art supplies, got my last Michelob out of the fridge, jumped in my Mustang and split.

WHEREAS: By morning I found myself in Tucson, Arizona. There I was. In Prickly Pear and Saguaro cactus country. Sand and pebbles as shiny as mother-of-pearl buttons. Rocks, boulders, mountains, canyons, strange looking lizards and rodents, such was the desert as I had never seen it.

On the way to the foothills I stopped for lunch at a Denny's. I asked the waitress if she knew of any places for rent in the vicinity.

"Look in the university paper," she said.

For that much information I left her an Honest Abe neatly folded under the ashtray, paid my bill, and set out to seek some shelter.

Sure enough in the university paper I found this under ROOM-MATES WANTED: Seeking responsible person to share a 3br 1bath house/walking distance/washer & dryer/$175permth half utilities.

The adobe house stood behind a couple of mesquite bushes and a fence far gone to rust. The house rested on a brick foundation. The name, B. TRISTE, was painted on the side of the mailbox. I opened the torn screen door and knocked. At first I heard nothing, then quick footsteps, and a young woman opened the door.

"The place still for rent?" I asked.

"Oh yeah," she said, "sure, come on in."

"Fuentes," I introduced myself, "Lucas Fuentes."

"Becky," she said. She had mossygreen eyes and caramel skin. No bra, so the nipples bounced around and poked at the cloth of her flannel shirt. When she started to show me the place, I got a good look at her small ass.

"Stop," I said. We came to a halt in the hall. "Look at this face and tell me I don't look responsible?"

She flashed a you've-got-to-be-kidding smile. "Oh, you do," she said, "but please look at this place carefully. See if you like it first."

Becky showed me the rest of the house, pointing out what couldn't or would be fixed. Cracks on the bedroom walls. Stains on the ceiling. In the extra room (she used it as a study) paint had sealed the windows shut.

"Are you a student?" she asked in the bathroom. Her voice echoed among the broken tiles and faucet-leak stains.

"Nope," I told her. "Left L.A. and came here to work on my painting."

"You're an artist?"

I asked her what she did for a living.

"Sing opera," she said as she led me back to the living room. "I'm a voice major at U of A. Getting my Master's in two more semesters."

I asked, "Opera?"

"I've played Musetta in *La Bohème*. Smaller part in *Cosi fan Tutti*. Next semester I expect to get a leading role in *La Traviata*."

"Luciano Pavarotti's all I know about operas," I said.

"That's a start," she said. "He's good."

"I need a place," I told her and backed to the door.

She went over the money arrangements slowly. I wrote her a check for $350 (money from an account I opened with what I made from the shoe sales), part rent and part deposit, and slapped it on the palm of her white hand.

"I'm easy to live with," I told her.

"Guess I'll find out soon enough," she said.

I left her standing on the porch and went out to get the stuff out of my car, which was covered with dust and dead insects, and moved in.

WHEREAS: Sunset after sunset I sat on the rotting porch steps and watched the sky blaze. In the desert the night came about quickly, bringing with it the noises of cicadas and crickets and of the wind sifting through the dry foliage. From inside the house, the sounds of Becky playing her flute, long, pipey whistles, rang in my ears. When it wasn't the flute, then her singing. She practiced by warming up fortissimo and mellowing down to a steady, hum-like bass.

Usually I sat there and felt happy that I was getting a lot of work done. For something wonderful began to happen to my work. Each canvas that I stretched, gessoed and added texture to came alive. Sepia, burnt sienna, raw umber, rust, and some of the lighter earth colors snuck onto my palette. The paintings began to look like ancient treasure maps. Blueprints to old civilizations was what they really looked like. Full of broken lines and shapes and things I cut up and glued on. Sometimes I took a spatula and smeared lots of paint on huge areas or I threw a handful of sand at the finished painting to give it a gritty texture.

I worked all afternoons until Becky returned from her part-time job at a fast-food restaurant, then I'd come out to talk to her.

During those first couple of weeks, I got to know her well. Sometimes she put on a classical record (Bach, Mozart, Beethoven, et al.) and walked out of the house and joined me on the porch.

"Missed it," I said, "a hawk landed on that mesquite. It had a frog hanging from its beak. It just—" I snapped my fingers. "Flew away the instant you walked out."

She told me about how when she graduated she was going to go to Miami and take lessons from a voice teacher and teach to support herself.

I mentioned as little as possible about my life, about my parents and how their divorce changed my life, because I no longer felt connected to anything. At one time their marriage was my foundation. As soon as my father moved out of the house and my mother drafted the divorce settlement and they both signed it, I didn't care anymore what I did or where I went.

One evening Becky brought out a miniature calumet and we smoked grass. She kept asking me what I was going to do for money.

"Work," I said, "but I haven't run out yet, so why worry?"

"I like you," she said. "When I first saw you I knew you were going to be easy-going."

I asked her to close her eyes and try to describe what she thought I looked like.

"Umm," she said. "Can see your eyes. The way wrinkles form on the edges there." She touched the corner of my eyes with her finger. "Chicken-scratch like. Let's see. Color? Color?" She opened her eyes and looked at me.

"Black," I said, "habit black. I hate them."

She grew quiet for a while, then told me that for the longest time she had wanted to move away from home, and now she was content to be out on her own.

WHEREAS: Jogging one night, I raced her back to the house and she beat me because I fell and scraped the upper side of my right leg. A bad slide. Anyway, the bruise burned and itched like crazy. She helped me up into the house and sat me on the sofa, left the living room, and returned with a first-aid kit.

"This is going to hurt," she said and pulled my shorts down.

Pain shot up my leg and I twisted and turned, my hands folded into tight fists, but I took the pain while she cleaned the scrape, then cotton-swabbed it with iodine.

Her face drew too close to mine. I grabbed her by the hood of her sweatshirt and kissed her, "I couldn't take it anymore, you know," I said.

She took me by the hand and helped me get to her bed. She helped me undress.

"Go slow," I said.

"This," she said, climbing into bed, "heals all. Cures all."

WHEREAS:

October 16, 1984

Dear Mother:

Made it out to Tucson okay, and plan to stay. Nobody's fault, you understand? I'm happy. You're happy. He's happy. Happy, the all-American adjective. Say hello to Mr. Century 21, the real realtor himself. Just in case you're wondering what I'm up to, I've met an American girl, diva-to-be opera singer. Anyway, love's brewing. Take care.

Still Cultured,
Rattlesnake

&

ESPERANZA L. MURILLO

October 29, 1984

Dear Son:

Ever since you left, I've been praying to Saint Jude. Know who that is? Patron Saint of hopeless cases. I've heard via one of the girls who called to find out where you were what you did at the store. So that's how you managed to support yourself, eh? Your father doesn't know. Here's a check for five hundred, half mine, half his. We both took a guess at your present living conditions. Chasing women still? Now it's an American Tweetybird. Who will it be tomorrow?

Love,
Misunderstood Mother

WHEREAS: We wasted no time planning camping trips. Three in a row, since she didn't work on the weekends and wasn't rehearsing for any opera parts.

Weekend #1: To Sabino Canyon, not too far from where we lived. Nice place with a ravine banked with beds of purple and yellow, wild flowers and fishhook cacti. We played see-who-spots-the-most-animals games.

She saw deer, roadrunners, an owl, a couple of hares, and a fox. I found some kind of lizard sunbathing on top of a rock and asked Becky what it was.

"Gila monster," she said. "Come to Illinois with me for Christmas?"

"What's there?"

"I want you to meet my parents."

"Let me think about it," I said, then asked her what she thought of the Saguaros.

"See how they stand?" she said, "With their arms bent up like that? It looks like they're saying, 'Don't shoot! Don't shoot!'"

Weekend #2: It was colder at the top of Mount Lemon when we finally drove up. We set up camp in the middle of a circle of pine trees, started a fire, and cooked hamburgers. In the night, after we made love she told me how much she really wanted me to visit Illinois.

"We can go Greyhound," she said, "that way you won't have to drive."

"In my book that's still two whole days on the road," I said, watching how the shadows moved on the canvas tent.

"C'mon, you'll love Illinois," she said. "I can take you down to Edwardsville. There are lots of old, run-down barns you can sketch. We can visit St. Louis. The zoo. The arch."

"I'll think about it," I said.

She rolled over away from me and fell asleep.

Weekend #3: The trip to the Grand Canyon took longer, but, after a stopover at Flagstaff for lunch, we got there. All the campgrounds were full this time of year. No reservations, no stay. That night we had to sleep in the car, then spent all of the next day and part of Sunday going down and then back up a narrow trail. Becky seemed pensive and withdrawn.

Mules passed us on the way, snorting and wagging their tails. They made the air reek of piss. We had to keep looking down at the ground to make sure we didn't step on mule shit.

"How long would we stay?" I said.

She looked up at me (on the way up she was walking behind me, sometimes holding on to my belt) and said, "Where?"

"At your parents'," I said.

"Three or four days," she said, "no more than that, okay?"

"Go Greyhound," I said, "and leave the driving to us!"

This made her so happy that when we got to the top she took me to a gift shop and bought me a cowboy hat with a leather band around it on which she pinned an I CLIMBED THE GRAND CANYON button.

I wasn't too excited, because I felt that to meet her parents would be letting things get more serious than they should be at this stage in our relationship, but I gave in just to please her. That night, she let me sketch her in the nude, and we drank two bottles of wine and got drunk.

WHEREAS: The trip. I found myself sitting next to Becky on the very front seat of the bus behind the driver who, from Tucson to El Paso, chewed tobacco and spat into a Styrofoam cup.

There was also this old woman sitting behind us who repeated, "I will take my cars and clothes and take them to the Salvation Army. He'll see." This became a litany. She chain-smoked, so the driver had to tell her to go to the back of the bus. Probably some woman who was getting divorced, I thought. It seemed like everybody in the world was getting divorced, so why get married?

Shortly before we arrived at the station in El Paso where we were supposed to change buses, the woman returned, sat behind us, then reached over and tapped me on the shoulder.

"Do you read the Bible," she said. "The Psalms?"

"Read them all," I told the woman, and this made Becky laugh so hard she had to hide her face. The woman left us alone after that.

WHEREAS: Her parents were waiting for us at the station in Peoria. I couldn't guess who they were in the crowd of people there until this couple approached Becky from behind. I stood back while they took turns hugging and kissing their daughter.

Her father was a tall, white-haired, broad-shouldered man. He shook my hand and eyed me over. I didn't like the red and blue veins on the tip of his nose.

I took Mrs. Triste's mittened hand and shook it with both of mine. She didn't let go right away, instead she held them and told me how utterly wonderful it was to make my acquaintance.

She had a small, round face, yellowish hair which hid under the hood of her coat, pudgy nose, lips the color of frozen meat.

"Happy to meet you," I said.

Snow covered the ground up to my ankles outside the bus station.

Her mother told us to get inside the car, that we were going to a restaurant for dinner. Feeling tired, dirty from the two days without a shower, I sat in the back of the Buick Regal and closed my eyes.

We arrived at the restaurant and Mrs. Triste was still talking about John Deere shutting down their plant. "A lot of people are leaving Peoria," she said, "and a lot of them come to Fred for counseling."

Becky's father was a marriage counselor, Ph.D. in Psychology. And her mother taught at a school for the mentally handicapped.

The conversation continued over dinner; I ate quickly my sirloin steak and mashed potatoes. Mr. Triste wasn't saying much. Mrs. Triste asked me where my parents lived.

"They're divorced," I said.

An opera buff just like his daughter, Mr. Triste started talking about what a terrible fate young Italian boys who were sopranos had in the eighteenth century. "Castrati sopranos," he said.

"Castrated sopranos?" I said. Mrs. Triste and Becky smiled, but Mr. Triste grew serious.

He didn't like me, I thought, because he probably figured I wasn't good enough for his daughter.

Dinner over, we drove to the house, a two story, four bedroom place. They had bought it cheap, and were planning to restore and remodel most of it by next summer. I was glad to be getting out of the cold.

Mrs. Triste made hot chocolate and served it on the dining room table under which the wooden waxed floors shone. Mr. Triste grew tired and said he was turning in.

"Make yourself at home here," was what Mrs. Triste said to me before she left, then to Becky, "Becky, show him to his room downstairs. Get a fire going in the fireplace if he wants. If not, get the portable heater out of the closet."

"I'll take care of him, mother," Becky said.

Her mother said good night and left.

"I want to go to sleep," I said.

"Party pooper."

Becky led me downstairs to what was to be my bedroom, started a fire in the fireplace, placed the screen in front of the flames, and fixed my bed.

"He doesn't like me," I said.

"Who? My father?"

"Did you see the way he kept looking at me?"

"You're crazy," she said, kissed me good-bye and left.

WHEREAS: After dinner the following night, Mr. Triste asked me to accompany him outside to get more wood for the fireplace.

The cold snuck in through the cuffs of my Levi's and made me shudder as I followed Mr. Triste to the woodpile. There he brushed the snow off, picked up a couple of logs, and handed them to me.

"Never been in this kind of weather, eh?" he asked.

"I prefer warmth," I said.

"We want Becky to return here after she graduates," he said, putting three more logs on my arms.

"She plans to go to Miami and take voice lessons," I said.

"And you plan to follow her?"

I told him I didn't know.

"Well, you should know," he said, and picked out some logs for himself to carry. "Both of you must realize that it's going to be hard."

I asked him what he meant by "hard."

"You come from a different world than she does," he said, "and you're bound to have disagreements. Lots of them."

This made me angry, so I told him, "Becky's a big girl now, Mr. Triste. I think she knows what's good for her."

He walked back to the house in silence. Inside, he stacked the wood by the fireplace, washed his hands in the kitchen, and went to his room.

WHEREAS: At 11:42 AM Becky woke me up. "Hey, sleepy head," she said and kissed me. "I have a surprise for you." She walked over to the stereo. "We have the house all to ourselves," she said, searching through the records. She found the one she was looking for and put it on the turntable.

Becky removed her terry cloth robe and dropped it on the rug. "Listen," she said, climbing onto the bed, "and make love to me."

Wagner's *Ride of the Valkyries* started. It was loud. "I don't feel comfortable doing this," I said. But she already had me pinned to the mattress.

I rolled her over and got on top. To keep myself from coming too fast I thought of the movie *Apocalypse Now*, Marlon Brando sitting in the dark sponging water over his bald head, reading his poetry.

Mr. Triste's bald head stood in the doorway, red in the face. Becky pushed me off and stood up.

I saw in the movie the native's machete fall and chop the sacred cow's head off. And I thought, God, was I stupid for letting my desires mess everything up. I felt embarrassed and ashamed for taking advantage.

Mr. Triste went upstairs.

Feeling a little dizzy, I stood and watched Becky put on her robe.

"Jesus," she said, "fuck! We had our asses to the door. He saw it all."

She rushed out of the room and I heard her go upstairs.

"I want him out," Mr. Triste said. "That son of a bitch."

"It's my fault," she said.

I felt like going upstairs and apologizing, but what good was it to say that I was sorry? There was nothing left to do but pack and get out of the house.

Becky returned, saw me packing, sat on the bed and didn't say a word.

"Drive me to the airport," I said, "I'm catching the next flight out."

"I'm sorry," she said.

"Bad luck," I said. "Maybe if I talk to him?"

"Apologies aren't going to change how he feels. We've betrayed him," she said.

"Let me talk to him," I said.

"You've got to go back to Tucson."

"I'm sorry," I said. This was the last thing I said to her, then she drove me to the airport and I flew back to the desert.

THEREFORE:

I. I did everything I could to save the relationship after Becky returned.

II. There was no sense in us staying together, pretending nothing had ever gone wrong.

III. Becky suggested we separate for a while to see if things worked out.

IV. We divided the stuff we had bought together: a light blue, reclinable reading chair, a drafting lamp, the collected poetry of Dylan Thomas and the complete works of Shakespeare, and the Steely Dan albums.

V. I told her to keep everything, including some of the paintings and sketches I had worked on.

VI. I returned to L.A. to deal with old ghosts and to prove to everyone I knew what I was doing.

The Clocks, Ribbons, Mountain Lakes, and Clouds of Jennifer Marginat Feliciano

Ed Vega

ED VEGA is the pen name of Edgardo Vega Yunqué. Born on the island of Puerto Rico, he came to the United States at the age of twelve. He is the author of *The Comeback*, a novel, 1985; *Mendoza's Dreams*, a frame tale novel, 1987; and *Casualty Report*, a collection of short stories, 1991. In Spanish he has written *Los Dinosaurios de Perico Colón*. Vega has recently finished *No Matter How Much You Promise to Cook or Pay the Rent You Blew It Cause Bill Bailey Ain't Never Coming Home Again*, a novel.

I

Arqueros
Los arqueros oscuros a
Sevilla se acercan.
Guadalquivir abierto.
Anchos sombreros grises y
largas capas lentas.
—FEDERICO GARCÍA LORCA
"Poema de la Saeta"

As he prepared himself to visit his ex-wife, Jennifer Marginat, summoned there to discuss their daughter's demand to leave boarding school, Paul Feliciano considered again whether, after he finally dealt with his ex-wife, he should write a letter to someone who was almost a stranger and confess what he had done. Feliciano had met Roger Mora in Madrid and they had traveled to Sevilla together. One evening, intoxicated by the adventure as much as by the wine, they crossed the bridge over the Guadalquivir River, reciting verses from García Lorca to each other in almost forgotten Spanish. As they walked at nearly 10 pm on a Sunday evening, the brilliant June sun of Andalucía blood red upon the water and the air the color of silver, they stopped on the bridge so that Roger could point out *La Giralda* in the distance. They had then crossed into Triana and sat in a flamenco bar and through the injured voices of the music Paul let his mind drift away in a gypsy fantasy of love and violence in which his ex-wife suffered unbearable pain. Returning to their hotel around two o'clock in the morning Paul Feliciano had felt an overwhelming sadness which he could not decipher. Everything about the feeling was familiar and yet new. He recognized love, regret, apprehension and fear within the emotion, but was unable to fathom what or who was causing him to feel as he did.

In writing the letter Paul Feliciano hoped to exorcise the demons that pursued him; telling himself that he'd have to apologize because, although they should, people didn't write letters anymore. Perhaps confessing what he was about to do to Jennifer when he hardly knew Roger was an imposition, but he had to tell someone and sometimes if people didn't know you well they didn't judge you as harshly. Considering the upcoming complications produced by his decision, Paul Feliciano felt as if he were in a large centrifuge spinning rapidly and his life becoming less and less distinguishable. He could now accept that his attempts to help his ex-wife Jennifer Marginat were part of an elaborate plan of self-deception, and that the only result of the subterfuge had been uncovering of emotions which he suspected existed within him only in a dormant state. Following her from one romantic disaster to the next, wishing each time to leave her alone for good, he began to see his life disintegrate under the weight of his well-kept secret. Their divorce, rather than creating a much promised distance, had compelled him to draw even closer and dance moth-like about her elusively brilliant complexities. As such he became her father confessor and hopeful savior, wishing simultaneously to rescue part of himself.

The last time he had visited her, more than a year prior, they had become involved in a horrible argument about her father. Like some dissonant symphony each detail of her father's life evoked themes of Feliciano's life. The entire matter had started when Jennifer insisted that Feliciano was monopolizing their daughter.

"Rebecca doesn't even miss me anymore when I don't visit, Paul," she'd said. "Have you spoken to her lately?"

He told her that he'd gone up to the school the previous month and that two weeks prior she'd spent the weekend at his apartment with a girl friend from school.

"Just before you got back from Barbados," he'd said.

Jennifer wanted to know if Rebecca had changed. He wanted to tell her that she certainly had, that she had stepped right out of the closet and into broad daylight and she wasn't offering any explanations to anybody about her choices and that she'd told him that next year she was marching in the parade with her friend, Meredith, who was this very earthy and quiet little blonde girl with wire-rim glasses from Chevy Chase, Maryland. And they had. Right down Fifth Avenue. Arm in arm, every once in a while kissing each other without the slightest self-consciousness. He had marched as a parent in support and felt hypocritical, dreading running into someone who'd unmask him. Jennifer could tell what was going on with him but seemed unconcerned. He couldn't tell Jennifer about Rebecca. Eventually she'd find out, but not now.

He'd then told Jennifer that Rebecca had changed a little and that she wasn't sure if she wanted to spend her last year at the school because, according to her, "the whole private school in Connecticut bit" had worn thin; that she wasn't learning anything and was tired of people calling her Becky and treating her like a child and could he see if they'd take her at Berklee in the fall. Jennifer wanted to know if Rebecca had filled out yet, and did she talk about boys. He said she had filled out, and that she had inherited not only Jennifer's good looks but her body as well. In his perception, his ex-wife was so self-centered that she would be deceived by compliments and he'd avoid having to answer the business about boys.

He said, instead, that she ought to hear Rebecca play. Jennifer replied that the last time Rebecca had stayed with her during the Christmas holidays she'd get up at eight o'clock in the morning, eat some Cheerios and play until nearly noon, when she got hungry. Everything from memory. Mozart, Bach, Debussy, everybody.

"You ought to hear her play Gershwin and Cole Porter. Her Thelonious Monk isn't too shabby, either," he said. He added that he'd asked Rebecca why she wanted to go to Berklee and she'd told him that they had a good jazz department.

"Paul!" she'd reprimanded him. She had a way of calling him Paul that angered him. He had described it to Roger as a horrid Upper West Side whine. "Jazz? Like Daddy?" the whine grating at him, and as if the word "jazz" were a swear word and shouldn't be repeated in polite company.

"Yes, jazz, like her grandfather," he said.

Mustering up as much sarcasm as she could, Jennifer said that she guessed genius *did* skip a generation. Her nose up in the air reminded him of her mother, who resented that Feliciano had *la mancha de plátano*, the dreaded plantain stain, which was the Puerto Rican euphemism for the intrusion of negritude into the pedigree. He did not deny his heritage but Doña Conchita Linares de Marginat, the mother, was obsessed with trying to convince everyone of his non-existent Caucasoid purity. Adding always words of praise for the Moorish tradition and blood ever present in the race. Feliciano often closed his eyes in desperation.

"Does Rebecca talk about me?" She'd wanted to know.

Feliciano'd thought for a moment of what he should say. Rebecca hadn't mentioned Jennifer. She basically loved her mother but at the same time realized she was too self-absorbed to bother with more than superficial maternal concerns. He finally opted for diplomacy and said of course she talked about her and had idealized her as the model of the new woman, complete with super-charged sex drive and control of her life. She noticed the bitterness in his voice but he didn't care. She didn't care either, her vanity getting the best of her. She asked him if he had dispelled that view. He'd lied and told her that he sometimes did and often explained to Rebecca that Jennifer struggled with herself like anyone else.

"I told her you're not as notorious as your reputation. That you're very conscious of AIDS and took good care of yourself," he said, and felt ugly even though he had not yet been tested, but had begun worrying. "The way she sees it, you're the luckiest woman in the world."

She'd thrown back her hair and reached for a cigarette. Feliciano recalled sitting with Roger in the cafe in Triana, with the breeze coming in off the river, when he told the story and saying: "Don't you wish you could do that? Right in the middle of a diagnosis or explaining some goddamn CAT scan to someone?" Roger Mora was eye-and-ear in some very rich clinic in Milwaukee. "Just throw your hair back and reach for a you've come a long way, baby, Virginia Slims," he'd said and Roger had laughed a little too loudly. Both of Jennifer's actions were designed to lessen the effect of her words on herself. When she released the first gray cloud from her lips, she did so slowly, letting the smoke drift up to veil her face.

She went on attacking the cigarette and began talking about the silences; telling him she couldn't bear them; knowing she could get to him by talking disdainfully about her father, telling him how she used to fill their own marital silences with memories of her father at the piano playing his heart out after an argument with her mother. Jennifer said her mother would go off and cry in the bedroom and she'd sit in the kitchen alone because the rest of the house seemed so dark.

And she'd listen to the music; anticipating each new theme; thick, melancholic Hungarian things dripping with pain and full of anger.

"He could never play like that on stage," she'd said, as she always did when discussing the subject, reiterating for him that her father knew what she thought about his failure and hated him because she felt he was weak trapped by his own hang-ups.

Feliciano reminded Jennifer that her father had been a good man, recalling his kindness toward him and his stories about coming from the island during World War I. His father-in-law's father was a cigar maker, a Spaniard, from Cataluña. His mother was a native of the island, her family having arrived from Galicia in the 1820's. Ignacio Marginat, his late father-in-law, was already a proficient pianist at the age of ten when the ship docked in New York from San Juan in 1916. His father went on to establish contacts with Cuban business-men and in a short time they began to take advantage of the embryonic cigar making industry in the small but growing Puerto Rican and Cuban community in Brooklyn and Harlem. "In those days there was a lot more respect between Cubans and Puerto Ricans because both had struggled for independence together," Ignacio Marginat had told him about six months before he died, the cancer in his throat making it nearly impossible for him to swallow his own saliva and his room always dark so that you could not look at his nearly skeletal face and hands.

Skilled as businessman and entrepreneur, Ignacio Marginat's father's trade in fine cigars flourished. Even though he was from Puerto Rico he deferred to his Cuban partner and the beautiful boxes with evocative scenes of Caribbean life (Feliciano still had several in which he kept photographs of his childhood) said in English, "Marginat & Flores Fine Cuban Cigars." Even though the cigars were no longer manufactured he'd suggested to Roger that he ask his older relatives if they remembered the boxes so they could verify the provenance of his story. The elder Marginat, don Alfredo, became wealthy within two or three years, investing in real estate and allowing young Ignacio and his two sisters Elba and Laura to study and enjoy a life of luxury.

The town house became the center for Puerto Rican social activity in New York in those days; people were still upset that the island had not gained its independence as had Cuba after the Spanish-American War, and felt insulted that the U.S. had officially changed the name of their homeland to Porto Rico in 1899. It wasn't changed back to Puerto Rico until 1932. He was told by his father-in-law that in those days the Marginat house was one of the places where Luis Muñoz Marín, who later became governor, came with his first wife, Muna Lee, when he was working as a newspaperman and living down in Greenwich Village after WWI; and that as a teen, his father-in-law had played the music of Morel Campos and was always praised for his interpretation of the compositions.

Paul Feliciano had played the *danzas* for Roger on his extra miniature Walkman as they traveled on the train from Madrid to Sevilla. A businessman from Asturia had inquired about the Walkman, it being the first he'd seen of that size. Upon hearing them speak rather poorly in Spanish, the businessman had said he knew they were Americans but wanted to know if their families had been originally from Andalucía. Roger had looked at Feliciano and Feliciano had explained that their families were from Puerto Rico. The businessman looked puzzled for a moment, and then earnestly said they looked too white to be Puerto Rican. Roger had been furious and turned away to stare out of the train window at the barren, rocky landscape. Feeling superior, Feliciano, with just the slightest bit of sarcasm, apologized and said that he had very white and very black relatives but that they hadn't been able to accompany him on the trip and that he hoped it wasn't too much of a disappointment. The businessman emitted a small embarrassed chuckle, and returned to his newspaper. When Feliciano looked at Roger, his eyes were closed, his head was turned to one side and his cheeks sunken in a mask of derision. He released a huge sigh and then shook his head in disbelief at the crassness and effrontery of the man.

Feliciano thought again of meeting his father-in-law for the first time. Back then the Marginat wealth was so magnified in his mind that when he met Jennifer at an Upper West Side party during his first year at Columbia Medical School and they started dating he was totally gaga. He was so impressed the first time he picked her up at her parents' town house on Riverside Drive that he assumed wrongly that she and her family were Sephardic Jews. It took him a number of years to overcome his private embarrassment, because he had even recognized Marginat as a Catalan name and also recognized that she had some sort of Spanish background, since he'd seen a photo album of her mother's family and the settings and dedications were in Spanish. He knew now that subconsciously he hadn't wanted Jennifer's family to be Spanish speaking, certainly not Puerto Rican.

One side of her mother's family had arrived in New York directly from Spain, from Santander on the northern coast of Spain, near the Basque countries. The album had photographs taken in Santander before the Spanish Civil War in the '30s when her family emigrated to New York. Her mother and her grandmother were *Casa de España*, middle class people. Her maternal grandfather was an accountant, born and reared in Matanzas, Cuba, a poor relation of the cigar-making Floreses. He helped the Goya Products people start their business when they were simply importing olive oil and olives and capers for their *alcaparrado*.

Jennifer became very upset when she caught him casually looking through the photo album while he was waiting for her to finish getting dressed to go out one evening. He had been puzzled by her reaction, but had backed off without asking about her anger. Her reaction had shaken him. He was even more shocked when one day her father spoke to him in Spanish and informed him that he had been born in Puerto Rico. Up to that time his future father-in-law had spoken English articulately with a nondescript, educated accent.

"In Cacimar," his father-in-law had said. "Up in the mountains. Tobacco country. You must go there sometime." Feliciano replied that his mother had been born in the same town, in the mountains. Ignacio Marginat had been ecstatic. His mother, however, nearly fainted when he mentioned the Marginat name. She told him the Marginats owned every bit of land she had known when she was a girl, and that her father had worked at picking and curing their tobacco up in the hills. Even though everyone had treated her well at the wedding, his poor mother had been a bundle of nerves and made it very obvious that she was ashamed to be there because she felt she didn't belong. And yet Jennifer's father would've accepted him into the family even if he'd had three eyes. He knew now that he'd married Jennifer in part to please Ignacio Marginat. His attraction to Jennifer was an attraction to an ideal and not truly to her as a person. They had been married about three years when, one Christmas after they'd had too much eggnog at a ski lodge in Vermont, she admitted to him that she was ashamed of her background and wished she could simply be American.

As Feliciano had done on a number of occasions he'd defended her father. He told her that her father had been a good man and a great inspiration to him. It didn't take much to get her quieted down because, in spite of her filial dissatisfaction, her father was never cruel to her and no man could love a daughter more. Feliciano never pretended to understand his father-in-law, but in a way he often thought that what bothered Jennifer most was her feeling that her father had very little ambition. He couldn't pass judgment on Ignacio Marginat, but neither could Feliciano explain that even though his father-in-law had been friends with the American composer Aaron Copland and had met the Russian composer Igor Stravinsky, both of whom had encouraged him to continue to pursue his career as a concert pianist which he did for a time, performing at Carnegie Hall and touring Europe as a young virtuoso, those experiences meant little to him. Ignacio Marginat was proudest of three experiences in his life.

An avid baseball fan, one of those cherished events was playing "Two Little Babes in the Woods" for the great Babe Ruth and a voluptuous redhead when they came into the Roadhouse Inn where his father-in-law worked in New Jersey four evenings a week, because the market had crashed the year before and he was convinced that his father had lost his fortune. This was not the case, since people went on smoking cigars and living in the buildings owned by the elder Marginat. The excuse, however, gave the young Ignacio an opportunity to get away from what he felt was his parents' stifling influence.

Having obtained permission from Colonel Ruppert to have a cab bring him back to New York, The Bambino had stopped off to get something to eat on his way from Philadelphia, after a series against Connie Mack's Athletics, towards the end of the 1930 season, when the Athletics were headed for the pennant and eventual world championship. The Babe had removed his big, newsboy cap and tapped Ignacio Marginat on the back as he sat at the piano. "Hey, kid, can you play 'Two little Babes in the Woods' for me and my friend?" Ruth'd said, pointing his thumb back at the table where the redhead sat smiling the brightest smile young Marginat had ever seen on a woman.

He would have to mention an even more important fact to Roger because his daughter, Rebecca, had inherited her considerable musical talent from her grandfather. Late at night Iggy Marginat would leave his parents' town house or go directly from his job in New Jersey and end up in Harlem to visit the Negro clubs like Smalls' Paradise or The Nest or The Cotton Club. Everywhere he went they called him the "Spanish kid" because he sometimes translated for the Cuban musicians. In more jocular moments the black musicians called him, good naturedly a "high yella boy." But he didn't care what they called him because he was fascinated by the "blues" and couldn't get enough of a music which he saw as much more challenging than that of his classical training.

After most of the white patrons left he'd sit in at the piano with the black musicians and they'd play jazz. Sometimes he would simply listen, his entire being soaking up the music, completely spellbound when one of the piano greats like Eubie Blake came in and played ragtime for hours. Some nights he'd walk in at three a.m. and sit at the piano and jam with the other musicians and early in the morning, after a breakfast of eggs and grits, feeling dazed by the reefer he'd smoked as part of the wonderful life-giving ritual that was jazz, tired but full of life, he'd drag himself home, the dawn, pearly gray behind him and the Hudson River blue and silver in the morning sun as he walked. He had been happy then.

Ignacio Marginat's third accomplishment was that he spoke Spanish well until his death and was proud of it, and that during that same period of time when he went into Harlem, around 1929 or 1930, he had met a young Spanish poet, whom he always referred to as Federico, who was a writer in residence at Columbia University. They had become friends and oftentimes Ignacio Marginat traveled up to the university, picked up his friend and they walked down the hill on Broadway, crossed 125th Street and entered that wondrous world of Harlem. Whenever Feliciano had asked his father-in-law whether he was talking about García Lorca, Ignacio Marginat had smiled lovingly at him and said that was a secret, but admitted that his friend, the Spanish poet, had visited the house and written about his time spent in New York. Only then, as he argued with Jennifer, did it dawn on him that perhaps his father-in-law and García Lorca had been more than friends. Had his father-in-law seen himself in him back then? Was his love and admiration for him more than paternal concern? The notion pained him.

Feliciano'd asked Jennifer if she had known how much her father had loved jazz. Somewhat sarcastically, she'd said she certainly did since that's what he'd taught Rebecca when she and Feliciano were too busy to take care of her. He told her that wasn't true. That he'd taught her many different types of music, including classical and that no child could've had a finer, gentler and better teacher. She argued that from the time she was three years old her father was teaching Rebecca jazz. And what was she going to do with that? Jennifer'd asked. End up the same as her grandfather? A nothing. She said her father taught her jazz and she soaked it up because children can tell what's really important to adults. He said she was probably right, that it explained her love of the music and he thought of how beautiful a girl Rebecca was and how she had her grandfather's large, beautiful hands. He smiled inwardly recalling that even when she was a little girl she seemed to have big hands.

Feliciano again insisted that he would always be grateful for Ignacio Marginat's friendship and counseling.

"He was a great man," he said, knowing that the justifications he was making for Don Ignacio's failures as a mediocre concert pianist were the ones he was making for his own failed life.

"I don't know," Jennifer said, meaning she wasn't sure she agreed with him. She shrugged her shoulders and said maybe she'd judged her father too harshly but that growing up she'd always thought he was weak. She said that she guessed that's why she'd drifted towards Feliciano. "I saw freedom in you," she said. "I didn't care if you had known poverty. You started with nothing and were determined to claw your way to the top. You were going to be the best surgeon ever. You stressed that. I've always remembered that. I was so proud of you. I could see the determination in your eyes and it would make my heart feel so much love for you."

"Jennifer, please stop romanticizing my life," he'd said.

"Sure, go ahead and reject my admiration for you," she'd answered.

They had gone back and forth a few times before he ended up calling her a selfish bitch and stomped off with her yelling at him that he was the selfish one since he'd stolen their daughter from her.

II

El Rey de Harlem
!Ay, Harlem! !Ay, Harlem! !Ay, Harlem!
No hay angustia comparable a tus rojos oprimidos,
a tu sangre estremecida dentro del eclipse oscuro,
a tu violencia granate sordomuda en la penumbra,
a tu gran rey prisionero, con un traje de conserje.
—FEDERICO GARCÍA LORCA
"Poeta en New York"

So that evening, several months after his return from Spain, Paul Feliciano walked in the November twilight the twelve or so blocks of West Side Manhattan solitude to Jennifer Marginat's home. She greeted him as always warmly, kissing him on the cheek and lingering near him long enough to let the fragrance of her body envelope him. She offered him a drink and immediately asked him why he still bothered with her after she'd been so ghastly. She had actually used the word and added a great theatrical gesture, which made her turn her head and have a subtle shudder issue from her shoulders.

He ignored her question and watched shadows in the lifeless winter park. The distant Jersey lights were a persistent reminder of the humanity struggling to find itself in the darkness of what he, having lost all hope of redemption, perceived to be a heartless and crippled America. In what he categorized as her asinine manner, she asked him again why he still cared what happened to her. He replied that he wouldn't bother if he didn't think she was making a supreme effort to destroy herself. He told her it wasn't like the two of them were strangers, that he did have a responsibility to their daughter.

With utmost sincerity and the tremulous tones which signaled
that she was uncomfortable with the truth, she suggested that perhaps he still loved her. Standing by the window, his back to her, Feliciano shook his head patiently. The remark offended him. Its lack of
intelligence actually caused him physical repugnance. He turned
around and walked across the living room to where she was sitting.
Legs curled up under her small figure, Jennifer seemed lost in the
large chair.

He looked at her a while before saying there was always a possibility that he did still love her and that the notion cropped up from
time to time. He explained, without the least equivocation, that it
wasn't as if he was in love with her, however. He made the remark
more as a boast than as a statement of fact and hated himself for saying so, knowing the words would have an impact. He felt truly evil in
beginning to set his trap. Why did he feel the need to seek revenge,
the results of which he would likely never live to see? His resolve
weakened for a moment and Feliciano thought that perhaps she, as
his ex-wife, had a right to know his condition and what the tests had
confirmed. For a moment he considered telling her the truth. Before
he had an opportunity to act on the urge a powerful wave of anger
pushed out from the center of his body and he changed his mind.

She earnestly informed him that there were other kinds of love.
The words echoed in his brain. They rattled like old bones come
upon by accident, he imagined, were he on a dig, a cave dig, something which had persisted in his life as a fantasy of the archaeology he
wished he had studied instead of medicine. Other kinds of love, he
mused without articulating the remark, ever fearful of letting his sarcasm take over. Other kinds of love. They were old words heard
thousands of times by tired men and uttered by desperate women.

"Jennifer, whatever you do, please don't start your games," he
said, feeling his anger subside to a razor-thin edge. It should've been a
coded warning but it wasn't. She insisted that there were other kinds
of love, her eyes betraying the righteousness of her beliefs and her
mouth set arrogantly like that of an animal who sees an upcoming
attack as unavoidable.

Feliciano sat down on the sofa and attempted to concentrate on
the articles in the large room. The fine lamps and end tables still
dusted religiously by the housekeeper, the furniture refurbished peri-
odically to maintain the pre-WWII elegance of the Riverside Drive

town house, the glass chandelier, the immense Oriental rug of the vast living room on the second floor, the original paintings bought speculatively and with little concern for their aesthetic worth by Jennifer Marginat's grandfather, all exuded staid but tired wealth. His eyes came to rest at last on the grand piano, a symbol of her father's supposed impotence.

Feliciano said he wasn't talking about that kind of love, the words dropping one at a time in what he had no choice but to characterize as resigned petulance. For a moment his hand hung limply in the air before he quickly brought it down.

"What then?" she said.

His rage subsided, but he could no longer point out her naiveté, nor could he outline for her the canons of intellectual integrity and courage. Her question was as fresh as if it had been asked the first time they discussed the subject of love eighteen years before. He didn't attack her verbally, because he had come there to deal with her once and for all, no matter how ignorant she might be. It hadn't even been a case of protracted bad judgment this time. Ted Sierra, in spite of his success in business, was a cripple; not only physically, but in spirit.

Jennifer had deceived Ted and herself in making Ted believe she was devoted to him; needing his helplessness until she became frightened and had once again run away. Her pretense for flight had been as transparent as the sheer robe she now wore and which, for all his overt protestations to the contrary, still drove him to attempt a furtive look at her body. The feeling pleased him; it made him relax for a moment, knowing the desire would make it easier for him to accomplish his goal.

He asked her why she had taken off as she had, leaving Ted that way. She said that Jack Cabrera had asked her to come and see him. She explained that Jack was working on a project in Hong Kong and thought she might be interested. There was no need to go into detail about Jack in the letter to Roger, since he had already described him personally: super handsome stud, Yale Law School, played tennis against Charlie Passarell in P.R. when they were growing up. In Paul Feliciano's scheme of things, Jack Sierra was the biggest phony anyone would ever want to meet. Jennifer now told him that Ted knew about her and Jack, and said Ted had no problems with this, that he understood.

"You offered him little choice," Feliciano said.

She laughed and threw her head back so that her black hair flew away from the delicate, rose-petal skin of her face; her eyes flashed brilliantly above the high cheekbones for a moment to make desire return; urging him to seize the thick mass of hair and, thus holding her, enter her body once more. That would serve as enough revenge. No condom, no protection of any kind. But that would be rape and would not suffice.

As he watched her Paul Feliciano felt thoroughly ashamed and knew it would be impossible for him to reveal his feelings in the letter. Not because he was a physician, but because of the baseness of his motives. No, rape would not do. He had to gain her trust once more and achieve his ends through artifice. She smiled innocently and reminded him that he had always said a human being had choices. There was a coyness in her remark, but absolutely no malice in the smile, no expected touché. He wanted to recite the formula again, but the words would sound hollow, pompous, out of date. At certain times in life, he had told her too often to recall, one is asked to choose between two positive alternatives. As one matures and time passes, one is cast into situations where one must choose between good and evil. And finally, when life and death become fused, when one accepts one's mortality and is faced with the spectre of eternity, the choice is often between the lesser of two evils.

Smiling reluctantly at her, he said she was right and went into his stale, sarcastic, two-drink imitation of Howard Cossell, spitting out the words with staccato precision. You know, you're right, Jennifer. For once you have displayed a rare glimmer of intellect so commonly absent from previous encounters with matters of the mind. Cossell had been gone from the sports scene for more than ten years, and yet Feliciano still clung to those times as a male suit of armor to disguise his secret life. But something else was at work besides his covert life, something much deeper, because lately he yearned for the Beatles and sit-ins and the now-sterile hope of the flower generation. She laughed right along with him, and he hated her even more because she could not recognize his insult.

He recalled those days in their small West Side brownstone apartment no more than a few blocks from her parents' town house; rejecting, at her insistence, her father's offer of a larger apartment in one of the buildings owned by the family, because she'd wanted them to succeed on their own; flaunting all of their madness; she pursuing her painting career, working feverishly at the Art Students League; he garbed in the white clothing of his internship; their bed like a revolving door after Rebecca was born and they decided that was it for children, both believing that they should not overcrowd the planet; admitting and discharging lovers; wanting desperately to create the new marriage before anyone had coined the phrase; swallowing his male pride when coming home he found her in bed, her mouth still swollen and her face delightfully flushed, spent like a female cat, playfully gentle, purring almost, so that her skin felt strangely electric; wanting then to act maturely and not ask who it had been; having to guess and never knowing; making the jealousy diffused and directed at objects in the room; his ego splattered all over the walls, dashed against the uncovered fireplace in front of which they had conceived Rebecca one spring afternoon after walking in Riverside Park, back before they decided to explore different relationships.

The experience was frightening because, when they tried to patch up the marriage, the more effort they made the farther they seemed to grow apart. He told her he'd wanted something beyond the marriage and he didn't blame her, but that he had quit seeing other people two years after Rebecca was born. After someone named Roberta. She was a ceramicist from Ohio. Atkinson. Roberta Atkinson. He hadn't wanted anyone else but Jennifer. He was scared. At that point in his life he believed he knew what was happening to him and denial set in. Rather than admit the obvious his answer had been monogamy. He'd wanted to stop seeing other women and did so. He had thought he'd fall apart at first.

"You're too much," she said, giddily, trying to wake him from his reverie.

"Have you seen him since you got back from the Orient?" he said.

She asked him if he meant Ted, and Feliciano said that's who he meant. She said that they'd had dinner several nights before; cooing, playing the little girl to perfection; explaining how Ted had been turned on about her experiences in India and Nepal; the backpacking with Jack and how they'd stayed at a Buddhist monastery, explaining that the monks had been refugees from Tibet; that Jack said that the Chinese had taken over Tibet and that Jack had met the Dalai Lama; proudly stating that Jack was helping Richard Gere and other celebri-

ties with a benefit to help him raise money for Tibet. Jennifer mentioned a few people, emphasizing that they were pop stars, but they
were no one he had heard of.

Anyway, she went on to tell him that Ted took her to a little Ben-
gali restaurant on the Lower East Side. She pronounced it Bengoli,
reassuring him that this was the right pronunciation when he corrected her. He backed off from challenging her linguistic explanation,
admitting to himself that there was always a ring of certainty to her
voice when she was correct about an issue.

And yet he was unable to leave things be, to allow her the room
to be correct, even in an insignificant area. He needed to test her emotional perception; wanted to deny that she was still damaged; a part
of him needing for a miracle to have taken place somewhere between
Rangoon and Katmandu; knowing, however, that no amount of philosophy, enlightenment, travel, religion, Eastern or Western, could
break through to her. He asked her how Ted was. She said he seemed
all right and then he asked her if Ted had given up on her. The question was blurted out, but not withdrawn or apologized for, since the
meaning described his frustration and he wanted her to see its extent.

"Pretty much, I guess," she said. "But not really."

And then feeling the tightness in his throat and the painful sensation in his lower abdomen which once again brought on arousal, he
asked her if she'd slept with him. She began to protest the intrusion
but smiled knowingly, as if suddenly deciphering that he thrived on
knowing about her lovers.

"As a matter of fact, I did," she said.

"Christ, Jennifer, you were gone an entire year," he said, feeling
the moral outrage pouring out of him. He examined his own motives
against the moral outrage, but was able to rationalize them and went
ahead with his indictment. "Didn't Ted ask for an explanation?"

"No, he was just glad I came back," she replied, puzzled.

"Did you know he tried to kill himself?" he said, accusingly.

"Really?" she said, uttering the word as if someone was telling
her about the benefits of a new skin cream. More than surprise, there
was a look of amused hurt on her face.

"Sleeping pills. Didn't even bother leaving work. They found him
in his office the next morning."

Absently she said Ted had not mentioned it. Feliciano explained
that Ted wanted to go back to his wife, but she wouldn't take him.

This time she said she knew; that Ted had broken down and begged Marissa, but that she wouldn't budge. She then told him that Ted wanted her to move in with him again. Paul Feliciano knew that if he detailed everything in his letter it would sound like some horrible Spanish television soap opera of the type his mother watched daily. But he had to tell someone and Roger seemed so attentive.

"And?" he said, "are you going to do it? Move in with him?"

Pausing for a moment, she became pensive and began talking about the two of them, herself and Feliciano, and how different their life together could've been; telling him that she enjoyed herself in bed like never before but that it was a temporary release. A body thing, she called it like in the old days, explaining that there was no connection from one time to the next, from one person to the other, and that it drove Jack crazy and he finally had to go back to Hong Kong and his travel book business; Jennifer surmising accurately, although he categorized her analysis not as developed acuity of perception, but as a one-time hit and miss occurrence, that Jack had become frustrated when she remained invulnerable and he couldn't reach her. To his question about moving in with Ted, she said she didn't know, and that her shrink said she had a healthy sex drive and that at the age of thirty-nine sex *should* be important; that for her it almost didn't matter who it was with. She reconsidered the statement and said she hadn't meant it the way it sounded.

"It does matter, but in a way it doesn't," she said.

A typical female response, he thought as he watched her. And then the disclaimer that she didn't think she was explaining herself well. Following that with the quick two-step away from the issue, she said that things hadn't worked out with Jack Cabrera, but that she was trying to sell the travel books for him here in the States.

Her words made his insides burn with desire, his mind's eye seeing her naked body and the men she had known, driving their organs into her, grinding their groins against her pubis, punishing her mercilessly, seeing everything physiologically, the gorged genitals, hers and theirs; his mind ablaze with a combination of lust and rage. But he listened intently, hoping for a faint glimmer that she was truly beginning to understand her life. In a way he admired her courage. She had often been on the verge of a realization, only to fall back, struck dumb by yet another question, yet another possibility to be explored, another door to be opened.

He was obsessed with her stupidity and asked her if she understood what kept happening to her. She said she sort of understood, but didn't seem to be able to stop; that she didn't feel one way or the other about it. He told her she had to be denying something; that it was the old equation. Trauma plus denial equals emotional deadness. "After a while it's impossible to recall anything of emotional importance," he said. He added that he had gone through it. There were blanks where there should've been something of importance, but that he was able to go back, carefully, step by step and put things together. "Everything is stored in the mind and all one needs is the courage and determination to go back through the endless banks of data to come up with the answer," he said to her, grasping for something that she could understand.

She stared blankly at him, and then the enormity of the truth hit him all at once. She had no concept of how her mind worked, how it was arranged, how information was separated and filed. He saw clearly, for perhaps the first time, her disorganization, her inability to piece even the smallest bits of information together if she was threatened emotionally; shielding herself from injury by pretending events had not taken place, not able to handle the imperfections of life and therefore not bothering to repair even the smallest breach of the social contract, violating trust on the one hand like a rebellious child and becoming irate when trust was violated and she was the recipient of the injury. She appeared straight-laced and unconventional at the same time.

He asked her how she saw her life? He knew his voice was filled with condescension, but it was the best that he could do. He asked her how she saw everything that had happened to her.

"Like a mess," she said, as if that were the required answer. "Like an awful, confusing mess."

"No, no," he replied shrilly. And then breathing deeply and trying to relax, he attempted to explain what he meant. If she were asked to portray graphically events that had taken place in her life, how would she do it? "For example, your thing with Jack," he said. "Here Jack is ready to make a full time commitment and you're still messing around with Ted."

She shook her head and formed a circle with her hands.

"It's like a clock," she said, shyly, certain that her example would be ridiculed. "Twelve on top and six on the bottom and things just keep turning and happening in the same way, going around and around, never changing at all."

Feliciano explained that this was part of the problem and went on a trip about her concern with a static time element, telling her that it seemed to him that space had no relationship in her scheme of things, in her world view. For a moment the words seemed to have meaning, and then the significance was gone, and from afar he saw himself mocking what he had become.

"What do you mean?" she said, sensing his discomfort.

He tried again, not caring anymore if he spoke in clichés. "Well, just try and tell me how you see events, things that have happened to you. How would you paint them, draw them, to illustrate to someone else their significance in terms of your overall time spent on the planet?"

"Like what?" she said.

"Like your first sexual experience," he replied. "Or our marriage, Rebecca's birth, the divorce, or your father's death. You know, significant events."

In the almost dream-like light of the room, the dark mahogany of the paneling, shiny in places, shadowy in others, her eyes seemed to produce a spark of awareness, and she said she thought she understood and went on to say that the clock was there going around and then she saw clouds; that if the experience was pleasant she saw a mountain lake; that if it wasn't then it was a cloud and that sometimes the experience was pleasant but she couldn't remember it too well and then the cloud was clean and fluffy.

He stood up and walked to the window.

She asked what was the matter, and rising, joined him as he stared out into the night, inquiring again if there was something wrong. She touched his arm and he turned to look at her, pitying her innocence.

"Is that all you see?" he asked.

"Yes, that's all," she said.

"And that's why you see one event as being different from the other, without any connection?"

"That's right, I guess. Time goes around and around and a cloud never comes back."

"But there must be some continuity, some way to check back and see where you went wrong."

"I suppose there is," she said, abstractly removed from the moment, her mind already relegating the subject to the insignificance of chatter.

She stared blankly at him, waiting. He held back, not wanting to speak, hoping something would go off in her brain to keep him from debasing himself again by instructing her. After a few moments he turned and asked her to sit down again. He reached deep inside himself to find some kinship with her and felt pride in his calm.

"Maybe I can tell you how I do it," he said. "I don't know. Maybe it'll help you."

She sat down, this time on the couch where he had been sitting. He crossed the room, his brow wrinkled, his face still tense with the severity of the situation, expecting a breakthrough, and sat down in the big chair, filling it and watching her curl up, her breasts outlined in the diaphanous fabric of her robe, her eyes suddenly sparkling as if she had been rewarded. He was silent now, thinking, his mind trying to control everything, his emotions regarding her churning inside of him.

"Is something wrong?" she asked.

"No, not really," he said. "I'm trying to fit the words together." He said his view of events in his life was different from hers; that he saw those events as ribbons, and that when something new happened another ribbon was connected, extending itself to the present, so that if he wanted to find out what went wrong he'd follow it. Sometimes he found a knot in the ribbon and then he'd have to spend time untying it.

"And what if it's something like Ana?" she said. "What happens then? Does the love keep going after death?"

"No, I suppose not," he said, unsure of himself, searching his mind, traveling back in time along that ribbon in his life to the place where Ana had stopped existing; back there at Bronx Science, having gone to the school like a freak, wishing to be anything but a Puerto Rican so that the cockroach jokes didn't hurt; never once feeling like a pioneer as Mr. Weissel had said; dreading the visits to the hospital to see a friend's life ebbing away; Ana's mother thanking him for the cards and flowers; doing research even then to understand the workings of the illness; leukemia; cancer of the blood; the life-giving fluid growing thinner each day and he unable to accept that someone so gentle and young could be stricken by the illness, not knowing then that he was in love with Ana Dávila, his concern hardly scientific but desperate, fighting the impotence of not being able to save her and resigning himself to the inevitability of the tragedy, recognizing now that fifteen was a fragile age and much too early in life to be confronted with either love or death on such a scale, but accepting it then in spite of himself and his need to cry out in anger. "No, I suppose not," he said again. "What happens is that the ribbon, that particular ribbon gets cut off. It just ends there."

Being questioned by her angered him.

"I see," she said, faintly amused by his seriousness. "You just cut it right there and then."

"No, not right there and then but eventually it's cut off, ended," he said.

"And there's no feeling?"

"No, none. I mean I can go back and see everything clearly, but I don't feel it now, if that's what you're asking."

"That's sad," she said. The concern puzzled him for an instant. It was more like that of an adult than it had a right to be. It was forgiving even when there was no sin involved, and for a moment he was jealous of one more feminine quality which he could not experience.

"What do you mean it's sad? At least I can recall what took place and see how one event is connected to the other."

"What color are the ribbons?" she said.

The question took him by surprise and he grimaced theatrically.

"C'mon, Jenny," he said. "Be serious. They don't have any color. Is my life supposed to be some sort of Disney spectacular? It's just a way of going back in time and putting things together to compare and recognize one event from the other, to separate them and see their similarities or differences."

"But they're all connected anyway," she shot back, petulantly.

"Don't be stupid, Jennifer," he said. He was reaching the boiling point, that place where the quick anger which exploded from him threatened to consume everything about him. "That's not the point. Of course they're connected. Why would I go to all the trouble of thinking of it if I didn't think they were connected. God, I'd go crazy if any time I wanted to recall something it came up in the shape of a cloud or a lake somewhere out there in the middle of nowhere. No place, no name, no dimensions or anything else."

"It's not like that at all," she protested. "I see the colors of the mountains and the trees around the lake, and if it's winter I see the snow and the ice and at night, when it's summer, the stars are reflected on the water."

"Well, why in the hell can't you see the connections?" he shouted. "Why in the hell do things keep happening to you?"

"I don't know."

"Jenny, what are you trying to do to me?" he demanded, speaking through gritted teeth. "If you want to have a tantrum, go ahead. If you want to relieve yourself of whatever it is that's making you unhappy, just start screaming and be done with it. Maybe then you won't have to think about this next mess you're getting yourself into. Whatever you do don't use me to get started."

He was almost on the verge of hysteria. The more he blamed her, the more elusive she would become and soon she would start defending even the most minute, irrelevant of points. Colors? Why did her ribbons need colors? He had to leave before she started asking if he was angry with her. He would strike her then, like he had the other times, when she was left with welts across her face and her arms black and blue like his mother and the other sad-faced women of his childhood and their daughters whom he now treated for the same abuses at the hospital.

He asked her if it could really happen with anybody and felt the sick, pleasant feeling in his lower abdomen, as he discussed the forbidden. He was happy he finally understood how important hearing her talk about her lovers was to him. She said of course not, chiding him faintly for asking a silly question. She said she had to know the person and did he know what she meant. He wanted to tell her that he didn't, that when the urge hit he had been totally indiscriminate. But that had not been true, because he had spared Roger, gently rejecting his advances, explaining his wish for friendship and inventing a monogamous lover back in New York. Instead, he asked her if she was saying that it could even happen with him again, feeling suddenly strong and in control of the situation.

She paused for a moment, recognizing, as always, that this was the place where she had always gone wrong, the place where she had to examine her emotions clearly and make a decision. She collapsed easily, quietly saying that with them everything had been her fault; that it was a misunderstanding on her part; that she'd wanted acceptance from him and got it confused with wanting to be understood;

that she couldn't figure out how he could claim to love her and still be so critical about little things.

Firmly, but perhaps a little too sharply he reminded her that those things were what *she* considered little things.

"Of course," she said. "I didn't bring it up to start anything, but I couldn't understand the way you behaved. It drove me out of my mind when you could be so understanding about who I was sleeping with and so upset about what I saw as trivialities. What did it matter if I forgot some appointment or a phone call or who was coming to dinner? Love should have taken care of all that. And I did love you. Probably still do. I trusted you. I believed in you."

"Sure, right," he said, looking away from her.

She was pensive again, and then said they shouldn't have split up. Feliciano watched her, understanding once again her allure. When she spoke this way she displayed a passion which he had known in few people. She was right. She had trusted him, believed in him. There had been a thirst in him to succeed that was unquenchable. Without her he wasn't sure if he could have gone far. He was going to be the best surgeon ever. Not the best Puerto Rican surgeon, but the best surgeon; he had stressed this over and over. And she was right. He had said those things. The best, so people would look at his hands and not his name. Then she said ever so softly, that she was sorry she had let him down. "I wasn't the smart girl you thought you had married."

"It's all right," he said, his voice soothing her, fearful for a moment that she had reached a breaking point, but angry that she treated him the same way she had treated her father. She still romanticized Feliciano's background, his poverty, the squalor of his childhood, pretty much the same way the society idealized that kind of life when someone manages to emerge from it. No one knew the hatred he felt when he looked back on the way he'd grown up; living in that awful East Harlem apartment with the constant threat of physical and sexual attack by his stepfather and the screaming and yelling between the bastard and his mother; the times when his stepfather walked in drunk and began accusing her of infidelities; using the charges as a pretext for beating her so that the next day her arms were bruised horribly from the beatings; pummeling her fat body without mercy and she stoically imploring him to stop; repeating that she loved him, that there was no one else in her life but him; his step-father, Humberto, calling her those awful names in English and in Spanish, and Feliciano helpless, cringing every time he heard the hollow sound of his fists striking her.

Before Feliciano was finished speaking Jennifer Marginat put her head down and began crying softly, her shoulders moving ever so slightly. A wave of repugnance attacked him, causing him to feel slightly nauseated. Why did he have to mention that she was careful about AIDS. Was he trying to protect her? What was the matter with him! His task was to catch her off guard, not protect her. Unable to hide his curiosity, his voice more intellectual than concerned, he asked if she was all right.

"Yes, please don't worry," she said. She wiped the corner of her eyes with a finger tip and told him she didn't even love Ted or Jack; but that she was involved anyway; that it was crazy; that love was so strange now; that she felt driven to people. Not gently and with a little flame burning inside of her, she said, but coldly, like a machine, and that when nothing happened she was always disappointed; that it satisfied something but she didn't know what it was. She stopped and looked at him.

"It isn't even sex anymore," she said. "You're right in telling Rebecca that I'm super careful because I am."

"I know you are but your involvement is a ruse, like everything else," he said. "The emotional risk in giving yourself is absent with Ted. Your risk is with Jack."

"You're probably right," she said, her voice filled with an awful resignation which he'd never heard before.

"He'll find out eventually," he said. "It's almost an emotional replica of what happened with us."

She was genuinely surprised, and wanted to know what he meant. She pushed her legs outward and sat demurely on the chair. Her question was genuine but it angered him. My God, he thought, they had discussed the subject countless times. For a long time he doubted the possibility of a woman like her understanding the problem. Now he was convinced of the futility in trying to make any woman understand the complexities of the issue. He had seen many who could pretend, but it was merely that, pretense.

It was indeed a male value, a moment-of-truth phenomenon, corny as it sounded, in which for a number of reasons it was impossi-

ble to turn away from a confrontation with the self. One either suc-
ceeded or failed but was never left in doubt about having tried. At
that moment one was alone with one's actions. There were no refer-
ees, no umpires, no judges or laws, no superiors, not even God. Left
only with the self to judge every move, weigh each action as to its
courage, its timeliness, its eventual consequences, a man could not
escape himself.

He weighed her question once more. He had to answer, had to
tell her again as if it were the very first time she'd asked. To do less
would be to go against himself. Having acquired, in the past few
years, a more conscientious view of the purpose of truth, he hesitated.
He told her he didn't know how to explain it anymore without causing both of them some pain. He told her, honestly, that he thought
most of it was his hang-up as a male.

"Do you know what I mean?"

She nodded, her quicksilver eyes brilliant, but empty of trust,
watching. He continued, choosing each word carefully, not allowing
his emotions to enter into his explanations, fearing the hysteria which
crept lately into his arguments if he was not understood. He
explained that of all of the human problems he could think of the one
he found the most perplexing was the one in which an individual,
male or female, faced with an equal chance of success or failure opts
for failure, even going to the trouble of manufacturing the ingredients
required for making the failure foolproof, fighting battles where no
battles exist, in order to forego the real conflict. He knew he sounded
as if he were lecturing but there was no other way.

He told her it had happened to him often enough for the recognition to be instantaneous, and asked her if she remembered the first
time he'd come up for promotion at the hospital. She replied that she
vaguely recalled the incident. She appeared lulled for the moment by
his impersonal tone, believing perhaps this time she would see everything he was attempting to say to her, pitying him at the same time
because he was trying when she herself knew it was hopeless. He
explained how there had been no need for him to get involved in
helping DeSpina with his battle, no need to become outraged by the
politics in surgery. All it did was throw him headlong into a confrontation with Lyons. He told her that his fear was that he was going
to be judged and ruled on. He couldn't stand the pressure and
released it someplace else.

"I understand," she said. "You were afraid you wouldn't be promoted."

Although he was momentarily distressed by her missing the point once more, he was able to manage a smile and explained calmly that it was more like a resentment at being placed in the situation; feeling he shouldn't have to be judged by them. She said she understood and that that's how she felt when they fought.

He wanted to tell her that their situation had been different, that it was one person's view against another's, that it wasn't an institution impinging on one's rights when he disagreed with her. And yet his analysis wasn't entirely true. He had become conscious, in the past few years, of secret institutions residing within each person, so that each acted like an agent against the other, fighting an all-out battle; the one bombing the other with complete abandon while the other, methodically, guerilla-like in her patience, waited. He hated the allusion to war. The fact that he'd wormed his way out of going to Vietnam still bothered him. Sole supporter of his mother; only son. Both lies. His sisters Rosa and Mildred were married, and William was living in Puerto Rico with his grandmother because their stepfather couldn't stand him and threatened to kill him when William stood up to him. God, the kid was only eleven and this bastard threatened to kill him. His mother sent him to P.R. He now drove a bus between Cacimar and Caguas.

III

Romance Sonámbulo
Trecientas rosas morenas
lleva tu perchera blanca.
Tu sangre rezuma y huele
alrededor de tu faja.
Pero yo ya no soy yo,
ni mi casa es ya mi casa.
—FEDERICO GARCÍA LORCA
"Romancero Gitano"

When Paul Feliciano worked at Mount Sinai he'd seen Sonny Maldonado coming at him, shuffling up the street, his head down, his entire body bent by the psychological pressure of the war which Feliciano had avoided. He crossed the street quickly to avoid his childhood friend and ducked into the hospital. Later on, he asked a patient at the hospital, someone who knew Sonny, how come he walked as he did. When he was told Sonny had lost a foot in Vietnam, Feliciano was filled with rage at the choice he'd made back then. It had been wrong. He should've gone. The chances of a doctor dying on the battlefield were minimal and he knew it, but the fear of not fulfilling his potential as a surgeon kept him home. And yet it hadn't been the right choice and he was now paying for his cowardice.

He asked her if she understood that it was the avoidance of that moment that caused her trouble. Genuinely perplexed, she asked him if he meant her in particular. He told her that no, anyone in the situation, but yes she in particular because they were talking about her. She said she understood, and shifted her legs back beneath her. She shook her hair once more as she ground another cigarette into a large, polished piece of marble hollowed out into an ashtray. He went on to say that it wasn't so much the fear of being rejected as of being scrutinized and seeing the self squirm under the pressure of not knowing the outcome of the situation, and having to decide to be courageous enough to wait until the problem resolved itself. He agonized over what he was saying, because more than ever the axiom applied to him as well.

Very slowly, with the same care which he had to employ when telling someone that the operation was a risky one, Feliciano told her that when he began changing, becoming committed to her, it forced her to weigh her role vis-à-vis him. Arrhythmically interjected, she stated that they knew each other pretty well. She was like a child again, her eyes open in the same innocent way he had learned to mistrust. It was her defense against knowledge. He lost his patience and said, Jenny, dammit and reminded her that they'd known each other superficially.

"Do you actually believe that things didn't happen between us?" he said. "Are you telling me that bonds were not broken; that there was no loss of trust or recriminations? We came from totally different worlds and the only thing that kept us together those first years was newness."

She again put her head down and he knew she was weeping.

He told her he'd hated her because she couldn't share her life completely with him. At first the resentment centered on not knowing what it felt like to carry Rebecca, shifting gradually to the childbirth itself.

"Not knowing what it felt like?" she said, and then recalled that they had talked about it and withdrew the question. "It was something else, wasn't it?"

He told her for the first time, feeling the shame flow over him like a fine liquid, not burning him or staining him, but nevertheless feeling the shame palpably, that it was the other; the sexual act and that he'd wanted all of her, her thoughts, her passions, her experience, everything; and that when he realized this he no longer needed to be with another woman, and he felt free and clean. "It was painful as hell, but I felt free," he said.

"But you couldn't tell me," she said, sadly.

He explained that he had tried telling her, and even saw her wanting to stop seeing other people, making attempts at getting closer to him and then withdrawing and hooking up with someone else. He told her that back then he'd loved her more then than he ever had; that he had been vulnerable and so had she.

She said she knew but couldn't help it. She corrected herself. She hadn't wanted to help it; that she could tell something had changed in him, but that he seemed so distant, so superior. She laughed and said she missed the arguments, the fights; that she needed them; that it was the only time she ever saw herself clearly and wasn't frightened by her feelings other than in bed. She said she still didn't understand the whole thing, but that Jack had explained it to her once; that Jack had said she was a counter puncher and didn't hit unless she was hit first. He told her he supposed Jack was right and that it was the best way to describe her.

"I'm sorry," she said, and her words pierced his heart, because they were spoken honestly. "I truly am, Paul."

"I'm sorry too," he said to his ex-wife and watched himself as he got up, walked to the couch, sat next to her and took her in his arms. She immediately fit into his embrace. She was like a child, trusting and starved for the warmth of human contact. He smoothed her hair, loving and hating her at the same time, her feminine fragrances like a sweet-tasting poison. Before he knew it, he was caressing her and she was moaning. There was no need to confess to Roger that he had been with a number of women. Some passionate and some like ice, but bar none Jennifer was the most highly sexed one he had ever been with. They had not held each other two minutes before she stood up, took his hand and was pulling him gently up the stairs to her bedroom.

His heart swelled with the immensity of the conquest. The feeling was stronger than any other time when he had pursued someone and finally persuaded the person to give themselves. Once in the bedroom she stood in the light of the lamp on the night table, and undid the robe to stand before him. Rather than the diminutive elfin-like fragility of her personality she was magnificent in her nakedness, her breasts, waist and hips as always perfect in their symmetry, the skin rose and amber in its tones, the pubic fleece merely an accent to the beauty. Her hands at her side, she turned her palms outward to beckon him.

"I don't have anything," he said, alluding to the need for protection, but walking to her and taking her in his arms.

"Don't worry," she said. "I trust you."

"You might get pregnant," he said, fighting the perverse desire making him wish to be within her, filling her with his poisoned life, fusing with her in destruction, knowing she had followed his advice and stopped taking the pill.

"Wrong time of the month," she said. "I'm safe," she added, her voice growing soft and enticing, backing up as if she were dancing him to the bed, their parents' huge bed where they had made love endlessly that first year when the Marginats had gone off to visit her grandmother's relatives in Spain and then gone to Cuba and then Puerto Rico; Jennifer giving the housekeeper permission to visit her daughter in upstate New York. They had gorged themselves on each other's bodies so that later, when they saw their friends' sexual manuals or the Masters and Johnson report, they had laughed uproariously at the supposed expertise of the authors; bragging that they could've written a much more interesting book. "Please," she said. "We can try again. I'll be good and study so that I don't embarrass you. Please."

She reached up to be kissed, but he held her and then the emotion hit him and he sobbed, the pain coming out in an agonizing spasm so that he slipped down to the floor and with his arms around her thighs buried the side of his face on her stomach, still flat and smooth and fragrant with her womanhood and he sobbed and sobbed.

"I can't, I can't," he said, repeating the phrase over and over, not as an excuse to her, but to himself.

"Poor Paul," she said, sinking down to the floor with him. "I can wait until you're ready. I won't see anyone else. I promise. I understand. Really, I do."

Paul Feliciano through his grief heard the adult Jennifer Marginat he had yearned for all those years, the ideal which he had always sought but had always eluded him.

"I know you do," he said, rising and helping her up. "Get dressed before I change my mind," he added, wryly, a bit of injured laughter escaping from his chest, the truly private joke monstrous in its significance to him.

She did not answer but disappeared into the walk-in closet. A few moments later she emerged dressed in a thick blue bathrobe and followed him out of the bedroom.

"Can I ask you something?"

"Sure."

"The ribbon for me. Is it cut off?"

"Yes, I suppose it is," he said stopping at the head of the stairs. He turned to face her. "No, that's not true," he corrected himself. "With you it's more than one ribbon. Some of them are cut off and others are not." He tried to smile but couldn't and felt as if his jaw were locked in place. "Why would I still want to see you?"

She touched his face, her hand almost childlike in its gesture.

"That's sweet," she said. "Poor Paul."

He wanted to touch her, to take her in his arms, to test again what he knew was impossible to recapture. His cheek was hot where she had touched him and the anger rose up again in him, flooding his body so that his fingertips tingled.

"I really have to go," he said. "I'll see you."

"Please don't go," she said, the voice cutting through him.

He descended the stairs, holding tightly to the bannister lest he faint from the spent emotion. He recalled again being in Sevilla; walking in the brilliant sun, the sky cloudless, the air dry and life-giving, the people speaking Spanish like Puerto Ricans spoke the language and their faces reminding him of his family and his friends, the blood of the Moors clearly visible, the dignity of the Arab culture prominently displayed in the reined-in passions, straining to be released but held in reserve, always there and demanding of respect. He and Roger had climbed La Giralda and looked out over the city. The mosque had been the most magnificent in Spain. It had been razed and in its place the Catedral de Sevilla had been erected. The largest Gothic cathedral ever constructed, it took its builders from 1402 to 1511 to complete. So spectacular had been the Moorish structure whose place the cathedral had taken that the Catholic king asked that the magnificent minaret, la Giralda, thirty stories high, remain intact and next to it was the cathedral erected. It was here in the cathedral that Christopher Columbus' remains rested. Feliciano had been awed by the history and was certain his relatives had walked through the cathedral as he had, for he was also certain the tragedy of his life had begun there in Sevilla.

He and Roger had eaten lunch in an outdoor cafe and then had taken a ride on a horse-drawn carriage, the hooves of the horse and the iron rims of the carriage wheels clattering over the cobblestones while the driver pointed out landmarks and recited their history until they reached Parque de María Luisa, where there are hundreds of gardens and fountains and winding trails where hardly any sun enters because of the height of its trees, some of them hundreds of years old. Roger had caressed his hand, but Feliciano had taken his hand back and patted Roger's knee gently. He had wished then that it had been Jennifer riding in the carriage with him and all at once he withdrew into a dark mood that had frightened Roger.

"I wished you'd change your mind," Jennifer said, her voice sounding absolutely mature. "I'm worried about you."

"I really have to go," he said bravely as he stepped outside. "Please don't worry. When Rebecca comes in maybe we can do something together."

"Sure, that'd be nice, Paul. Take care of yourself," she said and closed the door.

Out in the street he walked toward West End Avenue. Once there he turned south and began the walk home. As he passed one of the buildings a Latino doorman recognized him, called him doctor in greeting him and tipped his hat, remarking that it had grown colder in the past hour and it looked like it would snow. The doorman spoke in Spanish, and Feliciano saw each word clearly in his mind, each meaning separate but the unity of the words intact. He could not, however, determine whether the man was Cuban, Dominican or one of his own, having lost his capacity to distinguish their speech. The wind now slashed his face, so that he felt hot and cold at the same time. Colors. Why had Jennifer asked about colors? There were no colors to the ribbons. No need for them. As he thought, the ribbons turned into wires, thin, colored telephone wires, snaking in and out, twisting around each other all over the city, the voices alive as they meshed one into the other in a thousand tongues, their tones displaying every emotion, cursing one moment, caressing the next, imploring, begging, pleading, ordering, laughing and sometimes crying.

When he reached his apartment building the wires in his mind had turned to the roots of a tree. They twisted and turned in the earth, avoiding stones, housing insects and worms beneath them, absorbing rain and enduring cold, knocking into the roots of other trees, searching mindlessly, blindly. Once inside the apartment he tried to drive the thoughts out of his mind. It was useless.

His head was bursting with the images, the pressure causing his eyes to water. He lay down on the couch and stared at the uncovered fireplace, each brick seemingly separate from the others. The tree roots had now turned to the veins in his body as they coursed through every muscle and cell, to each of his vital organs, the connections seemingly random and confused as in a medical illustration, the blood blue and red, racing ahead, oxygenated, pumped by the heart, flowing aimlessly back and forth and around, supplying each organ without reasons or questions, changing itself to mucus or tears or seminal fluid, disguising itself to create illusions, carrying joy and sadness without knowledge of their consequences, and in those joys and sorrows carrying as well, illness.

His hatred became unbearable. On the one hand he was proud that he had shown restraint in sparing Jennifer. He had chosen the lesser of two evils although she had certainly made it easy for him to do otherwise. But why hadn't he told her? She had a right to know. Eventually, they would all know. He'd had the lab make his test under three different names and three times the results had been the same. First the Elisa test and then the Western Blot test. Positive. But he should've told her. She had a right to know. Or did she? Hadn't she ruined his life? Whose idea had it been, back then, to experiment? He was sure it had been her's, but it didn't seem likely. And it didn't matter. It was within him. Buried. Latent was the medical term. All his concern about her lovers had been nothing but a desire to experience what she experienced, so that eventually he had succumbed. As he lay steeped in self-disgust he thought about those secret ribbons . . . Conrad on that skiing trip to Boulder . . . Larry in St. Croix . . . Charles in Montreal during Expo . . . Hans, the muscular German, on Corfu . . . and the dozen boys in the baths down in the Village . . . down by the pier . . . in the men's rooms of bars . . . and he still didn't know what it was like for her.

He was sweating profusely now and his chest felt tight, his heart beating unevenly, so that he had a great desire to place a stethoscope there to listen, seeing the mass of flesh again in dissection. Who had it been? He had lost touch with all of them. Going from one horrible and saddened life to the next, laughing, pretending that everything was all right. Two years of a forbidden life, and then wishing to right things again and beginning to date women once more; tolerating their whims and listening to their boredom; once in a while truly charmed by someone's intelligence and wit; joining with them in "safe sex" and feeling a sort of antiseptic satisfaction, one free of guilt. But in spite of the safe sex it could've been one of them as well.

Only a corner of his mind remained cognizant of the rest of his body, searching for some place to grasp, to hold on to. But the blood kept rushing through him and he couldn't stop it, he couldn't look at it, examine it to find out what had gone wrong. It was like a bright red and unstoppable rapids which would eventually break through the skin and dot it with those awesome plum-colored blotches. It was his secret and no one had to know.

One evening in Sevilla, before they had gone out to eat, Feliciano recalled leaving Roger to finish getting dressed. He had walked alone in the failing light through the narrow streets near Plaza Museo. He turned the corner, and up the street walking toward him along the tiny sidewalk, was an exact replica of his mother as a young woman. She was small and delicate with jet black hair and large almond-shaped eyes, the iris and pupil indistinguishable in color. More than his mother, it was himself that he saw. He realized instantly that before him was a sort of female *doppelganger*, his female double as he imagined he would have wanted to look had he been a young woman, devoid of artifice, innocent and pure. The recognition struck him so deeply that he nearly swooned. The girl, strikingly beautiful in her simplicity and no more than sixteen, saw his surprise, recognized the resemblance to herself in him and smiled shyly. Within his chest his heart expanded and contracted and he nearly let out a sob. He was so shaken by the girl that he went and sat down in a cafe, ordered mineral water, and cried quietly for a few minutes before returning to the hotel. Now, the incredible sadness that had enveloped him, as he walked across the bridge over the Guadalquivir River coming back from Triana in the coolness of early morning with the sky dotted with stars, the sadness he had experienced inside the cathedral that felt as if he had been transported in time and was help-less to determine his fate, the sorrow that pierced his heart riding in the carriage wishing Jennifer was beside him, and especially the sad-ness he felt when he saw himself in the young girl in the streets of that alluring Sevilla dusk the previous June, assailed him and as if in apoc-alyptic cavalry those for instances were now riding against him so that within the realization he saw the overwhelming darkness that awaited him.

Like a moonless night that cloaks the land causing the most innocent of phenomena to become a mystery, the mind of Paul Feliciano, long accustomed to order, began to produce a fog-like grayness that gave everything he examined an edge of uncertainty. At first he imagined that like poor Victor, whose daily CAT scans showed less and less brain function until there was nothing left, he was developing encephalitis. He recalled his birthday, the names of geologic strata, obscure constellations, chemical symbols, made a quick inventory of his anatomical knowledge, named each of the Beatles' albums out loud, and decided his mind was intact.

He remembered again walking across the bridge over the Guadalquivir River the first time. He and Roger attempting to translate part of a García Lorca poem and not feeling satisfied with the translation: *Rosa futura y vena contenida*, Rose of the future and contained vein, *amatista de ayer y brisa de ahora mismo* Yesterday's amethyst and breeze of the present, *¡Quiero olvidarlas!* I want to forget them! Roger had argued that it should have been "breezes of right now" and Feliciano had insisted that the Latinate "present" was more poetic, closer to the Spanish. Roger had chided him and slapping his arm had said, "Oh Paul, please. You're such a proper spic." Feliciano had laughed and the two of them, intoxicated by each other and the beauty of Sevilla, had continued across the bridge along with the strolling couples of all ages, not caring what anyone thought.

Exhausted, Paul Feliciano closed his eyes and knew there was no need now to write the letter to Roger. He saw once again the young woman who had reminded him of his mother and himself and, as he had felt that evening, experienced the same longing for something lost. He promised himself that he would face whatever was to come with courage and dignity and if there was time he would return once again to Sevilla.

Fresh Fruit

Marisella Veiga

MARISELLA VEIGA was born in Havana, Cuba. In 1960, her family went into exile, and she was raised in both St. Paul, Minnesota, and Miami, Florida. Her poetry, articles and translations have appeared in numerous publications. "Fresh Fruit" was written in the silence and space provided in the Dominican Republic by the Altos de Chavon Cultural Center Foundation. Ms. Veiga currently lives, writes, and teaches in Miami, Florida.

I was up the first time about five, made coffee and heated up some milk for it. When I turned on the kitchen light, the dog came and stood near the stove. He seemed cold. Right before lunch I usually boil some meat and bones for him, but it was not time for that feeding, so I gave him a little warm milk instead. I snapped the light off and went to sit on the porch, where I usually have my coffee and listen to the roosters and the occasional car traveling along the highway.

The young woman across the street, Susana, went to work earlier than usual today. The driveway gate clanked loudly when she closed it, as if it was meant as a shout to someone inside the house, "There, you have it!" I'd like to see someone actually walk away from his home that easily.

She started that old car with tremendous faith. It's as loud as a motorcycle. Sometimes, as the car warms up, she looks over to see if I am on the porch and waves. In the morning she is relaxed, friendlier. By late afternoon, she is tired and a bit arrogant, thinking that what she does all day is more important than what I do. I can tell by the excuses she makes when I call her to come over for a short visit.

"I just got home from work and have to shower," she yells from across the street, one hand busy with a set of keys, the other holding a briefcase. Other times, when she's tired, there's a longer litany: "I'm hungry. There's no food in the house. I have to go to the market, then make dinner." There's a plea in her voice on those days, yet I do not do anything to alleviate her exhaustion. What she means is that there's no time for an old lady on the schedule unless a hot meal is included.

She'll push her plate away at the end of the meal, thank me, smoke a cigarette and five minutes later cross the street to her house without being any sort of company afterward. My husband Wilfredo is just like that.

Susana, of course, has the option to not make anyone anything. Every morning at the corner cafeteria she reads a newspaper while having breakfast. Someone cooks it and somebody else takes the dishes away when the meal is done. She does not even see the faces of the people performing these services. Throwing away money, that's all. I told her she could pay me less and have more delicious food, but I don't think she's interested in saving money either, or forming a home with a husband.

Why? For one, though I have advised her, she has not bothered to invest in a red dress. It's an attractive color that suits her, and would appeal to a man, and one never knows. A husband could help her along, and she, in turn, could help him. When I told her my idea, she said, "Red? I don't like that color at all."

When Wilfredo and I were first married, we rented a small apartment in this neighborhood, near the sea, and spent Sundays on the beach. Years later, he bought this house and a few years after that a farm in the mountains, so our home would not lack fresh fruit or vegetables. I haven't seen the farm in years; I don't leave the house, but he drives up there often and returns with the back of his jeep loaded with bunches of plantains. He hangs them on hooks to ripen in the garage.

I give them out to neighbors as a way of showing appreciation for their attentions to me. Whenever I tell Susana to take a couple, she hesitates. Oh, the diet she is currently on does not allow for much of anything fried, and that's how she likes them. A little prompting and she takes three thick ones home, hiding them in the briefcase. I know she eats them up fast, fried as *tostones*, not waiting for them to ripen for a sweeter tasting dish. No, she is an impatient sort who likes to take hard bites of hot salty starches.

She refuses things like custards, although I have seen her eyes widen when I've brought one out to the table and set it next to her coffee. No sweets. Give her salt, the sea, the beginning of the meal and she's happy. I know. Now I want the sweet, the fruit that comes after the meal is done.

He's home. I heard the car horn sound, a warning so I am not frightened when someone begins jiggling the padlock on the porch door. When Wilfredo returns in the evening, he greets me with a kiss on the cheek, though he is coming from his mistress' house. We have lived in this house for twenty years now, and she has lived in another one, which he also owns, all along.

I tolerate his nightly visits with her. I have no choice. In a way, they are a relief because he does not look at me anymore to satisfy his longing. He thinks I think I'm too old for sex. He doesn't leave her, won't abandon me, and the neighbors know that in the end he sleeps in this house every night. One might say I am no longer acting completely as a wife.

He does not allow his mistress to cook for him. That is why I believe that, after all these years, he loves me most because he comes home twice a day to my table.

The young woman across the street, despite all her American ways, which she learned at school, does not know how to do this. Yes, she is free to wander beyond her gate, to walk into a restaurant any time of day, like any man, and buy meals made by someone cooking anonymously in the kitchen. She has money, a way to ride around town. She speaks English and French and travels to the other islands. She drinks beer and sometimes stays out late, while I sit on my porch waiting for Wilfredo to arrive. I don't get bored.

Her house is empty all day until she walks into it. She can stroll along the shore of the sea anytime, but there, nobody gives a damn. There she goes, out to dinner alone again, taking a book along for company. I'll start frying up plantains. Wilfredo will be home in an hour.

After the meal and some conversation, he will turn off the lights in the dining room. I'll wash the dishes and close up the kitchen, and finally bring the dog inside the house for the night. We will go through the rest of the rooms, turning off the lights in the entire house, before going our separate ways.

Two Sketches

José Antonio Villarreal

JOSÉ ANTONIO VILLARREAL was born in Los Angeles in 1924. His family moved to Santa Clara, California, when he was six. He served in the U.S. Navy during the Second World War, and upon his return from the service earned a BA in English at the University of California, Berkeley. He also did graduate work at UCLA. Mr. Villarreal's classic novel, *Pocho*, is a watershed work that initiated contemporary Chicano literature as well as all Latino-American literature written and published in the United States. His second work, *The Fifth Horseman*, a novel of the Mexican Revolution, is an important link between the literatures of Mexico and the United States.

"The Last Minstrel in California"

Crispín Soriano came from nowhere. He just arrived one day out of the Santa Cruz Mountains on a buck mule, bringing with him only a bedroll and a guitar. He sat on a heavy blanket for he had no saddle, and he wore huaraches which had but two eyelets, and my father said that this meant he came from a very low station in life to have only one thong on his huaraches. He even wore a sarape and a straw hat. He was a ludicrous figure coming over the rise of a hill down to the boxcanyon where our tents were.

Although at the time this occurred it was not considered unusual to see horses and wagons on the streets and highways, my father said that it was indeed a strange thing to see someone come riding in that manner. It was a common occurrence in his own country, he said, but not here and in that dress. We children thought it immensely wonderful, for Crispín Soriano had a bi-lateral lisp and a high voice so that in his costume, for it was a costume to us even though we knew that not too long ago our parents had dressed in the same manner, he was fantastic.

He was a clown; a very happy clown.

Crispín Soriano captivated not only the hearts of the children but of all the people in the camp. We were camped in the Los Gatos hills where my father had contracted to pick eighty tons of French prunes and thirty tons of Imperials from a mountainside. I was still quite a little boy at that time but was expected to do my share and I did it, although quite reluctantly, for though I was a good worker I had no liking for work. In the hot sun as I worked uphill and my knees became more sore, I looked forward to the day I would descend upon the state legislature and demand that every rancher who farmed a hillside be required to have his entire orchard paved, and place a gutter at the bottom of the hill to catch the fruit. Then we would come along the gutter and pick the fruit right into boxes. At that time I was always concerned with how I could make it easier for the prune picker, for I had a vague idea that this would be my life's work. Why not, I had a trade and was secure.

But Crispín Soriano changed all that for me.

From the first night I saw him I knew I wanted to be just like him. He was a real cut-up and his eyes glittered in the dark. He joked with everybody, and even the men laughed through the ache in their bodies from the hard day's work. He did intricate little jigs and talked in inanities, and after he had eaten he played his guitar and sang ballads. When he sang he did not lisp. He sang about children and about grownups, about animals and about angels and spirits, and in short about everything, but somehow all these songs had a theme of unrequited love or love betrayed. Death was always present and it was made beautiful by his words. There was always a man—a strong man—forsaken by his woman in one way or another, and he was either killed by the lady's new lover, drank himself to death, or was pining away to a very pale death from a broken heart. He sang a corrido about a mountain lion who had found his mate shortly before the season of the rut. The lion had been extremely careful as he waited for the moment that he would mount the female, because he was young and this was the first time for him and his instinct told him that an older, larger male would arrive and that he must fight for his mate. And the other arrived at the precise moment the female was ready and the young lion lay on his side with his entrails still attached to his body before his open belly, his eyes strange with what we could not understand, and I cried.

Sometimes the protagonist was drunk and the ballad was in the first person and Crispín Soriano sounded just as if he was drunk and the tears streamed down his face as he sang and we cried too, even the men, and then sometimes the man was big and strong, stoically resigned to a life without the woman and Crispín Soriano grew in stature and seemed to be a huge man although he was just a little fellow.

Crispín Soriano slept in a shack a few hundred yards from the camp which had once housed workers but was now haunted. He would not work. He had never worked in his life, he said, and when the men were disgusted at this, he said he did not need money, had never needed it, in fact. He remained in the camp all day, occasionally helping a woman with her crying child or another one with the wash. He was very handy around the camp during the day, and the different families fed him. The men when talking among themselves said he was a maricón doing women's work and not working like a man. He could sew and knit and once even made pan dulce in a makeshift Dutch oven.

But in the evenings, everyone welcomed him with open arms, for he led them out of their real world for a while, and they loved the fantasy he wove for them. They were back home in their own countries every night.

He had an ambition, Crispín Soriano said one night, and that was to be the last minstrel in California. Perhaps even in the whole of the North American United States. He had followed crop workers for a year and everywhere he went he found Mexican camps. He had come from Watsonville and Castroville, towns near the ocean, where were grown the funny little plants called artichokes. He followed the coast and ate fish and seaweed. I am from the coastal regions, he said, in a place called Veracruz and I know the things from the sea that are good to eat. My father told me that indeed he had known Crispín Soriano was from a place called Veracruz on the Gulf of Mexico, and that place had a very Indianated population, he said, with a trace of the black blood in it from the islands. My father was very fair about Crispín Soriano and did not look down upon him because he came from Veracruz nor because he did not work. He was a bit contemptuous only because Crispín Soriano rode a mule just as he was contemptuous toward Americans for using a horse for field work. At one time my father had been a great horseman but now he was in the prune picking business.

By now I knew that Crispín Soriano would not be the last minstrel in California because that would be I, but I did not tell him, because it would have made him sad and anyway the prune season was almost over and soon the camp would be breaking up. Some of the people in camp would undoubtedly see him again, for they would go to Parlier in the San Joaquín valley to pick cotton and he was going there also, but we would be returning to Santa Clara, for I had to go back to school and would never see him again, so it did not matter to me that he would go back to Mexico thinking he was the last minstrel.

Then one day Crispín Soriano's heart swelled and he died in the bushes near the creek. The woman was undoubtedly very frightened, but somehow had the courage and strength to push him away and crawled from under his body. She straightened her clothes as best she could and picking up her wash, walked to her tent. No one had seen her. The men found Crispín Soriano when they walked back from the orchard. For the next few days until the camp broke up, they made it a point to not talk to one another. They were angry and embarrassed, for they did not know which one had been betrayed by his woman.

"The Laughter of My Father"

For Carlos Bulúsan
   Requiescat in pace

The man from Chile had been in Santa Clara for a year or two before we came to live there. Until he left the town some three years later, my father was the only person in our family who spoke to him. True, we saw him often, my mother, my sisters and I, but they, of course, being women, had no reason to speak to him. In fact, it would not have been proper for them to approach him nor for him to speak to them. I did not speak to him because, like my new play-mates, I was afraid of him. We suspected that there was something wrong with him, something mysterious or perhaps supernatural.

Our reaction was caused by his attire and his bearing. We saw him only when he was in the street, for we would never go near his home. Whether he owned the house or rented it we did not know, but we knew that he lived alone in a house large enough for a large family. He always wore black, except for a white shirt with ruffles on its front and at the cuffs. Even his hat was black and he wore a black bow tie. He was a bit rotund, although not what we would call fat, with slender shoulders and legs, so that he appeared to us something like a penguin except that penguins are not ominous.

Although we did not know the word *mystical*, we were all mystics because we were *good* Catholics. We believed in the existence of God and, thus, the existence of the Devil. And the man could not be God nor one of his Messengers.

The townspeople had little or no correspondence with the man. The few Mexican men in town thought he was a Spaniard, because his Castilian was different from ours. The Spanish people simply avoided him and referred to him as "el Brujo." We, the children, found the sobriquet as ominous as the man. We would never meet his gaze; in fact, we never looked at his face. When we saw him walking toward us on the sidewalk, we would turn and run in the opposite direction or across the street through the meager traffic. Once he surprised us as we waited for the box-office at the Rex Theater to open. We were skylarking and did not realize that we blocked his passage on the sidewalk. We looked up and were petrified because we looked straight at his face up close. It was a demonic face with a demonic smile. Long hair grew out of his nostrils and his pointy ears. He had one long eyebrow which extended completely across over his beady, glistening eyes. The ends curved down like a mustache. We recovered long enough to run pell mell every which way, stumbling over other boys who had been in line to buy their tickets. From a distance we looked back and el Brujo had the sidewalk to himself.

That night, as was usual for us, I sat at the kitchen table with my father and mother while my sisters were in the other room playing games or listening to the radio. I told my parents of my experience and they laughed. I was very serious, still frightened, and I resented their laughter. My anger at their response, if it was anger, was stronger toward my mother because she was the one who had taught me about the Devil and his cunning.

"Why do you laugh at me?" I asked.

My mother, who was extremely religious and superstitious, amazed me. "Because you imagine so much. The man does not look like a Devil."

"He does," I said.

"How do you know how the Devil looks?" asked my father.

"My mother has told me that the Devil has many faces and many bodies."

My mother's face now showed concern for me. Perhaps she was contrite because she had always frightened me with such statements as she tried to make me a good boy, or rather to maintain me a good boy, since I was never disobedient although in her mind I had thoughts that were bad. She placed a hand on the upper part of my arm. "Do not be so disturbed," she said. "God would not allow the Devil to frighten you in that manner."

"I begin to wonder," I said.

"Wonder what?" My father was out of it now. This part of my training was in my mother's realm.

"I wonder whether God really has control of the Devil," I said.

"What you have just said is bad," she said with a trace of incipient anger. "It is as if you believe that God is not all-powerful."

I could have said much more, but my instincts told me I should not.

There was a pause and my father said, "There is nothing wrong with the man. He is strange, but there is no mystery about him. And he is not a Brujo."

"But he *is* mysterious," said my mother. "No one knows anything about him. From where he comes. What kind of family he comes from. He does not have intercourse with anyone. He does not have a wife nor a woman in his house. Tell me that is not mysterious. And why do you say that he is strange?"

"Because of the manner in which he dresses. Because, as you have said, he is a solitary man and for other reasons."

"What other reasons? Is he one of those others?"

"Of course not," said my father. "I do know he likes women, he reveres them and is always searching for the one woman who will love him with the same passion he will have for her. That means that any woman who will love him he will love."

Now she was frightened, imagining things I could not, things I did not know. "Is he dangerous?" she asked.

"Dangerous how?"

"To women and young girls. You know what I mean," and she glanced toward me.

"I do not think so," he said, "but he has been here for almost five years and has never done anyone harm. And yet, I suppose that you are right. He could appear to be mysterious to anyone who does not know him. For example, he uses cosmetics like women do—not paint, but pomades and perfumed lotions. He believes that he will attract women with that odor. His house is filled with furniture and he has incense burning in every room. It is not a pleasant place."

"How do you know all this?" she asked.

"I visit him now and then and we converse. That also is not pleasant, because he speaks of nothing but women, past women and future women. Never current women."

"Why have you not told me that?" she asked.

He looked at her with that stare we all knew so well. It was not a look of anger. That was not necessary. He never raised his voice nor reprimanded us. It was only that look that told us we had somehow transgressed and my mother had indeed committed a transgression by questioning him in that manner. She was aware of the fact and her face filled with blood and shame.

And he asked in his soft voice, "When have I told you everything that I do?"

"Nunca, Juan Manuel," she said, and I knew that she would not speak again that night until they were alone.

The following morning I rose early and took my goats to graze in the outskirts of town. I returned and to my surprise I saw that my father was dressed for work. I had not been aware that he was to work that day, although at times he did work on Sundays. It was usual that, after six twelve-hour days at work, the Sabbath was his day. He would rise at an early hour, eat a light breakfast of soft-boiled eggs, a half dozen tortillas, a bowl of oatmeal with fruit in season and perhaps a small bowl of jocoque. He would then read *La Opinión* which had arrived from Los Angeles by the previous day's post, until my mother cleared the table and set his weekly bath. She then laid out his clothes while he luxuriated in a hot tub. After a time she went into the bathroom to soap and scrub his back and returned to the kitchen to have her breakfast. She had been to 5:30 Mass. My sisters were preparing themselves for church.

My father would come out of the bedroom shaved and with hair combed, dressed immaculately in suit and tie and lustrous, patent leather shoes, brushing his hat. At those moments I always noted how handsome he was and always felt somewhat inferior, for only my mother would ever call me good looking. His toilet finished, he walked to the center of town, where on the principal street across from the University was the pool hall. The proprietor had placed benches on the sidewalk for the older men to sit on and converse. At times there were some who bought a beer or glass of wine, but mainly they were there to talk, mostly on the same topic every Sunday. My father went there ostensibly with the hope of finding a Mexican man and converse about what he loved most, his country. That did not happen often, for few Mexicans lived in Santa Clara, but there were Spaniards, immigrants also, with whom he could speak, and despite his antipathy towards Spaniards because they had raped Mexico, he had a good relationship with them because they had also been peasants and because they spoke his language.

He would return home at midafternoon when we usually had our Sunday dinner, and when the entire family except for my oldest sister sat at table. But this day was different as I saw him in work clothes, and I felt despair because if he was to do piece work I must go with him. If he was to be paid by the hour, I would not go because I was too young to be paid for hourly work.

"You are going to work, Papá?" I asked.

"Eat something, we are both going," he said. In the car he said, "We will not be long."

"But you said we are to work."

"Well, I am working. You will help me for a short while," He drove off the road where the highway crossed the Los Gatos Creek. We walked down the bank of the stream which was nearly dry at this time of year. There was an occasional pool of clear water. He spoke to me but I did not listen. I remembered a time almost two years ago when he took me to a place near a creek in San Jose after midnight. We crossed the creek and parked in the shadows of a brace of walnuts away from the street lights. "Wait for me in the truck," he said. Although I always did what he ordered, I grew tired of waiting and walked down the embankment to watch the water flow. I became frightened because it was taking him a long time to do whatever he was doing, and I scrambled back up to the truck. I began to pray, and then saw three figures in silhouette carrying a large object. Following them was a fourth with something smaller. My imagination overcame me, and I knew that my father was doing something illegal, perhaps he and his accomplices had robbed a house. Whatever the booty was, it was carefully placed in the back of the truck. It now looked to me like a machine.

We rode a few blocks and I asked, "What is it?"

"An alembic," he said.

Another few blocks and I asked, "What is an alembic, Papá?"

He had a way of answering questions in a roundabout way. "The wine we have in the cellar is from last year. It is time we make more wine and I do not have barrels. I do not have money to buy barrels. I could bottle the wine. I have been told that it is better that way—that the wine matures, but I do not have money for bottles either." He had not answered my question and perhaps would not. I waited until we were near home before I dared ask again, knowing well how little he liked to be questioned.

"But the alembic?" I asked.

"Oh, that is an apparatus that makes brandy from wine. "He anticipated my next question and added, "Brandy is hard liquor. Aguardiente, similar to whiskey." He did not drink, so I did not know why he wanted brandy, and I had lost my opportunity to ask.

We were on the creek bed, and I remembered another time that we walked along a creek. What made me think of that was that although this happened during the day, we parked in the shade of two trees. We searched for tunas and edible nopales. This was the Guadalupe Creek, which passed near Campbell, wound around, and passed through San Jose near the downtown district. It was difficult getting down from the road, for there were dry, thorny shoots of wild blackberries and the poison oak was lush. Of course we were immune to the poison, having suffered from its effects several times, but we avoided it and reached the bottom alongside the trestle that we had just crossed.

"Let us cross under to the other side of the road," he said.

I stopped and said, "There is a man sleeping under there."

He looked. I wished to leave in the other direction, knowing that bad would come of this.

He went near the man and looked for a time, and then went to him and while on one knee, touched the face and closed the eyelids. He returned and there was anger in his face and I was certain that the man was dead. "Mal agüero," he said, "for the man to starve to death in this valley even during this pinche Depression. Come."

I followed him in my terror, for this part of the experience was not new to me, except that it was the first body I had seen of a person who died of hunger. He had always ordered me to see the dead and at those occasions, when I asked why, he told me that I should know my only destiny. And I followed and looked at the body and touched its face. I sensed warmth and I withdrew my hand quickly. "It is warm, Papá," thinking he might still be alive.

"No," he said. "He is dead. He expired a few minutes ago. He must have arrived from Oklahoma during the night."

I looked down once more and realized that I had not seen the color of the face I had touched. Without being told to do so, I walked away to find the nearest farmhouse, from where I could call the County Sheriff. My fright increased, for those people always had dogs. When the county police arrived I interpreted for my father and we took our buckets and left to pick our tunas and nopales.

I could not help thinking of that as we walked on the floor of the Los Gatos Creek. My father would stop every now and then to look at stones. At times he would bend over and pick one up, scrutinize it closely and either place it in his left hand or discard it. The words in my mind were in Spanish but I had learned enough English and was Americanized enough so that the words switched to English. "*Just what the fuck is my father doing?*" I wondered.

"Come here," he said. "Look at this stone. I need two more that look like this one. Oblong, but not flat. A bit thick, but not round." The entire exercise lasted about five minutes. We had the three stones; my father approved of them after having quality-controlled them. We sat and he took fine sandpaper from his pocket and for another fifteen minutes we sanded them and then he washed them in a puddle.

"All right," he said. "Let us go see the Brujo."

We were not far from town and we took less time to get there than to select the stones. It was a mystery to me, but I did not speak. Why speak? Why ask questions? I would know soon enough. I did not speak at all at the Brujo's home, although he spoke to me in a polite and pleasant voice, but I did reply when he asked me my name. He told me that his name was Caliban, but I had not read Shakespeare yet and did not associate it with evil. I was not afraid, for my father was with me. What my father had said about the Brujo's house was true. There were tables and chairs and sofas everywhere and there were chiffonniers and footstools and it was very dark inside. The windows were closed and tapestries, which looked like rugs hung from the ceiling, before every one of them. The only source of light was from votives and long candles burning before idols or pictures of Saints. The odor from the incense was oppressive. I sneaked a look into another room and it was the same.

My father was saying, ". . . the best one can find. I have been in the creeks, in the Santa Cruz Mountains and on the beaches from Half Moon Bay to San Gregorio. These stones are attracted to me, as you well know."

The Brujo held the stones in his hands, rubbing them and exchanging them from one hand to the other. "Yes, they are true magnets," he said. "I can feel their power. What do they cost?"

"Two and a half each. But you do not have to buy them all. I have another customer."

"I have always paid two dollars."

"These are two-fifty," said my father, "because I have never had stones with the power these have." He reached for the stones.

"No, no," said the Brujo. "I will pay what you ask."

Outside I had questions, but waited until we were in the truck. I had a vague recollection of my mother once having said something about the piedra imán, but I did not know what it was about. I asked, "Are we going home, now?"

My father was laughing as he turned the corner and could not answer. Finally he said, "We are going to San Jose and buy two sacks of flour and a sack of beans. Work will be slack now and we must have those staples for the winter. With the other dollar and a half you and I will have some apple pie and ice cream and with what remains, I will buy two gallons of gasoline and take your mother to the movies in Sunnyvale tonight."

"But you cheated," I said, finally getting out what disturbed me. "You robbed him."

He laughed again and then spoke with a sober voice. "No, Richard," he said. "It was but a trade. An honest trade."

"But how? You sold him what is worthless. Three little rocks."

"I tell you," he said. "They are not worthless to him."

"Why? Of what worth are they?"

"Every one of those little rocks will get him a woman. And that is because he believes that they will."

"No woman will come near him," I said. "He is repulsive and strange."

"You are wrong. In a man-woman relationship women are also strange. You will discover that some day. You see, those small rocks will give him confidence. With confidence he will not be shy near a woman. He will rub those rocks and light candles and pray and when you see him again, he will be different. He will not dress differently, but he will be different."

I believed him because he was my father, and said, "So that is the mystery of the Brujo."

"If there is a mystery, that is it." And he laughed some more, and then I laughed along with him.

Rights

About the Editors

DELIA POEY was born in 1966 in Mexico City, where she spent her early childhood. In 1973, she moved to Miami, graduated with a BA degree from the University of Florida. She taught English in the Dade County public school system, and is presently working on her Ph.D. in Literature at Louisiana State University.

VIRGIL SUAREZ was born in Havana, Cuba, in 1962, and later emigrated with his parents to Madrid, Spain. He arrived in the United States in 1974 and grew up in Los Angeles. He is the author of three books about the Cuban-American experience, *The Cutter*, *Latin Jazz*, and *Welcome to the Oasis and Other Stories*. Currently he teaches at Louisiana State University.

Mr. Suarez and Ms. Poey live and work in Baton Rouge with their daughter Alexandria, their two cats Rum Tum and Cuauhtémoc, and an aquarium full of fish.